Wild About You

SOPHIE LOXTON

Wild About You

**SIMON &
SCHUSTER**

London · New York · Amsterdam/Antwerp · Sydney/Melbourne · Toronto · New Delhi

First published in Great Britain by Simon & Schuster UK Ltd, 2025

1 3 5 7 9 10 8 6 4 2

Simon & Schuster UK Ltd, 1st Floor
222 Gray's Inn Road, London WC1X 8HB

Simon & Schuster Australia, Sydney
Simon & Schuster India, New Delhi

www.simonandschuster.co.uk
www.simonandschuster.com.au
www.simonandschuster.co.in

The authorised representative in the EEA is Simon & Schuster Netherlands BV, Herculesplein 96, 3584 AA Utrecht, Netherlands. info@simonandschuster.nl

Simon & Schuster strongly believes in freedom of expression and stands against censorship in all its forms. For more information, visit BooksBelong.com.

A CIP catalogue record for this book is available from the British Library

Paperback ISBN: 978-1-3985-3668-5
eBook ISBN: 978-1-3985-3669-2
Audio ISBN: 978-1-3985-3670-8

This book is a work of fiction. Names, characters, places and incidents are either a product of the author's imagination or are used fictitiously. Any resemblance to actual people living or dead, events or locales is entirely coincidental.

Typeset in the UK by M Rules
Printed and Bound in the UK using 100% Renewable Electricity
at CPI Group (UK) Ltd

MIX
Paper | Supporting responsible forestry
FSC® C013604
www.fsc.org

To Emily and Siân

Dear Reader,

I should let you know that this story
contains mention of fertility treatment and
childlessness. The subject has been treated
with thought and care, but I know it may
be upsetting for some readers.

With love, Sophie x

CHAPTER 1

'Goodbye, Anna. I'm so sorry.'

That was it. That was the moment.

I remember the tone of voice Sean used, as he said those words (in a very annoying, solemn manner, as if he was a politician, rather than the man I'd spent years sharing my bed with). I remember very clearly the sound of the door – our front door – as it closed.

I'm told change takes time, planning, baby steps. But that moment was all I needed to change. The old Anna fractured into a million pieces and fell away, to leave someone new standing there.

Full confession: before that door closed, I was the type of person who said yes to *everything*.

The old Anna ticked off activities as though life was one long to-do list. Report with a one-day deadline? *No problem.*

Charity sprint at the weekend? *Please find attached a link to my sponsorship page.* Hipster bar which flavours all of its drinks with chilli? *See you at six.* I bought and read all of those shiny self-help books. *100 Ways to Yes. The Extraordinary Power of Yes. How I Surrendered to the Yes and Changed my Life.* I was once voted Most Positive Team Member in my office. Which, now I come to think about it, is slightly nauseating.

Take a breath, Anna, I should have said. *Some things are beyond your control.* But no, my life was about plans, and goals, and positive thinking. Until that moment.

Just before Sean left, the axe had finally fallen on our hopes of having a baby after three years of trying. There were long words, and plenty of hesitation, as the doctor tried to explain what was unexplainable. And whilst there were gaps in the medical understanding – fertility seemed to comprise half hard science, half hope and magic – the essential point we all took from the conversation was this: it was me. My body wasn't doing what it needed to do.

There was a part of me that knew things had ended in the precise moment we were told. There had been a shift in the air, even as I gripped Sean's hand in the consulting room. We weren't holding onto each other; *I* was holding onto *him*. When he finally said the words, two days later, he felt awful about it, of course he did. That's what he said: *awful.* He loved me, but having a child was non-negotiable to him.

I think I took it pretty well at the time, in that I didn't say anything other than 'oh', before watching him leave, then carefully collecting my make-up bag, a handful of pants and a selection of loungewear and going to my sister Rose's house, where I became a sobbing snotty mess as soon as I walked through the door. There I stayed, setting up camp in her spare room rather than returning to the flat. As the evenings drew in that autumn, I found myself Netflix-and-not-chilling on a Friday, Saturday and Sunday night. Sometimes crying, sometimes quietly chipping away at a family-sized portion of tiramisu.

Sean and I were together for five years, and our relationship was so established, so central to everything, that it felt as though someone had kicked the main beam out from under my life when he ended it. I was assaulted by good memories: Sean massaging my feet after I'd spent the day in high heels; doing the crossword puzzle in bed together on a Sunday morning; the look of joy on his face when he'd knelt in front of me with the engagement ring in his hand. In an attempt to feel better, I'd dredge up the bad memories: the gag-inducing perfumes he used to buy me, which I always wore in an attempt to be nice; the way he criticised my driving; his habit of fading out if we had a difficult conversation.

Still, I moved through the classic stages of grief with denial at the forefront. This couldn't have happened, could it? Rose and my friends agreed: Sean was in shock, that was all. Once the reality of my absence came home to him, he'd see things differently.

One week passed, then two, then three, and he didn't see things differently.

My personal favourite of the grieving stages was anger. This hit me around Halloween, when I joked to my sister that I might spend the day dressed up as a murdered bride. Instead I knocked on the door of our flat and threw my engagement ring at Sean.

If I'm completely honest, the life I had pictured for myself had been slowly dissolving for some time, although I hadn't wanted to admit it. Holding onto it had felt like trying to hold onto water. Many of my closest friends from younger days had gone, disappearing into the world of motherhood as if they'd stepped through a doorway into a parallel universe. I'd spent the last three or four years trying to arrange coffee dates or baby-friendly days out, but had come to see that there were simply some people who didn't need me anymore. They needed their new friends, and those new friends were exclusively mothers. How ironic, then, that my fiancé now needed the same thing.

By December, when I thought of him or any part of our life together, it was with an empty deadness, as though it had happened to someone else. There was just a numb space at the centre of my chest, interspersed with the occasional stab of pain. I told my best friend Fi about this new feeling, thinking it was a positive thing. 'Oh,' she said, in a way that made me think she might be googling therapists for me at the same time as speaking to me on the phone.

One day, I caught a glimpse of myself in a shop window, and did a double-take at my worn, drained face. Fi's voice on the phone that evening echoed my sense of unease.

'Perhaps,' she said, 'it's best if you take a break from London. Find a calmer environment.' It was the same *perhaps* Rose had said as I lay next to her on the sofa and she stroked my hair, having watched *Bridgerton* with me for the eleventh time. It was time to leave London.

My managers at Mackenzie & Partners, the ecological and environmental consultancy where I was a project manager, were nonplussed by the changed me. For years, every time they'd thrown a project or a deadline in my direction, my first response had been 'no problem'. They were supremely unprepared for the new edited response of '*no*'. So they tried to be supportive. But I wasn't having any of it.

No, I did not want to write a bison reintroduction plan.

No, I did not want to meet with a millionaire and discuss his *vision*.

No, I did not want to be put forward for promotion that year.

No, I did not want to work there anymore.

They were quibbling about whether to accept my resignation in light of the 'difficult circumstances' they understood I was going through. Nothing I said seemed to put a dent in their armour-plated belief in my faithfulness to Mackenzie's. It was as though all my '*yes's*' added up over the years to the idea that I'd always, eventually, do whatever they wanted me to do. But this time I wouldn't.

'Where do you want to go?' Rose asked me.

'Nowhere,' I said.

Stonemore, an estate owned by some random aristocrat

(an earl, would you believe) set in a bleak, beautiful and hilly swathe of countryside on the edge of the Northumberland National Park, was my 'nowhere' of choice. It wasn't an entirely random selection – Stonemore was home to my beloved Fi and her husband Richard. Richard's family had always worked on the estate and Fi had gone there for love, having spotted Richard on holiday in Ibiza when we were twenty-one and swapped her high heels for wellies; she worked as personal assistant to the earl. She wore her happiness like a butterfly wears its colours, completely un-selfconsciously and without any need to take a snap of it for socials. During one of our tear-sodden conversations, she mentioned quietly that the lord of the manor (sorry, earl) wanted to rewild Stonemore, and how did I fancy some fresh air and wide-open skies? 'Yes,' I said, the answer coming out so quickly it surprised me.

I was interviewed for the role of rewilding manager on Zoom by Callum McGregor, the estate manager at Stonemore. When I say interviewed, I mean that Callum occasionally raked his hair out of his eyes and fired a question at me, looking more uncomfortable than I did, sitting there in his waxed jacket with a map behind him. Still, there was a definite glint in his eye when I mentioned my experience of managing species reintroduction. The interview was also attended by the earl, and co-ordinated by someone called Tally (Fi had opted out on the grounds of conflict of interest, as one of my friends). Tally was a frosty-eyed, blonde-haired woman who kept mentioning London with contemptuous

6

emphasis. As in 'Not too much green space in *London*, is there?' Towards the end of the interview, she asked if I'd ever worked for a peer of the realm before.

'No,' I said bluntly, trying not to appear defensive and probably coming across as chippy. It really didn't help that she spoke with a cut-glass accent, which, coupled with her chilly expression, had the effect of kicking my 'inferiority' switch on.

'I *see*.' She made a show of writing this down. When she asked Callum if he had any further questions, his 'no' was accompanied by a wry, relieved smile that made me think I would definitely get on with this man.

'And would you like to ask anything, Lord Roxdale?' Tally said, breaking into her first smile of the interview.

Throughout this process, my soon-to-be boss had kept his mic and camera turned off, remaining a black square with the words 'Jamie Mulholland' staring out in white.

We all waited a moment as he unmuted his mic. I surreptitiously took a screenshot.

'Nothing to add,' a male voice said, curtly. Which was the sole impact my new employer had on my recruitment.

Happy Christmas! came Fi's message an hour later. *You've got the job!*

As I drank my ninth 'calm blend' tea of the day, choking on its floral fumes, I messaged Rose.

ANNA *I've got the job.*

ROSE *Yes yes yes!! What was the Lord like?*

I sent her the screenshot of the video interview.

ANNA *Didn't get sight of him. He kept his camera off.*

ROSE *How inconvenient of him. That other guy looks like a bit of yeah. Time to get back in the saddle?*

ANNA ***Absolutely not.***

As I packed, I was rejoicing in the power of *No*, and all of its beautiful variations, turning down invitations to Christmas drinks and politely declining an exit interview at Mackenzie's. I started journalling to try and explore my emotions (no one needed to hear me say the same things again and again, plus it was an excuse to buy new stationery). *No* was the very first word I wrote in my new journal, and I liked it so much I coloured it in and outlined it with my new gold pen and glitter glue. Which is *not* the kind of thing I normally do.

CHAPTER 2

NO REGRETS was the heading on page two of my journal.

It was an instruction to embrace my new direction, and not to chicken out of my decision, even as I received multiple messages from my London friends and colleagues, all along the lines of 'if you're tired of London, you're tired of life'.

No regrets, I told myself when I packed up my possessions in the silent flat on a January afternoon, considerately vacated by Sean so he could go to an 'er, meeting', which I suspected was a date, from the amount of aftershave he was wearing. I had taken as many boxes as I could fit into the back of Rose's car, so I was selective: books, photographs, an ornament, a set of bath towels. All the time holding in my emotions, so tense that I felt as though my stomach and chest were bound tight in an iron corset.

I took the train to my new home and the weather steadily got grimmer and wilder as we journeyed from the softer landscape of the south to the wilder landscape of Northumberland (I was going to rewild it, so no problem there). I sat in the train, eating chocolate and watching the scenery change to a different kind of beauty, as though I was watching a film. 'Is that a tattoo?' the girl sitting next to me said at the slogan 'no regrets' I'd written on the inside of my wrist in biro as a reminder. I shook my head and smiled.

Fi met me at the station, and I saw the look of concern on her face as she opened her arms, enveloping me in a warm, incredible hug. 'Just in time,' she said, leaning back, taking my face in her hands and inspecting me as if she was looking for signs of damage.

'Yes,' I said, trying to smile as brightly as possible. 'Down, but not out.'

She drove me through narrow, winding lanes to the estate cottage I'd been allocated as a job perk. It was an impossibly sweet Neo-Gothic cottage built of pale grey stone, with mullion leaded windows. As I got out of the car, open-mouthed, I stared at its steep gables and fish-scale roof tiles. There were even gargoyles on the guttering. 'It's not as big as it looks,' said Fi, handing me the key. 'Basically one-up, one-down – it's 40 per cent attic. But it's cosy downstairs. I've had the wood-burner going this morning.' The door opened onto the main living area, a sitting room with a kitchen area at the back. The flagstones were grey and smooth, the walls plastered in a buttercream colour, with a navy blue sofa by the fireplace, and a pine coffee table and bookshelves. My boxes were sitting in the middle of the floor, having been brought up by van overnight.

I went straight to the one marked KETTLE and cut through the tape with my new door key.

Fi had put milk and a home-made lasagne in the fridge and a poinsettia on the counter to welcome me. 'I didn't know if you wanted to come round to ours this evening, or settle in?' she said, as I hugged her in thanks. I could see how carefully she was watching me, as though I was one of those ornaments that you had to pack in a box with the words 'THIS WAY UP' and 'FRAGILE' emblazoned across the box.

I glanced at the 'no regrets' on my wrist, which had already started to fade. 'I would love to come over tomorrow,' I said. 'But tonight, I'll unpack a bit, get settled.' I was determined that I wasn't going to be a burden; that despite the last few months of her mainly seeing me on video calls either sobbing, or mascara-less from *having* sobbed, this marked the beginning of a new phase. Strong Anna, capable Anna. She nodded, gave me another hug, and put on the kettle, just to delay her departure a few more minutes. I loved her for that.

I had a week to unpack, carefully building a small pile of self-help books on the floor of my bedroom and placing some more 'guest-friendly' novels on the small pine bookshelf in the living room, just in case anyone dropped by in future. I made a lot of tea and ate a lot of biscuits as I washed my crockery and cutlery, layered throws on the sofa, and decided where to place my various framed photos: one of me, Rose and Mum; a framed compilation of photos of friends; and some arty landscape shots I'd taken of various woodlands and marshlands near London where Sean and I had spent weekends escaping the city. I remembered how I'd initiated those walks, although he'd been happy to potter along with me as we'd discussed this and that, including playful mentions of our imagined future: where we would raise our family and what kind of dog we would get. Inspecting our relationship from a distance, I wondered whether he'd been in as all-in as I had been; if our positions had been reversed, I couldn't have imagined leaving him. Then, just when I had started hating him a little bit, I would remember the feeling of our hands clasped together, the sound of his laugh as we argued playfully over what kind of house we wanted. As I put the pictures on the wall, they helped, in their own quiet way; in the shots of trees silhouetted against the sky, or of water reflecting cloud, I caught sight of the essential Anna who had always been there, and still remained, even though so much of my identity felt stripped away.

The first night, I was kept up by the sound of mice scampering around above my bedroom in their lofty palace. So I put the bedside lamp on and got my journal out to write action bullet points, which then morphed into a shopping list:

Establish daily meditation practice, beginning with five minutes.

As you meditate, practise 'Sean' becoming smaller and distant in your mind. He can start off full size but should end up like a tiny stick figure, waving his arms on the horizon.

Start the day with hot water infused with lemon juice.

Buy humane mousetraps.

*

After a week of dozing, rearranging cushions and eating lavish meals at Fi and Richard's, my first day of work arrived. Fi picked me up and took me to the office by car, even though we'd walked the estate route once on my week off. 'You should arrive in style on your first day,' she said with a smile. 'Also, it's a muddy walk after all the rain. We need to break you in gently.'

The office was in the front corner of the manor house of Stonemore, a Neo-Classical mansion house a few hundred yards away from the ruins of a Real Life Castle. The Mulholland family had built the house in the late 1700s when the castle became too uncomfortable to live in. Its façade was impressive: built of honey-coloured stone, two vast fluted columns flanked the front entrance and its steps, with symmetrical lines of windows running either side. It looked out over a pristine carriage drive and a deer park. Its whole appearance gave the impression of precision and order; I wondered where wildness would find its place here.

It sounds glamorous, working in a mansion, but there were drawbacks, which I discovered within fifteen minutes. Air temperature: roughly the same inside as it is outside. Number of insect and mouse traps: many. And then there was Tally, who appeared as soon as I walked in the door, and was if anything even more brittle than when she'd interviewed me. She was the collections manager, which meant she was responsible for every single bit of art and furniture in the place, as well as all the volunteer guides. But she gave

Sophie Loxton

the impression that her *purview* (her word) extended to the entire running of the estate.

My desk faced hers, with Fi's desk at a right-angle between us. It was a big enough room – painted an institutional cream, but with lots of pictures on the walls and about four different antique carpets layered over the floorboards. Callum had an office next door. I realised immediately that my new colleagues and I were going to be spending a lot of time in close quarters.

'The kettle's over there, the blue mug is yours, the loo is first on the right down the hall,' Fi said, hawkishly watching her inbox update as she took her coat off. Then she double-clicked something on the screen, picked up the phone and dialled a number. 'When you say water ingress, do you mean a leak or a flood?' she said sharply, kicking off her trainers and putting her work heels on. 'Bear with me, I'll be there in five minutes. Anna,' she gave me a bright smile, 'I'll be back in a little while to get your computer set up for you, there's just something I have to deal with.' She was out the door in a moment, heading off through the innards of the house.

Sixty seconds after I'd settled into my desk chair, Tally narrowed her eyes and asked if Fiona had fully briefed me about the *etiquette* at Stonemore. At interview, she had identified gaps in my knowledge about this kind of thing. Did I know how to address Jamie Mulholland, 8th Earl of Roxdale?

I'm afraid her imperious look was like a red flag to a bull to new, negative, me. 'By his name?' I said. She looked as though she was going to implode, and shook her head in a way that should have been stern but made me want to start laughing. 'Just call him my lord,' she said, in a tone that was soft but severe. 'My *lord*.'

I didn't dare say I'd never heard of him until the day of my interview. To hear Tally talk, you'd think we worked for the king of England. It's all about correct *form* and the sense that the earl is *very important*. I said it didn't really matter what I called him, especially as it seemed I was never going to actually meet him. She gazed through me, as though I was dematerialising in front of her very eyes.

'We do things differently here, Anna,' she said. 'Whatever you did in *London*, it doesn't apply here.'

I smiled neutrally. She'd have to warm up eventually, right?

I felt positively jubilant when Callum took me out onto the estate that morning. We drove away from the house and its Neo-Classical neatness into the wilder part of Stonemore, bumping and jolting in an ancient green Land Rover. I loved this side of the place immediately: the expanses of heather, the vast hills, the wind-battered trees. The occasional shaft of sunlight on the browns and greens of the hills and the swiftly moving, constantly changing clouds. Callum parked the Land Rover beside a stream, the clear cold water running fast around grey boulders and rocks with a rushing sound that was astonishingly loud in the silence. The beautiful but unsparing landscape seemed to both match my state of mind and lighten it. And it was as far from my old life as it could reasonably be.

'What d'you think?' asked Callum as we looked out at the landscape we were going to be shaping and caring for together. And I felt a little tremble run through me – something like joy, and anticipation, which I quickly slapped down with a *take it slow, don't overinvest*.

'It'll do,' I said, and smiled at him.

'Glad to hear it,' he said, and handed me back into the Land Rover in a way that made me feel positively fluttery.

On my return to the office, I was enjoying my sense of calm as I settled down at my desk and took possession of the laptop Fi had got for me ('There's no IT helpdesk,' she said cheerily, 'just me.'). Despite Tally's evident suspicion of me, I was still very much in a 'no regrets' state of mind about the place in which I'd chosen to rebuild myself. I was searching the drawers of my (enormous, Victorian) desk when I became aware that someone else had entered the room, and looked up.

A tall man with short blonde hair and piercing blue eyes stood a metre from my desk, hands jammed into the pockets of his green waxed jacket (I made a mental note to buy one – it was clearly the uniform). I'm not going to deny it, my first thought out of the gate was – *he's hot*. The second thought was – *he's grumpy*. He stood there like an unhappy spirit blown in from the hills (if spirits could be that, er, ripped), wearing an ancient cable-knit jumper and black cords with boots that were caked in mud. And there was no doubt about it – he was glaring at me.

'Er, hello?' I said.

'Will you be warm enough in that?' he said, unexpectedly.

I mean, he was right. I was wearing a thin cotton blouse layered over a green vest top and black jeans, trying to look smart, and it was nowhere near warm enough. But there was something about his tone, a general dismissiveness, that riled me.

'I'll be fine, thank you,' I said crisply.

'Lord Roxdale!' Tally had re-entered the room and almost dropped her William Morris print mug on the floor, decanting some of her tea onto the aged Axminster carpet.

He flicked a glance at her then looked back at me and narrowed his eyes. 'I take it you have everything you need, apart from a coat,' he said.

Dear lord, I thought the hopelessly rich were meant to be incredibly polite. Wasn't that meant to be their saving grace?

'Actually, *my lord*,' I said, with a glance at Tally, 'perhaps we could meet to discuss priorities, and there are a few things I need, some stationery—'

Meaning: a whiteboard, some multi-coloured Post-it notes, coloured highlighters. I'd almost had a panic attack when I realised there was no stationery cupboard. *So I have an addiction.* No one's perfect.

'Tell Fi.' He was already turning away. 'I'm told you had an assistant in your last job – will you be able to manage without one?' He glanced over his shoulder. 'We all muck in here.'

I doubt that, I thought silently, then realised from his

17

expression that this was probably written all over my face. 'I'm sure I'll be fine,' I said brightly, with a definite subtext of *screw you*.

He raised his eyebrows. 'Well, don't come to me if you're not,' he said, and departed with a slam of the door.

I sat back down at my desk, waiting for my pulse to return to normal. And *that's* when I regretted coming to Stonemore. Because that was the moment I realised I was working for the most miserable man in Northumberland.

CHAPTER 3

'Why didn't you tell me how grumpy he is?' I wailed to
Fi that evening, with a large glass of red wine in my hand.

'Jamie?' said Fi. 'He's alright.'

'No, he's not!'

'His bark is worse than his bite.' She smiled at me as she
raked chopped vegetables into a wok. They gave a satisfying
hiss as they hit the hot oil. 'You'll get on fine.'

I sipped my wine fitfully and settled deeper into the faded
armchair near the table. I loved being in Fi and Richard's
kitchen. They bought the house as a near ruin when they
got married – a stone-built, eighteenth-century cottage
down the lane from the estate cottage allocated to me – and
over the years they'd extended it. The kitchen was in the
extension – it was the perfect mix of old-fashioned country
style and chic new: flagstones, pots and pans hanging from
the ceiling, a battered old sofa by the woodburner, but also

smooth white surfaces, soft-close doors and the largest picture window I had ever seen, revealing the hills beyond. I cringed when I thought about the first time I visited after the building work was finished, chattering away about the parties and gigs I had been to, feeling the epitome of both metropolitan chic and grime after a long day's work, my bag stuffed full with gifts of overpriced chocolate and different coloured sparkling wines. I remembered looking out of the picture window, wondering why on earth someone would choose to come and live somewhere so empty, so wild. Fi had smiled at the look on my face, helped me out of my coat, and plonked a stoneware mug of tea in front of me with a slice of cake so fresh it had steam coming off it.

'You wouldn't believe the sunrises,' she said, a look of calm, relaxed contentment on her face. And sure enough, as the days passed, I had unwound too. I stopped feeling so jittery; even my breathing became less shallow. That experience had stayed with me ever since – had brought me to Stonemore as much as my need to escape the past.

I was beyond glad I'd had a week off before starting work, as I'm not sure how I would have coped with grumpy Lord La-la when in the midst of emotional exhaustion. And as well as unpacking and journalling, I'd spent a good chunk of it comatose in my new home, mostly sleeping through the sounds of the wildlife outside the walls and within them (thanks, meeses), in the deafening silence of the countryside. The rest of it I'd spent in the kitchen I was sitting in now, staring at the flames in Fi and Richard's woodburner as we chatted. When I told Fi she had saved me, she said 'Ach,' and nudged me, but she had.

'What's going on?' Richard had been tempted out of his study by the smell of spices and garlic as Fi added them to the cooking vegetables.

'Jamie hasn't been an instant hit with Anna,' said Fi, giving him a mischievous smile.

'Do you mean you're not bedazzled by his rolling acres?' Richard stole a slice of carrot from the pan with a flourish. 'He's quite the eligible bachelor.'

'Are they rolling? More jutting, grim and rainswept,' I said. 'And I'm surprised he's not married already. I thought members of the aristocracy were betrothed early in life.'

'Maybe a couple of centuries ago.' Fi crumbled a dried chilli into the pan. 'Anyway, he was in a relationship until a few months ago. It's not been easy for him.' Her tone hinted I should cut the earl some slack.

'Who was she?' I asked, curious despite myself, as Fi emptied noodles into a pan of boiling water.

'Her name is Lucinda Fortescue-Menzies,' said Fi.

'Shut up!' I cried, and Richard snorted into his wine. 'I'm sorry, it's just I distrust surnames that aren't pronounced the way they're spelt. It's a trick to catch out plebs like me.'

Fi smiled gently and reprovingly. 'She's a cross-country rider and stables her horses on the estate. Ach, I feel bad talking about Jamie like this. Set the table, would you? It's almost ready.'

'Will do.' I got up to help. 'I promise I'll be nice to the

boss. I'll be working mainly with Callum, anyway. And he's far more acceptable.'

'I'm glad we haven't put you off entirely,' Fi said, with a raised eyebrow.

I wasn't feeling quite so cheerily capable the next morning. There was something about being at my desk at the crack of dawn, combined a with a faint but annoying hangover-headache, which made me feel the tiniest bit fragile.

I'd got home the night before at a perfectly sensible hour. The ten-minute walk from Fi and Richard's cottage to mine had felt unexpectedly peaceful, despite the fact that I was on my own in the middle of nowhere, having refused Fi's offer to drive me home. The route to my cottage was along a lane made hollow by centuries of boots and hooves, bordered by ancient trees with fields on either side. I enjoyed hearing the sounds of the countryside at night – the wind rustling through the branches, the crunch of my boots on the gravelly lane – and when I looked up, I could see the stars perfectly, tracing the small number I knew: three points of Orion's belt and from there, Bellatrix and Betelgeuse. It was only when a fox shrieked that I sped up and hurried home like the big scaredy-cat I am.

It was when I got there that the sense of warmth and comfort from my evening with Fi and Richard really wore off. The front door opened directly onto the main ground-floor room, and as I walked in I remembered I hadn't lit the woodburner earlier in the day, so the cottage was cold as well as dark. I clicked the light on and looked around at the room that served as my living room and kitchen, with a sense of emptiness. Despite the pictures I'd put up and my few belongings dotted about, it felt more like a quirky holiday cottage than a home. And there was something else missing too. In a vulnerable moment the week before, I'd texted Sean my new landline number, *just in case* he wanted to get in touch (I'd remembered there was very patchy mobile reception on the estate). When I checked the handset there were no missed calls and no messages. It wasn't as if I'd really expected it – not consciously – but the unmistakable fall in my chest, and my sudden sense that this place was less than homely, told me all I needed to know. Somehow, there was a small part of me that was still waiting for him to real-ise he'd made a mistake. Still waiting for one more chance to turn things around; putting together what I might say when he said he wanted to try again. Sean was like a word puzzle I hadn't quite cracked, floating around in the back of my mind as my brain attempted to piece things together. I was used to finding solutions to problems, and a small part of me refused to stop looking for one.

I did some tipsy journalling:

New boss is hot. Callum also hot. Clearly this is my disturbed brain processing the break-up and finding every available man hot. Must try to be less scattergun in my affections.

I carefully wrote the word 'Ice Queen' in the centre of the page, drew some branches out of it, and promptly fell asleep before I thought of a single icy precaution I could take.

Thanks to the alcohol, I only dozed fitfully and ended up getting up extra early with a headache, then got to my desk at stupid o'clock, because what else was there to do? I sat there, feeling queasy and slightly dozy, staring into the middle distance as my computer booted up.

'You should take more water with the wine.'

I was startled awake from the *very slight* doze I was in by the earl, yet again looming over my desk. He was dressed in a blue linen shirt over slate-coloured canvas trousers, and I considered asking him sharply where *his* coat was. I glanced at the clock on the wall. 6.30am. What the hell was he doing here?

'Do you always take a tour of your staff's offices before they get in in the morning?' I said, more sharply than I had intended.

He raised his eyebrows. 'Not always. Usually I just rely on the security cameras.' His gaze was steady, unblinking, not a hint of a smile in his blue eyes; I sensed in that moment, he was making a catalogue of my faults, and we held each other's gaze a moment too long. I realised I was giving him a hard stare, my heartbeat refusing to return to normal after the shock of being surprised. Luckily my rational brain kicked into gear with the thought *Anna, you've only said two words to him and you're already making an enemy of him. Be sensible.*

I got to my feet, pinned my best, most professional smile to my face, and held out my hand. 'Let's start again, shall we? Anna Whitlock, pleased to meet you.'

He hesitated, then shook my hand – his was warm and dry, the handshake firm. His eyes glittered, and I had the sense the assessment was still going on. 'Pleased to meet you, Anna. And there's no need for formalities. My staff call me Jamie.'

My staff call me Jamie? Nice touch, combining politeness with a reminder of status. I fear this thought crossed my eyes (my face is almost comically expressive, according to Sean, one of my least endearing features). It happened quickly: I saw his expression change at the sight of mine then I swung to sit down and knocked my travel coffee cup over. It wasn't a small spill. Unfortunately I'd left it in the open position and coffee went all over the estate map I'd been studying, as well as the leather-covered antique desk that I'd only been allocated the day before.

'Shit!' I cried. Then, 'Sorry! Bloody hell!' I tried desperately to mop up the coffee with anything – scrap paper, tissues from my bag.

'Don't worry.' Jamie threw a pristine handkerchief into the mix. 'It's just my great-grandfather's Chippendale desk.'

'What?! You're kidding!' I threw a look at him and saw a very slight smile, which showed me he was winding me up, then muttered 'Bugger' under my breath as I noticed a neglected pool of coffee seeping into red leather. How was there so much coffee in that cup?

'Nice range of expletives,' he murmured. 'Perhaps you'd like to try another one?'

I gave him an unwise glare.

'Hang on . . .' He headed off to the cupboard-like niche where we made drinks and returned with a wad of kitchen towel, whilst I tried to shepherd the coffee lake with two pieces of paper. Together we cleaned it up, then enacted a ridiculous little dance, me trying to take the sodden lump of coffee-drenched towel from him, him refusing. Eventually we disposed of it, a joint effort that involved me reaching for it and him lobbing it into Tally's desk bin, where it landed with a dull thwack.

'Great, now I'll be in trouble with her,' I said, regrettably out loud. I'm sure I was better at keeping my lip buttoned when I was in London. Heartbreak had removed all of my filters.

'What? From Tally?' He looked perplexed. 'She's a sweetheart.'

'Is she now?' I shot back, without thinking. Irritation flashed across his face and his expression hardened, all amusement leaving his eyes. Great – first I'd annoyed him, now I'd embarrassed him.

'I need a report for an area of the estate,' he said curtly, then said a name that sounded like pure gobbledegook to me.

'Right,' I was trying to write it down phonetically. 'Could you possibly pop that in an email to me?'

'No, I could not.'

'Okay.' I bit my lip. 'Perhaps you could spell the name for me?'

'Callum will tell you where it is. As soon as possible.' He was gliding away; the man had such long legs he could cross the office in two strides.

'But . . .' I said. Nope, he was gone.

*

Of course, Tally gave me her best snooty look when she stood over her bin on arrival and said 'What happened?' as though I was a servant who'd disappointed her. I explained the coffee catastrophe to her impassive face.

'Many of the artefacts here at Stonemore have been *in situ* for generations, Anna,' she said. 'You really must learn to be more careful.'

'Yes, sorry,' I said. I've never felt entirely comfortable in my rather stocky, wide-hipped frame. Occasionally someone has told me I have an hourglass-type thing going on, but I don't really think of myself like that. I do, however, notice it when I accidentally knock my stapler off my desk with my arse or trip over my little hoof-like feet. 'I've always been a bit clumsy.'

Tally shook her head pityingly.

'Where's Callum?' I said hopefully.

'Gone to check on groundworks,' said Tally vaguely. I looked longingly at Fi's empty seat – she was meeting a supplier about Stonemore merchandising for the small castle shop. I'd learned quickly that Fi was the key to almost every question at Stonemore. She was technically the earl's PA but in reality she played a part in almost every aspect of the house's organisation. And she wasn't here.

'Tally, can I ask you something?'

She sighed, raised her eyebrows.

'Do you know where this place is?' I tried to pronounce my phonetically spelt weird word.

She tilted her head at my lunacy. 'I have no idea what you're talking about.'

27

It would have to wait for Callum. I sat down and logged into my Forestcam. I had recently sponsored a planting of rowan trees in a reforesting project and liked to check in on the site. The charity had cameras all over the woodland to provide a live feed for sponsors. Every time I looked at them, whether they were still or moving in the wind, whether they were in golden light or grey, it reminded me that life would go on – *was* going on, at that very moment. Beauty was emerging, somewhere.

Callum recognised the place in a heartbeat. 'Of course, Belheddonbrae?' he said. 'You were only a syllable off.'

I glanced in Tally's direction and saw she was suppressing a little smirk. 'Thanks for that,' I called to her, and raised my topped-up coffee cup in a weary 'cheers'.

She straightened her face and continued tap-tapping on her keyboard. 'Just a little joke, Anna,' she said. 'Banter. You really must adjust to our country ways.'

'By the way,' I said, 'why do you hate *London* so much?'

She froze, her mouth twitching a little. 'I have no idea what you mean,' she said, her accent becoming even more posh.

Callum gave me a knowing look. 'I'll show you Belheddonbrae,' he said. 'No need to drive, it's close by.' As soon as we were outside, he cast me a shy smile. 'Don't worry about Tally. It's just a bit of town versus country. She thinks you might come here and dazzle us with your sophisticated metropolitan ways.'

'Right,' I said, thinking it was slightly unfair. Tally had been inspecting my every move as though I was about to fail in some way; I had the vague feeling at some point she would ask me which finishing school I went to. Which was fine, except the role of inspecting my failures was already filled by me. Attempting to quieten my inner critic was going to be even harder with an actual external critic constantly looking down her nose at me.

As we clomped down the length of the house frontage, past vast window after vast window, I had the feeling *close by* for Callum wasn't exactly the same by my measurement. In an attempt to be more 'country', I was wearing chunky boots I'd bought in preparation for hiking around the estate, and they felt like lead weights as I struggled to keep up with him.

Having exited the staff office at the front of the house, we walked the length of the frontage, then turned left and headed for the land behind the house. Before long, we came to the ruin of the medieval castle that had been the first habitation at Stonemore. 'It was a pele tower,' said Callum. 'A fortified tower, built in the 1300s for security against invasion. Three hundred years later, a member of the family added a wing to make it a manor house, then that fell into ruin, too, when the current house was built in the late 1700s.' He glanced at me. 'Do you want to have a look inside?'

I nodded, and had to suppress the desire to clap my hands with glee. 'Yes please.'

He smiled, and held out his hand to help me over a stony

mound. We threaded our way through a gap in the grey stone walls. I looked up at the ancient remains, gauging where the floor levels had been from the windows and arrow slits. The height of the tower meant it must have been possible to see for many miles. We walked onwards into the seventeenth-century wing of the house, also now a ruin, and I gazed through grand stone window frames now free of glass. I could imagine a log fire burning in this room, the family banqueting and dancing. There was something incredibly atmospheric about this place.

'Magical, isn't it?' His smile matched my own.

As we came out of the shelter of the ruins the wind hit us – hard. 'Wow,' I said, but my voice was lost in another gust. Callum glanced at me with a half-smile. 'You'll get used to it,' he said.

We were marching alongside high red-brick walls now. 'This is the kitchen garden,' said Callum. 'Most of the back of the house faces the formal garden, though. Mica and Keith are in charge of upkeep, but we have an army of volunteers and students on placement to help them. Have you seen the formal gardens yet?'

Trying not to pant, I shook my head.

'Let's just make a quick detour so you can take a look,' he said. We turned left and walked past the brick-enclosed kitchen garden to see the formal garden, an elaborate parterre. I exclaimed at the sight of it: ornamental beds in damask patterns, cut precisely into the level ground and edged by box hedges.

'Done in the nineteenth century,' said Callum.

'And best seen from above,' I said, glancing at the tall windows lining the back of the house. It looked sparse in the January light, but I could well imagine the beds in summer, softened by colourful flowers and herbs.

'It's a shame,' said Callum. 'Most of the upper floor on this side of the house is dust-sheeted – it's just too much money to keep it open.' He ascertained I'd seen enough, turned on his heel and strode back in the direction of the pele tower and – I presumed – Belheddonbrae.

'Right,' I said. I was working to catch my breath (another couple of items for my to-do list: 1 – buy waxed jacket. 2 – get fitter, much fitter). I was very glad when Callum eventually slowed, and unhooked a farm gate set in a traditional stone wall.

'Ta da,' he said.

I saw immediately that Belheddonbrae had once been a garden, although it was nothing like the disciplined, clear-cut parterre. There were trees and hardy shrubs, offering shelter from the wind, some bedraggled beds in the flatter section, long overgrown, and the remains of a lawned area.

'What was this used for?' I asked.

Callum seemed to be searching for an answer. 'The late countess – mother of the current earl – loved this area, made it her own when she was first married, I've been told,' he said eventually.

'Was she an enthusiastic gardener?' I asked. Obviously, I immediately had a vision of her, gleaned from costume dramas I'd watched with my mum when I was a kid: white floaty dress, drifting through the garden, gathering fruit and flowers into her arms as she glided on with the same long-legged imperiousness I'd seen the echo of in her son. Although it was bloody freezing out here so floaty dresses wouldn't be exactly practical.

Callum looked uncomfortable. 'No, not really. She held a lot of parties here.'

The vision disappeared. 'Garden parties?'

'Kind of. Once, there was a mini-festival, I suppose you would call it. She hired a rock band.' He named one of dubious 1980s vintage. I goggled at him.

'The guests trampled the borders. After that, the 7th Earl said she couldn't have access to it – the current earl's father. He padlocked the gate. They were divorced soon after.'

'She could have climbed over it fairly easily, I would imagine,' I said, looking at it. I was fairly sure I could haul my stocky little frame over it, so Jamie's mum (surely an elegant giantess?) would have no problem.

'She didn't seem to care too much,' said Callum. 'But it upset Jamie.' He cleared his throat. 'Keith's been here for years. He told me when Jamie came home from school and found it all ruined, there was quite a scene. He'd planted things with her, spent time here with her. It upset him.'

'Oh.' I digested this new piece of information. *Came home from school* – they must have sent him to boarding school. My stomach pitched at the idea – as a young child, staying

32

away from home for even a night had unsettled me. 'How difficult for him.'

'I'm surprised he's asked you to start here,' said Callum. 'This place is special to him – but also sad. It's his mother who named it Belheddonbrae.'

'Does it mean something?' I said.

He cleared his throat. 'Technically – Bel for beautiful, heddon for heathy hill, brae for steep hill.'

I raised my eyebrows and glanced at his face. *Beautiful heathy hill steep hill*? He shrugged.

'I suppose it has a ring about it,' I said.

I took my phone out and took snaps of the area from different angles. Then I made a quick sketch of the beds, identifying those shrubs and plants I could make out. It was a joy to focus like this, my mind seeking and noting information. When I finished, I realised that for the first time in ages, I had quieted the humming sadness that seemed to buzz behind my thoughts all the time.

Callum had watched me the whole time, and seemed to approve. 'I'll make you a hot chocolate when we get back,' he said. 'You've earned it.' Fi had warned me Callum's hot chocolates were legendary, involving cream, marshmallows and usually a drop of whisky.

'As long as you leave out the alcohol,' I said. 'Seriously. I've already got a hangover.'

He laughed. 'If you like. On the way back I'll introduce you to Keith and Mica, who look after the gardens. They're married and live in one of the estate cottages.

They do the cars too – Keith drives the earl to any official functions.'

'Just your normal, average workplace,' I murmured to myself. 'Does the boss have a Rolls?'

'Of course,' he said, and I couldn't work out whether he was joking or not.

CHAPTER 4

FROM: Anna Whitlock
TO: Jamie Mulholland

Hi Jamie, I have inspected Belheddonbrae this morning. Also the castle ruins, which were wonderful! I would suggest converting Belheddonbrae into wildflower meadow. Best, Anna.

FROM: Jamie Mulholland
TO: Anna Whitlock

Anna, was expecting something more innovative than that. I could throw a few handfuls of wildflower seed around myself without a professional's input. For discussion. JM.

P.S. The ruins are unstable. I hope you wore a hard hat.

I screwed up my face in the least flattering way possible, aware that Tally was watching me. I wondered why I had abandoned all attempts to appear glossy and composed: I'd always been extra smiley when I was working in London, in buildings made of glass and steel, in my uniform of black skinny jeans (or not-so-skinny jeans as Sean snarkily referred to them sometimes), sharply pressed white cotton shirts, and blazers. Oh, and my hair always cut every six weeks and expensively highlighted.

Yet here I was: 1) No haircut for two months, it was starting to straggle out of its sharply defined style, the natural curl breaking out. 2) Sharp wardrobe being eroded by 'country style', including my clodhopper boots and the holey old woollen jumper in Scandi pattern I was wearing today. 3) I was making no attempt whatsoever to hide my true feelings about anything.

I tapped my phone open and messaged Rose in London.

> *Help. All style and composure gone. Am turning into country bumpkin. Was stylish & cool once, wasn't I?*

Her reply came back ninety seconds later.

> *Clearly true self is now emerging. Hahaha. Wuv you.*

I pulled another face (hopefully a more enigmatic one) and watched Tally tremble into life, like a plant that's just been watered.

TO: Jamie Mulholland
FROM: Anna Whitlock

Jamie, a wildflower meadow can be an incredibly sophisticated ecosystem. I will provide further details. I'm sure it's the right choice for Belheddonbrae.

As I understand it, your focus is on large-scale rewilding and biodiversity. Presumably I can meet with you and Callum to talk more strategically?

Regards, Anna.

Take that! I thought, my finger hovering over the left click to send. Regards. We all know what regards means. *Get stuffed.*

I sat back without clicking. So far that day I had gibbered at my new boss, sprayed his antique furnishings with coffee, and was now on the brink of sending a snarky email to him. I should probably dial it back, I thought. I changed 'Regards' to 'Best'. The rest of it looked fine.

I clicked send. At that moment, Callum appeared. He was holding the most enormous mug I had ever seen, with a picture of a fluffy baby penguin on the side. The hot chocolate inside was topped by a mass of cream speckled with mini marshmallows.

'You are a legend!' I said, welcoming it with open hands. I leaned close, well aware that Tally was at the photocopier, crashing around with an auction catalogue she had been peering at earlier. 'Have you made Tally one too?' I whispered. It was going to take the edge off my pleasure if she was glaring at me as I consumed it.

'Oh no,' he said gravely. 'Moment on the lips, lifetime on the hips. Enjoy.' He twinkled at me and disappeared back into the office.

Tally returned to her desk in a cloud of Chanel No. 5. 'You've got cream on your face, Anna,' she said, paperclipping her photocopies together.

I made a vague questioning noise before realising I had dipped my face too enthusiastically into the mug of plenty. 'Thanks,' I muttered, wiping it off and checking my reflection in my mobile screen.

'Moment on the lips, lifetime on the hips,' she said, narrowing her eyes.

I smiled, nodded, and downed another mouthful of hot chocolate, wondering how I could possibly thaw relations. 'What are you working on?' I said, in as friendly tone as I could manage.

Her eyes narrowed even further. 'Nothing to do with you,' she snapped. 'Can't you concentrate on your trees and plants and things?'

'Right.' I decided to call time on my efforts to bond for

the day. I popped my headphones on, and turned on a podcast about ghosts. The supernatural felt like it might do me
less harm than the living, if the bad mood emanating from
Tally was anything to go by.

I realised the supernatural podcast wasn't such a good idea
as I hurried home that night. Callum had dropped me at the
end of my lane so I didn't have to walk through the deer
park, and it was only when I was on my own, making my
way down the lane in the blustery dark, that I realised my
heart rate was raised and I was a bit on-edge.

I crashed into the empty cottage, turned all the lights on,
and noticed a mouse dropping on the floor. Well, at least
I wasn't alone. Then I saw the blue light blinking on the
phone – an answerphone message.

It's-not-Sean, it's-not-Sean, I murmured to myself as I dialled into the voicemail, held my breath, and waited.

It wasn't Sean. It was my mum, calling from Spain, where
she and my stepdad live. She started as always by giving me
the temperature. It was a perpetual wonder to her that they
lived somewhere warm. She deserved it – my dad left when
me and my sister were two and four, and with two girls
and a part-time job, Mum struggled to keep the heating on
some winters.

The important business of weather reporting done, she
continued. 'Anyway darling, just wanted to see how you are,
we're worried you might be off your head, leaving London
to live in a castle? So call me back, but not tonight, we're

out with Les and Trisha, and not tomorrow, we're out with Pat and Eric, maybe Friday, or I'll call you? Anyway, love you, love y—' End of voicemail.

Smiling, I saved the message, took my coat off and put the kettle on.

I'd spent the afternoon with my headphones on drawing my plan for Belheddonbrae. Before I'd focused on conservation and ecology, I'd trained in garden design, and painting was the best way of consolidating my ideas. Whatever I did, I knew the plan would have to look good to impress the earl. I opened my sketchbook and set up my watercolours, water pot and brushes. I'd created a neat plan of the garden and drawn detailed samples of some of the types of grass and flower I wanted to include; now I added colour to them. It was some of my best work: focused, detailed, colourful. Perhaps a bit OTT for a wildflower meadow plan, but who cared? The random earl couldn't accuse me of not putting the effort in. Plus I was loving it.

I was letting the plan dry, and standing in my kitchen area wondering whether to have cheese for dinner, when a face suddenly appeared at one of the tiny cottage windows.

I did the only sensible thing: screamed and dropped my mug.

It was Fi.

'Sorry love,' she said, when I recovered my wits enough to open the front door. 'Did you break it? You're a bit keyed up, aren't you?'

'Podcast,' I said. 'Probably shouldn't have binged on

ghosts and demons. The mug's fine – it bounced on the rug.' I waved it at her and went to fill the kettle.

'I've just come to drop this off. And I've never seen a ghost or a demon round here, if that helps.'

She was offering me a casserole dish. When I lifted the lid a wave of aroma hit me – slowly simmered veg, dumplings bobbing in the rich brown sauce.

'You have to let me make you a cup of tea now,' I said. 'To say thank you. I'll get out the best biscuits?'

She grinned. 'Oh, go on then, just one.'

I put the kettle on. 'This meal looks amazing, but I'm going to have to call a halt to you cooking for me,' I said. 'You've got enough to do.'

'It's just . . . I'd noticed you're not eating properly,' she said quietly. 'Snacking won't see you through the day.'

'Says the girl who lived off French fries when we were teenagers,' I said. 'I'm grateful, but you don't have to look after me. Besides, I had one of Callum's hot chocolates today, which provided a whole day's worth of nutrition.'

She laughed. 'Week One, and he's already made you a hot chocolate? You are honoured. I'm sorry I've been in and out so much. I've got the new merch to sort out and we're doing budget projections next week. Is Tally giving you a hard time? Callum messaged me to ask if you were okay.'

'Did he?' I felt touched at the idea of him looking out for me. 'It's fine,' I said. 'She's just a bit spiky.'

'She'll warm up,' said Fi. 'And Jamie, too – I know he

can be a bit forbidding, but he's a great boss once you get to know him.'

'Hmm,' I said, trying to smile.

'Anna?'

I gave a half-laugh, trying to keep things light. 'I guess – I just wasn't prepared for him, and her, to be so . . .' I screwed my face up. 'Posh, and *frosty*. I don't react well to it. I just automatically go into – poor person mode, like they're looking down on me. I start doubting myself.'

'Seriously?' Fi frowned. 'Hand me one of those good biscuits.'

I pushed the packet towards her.

'I can't believe we're even having this conversation,' she munched a chocolate-covered cookie. 'You're amazing at your job and Jamie knows how lucky he is to get you. And as for Tally, where do you think all of that iciness comes from? She's insecure, that's all.'

'I just don't react well when people look down on me,' I said. 'I remember when I first started at Mackenzie's, a well-off client asked me what school I'd attended, what university. When I told him – the expression on his face . . . It was like he was automatically deducting twenty points from my IQ. I just froze.'

'What an idiot.' Fi sipped her tea. 'Sounds totally deliberate to me. People do things like that to get you on the back foot. Jamie's not like that, and neither is Tally, not really.'

I nodded, but her words weren't hitting home.

She finished her tea. 'Look, you ever start feeling like this again, just message me Snookered and I'll be over here in two ticks to give you a pep talk.' When we were teenagers, Fi had gone out with a bloke who was mad for snooker to the point he dumped her because he wasn't getting enough playing time, leaving her sobbing in my arms on a Saturday night. Since that day, the word Snookered was our bat signal.

'Will do,' I said. 'Do you want to take some biscuits for Richard?'

'We're good for biscuits,' she said. 'Now, my love, eat *all* of the casserole. See you tomorrow.'

An hour later, I was aglow with warmth. Casserole eaten, garden plan dry and beautiful before me with its rainbow shades, wind dying down outside and the room toasty warm from the woodburner. I sipped my cup of tea and opened up the work email on my phone. If I sent Jamie an email now, he would see it at whatever ungodly hour he chose to start work.

FROM: Anna Whitlock
TO: Jamie Mulholland

Hi Jamie, I've put together a plan for Belheddonbrae.
May I take you through it at your earliest convenience?
It's probably best if I show it to you in person.
Best, Anna.

Job done, I snuggled under the crocheted blanket on the sofa and fell into a light doze, which was broken by a notification. I looked at the clock on the mantelpiece and saw that only five minutes had passed.

FROM: Jamie Mulholland
TO: Anna Whitlock

Hi Anna, I'd like to see the plan. Tomorrow at 9?
Please come to the flat – Fi will show you the way.

Best, Jamie.

P.S. I assume you're not allergic to dust, animal hair or woodworm. Mentioning that just in case. Living in a manor house isn't as glamorous as it sounds.

Surprisingly cheery! I just about managed to piece together: Hi Jamie, that's great, see you then – and no, not allergic to anything. Best, Anna.
I was wide awake now.
Plink.

Looking forward to hammering out the details of Belheddonbrae. And so is Hugo, who you haven't met yet. J.

I decided not to send a cheery response in case we were messaging all night, in one of those cringey, too-polite circles of correspondence where no one can bring themselves not to reply. When my phone pinged again I felt slightly nervous.

It was Callum: *Congratulations on getting through the first couple of days. Hope we're not putting you off.* 😊

I tapped back a 'smiley face' and 'strong emoji'. Then I realised I had a large smile plastered across my face. But I was *not* going to get my hopes up about Callum and his twinkly eyes.

CHAPTER 5

'Does Jamie have a son?' I whispered to Fi the next day, as we were striding our way through the back corridors of Stonemore. The house was open to the public, so we were banned from the grand rooms, which were currently being monitored by cheery stewards in navy blue sweatshirts monogrammed in yellow.

'What?' She frowned. 'No. Why did you think that?'

'He mentioned someone called Hugo in his email.' I didn't mention my late-night power-googling had yielded nothing for Jamie apart from a picture taken a decade or so ago when he was graduating from university (Cambridge, obviously). And the Earl of Roxdale's Wikipedia page had mainly focused on an ancestor who'd been a particularly brutal warrior in the wars against the Scots. When I looked for a Hugo Mullholland, all that my searches had produced were a LinkedIn entry for a hedge fund manager and an Ancestry entry for someone who'd died in 1626.

'Ha! Close, but no cigar,' said Fi. 'You'll see. Here we are.'

I'd been expecting the earl's apartment to be lavish, a mirror of the grand reception rooms below, with their oil paintings, cold-eyed portraits, gilding and grand furnishings. But we were standing in a corridor with a threadbare green carpet, by a front door with a brass '1' on it, like a normal flat. Fi knocked sharply and there was a flurry of fierce barking.

'I thought you said there weren't any demons hereabouts,' I said to Fi. 'It sounds like a hellhound.' She grinned in response.

I heard the pounding of feet on floorboards then the door opened a crack and Jamie's face appeared. 'Hello,' he said. 'Sorry, he's an enthusiastic watchdog.'

A small but stocky white and tan beagle launched himself at me and crashed against my legs. Despite the impact, I still had enough presence of mind to brace myself and offer my hand to a wet nose.

I glanced at Jamie's face. I might have been imagining it, but his hard, cold gaze seemed to have softened.

'Anna, can I formally introduce you to Hugo? Sorry, he'll want to sniff your face. He won't rest until he's done it. He won't lick you, don't worry.'

'Right.' I bent down and looked into Hugo's enormous dark eyes. 'Hello, sweet boy,' I squeaked to him, stroking his chest. His coat was so soft. Hugo delicately sniffed my hair line, eyebrows and mouth, then booped me on the nose with his own snout.

'Ooh.' I put my hand to the patch of damp he'd left behind. 'Is that good? Do I pass?'

'With him, at least,' said Jamie. 'But he's not the best judge of character.' He turned abruptly away.

I glanced at Fi and gave her a 'what did I do wrong?' look but she just smiled encouragingly.

We followed Jamie through a short hallway and then into a room which made me exclaim out loud. I remembered how Callum had told me many of the rooms at the back of the house were dust-sheeted; this apartment was at the front of the house on the second floor. Floor to ceiling windows looked out over the carriage drive, and the view beyond of the deer park, bisected by the long drive that led to the road. The walls and ceiling were decorated with Neo-Classical plasterwork in pale blue and white – it looked like an oversized Wedgwood plate. But as I looked around, I saw that the one vast room had been zoned into different areas: a couple of leather sofas covered with throws and the oldest TV I'd ever seen; an office area with shelves and a desk; a dining table with chairs and a bowl of fruit. I glimpsed a small kitchen through another doorway. All of it was bathed in glorious light. The most extraordinary studio flat I'd ever seen.

Fi was talking to Jamie about budgets, their faces grim, so I went to one of the enormous windows. Below, a coach was pulling up. Its doors opened and dozens of people spilled out, all of them looking upwards, snapping away with their cameras and phones. I suddenly had a flash of what it might feel like to live here; people constantly trying to consume little bits of Stonemore. Fi had told me they had found someone trying to chip a bit of cornicing off one of the rooms, claiming they wanted it as a souvenir. What must it be like, to look down on those eager, enquiring faces, day after day? I supposed being lord of the manor was compensation enough.

Lost in my thoughts, I hadn't noticed that Fi had gone.

'Hello?'

I swung round to find my new boss standing directly behind me, and was so surprised that I instinctively stepped back hard against the sash window.

'Watch out!' In an instant Jamie had grabbed hold of my shoulders and pulled me away from the glass. I stumbled (of course) and landed hard against him, the sudden proximity tripling my heartbeat and setting off a range of conflicting thoughts including *please no* and *he smells delicious*. Luckily, he didn't see my face for more than a second, because he released me as though I was on fire and turned away.

'Apologies for startling you,' he said, facing away from me. 'I didn't want you to fall against the glass. It's original, and not exactly tough.'

I caught my breath. 'I suppose plunging to my death in my first week here wouldn't be a good look,' I said, struggling to regain some composure. I was properly flustered. If only I had managed to complete my 'ice queen' mind map.

He turned back to me, a slight flush on his face, hands in his pockets, and just for a moment he reminded me of a schoolboy; there was a strange, uncomfortable look on his face, as though he was lost for words. Then in an instant his face turned back to its normal expression: cold, complacent inscrutability. Any vulnerability vanished.

I had a sinking feeling this meeting was going to be difficult.

'Shall we sit down over here?' he said, going over to the dining-room table and pulling out a chair for me with elaborate good manners. Then his expression changed sharply. 'Sit,' he barked.

I sat down, just about stifling the 'bloody hell' that rose to my lips.

'I was speaking to Hugo,' Jamie said. 'He looked like he was about to come and start pestering you.'

I glanced back to see a thoroughly awake Hugo sitting obediently on the sofa like a sentry on duty.

'Okay,' I murmured, busily unzipping my portfolio and drawing out the plan, shielding it with a plain piece of paper so I could build up to a big reveal. *Act professional*, I told myself. *No need to be embarrassed. No need to doubt yourself.*

Jamie drew out a chair opposite me and settled into it, crossing his long legs and clasping his hands in his lap.

'Explain to me your reasoning about the wildflower meadow,' he said, fixing his eyes on me, level and unblinking. This man had been to staring school. It was probably lesson number one in boarding school: how to stare down a working-class person.

I began my prepared speech – the terrain, the flowers and

grasses that I would recommend; the complexity of it as an ecosystem; the pollinators, which would in turn benefit the kitchen garden nearby. He remained silent. I wanted him to ask any questions before I showed him the plan, so when I had finished, I waited.

'I think I had something more formal in mind,' he said eventually. 'Structure, order. It's been a chaotic place.'

'Callum said there was some history there,' I said, trying to look as sympathetic as possible.

He raised his eyebrows. 'Really? I expected him to show you the plot, not gossip about me.'

I cringed inwardly. 'He wasn't gossiping. I asked him for context, and the history of how it had been used.'

'It was once beautiful, and now it's not,' he said flatly. 'That's all you need to know.'

'Right.' Movement caught my eye, and I looked behind me. Hugo was watching attentively, his head cocked.

Old Anna would give the earl what he wanted, and the 'yes' was on the tip of my tongue; change the plan, and smile the whole time. But it would be the wrong choice.

I looked back at Jamie and swallowed hard. 'If you want a formal garden, then that isn't what you hired me for, although I can make up a plan if you'd like me to. Or you can hand it over to Keith and Mica, who would be able to restore it as it was – the bones of the original garden are still there underneath it all. My recommendation is the meadow.'

'So it's your way or the highway?' he said crisply.

I blinked. 'That's not what I said. However, you pay

me for my professional opinion, and I think a wildflower meadow would be the best use for it.'

'I hired you,' he said, 'because you have a reputation for thinking outside the box and getting things done. Because the voluntary work you did alongside your corporate work showed you had passion for conservation and biodiversity. I wanted something exceptional for Stonemore, within our limited budget. If you think you've come here so you can daydream your way through the job, then think again.'

I pushed my chair away from the table. 'I'm a hard worker, and I've earned my reputation,' I said, hoping there wasn't a tremor of annoyance in my voice. 'I've never daydreamed through a day's work in my life, and I've never been handed anything on a plate.'

His eyes met mine; it was like two pieces of flint striking against each other, sparking dangerously. For a moment we sat in fizzing silence, glaring at each other. Stalemate. A tiny voice in my head, said: *Anna, you're pissing off the new boss again*, but I ignored it. The man deserved to be pissed off.

I couldn't help myself. 'You've seen my CV. You've seen the range of skills I have. Everything from project management to being really good with a chainsaw.'

'You don't need to repeat it to me.' He stayed totally still, hands still clasped in his lap, leaning back.

'But the key to all of it,' I ploughed on, practically *willing* him to look uncomfortable, 'is people. Getting on with people from all walks of life. Volunteers, farmers, scientists, contractors. And, of course, the occasional *landowner*.' I gave him a pointed look. 'I have experience with all of these, and I can see it's going to be a central issue here.'

He tilted his head and fixed me with his blue eyes. 'I agree.'

I tilted my head in echo of his gesture. *Touché*. 'Not that it really matters, but here's my impression of the wildflower meadow,' I said. I took the plain piece of paper away and pushed the drawing towards him.

He stared at it. I saw his eyes range over the plan. Still, that stony expression remained. I glanced over at Hugo, as though to say *no worries, mate, I'll be out of your hair in five*. Eventually, his lordship sat back and sighed.

'It's clear you're wedded to the idea of the meadow,' he said, his eyes fixed on my drawing.

I folded my arms across my chest. 'You're the boss at the end of the day,' I said coolly.

He drummed his fingers on the table for a long minute. I was thinking about offering to leave when he spoke.

'Right. I provisionally give the go-ahead to try this plan. But I reserve the right to change my mind.'

'I'm sorry?' I said. Had I *won*? It didn't feel as though I had.

'Belheddonbrae,' he said crisply, as though speaking to an idiot. 'I agree that you should begin with this plan.'

'Well, um, great!' I almost laughed with relief.

'Unless I change my mind in the next five minutes, which I might if you keep looking so pleased with yourself.' The suggestion of a smile flickered over his face. Then he got it under control and returned his gaze to its normal grumpy baseline, sheathing those brilliant eyes behind their mask of coolness.

'Thank you.' My voice caught on the words as I started gathering my things together. Despite all of my bold words, he was so unsettling. Best to leave now, while I was still ahead.

'One thing.' He put his hand out, touched the meadow plan with the tips of his fingers. 'Can I keep this? Do you have a copy you can work from?'

'Of course. I scanned it this morning.'

He nodded, and let his gaze rest on it.

A thump indicated Hugo had jumped down from the sofa. As I tucked my papers and pen away, he came over with a slow tail wag and leaned against Jamie's legs.

'He really is lovely,' I said.

'Yes.' Jamie fondled the beagle's ears and Hugo looked up at him with devotion. 'He's also mad. Hates other dogs. Can't fit in with the pack.'

I remembered how isolated I'd felt from my friends in London as they'd settled down and had babies; the quietness of my phone after my break-up with Sean. 'I know the feeling,' I said.

'Me too.' His face had softened when he looked down at Hugo. When he looked back up at me, I thought I might see the human being again. But the wall was back up. It seemed his nice side was reserved for dogs only.

'Oh, by the way,' I said. 'I'm planning to survey the section of ancient woodland near the upper reaches. Callum's shown me where it is on the map. I thought I'd drive up there this afternoon for a first look.'

He raised his eyebrows. 'On your own? The terrain is difficult. Don't overreach yourself.'

Lord, this man was annoying. 'I think I'll be fine, thanks,' I snipped.

He said nothing, just raised his eyebrows then looked at his phone with a faint look of amusement on his face. 'Whatever you say, Miss Whitlock. But do stay away from any large windows you might come across.'

'Thank you so much for your time this morning, *my lord*,' I said grittily. 'No need to see me out!'

I bounded for the exit, and was out the front door before even Hugo could catch up with me. The flat door closed heavily behind me.

I was standing in the corridor, trying to remember the way back to the office, when a blonde-haired woman appeared from a doorway on the right. She was dressed in full country gear – jodhpurs, wellies (pristine), quilted gilet and (of course!) a waxed jacket. Her features were so symmetrical and her figure so willowy, she looked like a model from a countrywear catalogue, the type where you can't buy a sweatshirt for less than three figures. She was even wearing pearl earrings, for goodness' sake. I gaped at her.

She smiled. 'Hello?'

'Hi!' I made a quick recovery back to full consciousness. 'Sorry, I'm new here and I'm lost. I've just visited the earl for the first time. I should have dropped breadcrumbs on the way here.'

She laughed politely. 'The old place is a bit of a rabbit warren. Where are you trying to get to?'

I explained and she patiently gave me a list of directions. Then she glanced at Jamie's door. 'Is he in a good mood?'

'Um, to be honest, I have no idea.'

She laughed again. 'I'll take my chances then. Nice to meet you . . .?'

'Anna.' I held my hand out. 'I'm working on the estate management with Callum. Rewilding, environmental management.'

'Really?' She shook my hand. 'So Jamie's finally getting around to it. Good for him – and you. I'm Lucinda, I stable my horses here. You'll see me around.'

I froze. *The ex.* 'Nice to meet you,' I burbled. And then I hurried off as fast as I could. I'd already had enough awkwardness for one day.

CHAPTER 6

Obviously, I got lost. I remembered approximately six of the eighteen turns I was supposed to make to return to the office. I found myself staring at a door in a green corridor, gazing at the brass doorknob so hard I was surprised it didn't glow red-hot.

I was absolutely sure this was the door. It had to be. I turned the knob and opened it.

It wasn't the door.

I had opened a secret door built into the panelling, and it let me into one of the main rooms. My sudden appearance behind the ropes scattered a startled group of tourists, and I heard someone shriek.

A helper wearing a monogrammed polo shirt appeared. 'What are you doing here?' she hissed. 'You almost gave me a heart attack, let alone them. And I don't have the defib here. Vicki's got it in the orangery.'

I apologised and explained where I wanted to go in a whisper. 'I'd need a pen and paper to explain,' she said, alternating her furious face with a brittle smile for the tourists. 'Just climb over the rope and go out of the front door. Walking around the outside might be simpler.'

'Okay, thanks.'

'Not that way! You'll set off the alarm on the Caravaggio!'

Nerves shredded, I finally found my way out of the room, watched with curiosity by the visitors. But somehow I managed to set off on a route that did not take me through the front door, and after wandering around for another five minutes I finally emerged out of what was definitely a *back* door. I was relieved to be out of the building, although there were drops of sleet in the air. And, tragically, my waxed jacket was still in the post.

As I was walking along the back of the building, past the kitchen garden and formal garden, I heard it. The baying. The combined voices of beagles.

Instead of carrying on around the side of Stonemore to the front – the staff office was in the front corner of the house – I followed the noise and drifted away from the manor. The noise was coming from an enclosure a good distance from the house, set away from the main drive – another area with high brick walls and a wooden door, like a secret garden. I went over and peered through a crack in the door. There were at least a dozen beagles, racing around a mowed field excitedly, sniffing, baying, and generally being houndy.

I turned away and leaned against the wall, remembering

Jamie's words about Hugo not fitting in with the pack. *The man actually had his own pack of hounds.* I shook my head in silent disapproval. Damn these posh boys. They practically came from a different planet to the one I inhabited. And hunting? I felt slightly sick. I knew about the countryside. But I'd hoped to ignore the reality of it for as long as possible. Perhaps I really wasn't suited to living here at all. Metropolitan Minnie had better get back on the long-distance train.

'Finally!' cried Tally, as I stomped back into the office, wondering if I could cancel my waxed jacket order. 'She's here, Callum!'

Callum appeared, so calm and unhurried that I wanted to hug him. 'Anna. Jamie messaged me. He said you wanted to drive up to the upper reaches? I've got the newest Land Rover out, and it's got a full tank. I'd head off as soon as possible if you wanted a quick look. The weather's not looking great.'

'Great,' I said flatly. In truth, those few drops of sleet had made me wonder if I should go another day. But there was no way I was backing out now, so Jamie could laugh behind his hand at his snowflake new employee melting under pressure. I could sense Fi watching me, but I didn't even have enough cheeriness in me to direct a reassuring smile her way.

'When he says "newest Land Rover",' said Tally cheerfully, 'he means it's twenty years old rather than thirty.'

I nodded and swallowed hard.

'You don't have to go now if you're not up for it,' said Callum gently.

'I'm 100 per cent up for it,' I said, and forced a smile.

It was then I noticed a text had arrived on my mobile, alongside the usual cheery messages from my sister and London friends asking about how the 'wilds' were. I'd put the phone on silent during my meeting with Jamie. The name froze me on the spot.

Sean.

'I'll just be a minute, Callum,' I said, and dashed out and down the corridor to the loo, a freezing cold room where the window was constantly open. I locked myself into the single cubicle and prodded my phone screen, my hands shaking.

Hey. Was just wondering how you are. Sean.

I stared at it. I bit back my first, instinctive answer:

Fine thanks. Just working through my newly acquired self-help library on how to deal with childlessness combined with heartbreak.
PS there's no need to sign off with your name. I know who you are. And I've seen your sex face, remember?

Bitterness aside, the core of my imagined message was true. I had a full crate of books on childlessness and grief. I was chipping away at them with my coloured pens and Post-it notes, alongside my journal. *Open your heart to grief,* I'd written the night before, *don't stay rigid, don't fight it.* Some days it felt as though I was making progress, that my brain was processing things in the background. Acceptance might be in the far distance, waving a little flag, but at least it was within sight. On other days I felt like I was in a black hole, numbly searching for a foothold that wasn't there.

I typed.

> *Fine thanks. You? A.*

His reply appeared almost immediately.

> *Good thanks. Could you let me know a landline number I can call you on? It would be good to have a chat. I tried this one the other night but it kept going to voicemail. S*

I glared at the message. It was so typical of him to have lost the number. He cared so little about me, was so lazy—

The door creaked open.

'Anna?' It was Fi. 'Are you alright?'

I opened the cubicle and peered out. 'Sean texted me.' I made an emoticon-style sad face. It was better than speaking properly. Admitting how sad I actually was.

'Oh, love.' She looked stricken. 'Saying what?'

'Nothing really. I'm fine.' I came out, and looked at

myself in the mirror. My eyes were glistening with all the tears I couldn't bring myself to cry. Despite my journalling, it looked like I was still sticking with the rigid approach. 'Stiff upper lip and all that.' I splashed cold water on my face. This place was a waste of make-up, anyway.

I went back to my desk to find a large package sitting in the middle of it, my belongings fanned out around it as though it had been dropped from a great height.

'There's been a delivery for you,' said Tally, swishing past.

'You don't say,' I said, fishing my scissors out of the desk drawer and beginning my battle with layers of packaging. Five minutes of hacking later, my waxed jacket was revealed in all of its olive-green glory.

'Go on, put it on!' squeaked Fi, clapping her hands. I raced down the hall to the loo. No way was Tally getting a look at 'country' me until I'd prepared myself.

I cautiously put the jacket on, wondering if it might transform me in some way – make me more at home in this manor house. I'd sized up because of my outsized hips, but the most important thing was I had to be able to do the coat up, so I was ready for *all weathers*. This had worked, but the sleeves were a bit too long and it looked baggy rather than sleek, as though I was hiding something. It seemed I had bought a coat which would encompass both my massive bitterness as well as my arse.

'Crikey.' Fi had arrived on the scene. 'You could fit two of you in there.'

'It's okay though, right?' I said. 'I can work the outsized look? I can't be bothered to send it back.'

'Plus you tore the packaging apart like a crazed orangutan,' she murmured. 'It would take an entire roll of tape to put it back together.' She tilted her head. 'You look cute, actually.'

I marched back into the office and did a twirl for Tally, who frowned and said 'Did you mean to buy a marquee?' Cue return to silence.

Callum gave me the keys to the Land Rover and quietly took me through the route I should take to the upper reaches, advising me to pick up one of the estate long-range walkie talkies on the way out. He'd already told me the route the day before, but I could tell he sensed my nerves. When he finished, I looked at him in a way that I hoped conveyed utter confidence but the slight frown on his face told me otherwise.

'It's all fine,' I said, in a voice I'd aimed to come across as cheerful, but which sounded brittle.

'You won't need it, but there's an emergency kit in the back of the Rover,' he said. 'And the car's got a tracker on it.'

'A tracker?' I said. 'Do you, er, lose people very often?'

'You'll be fine. Look, I can come with you if you're at all uncertain. I've got stuff to do, but—'

'It's fine. Thanks.'

He smiled, that slow, easy smile which had persuaded me at my interview that we would be friends. 'Great. And Anna?'

I turned back. 'Yes?'

'I like the coat.'

Finally, a man who had something complimentary to say.

The temperature had dropped outside and the last of the tourists were meandering towards their cars and coaches. The house closed at 3pm in winter, so there was more than an hour to go, but the weather was putting people off. Icy blobs dissolved on impact with my face.

I had to tough it out. I tried one of the breathing exercises I'd memorised when I was trying to meditate Sean's face out of my mind. In for three, hold for three, out for three.

I got into the Land Rover. It smelt reassuringly of leather and fresh air, greenery and soil – the smell I'd already come to associate with Stonemore. As I put the key in the ignition, I could feel my own heartbeat, pounding with anticipation and fear. In for three, hold for three.

Then I glanced up at the house. Jamie was standing at the window of his flat, looking down on me. Even from a distance I could see the smirk on his face.

That did it. I released my held breath with a puff of indignation. With a flourish of annoyance, I turned the key, balanced the clutch, and roared out of the drive like a teenager heading out to do handbrake turns on a Friday night.

I'm not going to deny it, I was pretty damn terrified, but also exhilarated, as I drove up the pale gravel track in the direction of the upper reaches. Away from the controlled splendour of the house and deer park, the wintry landscape felt more unforgiving, the hills dark browny-green against dense white and grey clouds, the wind buffeting the car in gusts as I drove. One of the tracks through the edge of a wooded area took me past uprooted and broken trees from a recent storm, the clouds lying dense against the higher peaks of hills in the distance, splodges of icy water against my windscreen.

As I got higher and higher, the weather started to worsen.

Snow. Yes, this was definitely snow. I slowed the Land Rover, then finally stopped. I snatched the map up from the passenger seat and inspected it. I'd memorised the route but was beginning to think I'd made a mistake at some point. Callum had mentioned a fence line with red markers on the posts that I definitely should have reached by now. I looked at the fence ahead of me.

No red markers.

'Right,' I muttered, under my breath.

When I looked back at the map and directions, I struggled to focus. I tried to think logically about the route I'd taken so far, to work out where I'd gone wrong. But somehow I couldn't slow my mind down. Had I taken a left or a right? Had I seen that five-barred gate he'd mentioned, or hadn't I? My Land Rover felt tiny, insignificant against the vastness of the dark slopes around me, as visibility dissolved. When I tried to focus on the map properly, its symbols started to blur.

Oh God, this was actually happening. What an excellent time to develop a talent for panicking.

I tried the breathing exercise, but it wasn't cutting it. I got out of the car and looked at the landscape. It had stopped snowing (good news!), but there was no sign of the house and castle (bad news!). Although the weather wasn't worsening, visibility was limited by the swirling grey vapour in the air, the landscape reduced to bare outlines. No waymarkers. And I'd forgotten the walkie talkie. In the midst of winding myself up about Jamie, and feeling a little flutter about Callum's compliment, I had forgotten the bloody walkie talkie. I dug my phone out of my pocket. No reception. No data.

Swearing under my breath, I climbed back in and started the Land Rover again, to begin the laborious process of turning the vehicle round. I mean, I had to get used to this off-road driving, didn't I? Slowly and carefully, I edged it round in a ten-point turn. I had just completed the manoeuvre and was starting to accelerate gently away alongside a line of trees when, out of nowhere, a pheasant flew across the windscreen in an explosion of wings and copper-coloured feathers.

It was sheer instinct: I jerked the steering wheel to the right to avoid it. As I did so, one side of the vehicle dropped dramatically, and its wheels started spinning. Heart racing, I turned the engine off and climbed out of the car. I had steered it half into a shallow ditch. It wasn't sinking, but it was at a crazy tilt and there was no way I was getting out of there without help. The pheasant, meanwhile, was totally fine, and abandoned me to my fate. 'No,' I moaned, and leaned against the car, shivering in the cold.

Taking deep breaths, I opened the back of the Land

Rover and dragged the emergency kit out, then got back in the front to inspect the contents. Blanket, bottle of water, chocolate, rope, torch. I didn't look much harder. Chocolate and water was the go-to for me. I just needed to stay calm.

You are *not* going to panic, Anna.

A moment later there was a rushing sound in my ears.

No, no, no, I said in my head, and put my head to my knees.

Thankfully, after a moment or two, I started to feel more normal. Eventually I edged my way up until I was sitting in a normal position in the driver's seat. I looked at my watch. Beyond the Land Rover's window, the light was fading. I closed my eyes against the vastness of the landscape, the fierceness of the wind.

Things were getting better though – I wasn't shaking, and my breathing was slowing down. I just had to inure myself to the idea of staying the night in the car and finding my way back in daylight. It was perfectly fine, and I'd laugh about it one day, tell the story at dinner parties, that kind of thing. I wrapped the blanket around me and settled back in the seat. Took a square of chocolate. Then another one. Had a swig from the bottle of water. Let time pass as I watched the snow continue to fall.

It was almost six o'clock when I saw the headlights, coming from the vague direction of Stonemore. When I realised it was a Land Rover, I turned my own lights on and flashed them repeatedly. The vehicle approached at crawling pace, parked alongside me, and Callum jumped out, smiling as though he was on a Sunday afternoon drive.

'Hey!' I said, getting out to meet him, and trying to keep my voice light. I still had the tartan blanket wrapped around me, but I pushed my hair behind my ears and tried to look nonchalant. Callum sought my gaze and put his hands on my arms, then gave a me quick squeeze. 'Good to see you,' he said.

'Hey,' said another voice. 'I see you managed to get yourself lost after all.'

It was Jamie. He was climbing out of the other side of Callum's Land Rover.

Humiliation complete. I looked at the ground but, sadly, it did not open up and swallow me. 'Thanks,' I muttered. 'How did you find me?'

'We just looked for the enormous vehicle at walking distance from the house,' said Jamie, and I wanted to slap him so badly I gritted my teeth.

'I'm joking,' he said stiffly. 'You'd been gone a while. We checked the tracker and saw the car wasn't moving, so we came to see if you needed some help.'

'Right,' I mumbled. 'Thanks.'

'You doing okay, Anna?' said Callum softly. He was inspecting the front of the Land Rover.

'Yep, all good,' I said. 'I hope I haven't damaged it. There was a pheasant. I guess I'm used to London roads. Less wildlife. I'm glad to see you both. I was getting ready to bed down for the night.'

'Don't tell me you've already broken into the chocolate?' Jamie said, raising an eyebrow. I noticed he had another blanket in his hand which he now offered me from a distance, with an air of distaste. I snatched it from him grumpily and doubled it round me.

'Sure, it's fine,' Callum said. 'Why don't you get in the back of ours. Warm yourself up – I've had the heater on full blast.'

Feeling a bit feeble, but also grateful, I climbed in and watched Callum and Jamie inspect the Land Rover I'd deserted in a ditch. Eventually they came back and climbed back in. 'We'll get it in the morning,' said Callum.

'I'm sorry for your trouble,' I said lamely.

'Ach, don't even think about it, I did the same thing last winter,' he said.

I glared at the back of Jamie's head, he who was staying stonily silent with blame emanating from him. But I couldn't stay annoyed for long. I felt a rush of relief, followed swiftly by exhaustion. Lulled by the rocking of the Land Rover as we descended towards Stonemore, I fell asleep.

I came to when I felt a hand on my wrist, and opened my eyes to see Jamie. He was leaning round the seat, gently shaking my wrist. As I opened my eyes and stared at him in surprise, he pulled his hand away as though he'd been burned. 'Your phone,' he said.

It was buzzing on the seat beside me.

Sean's name, in white font on black. I stared at it.

'Shouldn't you get it?' Jamie glanced back at me, frowning.

I hit answer.

'Anna? It's Sean.'

I swallowed hard. 'Hi.'

'Are you okay? I thought we were going to speak.'

'I'm fine. There's been a situation at work. I'll call soon.'

He tried to interrupt me but I was having none of it. 'Okay, well—'

'No Sean, not now.' I saw Jamie and Callum glance at each other. I heard, and felt, the beat of silence. Had I ever said no to Sean before? I spoke into the silence. 'I'll call you later. Bye.' I hung up.

I tried hard to look calm, and tucked the phone away in my pocket. We took the rest of the journey in silence. I was pleased to see the house. 'Civilisation,' I announced, and saw Callum's mouth twitch in amusement.

As we clambered out of the Land Rover, I wondered what Tally would say the next morning. 'I guess I'll get some teasing tomorrow,' I said.

'Work from home,' Jamie said. 'And don't push yourself. Make any phone calls you need to make.'

'It's fine,' I said. 'I'm fine.'

'Don't make me use my Hugo voice.'

Was he actually being . . . nice? I ventured a glance at his face. Nope, he was gazing over the top of my head at the middle distance, as if our conversation was boring him to death. 'Thank you,' I said quietly. 'I'll get my laptop.'

'And,' he lowered his voice as Callum jumped out and checked the wheels. 'You sounded pretty angry with him, whoever he is.'

I gaped at him. What a cheek! To openly listen in to my conversation.

'Maybe write him a letter,' he said, his gaze cool and even. 'The kind you don't send.'

I gave him a tight smile but was luckily spared from replying by Callum arriving at my side.

'I'll give you a lift home, Anna,' he said. 'Grab your stuff and jump back in.'

CHAPTER 7

The next morning, as I descended the creaky stairs, padded my way across the cold flagstones and flipped the kettle switch on to make tea, I decided *not* to work from home. I was ready to begin the rewilding strategy for Stonemore Estate. Ready to deal with Tally's snarky 'jokes'. Definitely ready to spend more time with Callum, the man who had saved me from exposure on a hillside. Revitalised.

Plink. Sean.

Anna, can we—

Delete, because deleting him was a kind of 'no', wasn't it? I had to move on from the past. Give myself some tough love.

Although, perhaps he'd cottoned on that I'd taken one of his sweatshirts, which I occasionally wore when I was feeling particularly sorry for myself.

Tally looked cheery when I went into the office. She was wearing red lipstick which must have taken her an age to apply and a houndstooth suit that made her look like Jackie Kennedy circa 1962. Meanwhile I was lowering the bar again: jeans, fleece, enormous waxed jacket, barely brushed hair.

I'd just logged into my computer and made a round of teas when Callum popped his head around the corner. 'Anna, can I have a word?'

'Of course.' I picked up my notebook and my cup of tea. My stomach dived at the awkward look on his face as I followed him into the office.

'Is everything alright?' I said.

'Yes.' Callum was sitting up military straight, his hands folded on the desk in front of him. 'Please, take a seat.'

I sat down and took a calming gulp of tea.

'Right ...' Callum was looking as uncomfortable as he had when he interviewed me. 'It's just a small thing. Jamie's asked that you report directly to me from now on, rather than him. I can pass on any headline points, but things should go through me.'

Right. Not a disaster, but perplexing. 'That's fine by me,' I said. 'But I thought rewilding was very much his project?'

Callum shifted in his seat. 'It is, but he has lots to attend to at the moment. And as I said, I can pass on anything you need. He'll read your strategy document when it's ready, and feed back his thoughts to you.' He cleared his throat. 'Through me.' He hazarded a slight smile. 'Unless you find working with me objectionable?'

I tried to ignore the little flutter in my chest and laughed more loudly than I should have done. 'Of course not!'

He smiled, and bit his lip. 'Good. For the record, I'd prefer you to consider me a colleague, rather than a manager, even if I am a conduit for Jamie's instructions.'

'Will do,' I said, answering his smile with my own.

He gave a sigh of relief. 'Now that's done, would you like a hot chocolate?'

'I don't think I've done anything to deserve it yet. I'll make a start on the strategy right away. This afternoon we're going to begin removing the top layer of soil at Belheddonbrac.'

'By hand?'

I shrugged. 'There's no way of getting a digger safely in there. Don't worry, I love doing this kind of thing. Oh, and I've already initiated contact with that charity I mentioned at interview – about reintroducing beavers.'

'Grand. But don't rush – we're not on your London time here.'

I went back to my desk. Fi had arrived and was looking flustered. 'You alright?' I said to her.

'Fine. You?' She was distractedly putting lipstick on.

'Yep. I'll make you a cuppa,' I said.

'Are you obsessed with hot drinks?' said Tally brightly.

'Yes,' I said, sweeping past her.

'I'm surprised you're still here,' said Tally. 'Jamie looked so grim this morning, I'd assumed you were for the chop, but I'm glad you've been given a second chance.'

'Doesn't he always look grim?' I said, prodding Fi's teabag

into life and trying to ignore the anxious lurch my stomach had taken at the idea I'd annoyed Jamie again.

As I carried the tea over, Tally lined her pencils up on her desk. 'You could have made me another one.'

'I'll make you another one when you play nice,' I said.

'Oh shut up, the pair of you!' Fi snapped. Her outburst was so surprising, both Tally and I did shut up. Each of us quietly turned to our computers and started work. Fi put her AirPods in and fixated on a budget spreadsheet.

The peace lasted all of two minutes. I was just opening a fresh Word document and typing the words 'Stonemore Rewilding Strategy' when I heard Tally give a piercing scream. I looked up to see a flash of white and tan as Hugo, ears flapping, sped past. Like a stealth raider, he had run silently across the carpeted floor and snatched something.

'He's got my cereal bar!' squealed Tally. Fi shoved the door shut as Hugo made a bolt for it. He came to a halt and looked up at her, mouth full of a cereal bar still encased in its wrapping.

'Give it back!' said Tally.

'I'm not sure he understands that particular command,' I murmured.

But Hugo certainly knew what she meant when she approached him. His ears dropped, his eyes grew distinctly darker in expression, and he emitted a low growl from the depths of his throat. 'Oh, you little shit,' said Tally, in such a posh voice that I almost laughed out loud.

It was at that moment that Jamie opened the door a crack and peered round. At the sight of Hugo, he visibly relaxed.

'There you are,' he said, swiftly entering and closing the door before Hugo could get round his legs. Hugo stopped growling, but stared mulishly at his owner.

'He threatened to bite me,' said Tally, in a severe voice.

'Did he?' Jamie wasn't even looking at her. 'He does sometimes exhibit guarding behaviour.'

'Just let him have it.' She sat down heavily and tried to look unflustered. 'I mean, he's a sweet little thing really, aren't you, Hugo?'

Hugo glared at her.

'Does it have raisins in it?' said Jamie. 'They're very bad for dogs. Come here, you ingrate.'

Hugo refused to budge. Jamie reached in his pocket and took out a biscuit. 'Thankfully I'm prepared for this situation ever since he ate Lucinda's sunglasses.'

Lucinda. My eyes flew to his face. Perhaps Lucinda might be the key to his misery. His face was its usual set mask of chilliness.

Hugo was delighted at the appearance of the biscuit and immediately dropped the bar, which Jamie kicked clear as though it was a loaded gun before giving him the biscuit then bundling him into his arms.

'Sorry for the interruption,' he said, and caught my eye. 'I thought you were working from home?'

'I felt like coming in,' I said.

'Congratulations on finding your way,' he said.

It was all I could do not to throw a stapler at him.

*

I made good headway on my strategy document but was also well aware that things were not right with Fi. Her expression was stony after Jamie left, and it was clear she wanted her space, so we all worked in careful silence. Halfway through the morning I happened to look up and saw that her eyes were full of tears.

I looked away immediately. Everything about her indicated DO NOT DISTURB and I didn't want to initiate a chat in front of Tally. But when she got up to go to the loo, I waited for a few seconds then followed.

I caught up with her in the cold hidey hole of the loo, window open, obvs, even though there was still snow on the ground. Perhaps Mr I'm-a-poor-earl could save some money on the heating if he occasionally closed a window.

'Anna?' She turned to me, her expression neutral, the shutters still closed over her eyes. 'Has Sean been texting again?'

'Nope,' I said. 'That is, yes, but that's not why I'm here. What's wrong? Are you okay?'

'I'm fine.' But her normally sunny face was trembling, her lips pursed with the sheer effort of trying not to cry. There was something slightly scary about seeing Fi crumble in front of me. Her default setting was strong; I sometimes felt she was made of beautiful, durable York stone whilst I was made of chalk.

There was only one thing to do: I put my arms around her, and she sobbed on my shoulder. I had to stop myself from squeezing her tight, like she was a little child.

'Sorry.' Eventually she emerged from my shoulder and gave me a weak smile.

'No need to apologise. I'm a veteran of the toilet sob at work. You should have seen the loos at Mackenzie's after a restructuring announcement. Scores of men and women weeping, and it usually happened at least once a quarter.'

She smiled. 'It's all the bloody hormones I'm taking.' She wiped her face on her sleeve before I could get a handful of tissues out of the holder.

I nodded. I knew Fi and Richard were having IVF; we'd chatted around the borders of the subject but not ventured into the depths of it. It's weird what is veiled in secrecy, or is it shame? I could talk to her about weight gain, sex and periods, but not the relentless scramble to have a child. I'd been advised IVF wouldn't help me, but that wasn't the reason I avoided the subject. Every time it was mentioned, Fi's shutters came down, as if she couldn't admit it might fail, and couldn't relax until the baby was there. Their baby – the one that already lived in her mind, name picked out, features decided. I knew about the pain of that.

'This attempt,' she said. 'It hasn't taken.'

I looked her in the eyes. I knew she needed a witness, not for me to look away. 'I'm so sorry,' I said. We shivered together in the icy draught from the window.

'It will happen, won't it?' she said. 'Eventually? Before our savings run out?'

I paused. The truth was, I didn't know; IVF success rates were perilously low. I'd always told myself I would have kids; told myself that even as the odds shortened, until finally they crumbled to zero. But looking at Fi's face, I knew she didn't want hard truths. Right now, in this moment, she just needed reassurance.

'Everything will be fine,' I said, hugging her again, so she couldn't see my face. 'I promise.'

It was a white lie, but sometimes we need those, don't we?

There are some days when I wish I smoked. Or at least had a reasonable excuse to go outside and scream into the wind whilst doing something vaguely elegant with my hands.

After I had settled Fi back at her desk, wrapped her up in my chair blanket (so I have a chair blanket, what sane person doesn't?) and made her another tea with about five sugars in it, I went outside to have an imaginary smoking break, and walked to the ruins.

The winter sky was incredibly beautiful: the brightest forget-me-not blue, with black and white clouds scudding across it. I admit that within fifteen seconds my hands were so cold they felt like they'd been flayed, but I pulled my fleece sleeves over them, and everything was fine. Perhaps it was good I didn't smoke because I'd get frostbite in no time. I stared at the castle ruins, fragments of sky visible through windows empty of glass.

'Penny for them.'

I turned to see Callum. He was holding the penguin mug in both hands.

'It's chocolate,' he said, 'but I can't promise it's hot

anymore.' He handed it to me, then passed me a blanket he'd tucked under his arm. 'As Fiona is using yours, I thought you might need one. We don't want you catching a chill.'

'Thanks.' I tried to tamp down the little thrill in my chest at the sight of his smile, but there were some things, I was learning, that even my 'No' mantra didn't take the edge off. His presence was so comforting after the emotional upheaval of the day. And yet he was – undeniably, if not obviously – sexy. Yep, Callum was sexy.

I took a mouthful of hot chocolate and almost choked on it. He patted me on the back as I coughed.

'Thanks again,' I was laughing as I emerged out of the coughing fit. 'Aren't you cold?' He didn't even have a coat on.

'Nah.' He looked out at the estate. 'Got my long johns on.'

I gave a cry of laughter, half inhaled another mouthful of hot chocolate and descended into another coughing fit. When I looked back at him, he was smiling at me, and I didn't know how to arrange my face.

Honestly, it was as if *I* was on hormones, as well as Fi.

CHAPTER 8

I decided to deal with my difficult emotions by attacking the preparation of the site at Belheddonbrae like a demon, alongside a (bemused) set of volunteers. Together we took up the patchy grass of the lawn, working by hand with spades and rakes. That week we managed to reveal the subsoil, and I'd taken to getting up extra early to weed the ground, working on a square metre per morning.

After a day or so of fresh air, I decided it would be mature of me to speak to Sean rather than avoiding his messages forever. He called on my landline and we had ninety seconds of stilted conversation, before he admitted he wanted one of his CDs back, and asked whether he could buy it using my Amazon account, because he still had the password (classy). I agreed, and the conversation ended. When I hung up the phone I didn't feel as desolate as I thought I would.

The thing was, I was getting used to Stonemore. After

the anonymity of London, it was strange to live somewhere where the local grocer said, 'You're wearing that nice green coat again.' The fact that she knew my name, let alone noticed what I was wearing, seemed mind-boggling. It also helped that the village was so picturesque: quaint, grey stone cottages clustered around the river, with a local grocer, baker and post office where people gathered to chat – and of course, the Rising Sun pub. Everyone knew everyone.

I admit, the first time my neighbour (from across the field) said 'You were up late last night,' it seemed *really weird* that they'd noticed the time they saw a light on in my bedroom window. But, nosiness aside, it was also the kind of place where, if you were running for a train, the guard would patiently hold it for you – and no one would mutter and look at their watch when you got on. I hadn't really believed places like this existed, but when I witnessed it I felt a rush of goodwill and affection.

The cottage was already starting to feel more like home; I'd got used to its Gothic character and its one-up/one-down layout. I'd learned the creaks in the stairs, the knack of getting the shower in the tiny bathroom extension to produce hot water for thirty seconds, and I'd even started giving the mice names (they all looked identical, but it felt better to shout 'Shut up, Gerald' in the direction of the attic at midnight rather than quaking at the sound of them skittering across the upper floor). I didn't hear them as much as before, because for the first time in years I was sleeping soundly, from the fresh air and hard physical work.

There'd even been a ceasefire with Tally, who had grudg-
ingly accepted I wasn't 'too annoying, for a Londoner'. I'd
started baking treats for the office, and always did an extra
batch for Keith and Mica. Despite having been at Stonemore
for decades, they had embraced my schemes with enthusiasm, and organised their team of volunteers and students to
do my bidding with such kindness and lack of drama that I
felt I should start worshipping them as deities. I was heaving
an enormous bag of flour onto the counter to make a batch
of scones for Mica when my phone chimed.

Any excuse not to begin the terrifying process of scone-
making, so I went to my phone. It was a message from Tally
on the work group chat.

> *4got to tell you @anna, the WI called,*
> *they kindly requested that you give them a*
> *presentation on wildflower meadows at their*
> *mtg next wk.*

Plink.

> *I would advise you to accept.*

Plink.

> *It is important for the reputation of Stonemore.*
> *Over and out.*

I went back to the scone-making. Although giving a PowerPoint presentation to the Women's Institute in a draughty church hall on a weekday evening wasn't exactly my idea of fun, I'd had far tougher crowds. As I kneaded the dough, I remembered a conference paper I'd given two years before, with 500 delegates watching. Me: shiny, smiley, new engagement ring sparkling on my finger, manicure, sharp suit, not a hair out of place. The Anna that said yes to things. An entirely different person. So cheerful, so sure of what the future held: a houseful of children, a happy marriage, a successful career. Not baking scones for an empty house dressed in old jeans, a fleece, and with a dozen mice checking their watches upstairs to see if it was time for them to start dancing around the house and disturbing my evening.

The books all told me I should journal my feelings and face them, but for the last week or so I'd pressed pause on it, because it seemed to send me down a rabbit hole. I was happier rubbing butter into flour and mainlining podcasts; watching Forestcam and trying to forget that the only thing my ex wanted to talk to me about was not the fact that he missed the smell of my neck (I missed his) but that his Stormzy CD was missing. The only bright spot was the cheerful, buzzy feeling I had when I spoke to Callum, when he smiled at me in that twinkly way he had. And it was fine – I was *not* in the market for a new relationship. But a tiny flirtation couldn't hurt, could it?

*

Stonemore Church Hall on a Monday evening was a surprisingly intimidating prospect once I got there. There were
many more women than I had thought would attend, and
although lots of them were smiling and chatting, a few were
gazing at me with stony expressions as I set up my laptop
with the projector.

'I hear she's some kind of environmentalist,' one woman,
wearing pearls and a pale pink twinset, said rather too loudly
to another. 'She's probably involved with that Just Stop Oil
lunacy.' My smile fixed, rictus-like, on my face. *Great*, I
thought, *time to be inspected and found wanting.* I'd told myself
these would just be normal, friendly people, but here I
was with a woman looking me up and down as though I'd
wandered in for the free cake. At least I was wearing smart
clothes and had made an effort with my make-up. *Lump in
my throat, check. Dry mouth, check.* Kate, the lady who'd invited me, was flitting about, smiling and talking to people.

I went over and tapped her on the shoulder. 'I'm just going
to pop out for a breath of air,' I said. 'Won't be a minute.'

She smiled and nodded, then carried on talking. I made
my way out past more curious faces and emerged from the
door of the hall, facing onto the main street of the village,
the hills beyond. I'd hoped for a glimpse of the Stonemore
hills, but of course it was a dark winter evening, so I only
caught the faintest outline of them. Still, the air was cold
and clear and it was good to be on my own.

I'd taken a few shuddering breaths when I became aware
of two figures crossing the road and coming towards me.

No.

Please, no.

Callum and Jamie.

'What are you two troublemakers doing here?' I said, as cheerfully as I could, hearing the slight note of hysteria in my voice.

'I heard there's a presentation on wildflowers here tonight,' said Jamie. Was that a very slight flicker of a smile on his face? Then I realised it was the poor light and I was imagining it.

Callum was standing, looking diffident, a faint, shy smile on his face. 'We're just moral support,' he said.

'We'll try and stay awake,' said Jamie, sweeping past.

'Er, thanks,' I said.

After they'd gone in, I took a few more deep breaths and gave myself a silent pep talk: *You've got this. No problem. Perspective: in 100 years we'll all be dead.* When I walked back inside, smile pinned to my face, it felt as though everyone could see my nerves, and yet I also felt a spark of defiance, a distinct *take your best shot* feeling towards anyone who was looking down their nose at me.

I allowed the smile to drop. I'd read once if you looked really miserable at the beginning of a presentation, then smiled five minutes in, you'd have an audience eating out the palm of your hand.

Kate stood up and gave a short introduction whilst I stood behind her, gimlet-eyed. I looked at my hands: my short nails, scrubbed free from dirt after an afternoon of weeding, painted with a bright orange varnish that I'd dug out from the bottom of my make-up bag. Battle paint. Then Kate turned the lights out and my first slide sprang into view. My mouth felt like sandpaper. I took a swig of water. As I opened my mouth to speak, for a moment this all felt impossible: the last year, every loss and failure that had brought me here, waiting to leap out of the corners of the room.

'Good evening everyone, my name is Anna Whitlock and I am the rewilding manager for Stonemore Estate. This evening I'm going to be talking to you about wildflower meadows, both as aesthetically beautiful sites in the landscape, but also as diverse habitats, capable of enriching and assisting conservation areas in a variety of ways. Particularly important since the UK has lost 97 per cent of its wildflower meadows since the Second World War.'

My voice echoed out into the darkness: strong, confident, no hint of hesitation. Somehow I'd clicked into the part of my brain that could perform.

All of my preparation paid off. I paced myself, moving smoothly through the slides. Once or twice I dried up, but my experience told me to carry on boldly and I did. Occasionally I allowed myself a glance at the audience – a risky strategy – but I saw enough to show me that most of them were interested and concentrating, the bright colours of my slides lighting up their attentive faces. Just once I caught lady-with-pearls rolling her eyes, but I filed that and carried on. And mercifully, I couldn't see Jamie or Callum – they were sitting in the back row, and once the lights went out they were lost in the darkness.

'Thank you.' I concluded my talk and was gratified to hear a healthy round of applause as the lights came back on. Kate rushed up, her face wreathed in smiles, and gave a brief thank you speech before opening the floor for questions. Hands shot up. Possibly the most enthusiastic audience I'd ever had – who knew? Perhaps I should have run away from London earlier.

'Could you talk a little more about the red deadnettle?' asked one nervous, sweet voice. 'And show the picture again? I think I've got it in my garden.'

Most of the questions were like this: well intentioned, kindly meant, easily answered. I noticed that lady-with-pearls was putting her hand up again and again, but not being chosen by Kate. Eventually she was the last woman standing and cleared her throat loudly.

I heard Kate give a tiny sigh. 'Clarissa,' she said.

'Thank you, Katherine.' The woman's accent was as cut-glass as I remembered, and she rose to her feet in a stately fashion. 'An interesting presentation, Ms Whitlock. But I have no idea what relevance it has to the Stonemore Estate, which already has vast tracts of wild land.'

The audience turned their eyes upon me. I smiled. 'An excellent question.' I ignored the fact she hadn't asked a question. 'But perhaps the land you see as wild, isn't quite as wild as you think. There is, certainly, a small amount of ancient woodland on the estate. That needs careful management to ensure that it survives and flourishes. But let me be clear: I am not advocating stripping away what we currently have, and aggressive replanting. What we are aiming for is a careful process of gently managed natural regeneration. And the development of a richer ecosystem which will benefit the whole estate. Furthermore—'

'Yes, yes, yes.' The woman flapped her hands and gave a laugh. 'I heard you were some kind of environmental person. It all sounds like the emperor's new clothes a little though, my dear, doesn't it?'

I persevered. 'Not at all. It's a critical time for the healthy future of the estate—'

'Yes, yes, yes . . .' This seemed to be her standard response to me. 'We must let the gentlemen have their fads, dear, mustn't we? And if we profit from it, that doesn't hurt either.' She gave me a sly smile, as though we secretly understood each other.

I converted my expression from one of friendly openness to stony puzzlement. Not a stretch, I can tell you. 'I'm sorry,' I managed in a frostily polite tone. 'I have no idea what you mean.'

'Our earl,' said Clarissa slowly, as if I was stupid. A small ripple moved through the room, as the half of the audience which knew Jamie was there attempted to communicate with the less aware half. Which obviously included Clarissa.

Unfortunately for her, she seemed to take the ripple as agreement rather than warning, and built up some momentum.

'You're a very pretty manifestation of his latest fad,' she said, her eyes glowing with malicious merriment. 'But I can assure you he will be moving on very soon. I have rather more insight into his character than you do, dear.'

'How interesting, Clarissa.' Jamie's voice boomed out suddenly. He got slowly to his feet, and smiled to the audience. Not the sweet smile I'd seen him give Hugo; something rather more steely. 'I would be fascinated to hear these insights. Perhaps you wouldn't mind sharing them?'

I had to give it to her; she kept her pale, perfectly made-up face completely still. Only her eyes looked wild, like a pony that might be about to kick. 'My lord,' she said. 'I had no idea you were there.'

'Evidently.' He continued to smile. 'Perhaps everyone could discuss your opinions over tea and cake? I'm sure we're all interested in your study of my character.'

Another disturbed ripple, although I detected definite signs of glee in the faces of those nearest to me. The audience had got more than they bargained for: wildflower meadows plus drama and then some. Those who'd stayed at home would live to regret missing this legendary evening.

Clarissa had temporarily lost the power of speech. In London, someone would have been recording her on a mobile phone. Here, everyone was trying to forge every detail into their memories, for further embellishment later.

'Thank you, my lord,' I said crisply. 'Any more questions?'

There was silence. Kate gave an extended thank you and there was a hearty round of applause before the audience were released into bubbling chatter.

I let everyone rush the tea and cake table like a mosh pit

at a concert. Deliberately slowly, I shut my computer down and drank my glass of water. Then Kate reappeared bearing me a cup of tea in a green glazed cup, and a large slice of chocolate fudge cake, along with two friendly WI members who praised the talk as I sipped. I took a bite of cake. Good lord, it was heaven, utter heaven. I had to stifle a moan. As I chewed, I looked over at Jamie – he was attacking a slice of Victoria sponge whilst chatting with a large group of adoring women, whilst Callum inspected a rock cake. The look Callum gave me when he caught my eye was so comical, and I was feeling so high after completing the talk, I had to snort back laughter, and nearly inhaled a piece of cake. Oh well, you've got to die of something.

My companions continued talking politely as I recovered my equilibrium. When I had, one of them gently nudged me. 'Don't take Clarissa personally,' she said. 'She's not Jamie's biggest fan.'

'Only because she thought her daughter was going to be Lady Roxdale,' said the other.

'Sarah!' The other one looked scandalised. She lowered her voice to a whisper. 'You can't say that.'

I caught Jamie's eye across the room, and widened my own in a silent 'goodness this is interesting' look.

'Why not, if it's true?' said Sarah, although she too had lowered her voice. 'It's not Lucinda's fault if her mother's been acting like some latter-day Mrs Bennet.'

'I can see there's a lot more to Stonemore than meets the eye,' I said encouragingly.

'You wouldn't believe it,' Sarah hissed, and I leaned in. 'The things they do to get their daughters in front of him. The poor man should—'

'Can I rescue my newest employee?' Jamie's voice rang out, and Sarah turned the same shade as the cherry on her Bakewell tart. But he showed no sign of having heard anything, only asked after their families as I shovelled the last of my cake down and thanked Kate. When I'd finished, he turned to me and said in an undertone, 'Sorry if I interrupted – I thought you might be ready for all this to be over. Callum said he'd see us outside.'

'I am absolutely ready to go,' I said quietly. 'Thank you. I'm meeting Fi for a quick drink.'

'Right.' He took my cup and plate from me, then helped me into my jacket. When I pulled my arm back to put it in the sleeve, I winced. 'Are you okay?' he said.

'Fine, thank you,' I smiled. 'I'm a bit stiff. All the weeding at Belheddonbrae.'

'I thought you'd just leave it to go wild,' he said.

'No, it's important to get all the nettles and docks out before we start planting the wildflowers. And you have to do that by hand, really. But that's my dirty secret – I love weeding.'

'Duly noted,' he said. Was that a slight twinkle in his eye?

I became aware that people were watching us. Clarissa was long gone but most people were still chatting, and it was clear we were now a topic of conversation. 'Is this what it's like being a member of the royal family?' I murmured to Jamie as we strode out, side by side. 'All those eyes on you?'

'I have no idea,' he said, and I saw his expression had hardened.

We walked silently out into the darkness, into the rush of cold, clear air. Callum was vaping, and a faint miasma of bubblegum scent filled the air. 'Did you enjoy the rock cake?' I said.

He fished it out of the pocket of his waxed jacket, whole, and tapped it disapprovingly. I am disappointed to report that I giggled like a schoolgirl.

'Did I say well done?' said Jamie abruptly.

'I don't think you did,' I said, startled.

'You were very convincing,' he said. I should add that he wasn't looking at me, the whole time; his gaze was fixed on the distant hills, or an approximation of where they were in the winter darkness, whilst Callum puffed away on his vape and nodded in agreement with the sentiment.

I gave a mock-curtsy. 'I'd better go,' I said. 'Fi will be waiting in the Rising Sun.'

'Sure, I'll walk you down,' said Callum.

'Thanks.'

'Bye,' said Jamie, and before I could reply, he had turned and stalked off in the other direction. I don't know why I was taken aback by his rudeness – I should have been used to it by now – but when I looked back at Callum, he was smiling at me. 'Come on,' he said. 'Work's over for the day.'

We walked in parallel down Stonemore's main street, past the closed grocery shop and bakery, and along a row of quaint grey stone cottages. Occasionally I'd feel the bump of his arm against mine. With the combination of adrenaline from the presentation, plus cake and caffeine, I was feeling pretty good.

'Stonemore sure is dead on a Monday evening,' said Callum, guiding me onto the pavement as a car passed. 'How're you finding it? Getting any yearning for the big smoke? Newcastle, at least?'

I laughed. 'Not at all! How about you? Do you like the quietness?'

'It's all I've ever known. Came here from the Highlands.' There was that slow smile again. 'And quiet doesn't mean boring. It depends on the company.'

'It certainly does. I'll need a night or two at home under blankets to get over the drubbing Clarissa gave me.'

He laughed. 'Happens to the best of us. She had one thing right though – you're very pretty.'

I blinked. Really? Had he really just said that?

'Callum McGregor, are you flirting with me?' I said, as teasingly as I could.

'No, no,' he was half laughing, and gently he pulled my elbow to turn me towards him. 'Just stating the plain truth.'

'I see.' We were staring at each other now, his hand poised on my arm. I suddenly regretted there not being a shot of vodka in my tea. My first kiss, after Sean? *Courage, mon brave*! Callum was drifting slowly, too slowly, towards me. I couldn't take the tension. I pressed myself against him and ducked my face towards him, ignoring the fact that landing a first kiss takes about as much delicacy as docking a space station. Instead we came at each other at the wrong angle and our teeth clashed. We bounced away, smiled, then as I moved towards him and he suddenly came towards me, I landed him with a near perfect headbutt.

I jerked myself away, feeling the heat rising in my face. 'I'm so sorry!' I said, stifling the urge to flap my hands around.

He was laughing, and I caught that faint bubblegum scent. 'It's okay, Anna. It's okay.' I wanted the ground to open up and swallow me, but he didn't seem uncomfortable at all.

I was rubbing my forehead and just about gathering my wits when I glanced to my left and my hands closed over Callum's arms in a grip of terror. A woman's face hovered at the window of the cottage, barely a foot from where we were standing. As I stared at her face in horror, her mouth formed a perfect 'O'. She reached up, undid the catch and cracked open the window slightly.

'Oh, hey Heather,' said Callum cheerfully.

I opened my mouth to follow his lead but a small croak came out instead.

'My apologies,' Heather whispered, inspecting me. 'Nothing happens here normally, and that was so dreadfully entertaining.'

As I stared at her, she re-closed the window and mimed zipping up her lips. Callum gave her a thumbs-up, and gently guided me on down the street as I tried to work out what happened. 'Village life,' he murmured.

I shook my head in disbelief.

95

'This is me.' He tapped the battered Land Rover. We looked at each other. The moment had definitely passed. But he was smiling, and when he reached out and brushed a curl of hair off my forehead, I was relieved to see that relaxed twinkle in his eyes. 'I'll see you tomorrow, Anna,' he said softly.

'See you,' I said, simultaneously smiling like an idiot and feeling as awkward as.

As the Land Rover roared off, I pounded over the grey stone bridge and towards the lit, half-timbered frontage of the Rising Sun. I really needed a drink now.

You would have thought the extra-large Jack Daniel's and coke I ordered would have been enough to loosen my tongue about what had just happened between me and Callum. But I didn't tell Fi. It would have been selfish to catastrophise about a failed kiss after what she had just endured. Instead I settled down with her in a nook which was lavishly decorated with horse brasses, ordered drinks and double crisps, and at her request told a comical version of the evening's events, leaving aside the five minutes when I'd lunged at Callum.

'That was nice of Jamie and Callum to come and watch,' said Fi.

'Yes,' I said, and decided to venture it. 'Is – er – Callum single, by any chance?'

She put her wineglass down and wrinkled her nose. 'I don't think he's seeing anyone at the moment.'

I tipped my head at her. 'Your face looks weird,' I said. 'What aren't you telling me?'

She gave an embarrassed huff of a sigh. 'It's just – if you're looking for another relationship, Anna, I wouldn't go for Callum. He's a nice enough guy, don't get me wrong, but he's not one for commitment.'

'Absolutely not looking for a relationship, mate, so I'm fine then,' I said, although I felt surprised that she thought of Callum in such terms.

'Anna.' Fi stared hard at me. 'You've been through a lot. I don't want to see you get hurt again. And you said my face looks weird? Well, you've got that slightly dreamy look on *your* face that tells me you're in the early stages of an infatuation.'

'No, I'm not!' I cried, so loudly that the people at the next table looked over. Sometimes it was inconvenient having a *very* best friend. They don't let you get away with anything.

She sighed again and gazed at me.

I leaned close to Fi. 'I mean it,' I said. 'I don't need commitment right now. I need a bit of fun. To get my mojo back. I don't want to be moping around the cottage thinking about the past.'

'The only way out of that is through,' said Fi, crunching a handful of crisps. 'Callum's not your shortcut through heartbreak, I can promise you that.'

'Come on, you have to tell me more than that.'

Sadly, Fi wasn't a gossip. She shook her head and I made an internal vow to get her drunk one day and get all of the details about Callum out of her. She sat there, in a faint air of disapproval and concern. I squeezed her hand.

'He did rescue me the other day,' I said. 'He was a bit of a hero, if you ask me.'

Fi swallowed a mouthful of her drink with a frown. 'Jamie rescued you, more like.'

I paused, a crisp halfway between the packet and my mouth. 'What do you mean?'

'Exactly that. Jamie was watching the Land Rover on the GPS and told Callum they had to go and get you. Callum didn't have the foggiest idea how long you'd been gone. Loses all track of time.'

Recalibrating my vision of Callum coming to my rescue, I pushed the crisp packet away. Perhaps Mr Relaxed was a bit too relaxed.

'So,' said Fi. 'Who's the hero now?'

'I wasn't after a hero,' I said huffily. 'According to my therapy books, I'm perfectly capable of saving myself.'

'I'll raise a glass to that,' said Fi.

'Finally, something we can agree on,' I said, raking another crisp out of the packet.

CHAPTER 9

If I'd felt I was starting to settle into life at Stonemore, the following morning corrected that opinion. It started with Tally complaining that Jamie wasn't being communicative. She had been muttering for some time and I'd sadly forgotten my headphones to block out her tuts.

'The earl won't get back to me about the painting conservation,' she muttered eventually, some sense resolving out of her murmurings. 'And he's giving me one-word replies about other things.'

'We have to be careful with that conservation budget,' said Fi, who was in the middle of attempting to edit the website. 'We might need to divert some money away to essential maintenance. And I think Jamie wanted a quiet day – he has lots to consider before the financial year-end.'

Another half hour, and Tally started again.

'I bet it's your fault, Anna,' she said sulkily. 'You've said something to upset him.'

'Come on, Tally,' said Fi.

'You think I said something upsetting about wildflowers?' I carried on typing, my eyes not leaving the screen. But I had to stifle a sigh. A *here we go again* feeling rose up in me.

'I hear you got a lot of people's backs up at the WI meeting,' she said, narrowing her eyes.

I took a breath, trying to ignore the dagger-like sensation in my stomach. 'I thought we were playing nice. And I don't think I got anyone's back up.'

'Stonemore is a delicate ecosystem, Anna,' she said, as though speaking to a small child.

'I'm not sure you're the right person to be talking about ecosystems,' I said.

'I mean socially.' She twirled her pen in her hands. 'Also. *Callum*. A little birdie told me you're getting a bit too friendly.'

I looked up sharply.

'Not me,' said Fi, hands in the air.

I stared at the geometric pattern on the antique carpet. Took a breath. Yes, this was definitely a stately home, the air infused with the slight smell of drains. 'Just save it, Tally,' I said. 'You're not the only person who can lose their temper.'

'Anna, threats are not professional.'

'Neither is repeating village gossip, but I notice that's not stopping you.'

Primly, she reapplied her scarlet lipstick. 'I'm just trying to help,' she said, completely recovered now she had riled me.

I got up from my desk and threw my jacket on. 'Try

harder,' I snapped. 'And while you're at it, if you could stop talking to me like I'm a piece of dirt on your shoe, I'd appreciate it.' I walked out and slammed the door.

Once I'd found a space on the carriage drive that wasn't directly viewable from the office, I paced backwards and forwards to get some of my nervous tension out. I hated, *really* hated, arguing with people. In the past I'd been so conflict-avoidant it had worked against me. But having my heart broken seemed to be shifting something in me; it had been weirdly easy to bite back at Tally. Maybe, I thought, it was easier to be nasty because I now had an immense reservoir of anger and bitterness to draw upon.

Great.

As I breathed the clean air, I started to feel better, even if the knot remained in my stomach. And as I stood there, watching a family take a picture of the exterior of Stonemore, I noticed it was lighter than it had been at the same time yesterday. The prevailing colour of the sky was still grey, but there was a very slight softening of the air.

The family finished taking pictures and glanced at me, smilingly curious as they passed. I smiled in return. At least I looked the part in my country outfit: cable knit sweater, jeans, boots, waxed jacket. Today I'd managed to brush my hair, spray on some perfume (a lovely one, which claimed to contain 'essence of jasmine') and (hooray!) apply lipstick. Who knows, I thought, tomorrow I might actually reapply it at some point during the day. Goals, Anna, goals. I'd drawn the word in swirly writing in my journal, having started a fresh page that week, and I'd be adding to it this evening.

GOALS:
Lipstick every day.
Learn to say no without going OTT and being mean.
Breathe through thoughts of inferiority.

When I caught sight of Jamie, striding out of the house and across the drive towards the deer park, Hugo alongside him, I made a split-second decision to build bridges.

'Afternoon!' I called to him. He heard me – I swear he heard me. But he didn't acknowledge me. When Hugo turned his head, Jamie twitched his lead and carried on.

'Jamie!' I called. When he ignored me again, I thought *oh come on*. Then *I'm not having that*. Even though another, perfectly sensible, voice was in my head telling me to leave it, I found myself sprinting towards his retreating back.

He didn't turn. Not until I put my hand on his shoulder. He flinched, turned, and the look of irritation on his face made me step back.

'Anna,' he said. 'What do you want?'

I froze as I looked into his face. Why did he look so angry?

'Sorry for disturbing you,' I said. I felt small, reduced. All that toughness I'd been nurturing? Gone in an instant. I looked down at Hugo, instinctively going to stroke him, but Jamie kept the little dog on a short lead.

'If it's to do with work, feed everything through Callum,' he said sharply.

'It wasn't to do with work,' I said. 'I just wanted to say hello, you know, be polite. Say thank you for coming along last night.'

'Really?' The frown was sardonic as well as hurtful. 'Seemed to me like you couldn't have cared less whether I was there or not. And I didn't hear anything new – wild-flower meadows. More of the same. I guess I'll have to wait for some of your original thinking. Tick tock.'

I felt something snap in me. 'Why do you have to be so *rude*?' I cried. 'They asked me to talk about wildflowers. Do you think they care about land management, or drainage, or reintroducing species into the landscape? You might, but they don't. And I *could* talk to you about all of that, but you don't even want to speak to me!'

He was staring at me, lips parted, but his expression was impenetrable.

'Forget it,' I said. I was already walking away when I heard him call my name.

Technically, he's still my boss, I thought. *Technically, I'm on his time*. I stopped and turned around.

'Hang on,' he said, striding towards me, Hugo trotting alongside him.

'It's fine, let's just leave it.'

'Okay, okay.' He passed a hand over his brow. 'We've got off on the wrong foot, Anna.'

'Do you think?' I cried.

'I guess Callum's had the conversation about the reporting line?'

'Yes,' I said. 'Understood. Just—'

'What?' he said quickly.

'I don't know how we've got off on the wrong foot,' I said. 'I didn't intend to annoy you, or make you not like me.' It sounded so pathetic as it came out of my mouth. But I was honestly perplexed. I'd been ruder to this man in the space of a few days than I ever had to any other colleagues, put together. Was it my fault? Was he really as grumpy and pig-ignorant as I thought? No one else seemed to dislike him as much as I did. Maybe the whole upper-class thing really was skewing my judgement. Plus, I was second-guessing myself. Everything that had happened in London made me question everything that had happened since – I doubted my instincts.

'Hey.'

I looked up. He was staring at me, steadily. My breath caught as our eyes met.

'I don't dislike you,' he said. The words were said with effort. 'I rub people up the wrong way sometimes. It's just the way I'm made. That's why it's better you work with Callum.' He smiled tightly. 'It's obvious you get on better with him.'

I stared at him, nonplussed, feeling heat rising in my cheeks. There was so much energy in his gaze. The truth was, his eyes were hypnotic. Especially when he was glaring at me with such intensity.

'Right ... You know,' I said, trying to keep the mood light, 'my mum always said, you can't put a hot pan on a cold stove. That's probably why we don't get on.'

'I'm sorry, what?'

I looked him in the eyes. His super-intense blue eyes. 'We're from very different backgrounds,' I said. 'I'm working class, and pretty proud of it, to be honest.'

'And you think I'm what? Super-privileged?'

'I think you're from an entirely different world,' I said carefully. 'A world I haven't really experienced. We come at things from completely different perspectives.' *Plus, you're a bit of a dick*, I thought. A thought that probably relayed itself to my face.

'I see.' His expression was shuttered. 'I'll let you go then. Feed everything through Callum, and I'm sure we'll get on like a house on fire.' But it didn't look as though he was going anywhere, and he was staring at me in a way that made it hard for me to tear my eyes away, mixing annoyance with other feelings that I couldn't quite identify. I opened my mouth to say something, but no words came out. 'I—'

And, cut, as Hugo started barking.

My whole body felt full of adrenaline. What was going *on*?

Jamie sighed as though he was releasing a whole lungful of breath. 'Excuse me. He wants his second breakfast.'

I choked back a laugh. 'Is he a hobbit?' I looked down at Hugo's enormous eyes.

'He gets very hungry. It's a beagle thing.' He stared at Hugo for a moment, his face softening a little. Then he seemed to steel himself, and turned away, taking the little dog with him. 'See you, Anna.' He threw the words over his shoulder as he strode away, without even a glance behind.

'Bye, then,' I managed. I turned and stalked back to the house.

As I sat back down at my desk, I couldn't shake my feeling of unease. We both wanted the same thing, didn't we? A better future for Stonemore. So why on earth was it impossible to have a civil conversation?

I got home from work at just past five, when it felt exactly like midnight. The afternoon had passed calmly enough on the surface. Tally had even made me a cup of tea and given me one of her cereal bars as a peace offering. But there was a sour feeling in the pit of my stomach. Had I made a mistake, coming here? I'd been feeling warm and fuzzy about Stonemore as my escape hatch, but some of that pleasure had curdled. If Tally was right, a bunch of people at the WI had hated me, and my boss seemed to be disliking me more each day. Was this really the right place to recover from the past?

I opened the fridge door. One red pepper stared out at me, a faint air of apology about its shrivelled appearance, reminding me I hadn't had time to go grocery shopping. I slammed the fridge shut. Toast for dinner, then. I'd got way too used to the London habit of ordering takeaway in, and I was suffering for it now.

I had more than one Achilles heel, it seemed. I really didn't like it when people disliked me. I knew I had to kiss goodbye to my people-pleasing past, and I knew I had to grow a thick skin, but it was still difficult to know there was a bunch of people who disliked me just for being myself. But this wasn't time to cave – I was not going back to yes-to-everything Anna.

I opened the bread bin and took a breath before inspecting the contents.

Plink. My phone trembled on the counter. I closed the bread bin and picked it up.

> *Hey. Are you busy?*

It was Fi. I smiled at the idea of being busy.

Nooooo. I offered a prayer up that she was going to invite me to hers for a relaxed evening by the fire.

> *Good. Jamie came by the office to invite everyone up to the flat for a drink, but you'd gone. Everyone's here and we're going to have something to eat. Please come.*

I stared at the screen. She could see the blue ticks. She could see I wasn't answering, but the truth was I didn't know what to say. Fi was typing.

> *Jamie says please come.*

She carried on typing.

> *Give him a chance, love. Give Stonemore a*
> *chance. You can't say no to everything.*

I snorted. *I think you'll find I can*, I typed and sent. She answered with an eye roll emoji, then:

> *Have you eaten?*

I took a breath, and typed.

> *No.*

> *Are you hungry?*

I walked around my little kitchen. Yes, I was hungry. No, I did not want to go back into the lion's den. I still felt angry, obscurely wounded, and was in no mood to be polite to Jamie. My phone trembled.

> *Please come. We all want you here. Xxxxxx*

I felt something shift in me. I stared at my journal, left on the kitchen counter. I opened it at the latest page, at the word GOALS, written in such hope. One of the bullet points I'd noted under it: *Do not be inflexible. Be open to every possibility.*

Picked up my phone.

Alright then.

And pressed Send.

Fifteen minutes later, Jamie's Land Rover was waiting at the end of the garden path. I swore under my breath as I pulled my coat on – I'd assumed Fi would come and get me.

The door swung open as I approached. I decided against trying to be graceful (there was a chance I'd get marooned halfway through an excruciating scrabble-up, like all those bar stools when I first came to London). Instead I enthusiastically hurled myself at the step and landed in the battered front seat with embarrassing momentum.

'Hello,' said Jamie. Even in the half darkness of the cab, I could see his face looked different. Marginally less grumpy than usual.

'Hi.' I couldn't bring myself to smile at him and concentrated on closing the door.

'Thanks for doing this.' He swung the steering wheel and turned the Land Rover, eyes on the road. 'I'm . . .' he cleared his throat. 'Sorry. If I've been a bit—'

'It's okay,' I mumbled.

He took a breath. 'Okay.'

Things felt strange – really strange. Until this moment I hadn't realised how much his anger had wounded me. Sean had never really got angry; on the rare occasion I disagreed with him, he'd always adopted a kind of faraway expression, as though he wasn't really involved. And I'd been extra careful not to upset people at work. Yes, that Anna had been so *agreeable.* When Jamie and I had clashed, we'd sparked off each other dangerously. Now, it felt as though we had to be careful with each other.

'Have you recovered from all the weeding?' he said.

'Yes, thank you,' I said, trying to sound cheerful.

'Callum says you're interested in converting some of the estate into scrub.'

'Yes.'

'Isn't that quite controversial?'

I glanced at him warily, but he looked curious rather than grumpy. 'It can be, but it's wonderful for insect and bird life. You're going to have to let the wildness in at some point,' I said, making an effort to smile so brightly that I probably looked deranged.

'I suppose I am,' he said quietly, turning off the road.

The estate felt entirely deserted as Jamie clicked a control to open the gates. The Land Rover scudded down the long drive, glistening with the damp of evening, through the deer park. I spotted the ghostly white shape of a deer as it lifted its head and ran, fleet-footed, towards the trees. Most of the lights in the building were out, including in the staff office; the front doors locked and bolted. Only two windows in the mansion glowed with light on the upper floor: Jamie's flat.

He parked on the carriage drive and we went in through an unobtrusive side door I'd never noticed before, through a back corridor with green peeling paint. Eventually I began to recognise the stairs and corridors. As we entered the flat,

Hugo greeted us with a flurry of barks and jumped up to sniff my face and stare at me. As his pup-eyes fastened on me, I felt something unlock in me. I had to blink away tears at the tenderness I felt.

'Anna!' Fi came to greet me, arms open. I accepted her hug gratefully. 'Come on.' I could hear the sound of conversation in the main room. I put my arm in hers and we went in.

Richard, Tally and Callum were in the middle of an intensely competitive game of Scrabble. 'I just don't think it's a proper word,' Tally was insisting. She was holding an enormous glass of something pink with an umbrella in it.

'Look it up, Tallulah,' cried Callum. It was the most animated I'd seen him. 'A liger is an offspring of a lion and a tiger.'

'Wine?' Jamie had appeared at my side.

'White, please.'

Just for once, he didn't say anything snarky and returned quickly with a cold, full glass. 'Dinner's coming up soon.'

'Great,' I said, hoping my stomach didn't produce an audible swamp-creature sound.

He disappeared off to his tiny kitchen.

I caught Fi's eye. 'You see,' she murmured. 'He's nice.'

I shrugged. 'For once.' I gave her a rueful smile then took a big swig of wine and sat down on the floor next to Fi, enjoying watching the rest of them bicker with each other. Jamie brought out plates of baked potatoes and salad and we all ate, cross-legged on the floor, collectively playing the game.

I saw all of them in a new light: Callum seemed animated, occasionally catching my eye and smiling; at one point, Tally laughed so much at a joke that she smudged her eyeliner with tears of laughter; Fi rested her head on Richard's shoulder and seemed more relaxed than I'd seen her for weeks. Hugo picked his way through the group, picking up titbits and strokes. There was a sense of camaraderie in the room, which was the complete opposite from how I'd felt just a couple of hours before. Once I even looked up and saw Jamie's gaze resting on me, in a dazed but not unfriendly way. He raised his glass to me and I did the same in return.

Callum was just setting up an oversized game of Jenga that Jamie had found in a cupboard when there was a knock at the door and Lucinda's head popped round.

'Hullo!' she piped. 'I was just exercising Jessamy and I heard you all laughing. Mind if I join?' She was still dressed in jodhpurs and a pristine tweed coat. There wasn't a speck of dirt on her.

'She looks like a princess,' I whispered to Fi as Jamie took Lucinda's jacket and got her glass of wine.

'She'll have been home and got changed,' said Fi, sipping her elderflower cordial with a knowing glance. 'Her mother will have dropped her off at the gate.'

Lucinda waited until Jamie sat down next to the Jenga, then joined him, draping her arm over his broad shoulders. He shifted, slightly uncomfortably, but looked as though he didn't want to embarrass her by shaking her off. I almost choked into my wine, then started coughing.

'You okay, Anna, love?' Callum pounded me on the back.

'Perfectly fine,' I said, recovering myself, and making a mental note that he had called me *love*.

At first we all concentrated on the game. Tally was highly entertaining, squealing every time she pushed a brick out of the structure. But before long, Lucinda began talking, and she introduced a truth or dare element into the conversation. It was a bit like being at school, only it was the cringey element of school, where you somehow let something slip that would be used against you for ever after. I stayed quiet as the conversation ranged over everything from favourite colours to how old you were when you first kissed someone.

'How about you, Tally?' Lucinda said, after Tally had removed a brick from the teetering wooden pile, squealing as she did so. 'Is there anyone special in your life?'

Tally blinked. I suddenly felt protective of her, with her smudged eyeliner and pink drink. Yes, she was spiky, but I'd seen a new side of her: throwing herself into games and laughing at full pelt. There was a twinge of vulnerability in her eye as she answered. 'No, I see myself more as a career woman.' I nodded in support. 'Like Anna,' she added fiercely.

All eyes swung to me and I hastily revised my new liking for Tally.

'Really, Anna?' said Lucinda kindly. 'Is that how you see yourself?'

I gazed into the depths of my wine glass. 'I think we're all multi-faceted human beings,' I said. 'But yes, I suppose I am quite focused on my career.'

'Oh, I don't buy that,' said Lucinda. 'You're just waiting until someone special comes along. That's what we all want, isn't it? A home? A family?'

I saw Fi look sharply down. In the past I would have said something neutral, non-committal. But now, I turned back into the full beam of Lucinda's gaze.

'Nope,' I said.

'What do you mean?' Lucinda said.

'Exactly that. Yes, I'd like a home, but I won't be having children.'

She gave herself a little shake. 'Oh, I'm sure you will.'

'No, I won't.'

'You say that now, but—'

'I mean it.'

'But—'

'I can't have them,' I blurted out, more violently than I'd intended to.

God, that silence was awful.

Luckily, at that moment the enormous pile of wooden Jenga bricks teetered and collapsed with a roar that sent Hugo barking and running off and Tally squealing anew. All conversation was forgotten as Jamie went after Hugo and the rest of us started to pick up the bricks, Fi yawning audibly and suggesting that we all go home. Callum said he was heading outside for a vape. As he left, I felt a pang. My confession had ruined the fun and I imagined I was looking less 'flingable' by the minute.

I busied myself by collecting glasses and plates and

ferrying them to the kitchen, where I found Jamie comforting Hugo. The little beagle had attempted to shelter behind one of the kitchen cabinets and Jamie was tempting him out with a piece of chicken.

'Hey,' I said, neatly piling the plates.

'Hey.' He waved a piece of chicken in front of Hugo. Hugo snatched it and bolted past me into the main room.

I took a breath. 'You pushed the Jenga over, didn't you?' I said. 'I saw you nudge it.'

He glanced up at me sharply in a way that told me all I needed to know.

'Thanks for the diversion,' I said, trying to process that he'd been my unexpected ally.

'I don't know what you mean,' he said, raising an eyebrow, then stood up and tutted. He looked so neat: his hair perfectly in place, his shirt pristine. It took effort to be so controlled. 'You clearly don't know how to load a dishwasher properly.' He wrestled a wineglass out of my hand and I was about to tell him not to start mansplaining when Lucinda bounced through the doorway.

'Helllooo!' she said. 'Jamie, Fi and Richard are heading off, they're taking Tally. Would you like to go with them, Anna?' She looked at Jamie, who was rearranging the contents of the dishwasher as though it was a game of Tetris, and leaned against the wall. 'I can always stay, J.' She raised her eyes from beneath the thick canopy of her lashes, and bit her lip.

I had never seen someone make such a blatant pass. I fear

my mouth may have opened like a goldfish. But Jamie was unperturbed, and nothing crossed his poker face.

'Actually,' he said, 'I'd told Anna I would take her home, to save Fi and Richard an extra leg of the journey.' I opened my mouth to say it was no distance at all, then shut it at the sight of the look he was giving me. 'I'm taking Callum anyway. Why don't you go with Fi, Lucinda? They won't mind dropping you off.'

'Sure,' she adapted smoothly, her smile just as bright as it was before, but a faint tinge of pink in her face.

I watched Jamie as he waved off Lucinda and the others, then we continued fractiously loading the dishwasher whilst we waited for Callum. I'd just slotted a plate into the lower section when I heard Jamie clear his throat, and looked up.

'I know you must have felt pushed into saying more than you wanted to, earlier,' he said.

'Oh,' I swallowed, hard. Tried to find my breath. 'That's okay.'

'And – I'm sorry. About all of it, you know?'

'Thank you,' I flapped my hands, thinking I could accept anything but his pity. 'It's fine. You've put that bowl in the wrong place.'

'I think you'll find it's the perfect place,' he said, and smiled when I narrowed my eyes at him.

I slotted a handful of teaspoons into the rack. 'You know,' I said, with the unnerving certainty of the slightly tipsy, 'if my situation has taught me anything, it's when happiness is there, we need to grasp it.'

'Right,' he said, twisting a mug so it sat properly.

'She seems like excellent countess material to me,' I said. 'Just saying.'

Jamie stopped fiddling with the dishwasher and turned a pair of flinty eyes full on my face. Unblinking eyes, full of such energy that his gaze startled me into temporary sobriety.

'I'm overstepping the line,' I said. 'Sozzo, as Tally would say.'

A faint smiled softened his hard features. 'How do you know what good countess material is?' he said.

We stared at each other.

'I don't,' I said.

'You don't?' he said softly.

'I mean . . .' Why was I not breathing? I definitely wasn't breathing. 'At a guess . . .'

He held my gaze, not moving, but it was as though the space between us was charged with tension. I saw his lips part, saw him take a breath. 'Yes, Anna?'

'Hey, you two.' Callum crashed into the doorframe, followed by a barking Hugo. 'Are you running us down the road, Jamie? If you drop us at the end of Anna's lane, I can walk her home then saunter to mine.'

Jamie stared at the floor for a moment. I tried to catch my breath. 'That's quite a walk for you, Cal,' said Jamie.

'I need it,' said Callum, laughing. He pulled me towards him and gave me a squeeze. I was still trying to process what Jamie had meant and made no attempt to resist being enveloped in Callum's bubblegum-scented atmosphere.

'Are you okay with that, Anna?' said Jamie.

'Absolutely,' I said, hardly hearing him.

'Excellent,' he said, and slammed the dishwasher shut.

Jamie was as good as his word, and dropped us at the end of my lane.

'Goodnight, thanks so much,' I said to him.

He glanced at me. 'Goodnight,' he said. 'Be good.'

I was still frowning at this gnomic pronouncement as Callum helped me out. Jamie took off, wheels spinning on gravel, and within moments his Land Rover was a distant roar in the deep silence of the country night.

We walked down to my cottage. The evening had been strange, but not unpleasant, even if I wasn't quite on top of all the feelings it had brought up. I was relieved I hadn't put Callum off entirely. The sky was an inky blue black, scattered with stars. It was so beautiful, so romantic. As I stood on the front step of the cottage, looking at Callum, things should have been simple.

Ask him in, Anna. Have a bit of fun, Anna. It's no big deal. This moment was so textbook it was practically one of the action points in my 'getting over the past' journal, although I hadn't explicitly added *have a fling* as a bullet point. But I found I was frozen. As Callum stood, faintly smiling at me, I could say nothing.

'Penny for them?' he said softly, stroking the side of my neck.

I gave a nervous laugh. 'Sorry. I'm a bit out of practice.'

He leaned in gently, and brushed my lips with his own. Luckily, I managed not to headbutt him. One kiss, then another, gentle, and kind, and soft, and for a moment I relaxed. But when his tongue gently dipped between my lips I froze again, my chest tightening as though a vice had closed over it.

'Anna?' he said, leaning back and looking into my face.

'Sorry, so sorry,' I said. 'I can't ask you in. Not tonight.'

If he was disappointed, he didn't show it. 'Hey, it's alright! Don't worry.' He put his arms around me and I buried my face in his lovely broad chest. He stroked my hair and I felt the urge to weep. Here I was, attempting to have my first one-night stand, to get over Sean, and I was acting like a girl who'd never been kissed, never mind . . .

'Look, I'll see you tomorrow.' He kissed me on the forehead. Bad, very bad. The forehead, like I was his niece and he'd just picked me up from school.

'Night,' I said.

As soon as the door closed behind me, I messaged Rose.

Just had first kiss with bit of yeah.

OMG! Verdict? she replied.

It was fine.

Fine?!

119

I wasn't swept away. But that's OK, isn't it? Maybe it's a good thing if we're just going to have a fling.

Flings are, kind of mechanical, aren't they? I typed.

Mechanical is not the word I have in mind when I think of a fling, she replied.

Oh dear.

It's fine. Next time have a couple of drinks and I'm sure you'll be swept away in no time.

I jabbed at the keyboard. *I did have a couple of drinks.*

Confused face.

I messaged her goodnight and made myself some toast. I went to the window to eat it, looking out at the hypnotically beautiful sky. Perhaps I was far more broken than I'd realised. It felt easier to be alone. Perhaps saying no should extend into my romantic life, I thought.

'Goodnight stars,' I said. 'Goodnight cottage.' And after I got into bed, and lay there in silence, I had just the time to think this was enough, perfectly enough, before I fell deeply asleep.

CHAPTER 10

'We're going to have a fete!'

Nine in the morning was too early to hear Tally screeching at her highest pitch. I unwrapped the round of buttered toast I'd put in my bag and took a savage bite. I felt awful – headachey and embarrassed. That would teach me for drinking a litre of white wine and confessing my infertility to the world. 'When?' I said, mid-munch.

'April 2nd.' Fi was smiling at Tally's glee.

'Bit risky, weatherwise,' I said gloomily.

'Perhaps we can hire a marquee in case things go south,' said Fi.

'Or north,' I said, taking another bite. 'What's the occasion?'

'The anniversary of the earldom being bestowed upon Henry Gervase Mulholland,' said Tallulah loftily.

'Oh *that*,' I said. 'Can't believe I'd forgotten.'

'It's an old tradition,' said Fi. She and Tally were smiling at me, so it seemed I'd kept withering sarcasm out of my tone. 'But Jamie hasn't done it for a while. He thought he'd revive it this year.'

'All the tenants, volunteers and estate workers are invited,' said Tally.

'Why would he revive it?' I said.

Fi shrugged. 'George and Roshni are visiting this weekend. Maybe he was thinking over old times.'

I raised my eyebrows as I munched the toast. I'd seen the names on the family tree that Tally had pointed at on my first day, hung prominently on the office wall with its beautiful calligraphy: Jamie's brother George, his wife Roshni, and their two little boys Kes and Jake. And if he was dwelling on the family dynasty, he might be ready to give romance another go. Prepare yourself, Lucinda.

'You okay, Anna?' Fi said.

'Fantastic,' I said, taking another bite of toast. 'I'm just about to go and rake over Belheddonbrae with Keith. We're preparing it, ready for planting. Almost there. You?'

'I'm not too bad,' she said, smiling. 'Make sure you pop back mid-afternoon. Tally volunteered to buy office cake today.'

'I did what?' said Tally.

George and Roshni arrived the next day in a hybrid 4x4 right in the middle of visitor hours. I noticed a streak of blue pass the office windows and looked out to see tourists scattering and gravel flying as it ground to a halt on the far edge of the carriage drive. Feeling a jab of nerves in my stomach, I took a few deep breaths. Was I ever going to feel confident about being around the landed gentry?

A strikingly elegant woman dressed in cream who I took to be Roshni, Jamie's sister-in-law, unfolded herself from the front seat of the car. 'I'm so sorry, Jamie,' she said, opening her arms as Jamie arrived on the scene. 'I shouldn't let George drive outside London. He gets overexcited.'

I didn't catch Jamie's response because two young boys were tumbling out of the car, talking nineteen to the dozen and addressing many questions to their uncle.

'Uncle Jamie, where's Hugo?'

'Uncle Jamie, is there cake for tea?'

'Uncle Jamie, are we going to go fishing?'

The man who'd been driving had now joined them, floppy-fringed with a broad grin. I saw the resemblance to Jamie – the clear-cut jaw, and piercing eyes – but he was much more smiley and younger-looking, and he was charmingly dishevelled rather than rigid and pristine.

The family tumbled through the office. 'Hugo's in the flat,' Jamie was explaining to one of his nephews. 'I didn't want him barking at the tourists.'

'I love Hugo,' replied the little boy seriously. 'His ears are so soft.'

'I love him more,' stated the other little boy. 'I love him so much I could eat him.'

'Hugo pie?' said Jamie. 'Sounds a bit hairy to me.'

Over the sound of their sons' giggles, George and Roshni each embraced Fi then waved hello at Tally, and asked after Callum, who had disappeared for the morning.

'Dear old Cal,' said George. 'Hates hellos and goodbyes, doesn't he? And who are you?' He had turned his very pretty eyes on me.

I extended my hand and smiled. 'I'm Anna, the new re-wilding manager,' I said, as confidently as I could.

'Wonderful!' George beamed and shook my hand.

'Pleased to meet you,' said Roshni, and did likewise. She smiled warmly, and something flickered in her face, as though she was slightly assessing me. 'Jamie said he couldn't believe his luck when he hired you. Weren't you involved in that groundbreaking rewilding project in Scotland somewhere?'

'Yes.' I named the project. 'But just on a voluntary basis.'

'Do you spend a lot of time at your desk? Somehow when I think of a rewilding manager, I think you should be out in the landscape.'

'Hugging trees?' said George.

'A lot of the job is strategic rather than practical,' I said. 'But I manage to get outside sometimes.'

Jamie had already gone, slipping away, his nephews' voices fading as they followed him through the house. 'That's it, bro,' called George after him. 'You put the kettle on.'

'Go ahead, my love,' said Roshni, brushing his shoulder with her hand. 'Don't let the boys tease Hugo.'

He grinned and went.

'Do you want to join us for tea, Anna?' said Roshni. 'Jamie is really enthusiastic about the rewilding project. We'd love to hear about it.'

'That's really kind,' I said, feeling slightly terrified about the idea of being under her analytical gaze, and mindful that Jamie wouldn't want me barging in on his family time. 'But I need to check on Belheddonbrae. I was just about to head there now.'

'Maybe another time,' said Roshni. She flashed a smile that was decidedly playful for someone wearing Gucci glasses and a pale cream trouser suit, blew kisses and departed, her energetic, graceful stride echoing her husband's.

I sighed inwardly, relieved the introduction had gone well. Excellent – they didn't seem to dislike me on sight, as Tally had. The scent of Roshni's perfume still hung in the air, sweet and musky. I wondered if she had got on well with Lucinda when Lucinda was dating Jamie; composed, groomed Lucinda, who strode through this house on her long legs with an air of calmness and confidence. I'd faked confidence pretty well during my London years, but it had never settled into my bones – not really. It had all been a sham. No wonder when disaster struck, I'd been knocked over like an empty plant pot caught in a storm. Perhaps it really was all a matter of class.

'How are you doing?' I said. Fi and I had linked arms and were walking to Belheddonbrae. She smiled at me, blinking in a rare shaft of sunshine.

'I'm good thanks,' she said. Then caught my expression.

'No, I mean it! Really good. We're just going to move on, try again.'

'That's great.' I couldn't think of anything sensible to say, so I squeezed her arm instead, and she squeezed back.

At Belheddonbrae, Mica and Keith were starting to plant the plug plants I'd ordered. Although there was lots of bare soil now, I could imagine it in the future, with swathes of sorrel, corn chamomile and prunella; melancholy thistle and yellow rattle, with paths mown through according to my plan, allowing the grass to grow long in certain areas. Keith smiled at me. 'Looking good, isn't it?' he said.

'Don't do all the planting without me,' I said, and we laughed. 'I'll be here all day tomorrow.' It didn't look much at the moment, but it was going to be beautiful. I dropped off a box of cookies to Mica in the potting shed. 'Thanks for the pruning you did on the shrubs, Anna,' she said. 'I came down on Tuesday and it was as though a little helper had visited in the night.'

'No problem. I was up early and I love hacking at things,' I said. I'd come in from my pruning session pretty much coated with mud and with a broad smile on my face.

Also rescued from the general mess was an ornamental wooden and wrought-iron bench with a curved back and arms. Keith had sanded down the slats and given it a coat of wood stain, and it sat resplendent at the highest point of Belheddonbrae. After I'd chatted with Keith about plans for the following week, Fi and I settled on the bench. Before us lay the hills and fields of the estate, beginning to transform as spring made its way through the countryside, but still breathtaking in their unforgiving silhouette: dense mossy green slopes delineated by grey stone walls and hedgerows, the sky its vivid, cool blue that pierced my heart.

'It's lovely, isn't it?' said Fi.

I nodded. 'Sure is.'

'You *are* happy here, aren't you?' She turned her straight-forward gaze on me. Nowhere to hide. Fi nurtured things, and people. She was an exemplary PA and manager, with her eye for detail and comfort, smoothing out the wrinkles in the running of the house. But I didn't want her to feel that she had to care for me too. She would be the perfect mum when the time came, and she needed to rally her resources for that.

'You don't have to look after me,' I said gently. 'Yes, it will probably be a while before you see me dancing for joy, but I'm doing fine.'

Fi slipped her phone out of the back pocket of her jeans and started swiping. 'I was going through some old photos the other day,' she said. 'I found this.' She turned her phone towards me.

It was a photograph of Fi and me. We must have been eighteen years old if we were a day, sitting side by side on a night out, arms around each other, smiling. What struck me first was our stupendous, dewy-skinned youth; how great we had both looked, and how little we had known it. Then, something more: the sweet, uncomplicated happiness of our smiles.

'Was that at your brother's twenty-first?' I said. 'I think I actually remember that night.'

'Yep.' Smiling, Fi looked down at the picture. She pointed at my face. 'I was looking for something to remind you. That's my girl. So confident, so full of hope and excitement for the future.'

'Yes.' I remembered that time. Remembered the future opening up in front of us, ours for the taking.

'What I'm trying to say is,' said Fi. '*That* Anna. She's still there. You just have to find her again.'

I felt a shaft of emotion so pure I knew I had to push it back for now. 'I mean, I hate to break it to you, but my skin is never going to look that good again, no matter how much collagen I take.'

She laughed and elbowed me playfully. 'Oh!' she said, and waved. 'It's Roshni. Now remember, do not panic, she didn't go to finishing school, and she's not a snob.'

'Send me that photo,' I said.

'I will,' she said.

Roshni had changed into skinny jeans, a checked shirt and a pair of red wellingtons. She was making her way smoothly across the rough ground. She raised her hand at us and smiled as she made her way over.

'She's been wonderful for George,' said Fi, putting her phone away. 'I'll never forget the first time he brought her back here. You could see how tense he was. But she just got out of the car, looked around, smiled and said you're worried about *this*? I thought you had a proper castle.'

'Hello!' Roshni had arrived by us before I could ask more. 'As you said you were whipping this area properly into shape, I couldn't resist taking a peek.'

'There's not a lot to see at the moment,' I said, and explained the plan, showing her my drawing on my mobile phone.

'Amazing. How on earth did you learn how to do this?'

I gave a half-hearted laugh. 'A circuitous route. My first job was in admin – a project assistant. I worked my way up to project manager, and studied at night to keep my interest alive. First, garden design, then wildlife conservation, so I could move in that direction in my career. Long story short, I ended up working for an ecological and environmental consultancy.'

'Which means?' Roshni's hair was caught in the breeze and she brushed it back. 'I'm sorry, I only really know about financial markets.'

I smiled. 'It means all kinds of things, from ecological appraisals and protected species surveys, to devising strategies for people who want to manage their land in harmony with nature. Luckily, the firm I worked for was big on their staff's personal development, so I got to strike out. I worked on a woodland management project with a contractor, and after that, I got involved with rewilding projects, sometimes in my own time, sometimes on secondment. In short, I can do a Gantt chart but I can also dig up a tree stump and replant a border.'

She nodded. 'I'm in awe. I love looking at beautiful trees

and flowers, but I can barely keep a houseplant alive. I'm more of a numbers kind of woman.'

'Anna is totally brilliant,' said Fi, putting her arm around me and squeezing.

I smiled, and tried unsuccessfully not to look awkward.

Roshni looked between the both of us. 'So you've checked the work here, right? You can both join us for tea and cake now? George says he can't recuperate from the drive without cake.'

'I – er . . .' I said, but then saw Fi was giving me a very definite look. A *just-go-along-with-it* look.

'Don't worry,' said Roshni breezily. 'My brother-in-law has agreed it and I've even invited Tally and Lucinda, who I found in the courtyard, loitering. No soldier left behind.'

'Come on, Anna.' Fi gave me a small and – she would have said – loving shove. There was no other place to go. I'd rather not have risked my fragile détente with Jamie, but I wasn't being given a choice.

'Jamie said your design skills are brilliant,' said Roshni.

'Did he?' I said, wondering how I was heading for the house at such speed when I'd declined the offer several times.

'I don't mean to impose, but if there's any chance I could discuss our little garden in London with you, I'd really appreciate it.' She was striding ahead and I was struggling to keep up. Fi was bringing up the rear.

'Of course.' I could feel myself running out of words, and I was aware that I was speaking carefully and crisply. My telephone voice, Sean used to call it. It was the class thing, again. Knocking me off-kilter, making me try to appear a different version of myself. *Don't do this, Anna*, I thought, gritting my teeth.

Roshni came to a sudden halt. 'Oh God, I'm galloping, aren't I? So sorry. Fi!' She held her arms out towards Fi, who gave her a rueful smile. 'Just shout at me when I do that.' As everyone caught up, we started off again. 'I can see it *is* an imposition, Anna,' Roshni said.

'What?' I broke out of my self-chastising thoughts. 'No, not at all, we can talk about your garden.'

We'd reached the side door. Roshni turned the handle and pushed the door open. She caught my gaze and her smile was sincere. 'Thank you. But only if you want to – I mean it.' She gestured towards the door. 'After you.'

We entered Jamie's flat to find Tally and Lucinda sitting at opposite ends of the green dilapidated sofa as Kes and Jake bounced up and down between them, the smell of baking pervading the whole place. Roshni shot me a meaningful look. 'I'll just check on the cakes,' she declared loudly. 'I'll leave you all to have a nice chat.'

I glanced at Fi questioningly. 'She's a bit mischievous,' Fi murmured, 'but well meaning.'

I sent Callum a text. *Family gathering in flat. Will you join?*

I was used to him taking several hours to answer, but this time it was instant.

No way hahaha.

Hugo was engrossed in the children, barking delightedly and stretching out his front legs, lowering himself into a doggy bow, showing that he wanted to be involved in their games. I'd hoped I might stroke him as a way of avoiding speaking to anyone, but I clearly wasn't going to get a look in.

Jamie was in deep conversation with his brother. Tally was concentrating on her fingernails and Lucinda was neatly positioned, legs swept to the side and crossed at the ankle, princess-style. She really was perfect for Stonemore. Perfect for Jamie.

'Such a lovely day, isn't it?' she said to me brightly.

'Oh yes,' I said. 'Beautiful.' She smiled in response, but I could see her eyes flicking towards Jamie every few moments. If she kept staring like that, the laser-like intensity would have the flesh melting off his bones before long.

'So you've adapted to this lovely place?' Lucinda continued. 'People tend to stay for their whole lives. That's always what I thought I'd do.' She was holding a long-stemmed glass containing something sparkling like champagne, which she was fitfully sipping.

Was Roshni trying to get us all drunk? As if on cue, she appeared, carrying a full glass for me.

'I thought it was just tea and cake?' I said, accepting it, then putting it down immediately. There was no way I was drinking in this situation. Her smile broadened, and she returned to the kitchen.

'Do you ride?' Lucinda said suddenly.

'Nope,' I said, wondering how many glasses she'd drunk. *Not many riding schools in our neck of the woods*, I added silently. I had once been taken on a trip for 'disadvantaged children' to a farm where I bounced around on a pony for half an hour whilst clinging to a neck strap. Utterly terrifying.

'That's a shame. You really should ride.' Her eyes fixed on the place she wanted – Jamie's face. 'Don't you think, Jamie? Anna should ride, shouldn't she? If she's going to stay at Stonemore?'

Roshni appeared in the doorway. She was holding a plate of fairy cakes but gave no indication that she was intending to offer them to anyone. She had heard Lucinda and come to watch what was developing.

'Jamie!' Lucinda half shouted, then gave a tinkling laugh. 'We're over here! Don't you think?'

'I'm sorry?' Jamie reluctantly joined us.

'Anna can't ride. But it's a skill one should pick up in the country, don't you agree?'

'I can ride,' Tally chimed in. 'It's not exactly a special skill.'

'Boing boing!' shouted Kes.

'Well, as I said, who knows how long I'll be here,' I muttered.

Jamie looked at me directly for the first time since I'd walked in, his blue eyes boring into my face. 'Don't forget you need to give three months' notice,' he said. 'Perhaps I should have asked for six.'

I picked up the champagne and took a gulp. Had I really

signed a contract that had a three-month notice period? Three months was a corporate amount of notice. Highly surprising for somewhere like Stonemore. Maybe, if I really wanted to go, I could claim I was emotionally compromised when I signed the paperwork. I had been so desperate to leave London, I would have agreed to anything.

But also, why had I just hinted I was leaving? I didn't want to go. Although with Tally and Lucinda bearing down on me, about to fight to the death regarding the level of their riding skills, resignation was looking more tempting by the minute.

'Three months' notice?' Tally looked aggrieved. 'I only have to give four weeks.'

'Or one month, as it's otherwise known,' I murmured, already emboldened by the champagne. Only Jamie heard me, and flashed me a look (and possibly Roshni, who seemed to be enjoying things vastly).

'Four weeks is standard,' said Jamie, sounding weary. 'Callum is three months too.'

'I can understand Callum.' Tally tilted her head. 'But why Anna?'

'Because she's vital,' Jamie snapped.

Silence fell. I could sense Lucinda looking at me with new interest.

'Maybe I'll make some tea,' said Fi loudly.

Jamie sighed. 'Yes, please,' he said. 'Roshni, you're failing in your hostess duties, you know. Shall we have tea and cake before George starts bending my ear about financial instruments again?'

Help me, I texted to Callum.

Hahaha, he replied.

'Uncle Jamie,' said Kes, playing with Hugo's ears, 'if you were a dog, what kind of dog would you be?'

'A beagle,' said Jamie, without missing a beat.

'I'd be a Labrador!' cried Lucinda, a little overeagerly. 'How about you, Anna?'

I put my hands in the air. 'I have literally no idea.'

She tilted her head. 'Perhaps a Jack Russell? Small.'

'They're quite yappy though,' added Tally.

Lucinda tinkled with laughter. 'Yes.'

I took a large bite of fairy cake and allowed the conversation to move off in another direction, wondering if that remark had been innocuous or the worst insult I'd ever received in my life.

A minute later, Roshni drifted past. 'Would you like another cake?'

'I'm fine, thanks,' I said.

'I thought Labradors were supposed to be friendly,' she said, in an undertone, her gaze set on Lucinda. 'But this one is definitely crossed with a wolf, don't you agree?'

Half an hour of stilted conversation later and Fi and I escaped into the open air. She had claimed an urgent photocopying errand needed doing and I had offered to help. We left Lucinda attempting to play a convoluted form of hide and seek with Kes and Jake, whilst Tally tried to interest Jamie in Poussin's early landscapes.

'What's going on with you and Callum?' Fi glanced at me, gimlet-eyed. 'That was him you were texting, wasn't it? You had that look your face again.'

Luckily, I was already breathless in the fresh air. I opened my mouth, trying to assemble a sensible answer.

'You haven't slept with him, have you?' shrieked Fi, as though we were teenagers again.

'No!' I cried. 'Not that it would be a disaster if we had. I could do with a bit of fun.' She glanced at me warningly. 'We did attempt a kiss, though.'

'Why didn't you tell me?' She wheeled around and caught my arm.

'Let's see,' I said. 'Number one, you've had a lot to deal with. Number two, it was just a kiss. Number three, it's not going to lead anywhere, and I'm fine with that.'

She stared at me in the early spring sunshine, the wind rifling her hair. 'Please be careful, Anna.' She stomped on. 'I can't believe you didn't tell me.'

'I didn't tell *anyone*,' I said. 'I'm trying, Fi – trying not to, I don't know, *bleed* over everyone! I might be walking wounded at the moment, but I don't want to bring other people into *my* issues. I've got to get on top of things and start dealing with things on my own. You know?'

She waited a minute, still assessing me. 'Right,' she said finally. 'But I'm always here. You know that, don't you?'

'I do,' I said. 'Come on, before I sober up completely and leave you to do that photocopying on your own.'

'Hug?' she said. I nodded, and we clutched each other.

She gives good hugs, Fi; I never trust a friend whose hugs are less than two seconds long, and she's a good three or four.

'You really unsettled Jamie,' she said, as she unlocked the door to the staff office. 'The way he looked at you when you said you might leave.'

'What do you mean?' I asked.

'Like you'd pulled the rug out from under him,' she said.

My stomach inexplicably did a back flip. Daytime champagne, never a good idea.

'He probably deserves it,' I said airily.

'So cruel, Anna,' chided Fi.

I smiled. I was definitely *not* going to start feeling sorry for Jamie.

CHAPTER 11

Why I agreed to get on a horse, I have no idea. I can only put it down to the fact that I hadn't had my second cup of coffee and was too bleary-eyed to really understand what I was getting into. Also, Jamie had annoyed me yet again, which seemed to be a determining factor in most of my actions.

I'd been worrying about not getting enough work done, before Fi pointed out that it was generally accepted that no one did any work whilst Roshni, George and their boys were around. They had brought holiday time to Stonemore. Bearing that in mind, I spent a good hour with Roshni discussing the difficulties of her London garden, and finally managed to recover the ability to speak rationally in her presence, largely because it was impossible to be intimidated by someone whose laugh was so raucous.

Each morning the boys tore through the house with Hugo, hallooing at volunteers, staff and visitors alike, followed cheerfully by Roshni who disciplined their descent ('do *not* touch that vase, Jake') and more slowly by George, who was usually complaining about the broadband – even though, as Roshni explained, she was the only one who had *important* work to catch up on. They would eventually end up in our office, where amusements would be arranged (the first full day involved a 'Land Rover safari' with Callum).

This particular morning, Hugo led the charge, appearing a good thirty seconds before anyone else and launching himself into my lap. I was busy stroking his ears when the boys arrived.

'Anna Annabel Annie!' Jake cried. He had an excellent, if approximate, memory for names. 'We're going on a horsey today!'

'Jake, don't shout at Anna.' Roshni and Kes had arrived, this time with George and Jamie. I smiled brightly at the family and tapped away at my computer.

'Lucinda's lined up a riding excursion,' said Roshni. 'Will you be joining us, Tally? She says there's room for adults too.'

The alarm on Tally's face was plain for all to see. Surely she hadn't faked knowing how to ride? I'd started to suspect her carefully cultivated façade of competency was just that. The previous day she'd gone into a meltdown when attempting to enter a calculation into Excel. But pretending to ride? Like rats in London, you were never more than three feet away from a horse at any given time in Stonemore. She must have known she'd be caught out.

'I can't,' she chuntered. 'I'm wearing vintage Chanel today. And I'm inundated with work. The paintings conservator will arrive at any minute. Maybe you can take Anna – she looks horse-ready – it's not as if she'll ruin her clothes.'

I raised my eyebrows at her for the unfair shot. So, okay, I hadn't managed to put any make-up on today (lipstick goal: failed). And I was still wearing jeans, boots and a Scandi-style sweater. But I was clean! I was wearing perfume! And there was no reason to throw me in the path of thundering hooves.

Tally's mobile rang and she hurried off with it.

'Looks like it's every woman for herself, Anna,' said Roshni. 'Will you join us?'

'No.' Jamie and I spoke in unison, providing a response so loud, and in stereo, that everything stopped. Even Kes paused from flicking his brother's right ear.

'I beg your pardon?' I said indignantly, finally letting myself look at Jamie. Either he'd been drinking whisky first thing in the morning or he was blushing with embarrassment. A definite first. As was the fact that beneath his waxed jacket, he was wearing jeans (posh jeans, no doubt), along with worn brown Chelsea boots and a copper-coloured sweater that looked as though it cost a month's salary (my salary, that is). Or maybe it was just him – his high and mighty attitude *made* things look expensive.

'What I meant to say is, Anna is busy,' said Jamie.

'I'm pretty up to date, actually,' I said (a blatant lie).

'Maybe I will have a go at this riding malarkey. How hard can it be?'

'This, I have to see,' said Callum, smiling. 'I'll go and make sure Lucinda saddles up a safe one.'

'That's my girl, Anna,' said Roshni. 'I'm going to take these terrors for a quick runaround first. Come on, Hugo.' She clipped the beagle's lead on. 'See you at the stables, Anna. George!' Her husband glanced up from his phone, nodded, and followed her. But Jamie didn't go. He stood, glowering, his hands pushed into the pockets of his waxed jacket.

'What was that all about?' he demanded.

'I could ask you the same question,' I said. I heard the churn of the photocopier down the hall as Fi prepared the steward rotas Tally had bailed on.

'I got you out of it,' he said. 'You looked like you didn't want to do it.'

'Well ...' I bumbled. 'Technically, you're correct. But you've reneged on being my *boss* boss, so speaking for me? It's a bit much.'

'Your *boss* boss?' he said, a flicker of amusement brightening his eyes. Against my will, I felt the ends of my mouth curving up into a smile at the idea I'd amused him. How annoying. Being made to smile when I was meant to be acting very angrily.

'I suppose I'd better go and look at the horse,' I said sulkily. I could hear Tally's heels clattering down the corridor as she spoke nineteen to the dozen. When she appeared she was followed by a rather puzzled-looking man, who was nodding at her narrative of the Poussin painting: layers of varnish, layers of smoke, blah blah. Tally formally introduced him as 'Darren the conservator, here to look at the Poussin'.

Jamie shook his hand and I became aware Tally was eyeballing me. 'Anna,' she said. 'I'm dreadfully busy – could you look after Darren?'

Darren gave me a weak, but faintly unsettling smile.

'Um,' I said. I automatically felt the pull to say yes: *smooth the path with Tally*, my brain said, *she might even start liking you*. I fought the feeling. 'No?' I managed. It definitely came out as a question. Tally tilted her head, ready to go in for the kill.

'We have something else to deal with,' said Jamie shortly, before I realised the *we* he was referring to was him and me. 'I'm sure you can deal with this, can't you, Tally?'

Tally's eyes widened with shock. 'Of course, my lord,' she said, practically curtseying.

'Great, thanks. Anna! You're with me.'

Just this once, I decided not to give him any lip, grabbed my coat, and followed him.

Jamie and I walked to the stables, which were behind the house at a diagonal from the formal garden and hidden by high privet hedges. I had to hurry to keep up with his long stride. 'I hope you don't mind me saving you from babysitting Darren,' he muttered.

'It was fine, I didn't need saving,' I said.

'Don't tell me he's your type. I'd better warn Callum he has a challenger for your affections.'

'What the hell!' I swung round and nearly slipped in a swampy puddle. Jamie caught hold of my arms to stop me from falling.

'I'm sorry . . .' The words slipped out as though he had no control of them. 'It's just—'

'Uncle Jay Jay! Uncle Jay Jay!' Kes came barrelling around the corner. Jamie released me. No sign of curiosity showed on Kes's six-year-old face. 'Ponies! You're missing everything!'

'Okay, mate.' Jamie's face broke into a smile. There was something very strange about that smile. Since that evening in the flat, I'd noticed it was ridiculously breathtaking – like the sun coming out from behind a cloud. Perhaps he'd been taught how to do it at boarding school, along with the staring, to use his smile as a deadly weapon, able to floor people at fifty paces.

I kept my gaze fixed on the ground and marched on behind them. When we arrived, Callum greeted me with a quick hug. 'Lucinda's chosen a lovely old codger for you to ride,' he said. 'She's gone to get him now.'

'Lucky me,' I said, glancing up to see that Roshni was watching me. She was sipping tea from a tiny cup. As Jamie lifted Kes onto a Shetland pony, who was rather worryingly known as Tyke, Roshni beckoned to me.

'You're glowing,' she said.

'Er, gosh! Thanks,' I said, and she gave me a smile that seemed to have layers to it.

'Fi arranged for tea and biscuits,' she gestured to

refreshments set up on a tarpaulin-covered table. 'Honestly, sometimes this place is heaven. I never feel more looked after than when I come here.'

I poured myself a miniature cup of coffee. 'It's certainly nicer than the corporate world,' I said. 'Even if we have a draughty loo and no HR department.'

'I suppose. Although aren't all workplaces just mud and gossip? I agree it is literal mud in this case.'

'Certainly is.' I raised my voice. 'Lovely ponies, Lucinda.'

Lucinda was leading out her beloveds. She gave me a sunny smile. 'Anna! I suspected you fancied a ride really.'

Callum gave a snort of laughter.

'I've had Kit saddled for you.' Lucinda nodded towards a bemused-looking piebald pony who stared at me with rheumy eyes. It was *not* love at first sight.

'I'll give you a leg-up,' said Callum, with a twinkle.

I thought I'd be terrified from first till last, but I almost enjoyed it. Kit was a game little pony, and although he wasn't nearly as handsome as the bay thoroughbred Lucinda had selected for Jamie (typically, he got the classiest horse), it seemed Kit was not going to be put off by the presence of superior beasts, and neither was I. So off we went at speed. It was easier to stay on than I remembered, even when Kit started cantering, apparently overjoyed to be in a fenceless field. It was only when I heard distant shouts that I got the hint we really weren't supposed to be going that fast. I gave a little tug on the reins but Kit hurtled on, oblivious to my wishes, as I bumped up and down and adjusted to the rhythm of his canter – which was, er, definitely getting faster. Scrub canter, try gallop.

I wasn't afraid, and that was refreshing. As we hurtled on, it crossed my mind there was nothing to cling to anymore – not the wreckage of my relationship with Sean, not our future plans – and there was no need to preserve myself to be someone's mother. There was a kind of freedom in being alone. After all, weren't we all alone, really – even if most people weren't confronted with it as harshly as I had been?

We'd been careering towards a hedgerow whilst I thought my la-la thoughts and for a moment I thought Kit was preparing to jump it (slightly terrifying), but instead he decided to implement an emergency stop. With breathtaking speed I flew over his shoulder, bounced off the hedgerow, and tumbled onto the ground, where I lay, temporarily stunned like a bird that's hit a windowpane.

There was a moment of silence. Just me, birdsong, and I thought for a moment I might be dead. Then I wiggled my fingers and toes, checked for pain (none), and started to laugh. I was still laughing when I heard the pounding of hooves and saw Jamie riding towards me, way ahead of everyone else. My heart was already beating pretty hard but, let me tell you, there is nothing like seeing a man galloping towards you on a thoroughbred with an expression of concern on his face to get the pulse racing. As he came to what I believe is technically known as a *screeching halt*, my laughter reached new heights of hysteria.

'Holy shit,' he said. He dismounted in one smooth movement, looped his horse's reins over its head and fell on his knees next to me. 'Are you hurt?'

I managed to stop laughing long enough to assure him I was not.

'Are you sure?' He put his hands on my shoulders, his eyes searching my face. The sudden physical contact coupled with the intensity of his gaze silenced my laughter. 'Anna? Did you hit your head?'

'No,' I said, trying to catch my breath. 'I'm fine.' He looked anguished; I smiled to try and reassure him, very aware of our proximity. 'Really. I promise.'

After a minute he seemed satisfied that I wasn't injured and sat back on his heels. 'Thank God for that.' A smile dawned on his face in answer to my own. 'You looked like a bloody Thelwell cartoon.' He seemed to suddenly notice that he was still holding onto me and let go, pulling away as though he wanted to put distance between us.

George and Callum pulled up alongside the field in a Land Rover and came running. Lucinda was off in the distance, proceeding at a graceful slow-motion canter.

'Crikey,' George said. 'That was quite a tumble.'

Jamie got up and put his hand out to me but I brushed it away, my fingers catching his for a millisecond. *Be brave, Anna,* I told myself, *don't go all fainting maiden now.* 'I'm 100 per cent fine,' I said. I got unsteadily to my feet, aware that Jamie was hovering beside me. 'See?' I said. 'No need to worry.'

Jamie nodded, and took a step back as I started to brush myself down.

'Look at the state of you,' said Callum, and started laughing.

'I knew you'd make an idiot of yourself,' said Tally, as Roshni and I traipsed through the office twenty minutes later. I was still pulling bits of hedgerow out of my hair, but managed to give a shocked-looking Fi – who was on the phone – a thumbs-up as I passed. Jamie had entrusted his horse to George and driven me back without saying a single word, whilst Callum sat in the back seat next to me, picking bits of foliage off me and pissing himself with laughter at my plight. Which had started off being okay but ended up being quite annoying.

'This is me,' I said to Roshni as we neared the loo. 'Thanks for seeing me this far – I should check the damage.'

'Uh uh,' she said, in the same tone I'd heard her use on her sons. 'You're coming up to the flat. You can use the bathroom there – and have a hot sweet tea. Possibly a glass of whisky. Also, you've got a scratch on your face. You need a plaster.'

It was true that after the first blissful discovery that I hadn't broken anything, I was now starting to feel it a bit, so I followed Roshni without protest. It was just her and me in the flat – the boys were still out with Lucinda, playing with the ponies. I'd given Kit an apple before departing, with the words, 'No hard feelings, buddy.' He had munched it happily but looked unimpressed at my attempt to make friends.

We discovered Hugo in the act of dismantling the throws on the sofa. 'He hates being alone, don't you, hon?' said Roshni, stroking his head.

I decided to give in to Roshni's care. I collapsed on the sofa, let her provide tea, refused whisky, and accepted her first-aid efforts: antiseptic lotion, arnica, and four spoons of sugar in the tea. When the phone rang, Roshni picked it up, and I saw her arch an eyebrow. 'Anna will be back down when she's recovered, Tallulah,' she said crisply. 'Thank you.' She put the phone down.

I stifled a groan. 'Have I annoyed Tally?'

Roshni smiled. 'Don't worry, I think she enjoys being annoyed. Also, she doesn't like me much. She tried to give me a tour of the paintings once, against my will.'

'I can't imagine that worked out for her,' I said.

'It didn't.' Roshni's eyes sparkled behind her large-framed glasses. 'In the end I had to tell her George had already given me a very *private* tour, and I said it in a way which left her lost for words.'

I could just imagine Tally freezing in horror and retreating to her neo-Chippendale desk.

'The thing I didn't tell her was that it was desperately romantic,' she said. 'We weren't wrapped in bedsheets or anything, though I think she thought we were. I'd just finished meeting his father, which George had painted as an epic ordeal, but he was enchanting once he'd got over the colour of my skin.' She caught my eye; I glimpsed the depths beneath her bright exterior. 'I went to Cambridge from a state school in Bradford. I've worked in finance since the day I graduated, sometimes managing only men. George doesn't really know what an ordeal is.

'Anyway, so I'd met my future father-in-law, and he'd retired to his brandy, then George took my hand and led me through the house. Jamie had de-alarmed it for us, opened some of the shutters, so I saw the Caravaggio and the Canaletto by moonlight.' She paused, and I saw again that glimmer of seriousness in her eyes. 'That's always how I see them in my mind. Not that he could tell me too much about them. So maybe we did need Tally after all.'

'Maybe we can ask her later,' I said. There was something about Roshni's easy familiarity that relaxed me. *Careful*, I thought. *She's still family – still a cut above. Act professional, Anna.* 'I don't remember there being a Canaletto.'

'There isn't, anymore.' Roshni topped up my tea. 'Jamie had to sell it at auction a few years ago. The house needed a complete rewire. His father had hedged around it for years. It meant Jamie was lumped with all the hard decisions.'

I sipped my tea, thinking that it must have been a wrench to sell something from the collection, when Roshni cut into my thoughts by slapping my knee.

'You're a picture,' she said. 'There's still several bits of hedge in your hair, you know.' We grinned at each other.

'Thanks,' I said. 'I think I've failed to entirely adapt to the countryside, as you can see.'

'Not at all,' said Roshni. 'You're exactly what Stonemore needs. And, much as I love my brother-in-law – and I do – it's good to see you keeping him in line. He needs a new perspective.'

'I don't think I keep him in line,' I mumbled.

'You'll have to take my word for it, then.' She offered me a biscuit.

'I think my suitability is yet to be proven.' I inspected the dregs in my teacup, and thought of ways to change the subject. 'If I'm not being too nosy,' I said, 'how did you meet George?'

She tried to suppress a smile, and failed. 'I was his manager in a City finance firm – where I still work. I'm used to handling the posh boys. It helps that I'm smarter than most of them, but I've had to be.'

I nodded. 'This doesn't feel like the real world to me.'

'I get that. I come from a working-class background, Anna. When I went to Cambridge, it was as though I'd landed on another planet. Half of the people there expected me to defer to them.'

'And the other half?'

She fixed me with an unblinking stare. 'The other half didn't speak to me at all. I wasn't worth their while. But I was clever. Very, very, clever. Anyway . . .' She poured me another cup of tea from the pink teapot on the coffee table, and spooned in more sugar. 'So there I was, managing teams of these boys, and managing very well. I had zero interest in any of them, romantically. I knew how perilous it was in that kind of environment – they were all waiting for me to fuck up, in any way.'

'So how did he manage to convince you?'

'There was a work jolly to Henley Regatta. I took a man I'd met – a lawyer, not from my firm. We'd been together a while. I was thinking of settling. He seemed like a sensible choice, just like I seemed like a sensible choice to him. Decent guy. Nothing to object to. Well, George got drunk and decided to have an argument with me. Out of nowhere. We were bickering away and then I thought, suddenly – *God, this is So Much Fun.* By the end of the day, I knew he would be important to me in some way. For the first time in a long time, I'd found a man interesting. Really interesting.'

We looked at each other, in the stillness of the flat, Hugo snoring between us. I was used to mischievous Roshni, but this Roshni was serious.

'The following Monday,' she said, 'he came into the office and declared his love. I told him to stop being ridiculous, that there was no way I was getting involved with someone from work. So he resigned, that day.' She gave a laugh, a little echo, it seemed, of the shock she had felt in the past. 'I suppose that's where money helps. I remember thinking how wonderful it was: that desire to declare himself, to be bold, to take a risk. Is that what you're looking for?' She gave me too much side-eye; I'd seen her keenly observing me as I hurled myself out of the Land Rover in the wake of a silent Jamie and still-laughing Callum.

'I'm not looking for anything,' I said, shifting in my

seat and causing Hugo to give a gargantuan sigh. 'I think I'm feeling fine now. Are you staying for the anniversary celebrations?'

'No, not this time.' She smiled. 'Lots to do at home, and if I'm away from my desk for more than a week, the City boys start rioting, or selling when they're meant to buy. So we're off tomorrow. But it's been nice meeting you, Anna. I hope we see each other again one day.'

CHAPTER 12

As soon as Roshni, George and the boys left, Stonemore moved smoothly into fete-preparation gear.

I had to give Tally credit; she really knew how to imagine a party into life. Despite the fact that it wasn't even remotely her job (Fi had been perfectly happy to arrange everything), Tally decided she would lead on designing the anniversary festivities and threw herself into the task with immense enthusiasm. Different kinds of stalls and refreshments, a photo booth, and an ice-cream van (frankly overly optimistic, given it would only be the beginning of April).

There were only two drawbacks. The first was, Tally was very much an *ideas* person rather than a *physical work* person. This meant that she felt having the ideas was the most difficult part, rather than actually putting them into practice. So whilst she loved brainstorming, mood-boarding and – slightly more practically – picking up the phone and ordering people around, she didn't enjoy sourcing table-cloths, raising purchase orders, or doing anything that might ruin her manicure. If I passed one set of gloomy volunteers attempting to tie the ends of countless shrivelled balloons, I passed a hundred.

The second drawback was that she had no desire to keep to budget. So when Fi, who was in charge of our finance system, flatly refused to raise a purchase order for a chocolate fountain ('think of the midges, Tally'), we later found her whacking it on the estate credit card that she had nicked from Fi's desk. In the corporate world this would have been a sackable offence, instead lovely Fi rolled her eyes and hid the card elsewhere to prevent future issues. However, when someone telephoned asking for Tally vis-à-vis the reindeer she wanted to hire, Fi took matters into her own hands. 'A bloody reindeer?' she said. 'It's April!'

'But I've always wanted one,' wailed Tally.

Fi, tight-lipped, marched off to see Jamie.

This was my cue to leave the office. In the fortnight since Roshni, George and the boys departed, Jamie and I had managed to avoid each other entirely. And life had been better. I'd been mapping the different habitats on the estate and taking soil samples. I'd finished the first draft of the rewilding plan for Stonemore Estate. Callum had submitted it to Jamie and the following morning he approved it by email. So it was time to start speaking to contractors about the gentle thinning of fir and spruce in the woodland, and the process of introducing beavers into the estate was already underway. In my downtime, I'd watched Forestcam, read a book a week, and mastered some of the healthy recipes I'd always wanted to try (crispy mushrooms in silky tofu sauce, anyone?).

Life was calm, life was quiet, life was good. Even if my flirtation with Callum had faded to practically nothing.

A week before the fete, Fi told me Tally had had her knuckles well and truly rapped by Jamie, who had marched into our office sixty seconds after I'd left it to work at Belheddonbrae and said, 'What the hell is that?' in response to the two foot by six foot mood board Tally had created for her ideal party. 'No more spending' had been the gist, 'and stop upsetting the volunteers. I heard you made Pat cry because she couldn't blow up a balloon.'

You'd have thought all of this would have cowed Tally, but she'd fully recovered by the time I'd returned, completely unrepentant and sharper than ever.

'Where have you been?' she asked.

'Working,' I said, gesturing to my mud-smeared jeans and the nettle leaves stuck to my fleece.

'Humph,' she snorted. 'Well, just to let you know, you're going to be on the candy floss stall.' She bowled out, leaving a cloud of Chanel perfume in her wake.

I switched on Forestcam. 'Candy floss?' I said to Fi. 'How did that get through?'

'Under the wire,' said Fi, and typed an email, striking the keys particularly hard.

*

Of course, the weather went against us. At 9.15 on the day of the fete, 45 minutes before opening, the ice-cream van gave one little jingle in a minor key and the heavens released a month's worth of rain. Which could have been predicted because the weather forecast had been telling us that, only Tally had chosen to put her hands over her ears and say 'la-la-la' every time it was mentioned.

But it wasn't that bad. Fi and I decided to move most of the amusements into Stonemore's vast Neo-Classical entrance hall, with its marble floors and honey-coloured stone interior, which included two vast fluted columns and a staircase. At least it was well lit, thanks to a vast lightwell in the middle of the room. 'We're setting up in here,' I announced to the massed volunteers' sad faces.

'You're not going to make me put paper chains together, are you?' said one as she passed Fi.

'Absolutely not,' said Fi, with her brightest smile.

Tally had disappeared, in mourning for her grand plans, so it was Fi and I who directed the set-up in the hall, whilst doing our fair share of lugging furniture around.

'The carousel's a dead loss,' said Fi, just before 10am, 'and we can't do any of the throwing games inside, but there are a few things, aren't there?'

I looked around: cake stall, tombola, crafts made out of 'found objects', tie-dye clothing, second-hand books, guess the weight of the sweet jar, and a few other things – including, of course, my candy floss stall, which was manned by a gnomic man called Jim dressed in a pink uniform to match his product. 'I do not do cash handling,' he said flatly, on arrival.

'That's me!' I said. He did not smile.

The ice-cream man had decided to open up his van outside the main door. 'People always want ice cream,' he said cheerfully, rain dripping off his white peaked cap.

'I think it looks good,' I said, and Fi nodded and went to update the socials to let the village know it was still happening. But the rain was still falling so hard that the sound echoed around the austere marble-floored hall, and everyone was looking glum, when a rattling sound made a few of us turn.

It was Jamie. He was pushing a tea trolley laden with several teapots, a coffee pot, a milk jug, and plates of biscuits and pastries. He also had Hugo with him, on a tight lead, although the little beagle was definitely eyeing up the goodies.

'You all need to keep your strength up,' announced Jamie. 'Come on, tuck in before we open the doors.'

I have never heard a collective sound of joy quite like it – half sigh, half contented babble. Everyone got properly stuck in, Jamie handed out steaming mugs of tea and coffee, and within a couple of minutes the gloomy volunteers who'd prepared themselves for a day of being shouted at by Tally were smiling, laughing and chatting.

Jim went to get tea, but I stood hesitantly by the candy floss stall, noticing how Jamie knew everyone's name, chatting to people naturally, young and old alike. And this time, he didn't look posh, or different: his navy cashmere jumper was worn thin at the elbows and his olive canvas trousers were workwear, as though he was about to go and do maintenance work on one of the dust-sheeted rooms. There was nothing showy about him as he smiled at a joke Pat made and handed someone else a cup of tea. Hugo wagged his tail as people spoke to him and fed him fragments of biscuit. I wasn't used to this version of Jamie, and it threw me; I was so used to having my defences up.

Pat appeared by my side, carrying tea and the most enormous chocolate-sprinkled croissant I'd ever seen.

'Jamie says you're looking peaky and need this,' she said. 'I told him you and Fi had moved all the furniture for us.'

'Thank you.' I took it gratefully. She smiled, patted me on the shoulder, and went to recommence stroking Hugo.

I looked up, and my eyes met Jamie's. 'Thank you,' I mouthed, and the slight smile that crossed his face made me look away.

I took a large bite of the croissant, which was all buttery flakes and dark, moist chocolate. It was good. Very good.

'Doors are open.' Fi returned from updating socials. Her hair was slightly damp and she had three pink wafers in her hand. 'Tally's hiding in the office. She says she'll come out if more than one hundred people cross the threshold.'

I saw a volunteer click in the first two. When I looked back, Jamie, Hugo and the tea trolley had gone.

Jamie returned later, because people expected to see the lord of the manor, but he skirted round my stall. Probably for the best, I thought to myself, as Jim wrangled several fistfuls of candy floss onto a stick for a beaming four-year-old and I took payment. I couldn't get over how much these people loved candy floss!

> *Are you coming for candy floss?* I messaged Callum.

> *Sorry, I'm busy. Save me some though.* ☺

A couple of hours in and Dorrie on the front door had clicked in 150 people. I didn't even know 150 people lived in the village. 'I was good with the hashtags,' said Fi, as she whizzed past with a clipboard. 'And people will come from miles around just to visit without paying the entrance fee. Everyone loves a free nose around a stately home.'

'But the other rooms are locked off, aren't they?' I said, gazing at Jim's violent churning of the candy floss.

'Yep, but that doesn't matter for some people, as long as they can say they've been here. And if they meet the earl, they get bonus points on social media.' She nodded in the direction of a group of thirty-something women who were taking a group selfie with Jamie.

Richard appeared in the doorway carrying two bulging shopping bags. 'I told her not to click me in, because I don't count,' he said, smiling. 'Jam doughnut and sticky bun delivery for the tea stall.'

'Thank you, thank you!' cried Fi, embracing him. 'We're completely out of carbs. And of course you count.'

They went off together. It was still raining, but someone had turned the lights on and it gave the room a warmer feel, helped by the low-level sound of people chatting and laughing, the clink of teacups, and a few excited children's voices (all hopped up on candy floss). It was a large, grand, austere space, but it suddenly felt cosy, as if it had been waiting for all these people to fill it.

A few minutes later there was a brief lull in candy floss sales and I noticed Tally had drifted into the room. She stopped to speak to Pat, who uncharacteristically gave her a disrespectful two-finger salute. I stifled a laugh – Tally's captive workforce were rebelling. I caught her eye and beckoned her over.

'See,' I said. 'It's going fine.'

She looked a bit sheepish. 'Maybe.' She took a breath. 'I'm sorry I bailed on you, Anna. I may have overreacted.' She always went extra posh when she felt uncomfortable. I felt a twinge of affection for her that I expressed through a playful shove.

'Well, I'm glad you're here. You can take over for ten minutes while I have a break. Or longer, if you like.'

She shook her head. 'No, I don't *do* customer-facing.'

'Yes, you do. I've been on my feet for hours and I need a break.' I took my apron off and put it on the table, then nodded my farewell to Jim. 'I'll be back in ten.' I charged off before she could say another word.

I cadged a cup of tea from the refreshments stall and slipped down one of the staff corridors that came out at the orangery. Phyllis, one of the volunteers, was lying down with her legs up the wall. 'Don't mind me, love, my ankles are a bit swollen,' she said when I stopped dead on the threshold.

'I can go, if you want some privacy?' I said.

She said not to and we chatted a little whilst I sipped my tea. Phyllis was usually a tour guide and she knew Stonemore inside out. She told me about the history of the orangery – a Neo-Gothic construction one of the Victorian earls had built for his wife.

'Really?' I said. 'It seems strange to have an orangery. Not quite the climate for it.'

'She wanted one, so he built it for her,' she said. 'Romantic, isn't it? You should see their tomb in the mausoleum. The inscription on it is wonderful. *Here I lie, beneath grey forbidding skies/Lost in the eternal present of your eyes.*'

I bit my lip, and looked at the rain, drumming against the windows. 'Hmm,' I said. 'So much to learn about this place.'

She said she'd be happy to tell me more at any time, and left me to finish my tea ('I'd best get back to name the teddy bear or Joy will have my guts for garters').

I glanced at my watch. Ten minutes and counting. But it felt so luxurious to be here, the rain rattling against the windows, the pale light streaming through the Neo-Gothic tracery. I sat down on one of the Victorian cast-iron chairs and savoured my last few sips of tea.

'Don't tell me you've sold out of candy floss.'

I almost dropped my cup. It was Jamie. Standing in the doorway, his hands in his pockets.

'You almost gave me a heart attack,' I said. Obviously, I was in flight or fight; I was so used to arguing with him, I went on high alert the moment he walked into a room. I made a mental note to re-institute the meditation practice I'd been attempting to establish.

'It's good to have a break, in the quiet,' he said, with feeling.

'Too many selfies with visitors?'

'Yes.' He smiled. 'The last one told me she would make an age-appropriate countess.'

I couldn't help myself. 'I suppose you are getting on. What are you, thirty-five? Maybe she thought you might be open to offers.'

'Thanks,' he said tightly. 'Always good to be slapped down.' The way he held my gaze with his piercing blue eyes set my heart spinning like a worry bead.

'Where's Hugo?' I valiantly tried to steer the conversation onto safe topics.

'He's snoring on the sofa upstairs. He was getting over-whelmed by the kids. He loves them, but after getting poked in the eye for the third time I think he fancied some alone-time too.'

I gave a cry of laughter and he smiled. But when our eyes met, I couldn't hold his gaze. Instead, I focused on the rain falling in rivers down the glass.

'Anna,' he said softly, sitting down opposite me. 'Are you okay?'

'What do you mean?'

'After the horse thing. I was terrified.' He blinked, changed direction. 'Thought you might sue me for broken bones or concussion or something.'

'Of course not,' I said stoutly. 'I normally behave as though I'm slightly concussed anyway.'

'Good to know.'

I smiled blandly.

'Looks like that scratch is healing, anyway,' he said. And he reached out and brushed my face with his thumb.

At his touch, a feeling trembled into life in me that I could not name. A connection that made me catch my breath.

'I'm glad you're safe,' he murmured.

'Employee safety is very important,' I murmured back. He was close to me now, and I could smell the fresh air scent of his skin. It felt as though my skin was humming. His hand was still on my face, the lightest touch. *What is happening*, I thought, as our eyes locked on to each other, enough electricity in our gazes to flip the trip switch of the house. Everything was tingling at the softness of his touch as he ran his index finger down the length of my face and tipped up my chin. Moreover, I didn't want to move away. I wanted to move towards him. When his hand gently brushed against the back of my neck I felt as though my veins were filled with liquid honey.

There was an enormous boom, as though someone had set a cannon off, and the room vibrated with a techno beat that sent us leaping apart. Someone in the hall had got the ancient boom box working and I thought I was going to have a heart attack. Again.

'Woah,' I gasped and started laughing.

Jamie had let go of me. He looked dazed, but he wasn't smiling; it was as though someone had slapped him.

'I apologise.' He got to his feet and stood soldier-straight.

My heart was rattling in my chest a ridiculous amount. 'Yes, best get out there,' I said. 'There'll be some potential countesses queuing up.'

The look of horror on his face silenced me. 'I'm joking,' I said forlornly.

'That was unprofessional of me, Anna.' He cut through any attempt at humour. 'Could we – forget that happened?'

My heart dropped in my chest. Really? I fought the urge to breathe on my hand and check I didn't smell of swamp or something. I'd been just as blindsided as him, but the way he was trying to get away was pure bad manners.

'No problem,' I said, in a small voice.

'Great,' he nodded, looking anywhere but at my face. 'I hope the rest of the day goes well. Make sure you sell all that candy floss.'

Luckily he wasn't looking at my face so he couldn't see the bewilderment painted across it as he disappeared out of the door.

'You've been *twenty-seven minutes*!' hissed Tally, as I staggered back to the candy floss stall, feeling very much like a Victorian maiden who might faint at any moment. I stood there for a moment, my face burning at the memory of Jamie scuttling back through the halls of the house as though I'd blown a raspberry in his face. The realisation was dawning on me: I had definitely wanted to kiss him. I'd been pretty sure he'd wanted to kiss me. And now, kissing him or slapping him was even.

'*Anna*! You left me for ages!' Tally's voice was like a pail of iced water over the head.

'And you've done fine,' I said, observing the empty candy floss box and Jim's thunderous expression; it was clear he and Tally had not got on. 'Do you think the children of Northumberland have had enough sugar for now? I can go and help with teas. They look a bit inundated.' As I glanced over, Pat mouthed 'help' in my direction. She wasn't the only one who needed help. I did.

'Fine,' said Tally. 'No one's listening to me anyway.'

I felt like pointing out to her that she'd abandoned her project when things got tough. 'It's worked out well though, hasn't it?' I said.

'I suppose,' she said.

'Why don't you go and get yourself an ice cream?' I tried not to sound patronising, but failed.

'I might, actually,' she said to my surprise, brightening up.

I released Jim from his purgatory then marched over to Pat and started to help with tea and scones. They'd been spreading the butter too thick ('spread on, then spread off', my mother used to tell me, when we were struggling to pay the gas bill), so they'd almost run out. I set about changing this and also halved the amount of jam being given out to punters. It turned out my working-class economising skills were useful at Stonemore after all.

'That Tally was eating all of the candy floss,' Pat said, nudging me.

'Can I have some sugar with my tea?' said an elderly gentleman. 'I did ask before.'

'Of course,' I said brightly, as Pat raised her eyebrows. Glancing up, I saw Fi and Richard disappearing off out of the front door, hand in hand and giggling like teenagers. It was so good to see them looking carefree. Fi had recently been wearing that tired, worn look that nights spent worrying gives you. I knew they were embarking on another cycle of IVF.

'I said coffee, not tea,' said another woman, who had a small child hanging off her arm, begging for more candy floss.

'Sorry!' I got her a fresh cup and poured her a coffee.

'Hey, trouble.'

I looked up from my daze.

Callum was there, smiling, damp-haired from the rain and with a twinkle in his eye. 'Thought I'd drop in. How's it going?'

I gave a little huff of relief. 'Good, thanks. Tea? On the house?'

'Don't mind if I do. How are you, Pat?'

'All the better for seeing you.' She winked at him.

I bustled round, getting Callum his tea. Then I felt someone's eyes on me.

Jamie, in a brief respite from greeting people and having selfies taken, was leaning against the wall and watching me.

I lifted my chin and carried on working as though I hadn't seen him, smiling brightly at Callum as he took a bite out of a biscuit and offered me the other half. Damn it, I even let him post it into my mouth then almost choked on it as Lucinda streaked past, clearly in pursuit of her earl.

I heard a door slam and when I looked back, Jamie was gone.

I could actually *hear* the blood thundering in my ears. Honestly, with these cardiac symptoms I should probably go and see a doctor.

Goal of the week, I wrote in my journal that night: *try not to have panic-palpitations every time Jamie walks into the room.*

CHAPTER 13

I found myself looking forward to summer at Stonemore. As the days grew longer, Fi and I took to eating lunch on a picnic blanket near Belheddonbrae when it was sunny, taking it in turns to create elaborate salads with increasingly outlandish ingredients. In the evenings, I walked across the deer park and down the lane to the cottage whatever the weather. By the time I got home, I'd usually forgotten any stress from the day (Sean had been texting but as he was probably trying to recover more lost CDs, I ignored him). If my mind kept returning to the weird moment between me and Jamie, the day job on his estate was an excellent distraction. Out on the hillside of the Stonemore Estate, things were much simpler. The air was so pure and clear, limpid as spring water from one of the estate's streams, but scented too, carrying with it faint traces of forest and newly turned soil. Along with

Belheddonbrae there was always plenty to do outside, whether supervising the work of volunteers or taking water samples from the estate's streams. Once a week, I toured the whole estate with Callum, and we discussed new initiatives and recent work that had been done, checking that all was as it should be.

The section of ancient forest, and its soft, lower light, was a haven. Spruce and fir had been carefully thinned to increase light levels and allow native species to recover. I'd worked alongside a team of contractors who were far more efficient than me, but nonetheless appreciated my efforts. With every small increment of change on the estate, I could feel my body and mind gradually strengthening.

I showed Callum what had been done in the forest. I wondered if he would try and dismiss it, or even say he couldn't see any difference, but he nodded gently as I spoke to him about it. 'It's grand,' he said softly.

'And some other good news,' I said, as Callum swept his gaze around the area, taking it all in. 'The beaver pair are being introduced to an area by the Claybeck stream next week. We've been surveying for the right spot, and all the experts are satisfied. The charity confirmed this morning.'

Callum said nothing. I gave a satisfied sigh and glanced back at him, then did a double-take. 'Are those ... tears in your eyes?' I said.

'No!' he said, and sniffed. 'Sharp wind up here today, that's all.'

I nodded and looked away. No point in arguing with

a man who said he wasn't crying. Then I felt him tap my shoulder. 'Sure, Anna. It's a beautiful thing.'

I nodded back, and found the sharp breeze had got to my eyes too.

He put an arm around me and gave me a squeeze, and I looked up at him. Slowly, he began to drift towards me, and I found I was bracing myself. This was what I had wanted, wasn't it? A bit of fun with Callum?

We managed a proper kiss this time, but my mind was scrambling, and not in the way it had with Jamie. I mean, Callum was very attractive, sure he was, but for some reason I could note this dispassionately. With Jamie, my reaction had been immediate, intense and physical. Undeniable.

Callum tilted his head and looked at me shyly. 'Do you fancy a drink tonight? At the Rising Sun?'

'Er, yes,' I said. 'That would be nice.'

He smiled, and nodded. 'Great,' he said. 'Great.'

Back at the house, the aftermath of the fair was still being 'processed'. Tally had been reined in from giving 'feedback' (criticism) to the volunteers and was raging that sticky fingerprints had been found on a Boulle cabinet, thus necessitating more restoration. 'From Darren?' asked Fi.

'No! He's paintings!' cried Tally. 'And if that ice-cream man calls me again, I shall go mad. He wants to set up here every weekend.'

'I'll mention it to Jamie,' said Fi, drifting out the room with a dreamy smile on her face. 'Get the restoration quote to me when you can, Tally. I need to assign it to the correct budget line.'

'You're very cheerful,' I said to Fi later, as I supervised a harried furniture conservator who had been summoned urgently from Newcastle in the pouring rain, only to find Tally was on the longest lunch break of her life.

She blushed. 'Things are so good with me and Richard. It's like we're on honeymoon again.'

'Spare me the details,' I said, with a grin. The furniture conservator had a gloomy look on his face as he inspected the sticky fingerprints on the black and gold cabinet and muttered to himself about 'little blighters' as he unpacked his kit on the polished floorboards.

'Have you,' Fi glanced over her shoulder, 'spoken to Jamie recently? He seems a bit down. He's been spending most of his time on long walks with Hugo.'

'Well, dogs are better than people,' I said, 'so I don't blame him. Also, we don't speak to each other, remember? Everything has to go through Callum.'

'Mmm.' Fi narrowed her eyes at me. 'No more arguments with him?'

'Nope,' I said, managing to combine looking innocent with feeling guilty as Fi looked at me suspiciously. Let's have a girlie night soon,' I said. 'Wine, takeaway, film?'

'How many children did you let loose on this cabinet?' piped up the conservator.

I began my long explanation about the fete, and the involvement of candy floss and ice cream. Fi received a call about a malfunctioning till and disappeared in the direction of the gift shop.

When the conservator had been pacified, I returned to my desk and switched on Forestcam for a quick hit of serenity. The faint scent of cherry informed me that Callum was vaping in his office as he answered emails. I was texting Keith about an upcoming delivery of lavender when an email from Callum landed in my inbox with the title: 'This is unusual!!!!'. It was so unlike Callum to use exclamation marks that I opened it immediately.

It was my proposal to establish a beehive near Belheddonbrae; Jamie's response to Callum's request for clearance. It had been sent at 5am that morning.

Hi Callum: tell Anna she can have whatever she wants. J

I sat very still and observed the faint thud of my own pulse in my ears. Why did that one-line email feel like something more than a work email?

Because I was crazy, that's why. It was simply the meanderings of my crazed brain.

Tally breezed in. 'Pat says you let the conservator in to look at the Boulle? I hope you supervised him properly.'

'Oh, knob *off*!' I said, digging through my bag for my pasta salad and a box of painkillers. I had a headache and I needed carbs, pronto.

'Someone's hangry,' said Tally, wandering back in the direction of the photocopier.

I was wolfing down my lunch in the niche, waiting for the kettle to boil, when Tally reappeared and gave a shriek, and I looked up.

Hugo.

He was sitting in my chair. Sitting up cheerfully, like a soldier about to salute.

'Oh God, I left some chewing gum on my desk – he hasn't eaten it, has he?' wailed Tally, dredging through her customary piles of paper. 'Jamie loves that flea-bitten idiot. I can't be responsible for— Phew! It's here.'

'Hello you,' I said to Hugo, leaving my lunch on the counter.

Hugo gave a single, low bark. But his tail thumped, to show friendly intent.

'Down,' I said, looking around to see if there was a spare dog lead anywhere. 'You have to go back to the flat, mister.'

Hugo looked at me.

'He won't listen to you. He never listens to anyone. Bloody beagle,' muttered Tally.

I tried perking up my tone a bit. 'Come on! Hugo! Hugues! Huggy bear!'

'You sound like an idiot. I'm going to record you for TikTok,' said Tally.

I held up a reproving finger. 'You don't have my permission.'

She slammed her phone down on the desk.

'Please, Hugo,' I said. He tilted his head and gazed at me with his oil-black eyes.

A sharp whistle sounded across the office. Hugo jumped down and galloped to the feet of Callum.

'Good boy.' He rubbed Hugo's sides. 'Sorry about that, Anna. Hugo's going to be an office dog for the next few days. If we could all keep an eye out when we're going in and out, so he doesn't disappear off exploring. Jamie's gone to London and Hugo's staying with me.'

'To London?' My stomach dropped. How long was he going to be gone for?

'Yep,' said Callum. 'He said, though, could you put some content together on the beavers? We need a short clip for social media.'

'The charity will share all their footage of the release. I'll ensure we get a social-ready clip.' I made a show of writing this down carefully. Tally was already batting away Hugo, who had decided that she was a food source of some kind. 'Callum, get him out of here!' she called.

Hugo cast me a melancholy look as Callum clipped a lead on him and led him to his office.

Callum and I had our date at the Rising Sun that night, and Hugo came along too. I decided not to try too hard with my outfit, and winged it with a pair of (clean) jeans and a nice jumper, which Callum complimented as being 'very holey'.

'It was made by a lady in the village,' I said. 'She has all kinds of looms and knitting machines.'

'Oh, Sandra?' he said, as Hugo pawed at my leg.

I fed the beagle a crisp. 'Yes, I think she's fabulous.'

'It is mainly hole though, isn't it?' he said. 'I'm not sure she should charge too much for materials. Not that I mind looking at your skin.'

'Er, thanks,' I said. This was way too weird. He'd paid me a compliment and all I could do was cringe. When he got up, I asked for another Jack Daniel's and coke, even though I had only just begun my second. Perhaps Rose was right. More drink was needed.

The thing was, I couldn't stop myself from being detached from the situation. *Oh look*, my brain said, *Callum is gazing at you. Oh look, he has put his hand on your knee. Oh look . . .*

Meanwhile, it felt as though I was on a date with two men rather than one. Hugo kept prodding me for bar snacks and when I tried to ignore him, focused on me with his seal-pup eyes, glinting in the half-light, so that Callum remarked that I was 'looking at the dog more than you are at me'.

We managed a kiss or two – clearly noted by the regulars – then we headed out into the night. Walking alongside each other, brushing against each other as Hugo sniffed trails on the pavement, I felt calmer. *I can do this*, I thought. So when Callum's hand brushed mine, I slotted my fingers into his, and was delighted to feel him squeeze my hand.

'Callum!'

The squeal sounded from far behind us, high-pitched and almost childlike, and I turned to see a woman running towards us. When she neared us, she picked up speed, then literally leapt into Callum's arms and wrapped her legs around his waist as he struggled not to drop her. Ten out of ten for athleticism, but I have to admit I felt slightly peeved at her clinging to him like a koala on a eucalyptus tree.

'Cassie!' he was saying, as he gently lowered her to the ground. 'Good to see you.'

'Long time no see,' she said, and glanced at me with a wrinkled nose. 'Er, hi.'

'Hi,' I said, as Callum handed Hugo's lead to me and the beagle attempted to drag me away from the squealing being, ears down.

'Anna, this is Cassie, Cassie, Anna,' said Callum, before embarking on a brief amount of small talk which covered stuff I didn't understand, such as 'did you know Mikey and Jolls were getting married'.

After she'd disentangled herself and headed off in another direction, we continued our wander home, but the rosy glow had worn off and I didn't attempt to take his hand again.

'Sorry about that,' said Callum. 'I didn't want to be rude to her. There's some history.'

'Mmm,' I said, nodding, 'I thought there might be.'

'Anna?' he said. 'You're not annoyed, are you?'

We'd stopped and I managed to hold his gaze. 'Of course not,' I said. The truth being: *I have no idea if I am or not. And although I've just watched a woman wrap her legs around your waist, I'm not entirely sure I want to do the same at the moment.*

Luckily, as we stood looking at each other awkwardly, Hugo lost all patience with our slowness and started barking, then baying, with a note of manufactured hysteria.

'Look, I'll let you go,' I said. 'I'd forgotten, I said I'd call a friend tonight.' I kissed him on the cheek. 'See you tomorrow, yeah?'

He shrugged, and smiled. 'Sure.'

That was the excellent thing about Callum. So easy-going. Perhaps, I thought, as I walked home, some of that easy-going attitude might eventually rub off on our grumpy boss, and make our lives so much easier. Bloody typical that I was thinking about him, when I should have been rolling around in bed with my lazily handsome, utterly available colleague.

'I did say before, Callum's not a good idea, Anna.'

Fi and I were eating noodles and discussing my love life, the film we'd chosen paused on the opening credits.

'Nnngh,' I said, levering a chopstick's worth of tofu into my mouth. 'Why?'

She sighed. 'Because he's a massive tart!'

Chewing, I attempted to process this information. 'But he's not chasing after people.'

'He doesn't have to, sweet. They're queuing up. He's got that whole oh-I'm-so-scruffy-and-helpless thing going on,' she said. 'I've never seen the appeal of it myself but other people certainly do. There's barely a woman under fifty in the village who wouldn't crawl over broken glass to get to him.' She put her arm around me and squeezed. 'I'm sorry. I know I sound like the fun police.'

'It's fine,' I said. She looked at me as though I was being

brave. 'No, really. I couldn't quite get into the swing of it. In fact, maybe it will help, knowing that it doesn't mean anything at all.'

'You keep saying that, but it's not really you.'

Gloomily, I helped myself to a spring roll or three. 'I'm trying to be a new me. And I'm not going to get attached to the first man I sleep with.'

'The real you is already wonderful. Stop trying to be something different. I've seen you get attached to a spider that's taken up residence in your bathroom. It's what you do.'

I shook my head. 'Anyway,' I said, 'I can name one person who is definitely not crawling over broken glass to get to Callum, and that's Lucinda.'

Fi sighed. 'Oh yes. She does seem to be still keen on Jamie, doesn't she?'

'What happened with them?' I topped up our glasses with elderflower.

'I don't know,' she said. 'He's very private about that kind of thing. But it always seemed to me that he was holding back, in some way. Lucinda was always very bubbly with him, very affectionate. And he seemed, well, happy, I suppose, but also – not.'

'I suppose we never know what's going on between two people,' I said. Jamie was an equation I couldn't quite solve. *That was obviously why my mind kept returning to him.*

She nodded. 'Look, back to you. Hear me out when I say this?'

I paused in the act of spooning more noodles onto my plate.

'Why don't you give internet dating a chance? One of those apps?'

'Oh come on!' I said.

'There are lots of perfectly decent-looking, absolutely normal blokes out there,' she said. 'What's wrong with giving real life a try again?'

I gazed at her dumbly.

'Because,' she said, 'all this dancing around after Callum suggests one thing to me. You seem to have a penchant for emotionally unavailable men, Anna.'

'No, I don't!' I said indignantly.

'Come off it,' she said. 'Sean was always blowing hot and cold on you at the beginning.'

I opened my mouth to say that he wasn't, but then closed it again. 'We can't all meet the love of our lives at eighteen,' I said huffily. 'Sometimes you have to compromise.'

'Exactly,' she said cheerfully. 'Shall we raise a glass to swiping right?'

After Fi had gone, I went and got my self-help books, my coloured pens and my journal. Feeling a bit like a teenager, I sat cross-legged in my pyjamas, opened the front page, and looked at the cheerfully decorated word: No.

I flicked through the pages, looking at the word maps where I'd tried to examine my feelings, to chip away at the grief about losing Sean and my dream of having a family with him.

Then I turned to a blank page, and wrote in gold:

Self-Sabotage.

It was time, again, to start digging around in my mind. To work out the many ways in which I'd tripped myself up. Starting, perhaps, with Callum. But as I jotted down thoughts, I couldn't think of my crush on him as a hindrance. He was calm, he was kind, and I wanted someone like him in my life. And it was strange that I always fancied him most when he wasn't there. I thought of him squinting against the sunlight as we looked at the woods together, and that slow easy smile beneath the thatch of unkempt hair.

And of Jamie, staring into my eyes in the orangery.

Second goal of the week, I noted. *Stop thinking about Jamie in* that *way.*

Maybe Fi was right. Even that weird moment I'd had with Jamie might just be me, attracting inappropriate men like a magnet attracting iron filings.

Gerald the mouse raced past, and I threw a book at him, half-heartedly.

CHAPTER 14

Jamie's absence stretched from a couple of days, to a week, to two, whilst Stonemore basked in summer. White clouds like torn cotton wool drifted across vivid blue skies, and the chill breezes combined with fierce sunlight. The beaver family had been carefully introduced to the Claybeck stream, and enthusiastically began their work on the surrounding trees.

It was a bright morning in the staff office, several weeks later, when Hugo gave a sharp little bark of a type I hadn't heard before.

'Shut up!' Tally squeaked, when there was the sound of feet on gravel, and the office door swung open.

It was Jamie.

Clean-shaven, looking almost metropolitan in jeans and a linen shirt beneath a grey jacket – not waxed this time. We glanced at each other, and I was immediately on edge.

'Hugo knew you'd arrived,' I said, my eyes fixed on my

computer screen as Hugo danced around his master's legs, barking hysterically, his tail wagging so hard he should, by the laws of physics, have taken off.

'He must have heard the car.' Fi was on her feet. 'Hello, hello!'

'Hi everyone.' When I glanced back at him, I saw he had the beginning of a smile on his face as he looked at Fi. 'Thanks for holding the fort.'

'No problem/no worries/it's a pleasure,' we all chorused. I kept my face neutral, until I felt a wet nose nudging at my ankle. Hugo. Whilst Jamie had been away, he'd spent at least an hour a day asleep in my lap as I typed over his head. Now, having greeted Jamie, he was looking at me in a questioning how–about–a–cuddle way.

'Hey you,' I said softly to him, stroking his ears. 'Not now. Your dad's back.'

'She's going to have to disappoint you, Hugo.' Without looking at me, Jamie scooped the small hound into his arms and carried him away, holding him close.

Life stayed calm. I deepened my experience of the estate from close observation of every copse and hillside, drawing on Callum's encyclopaedic knowledge of the landscape and his memory of every snowfall and flood. I even spent a day in the formal garden doing a beetle count, and was delighted to find a black and orange sexton beetle, although Tally didn't appreciate being shown a picture of it on my phone.

One afternoon I arrived back in the office after a morning

striding over Stonemore's acres with Callum, feeling unusually peaceful. I found Fi packing up to go and Tally's desk empty apart from its usual piles of catalogues and magazines.

'Where's Tally?' I said.

'She's doing a presentation,' said Fi, sweeping her notebook and pens into her desk drawer with an air of finality. 'They're considering a re-hang of the paintings. Tally has done a presentation on her thoughts and Jamie is going to provide tea and scones. They should almost be done, actually.'

'Employee of the month,' I said. Apparently it was only me who he couldn't stand to be around. I sat down and clicked Forestcam on.

'Right, I'm off.' Fi stood up, jingled her keys, and looked at me, apprehension in her eyes. It was transfer day; the moment when Fi and Richard's embryos were transferred into Fi's uterus and they began their wait to see if the embryos would implant. Rather than rest, she had opted to stay busy and had come to work before the procedure.

I got up, went to her and put my arms around her. I didn't know what to say, even though I'd been thinking about the perfect words to support her for several days now. I had to wing it. 'It will be fine, everything will go smoothly and brilliantly,' I said. It always felt so difficult – how to wish someone luck without building false hope? She rested her head on my shoulder for a moment. When she looked back at me, she was crying.

'No, no, no . . .' I took her face in my hands.

'Sorry, it's my frigging hormones,' she sniffed, trying to smile.

'It's a constant battle,' I said, because I didn't know what else to say.

'Richard's cooking my favourite meal tonight.'

'Lasagne? I'll be over at seven. *Kidding.*' She was properly smiling now. 'Off you go. No more tears. Tears are forbidden. This is going to be a good day.'

After she'd gone, I felt dull and restless. Where was Hugo? The little hound seemed to quite enjoy being a stress toy. But he was nowhere to be seen, and Callum was out, so there wasn't anyone to chat to.

I did a couple of emails then decided to check on Belheddonbrae. There'd been some spells of sunshine and showers, and I guessed the wildflower meadow would be showing progress. I also wanted to check whether Keith and Mica had enjoyed the cherry biscuits I'd made them the week before.

As I put my jacket on, I heard my phone chime.

SEAN *Are you screening my texts?*

I narrowed my eyes at the screen and tapped back.

You can't screen texts, Sean.

I left out the eye roll emoji I was tempted to add.

SEAN *I need to speak to you*

ANNA *Any missing CDs can be charged to my account.*

SEAN *It's not that.*

I put my coat on.

SEAN *I miss you.*

The gut punch of feeling almost floored me. It took me back, in an instant, to a London street the year before. All of life moving around me – traffic, shoppers, a lady with a pram tutting because I was in the way. Exhaust fumes and the faint sweet smell of fruit, stacked outside a corner shop. As I stood there, watching my fiancé turn away from me, unable to meet my eye, because we'd just heard the worst news together, hand in hand. But now, having left the doctor's office, he had let go of my hand.

For months, this text message would have been what I wanted to see. I would have broken down in relief and joy at the sight of it. Now, I felt . . .

Numb? Happy? *No.* Disappointed. *Really?*

I tried to breathe, as my self-help books had told me. I counted on the in-breath, counted on the out-breath. I tried to name the feeling that felt like a balled-up fist in the depths of my stomach.

Disappointment couldn't be right. Irritation? I checked again and again in those few moments.

Yep, I was disappointed and irritated that Sean had contacted me.

SEAN *Anna????*

I jabbed at the settings of my phone, and blocked him. I needed time to think, free from his messages.

There was no reason to delay going to Belheddonbrae, despite the fact that I now felt a bit shaky. So I locked up the office and went out into the fresh air, relishing the glances of some curious tourists. I loved the backstage, behind the scenes feeling of emerging from the staff office.

I heard the distant baying of the beagles as they took their afternoon play time in the enclosure, poor munchkins. Kept on walking that same route Callum had shown me on my first day, which was now as familiar to me as the walk to my own cottage.

I stopped dead at the gate to Belheddonbrae.

Jamie and Lucinda were sitting on the bench. Enjoying the view of the infant wildflower meadow, talking, a slight smile on his normally grumpy face as she spoke to him. Just as when I'd received Sean's message, I stood stock-still, an animal frozen to the spot.

What was this *pain*? A delayed reaction to Sean?

They were engrossed in each other. *Ugh.* Carefully, I turned, and began to move away, very slowly, trying not to capture their attention.

At that moment Keith appeared, carrying some *Verbena bonariensis*, the tiny purple flowers shivering on their long stalks.

'Hiya!' he said, smiling. 'Are you alright? You look like you're practising deer stalking or something.'

I bit my lip. 'Quite the opposite actually. I didn't want to disturb them.' I tilted my head slightly.

'Well, they're looking now. Do you want to come over there with me? I was going to show Jamie the verbena.'

'No, that's fine.' I noted the slight puzzlement on his face. 'As you were.' For some reason I'd started talking like a colonel on parade. 'Pip pip and all that.'

He looked puzzled. 'Are you alright, duck?'

'Hi Anna!' Mica came through the gate, wiping her hands on a cloth. 'You have to give me the recipe for those biscuits. They were incredible. Not that I got to eat many of them.' She nudged Keith.

'So glad you liked them,' I said. 'I'll send you the recipe.' I could feel Jamie and Lucinda looking at me. 'Sorry, I've just remembered something I have to do. I'd best be off – can we catch up later? I'd like your opinion on the parterre.'

'Sure,' she said, smiling. Keith carried the verbena off in the direction of Jamie.

I went back to the blissful silence of the office, and was making myself a restorative coffee when Tally came bowling through. 'Gosh, I'm exhausted,' she cried, picking up her bag. 'I went to condition-check the paintings in the music room, but I'm too drained. That presentation to Jamie was really tiring. Lucinda made some excellent suggestions.'

'Lucinda did?' I frowned at her.

'Yes,' said Tally, checking her lipstick. 'Looks like she's back in the fold, if you know what I mean. I think I'm going to finish early.' I heard her rooting around in her desk. Then she said my name. When I looked at her, she seemed uncharacteristically awkward.

'Fi said I should have a word with you,' she said, her tone particularly clipped. 'You were . . . very helpful at the fete, Anna. I appreciate it.'

'It's fine.'

'No, well, yes. Anyway. Fi said I haven't been . . . entirely nice to you. So I wanted to say that I'm sorry.' She gave an awkward little laugh. 'I suppose the truth is, I felt a teeny tiny bit threatened when you started working here. As a sophisticated woman, I am very much used to being the alpha female here at Stonemore.'

I clamped a hand over my mouth. I could *not* laugh at Tally's heartfelt apology. Luckily she wasn't looking at me; in her awkwardness, she was playing with the handle of her bag.

'So. Well. You seemed very capable, and very metropolitan. I could have been nicer,' she said, as though the words were being wrangled out of her.

In the time it took for her to finally look at me, I managed to get a hold of myself.

'That's very decent of you, Tally,' I said, a slight tremor in my voice. 'I accept your apology.'

'Well, yes, anyway, I'm very tired so I'm going now.' She was gone in under a minute, and I allowed myself a stifled cackle of laughter when I was totally sure she couldn't hear me.

Despite the diversion, as I settled back at my desk, a restlessness overcame me. I couldn't help my brain returning to Lucinda and Jamie in the garden. Every time I tried to refocus on a plan to rebuild old hedgerows with wild pear and apple trees, my mind returned to them. Sitting alongside each other, talking and smiling in a way that was so unfamiliar to me.

Name those feelings, I thought idly, as I poured the water into another coffee and stirred. *Go on, Anna. Name them.*

Irritation, check. Just like with Sean then.

Disappointment, check. But a different kind, somehow. And something else.

Jealousy.

Definitely jealousy. Was I really that much of a loser? Completely unable to support others in their happiness? Why shouldn't Jamie and Lucinda fall wildly in love? It wasn't hurting me. It wasn't their fault that all I had to my name was an ambiguous ex, a failed fling with Callum, and the serious creeps about the idea of jumping back in the dating pool.

I picked my mug up and clomped back to my desk: 3pm. Two hours until home. I could get lots done in that time.

*

189

After a week or two of thinking about further steps in our rewilding strategy, but not actually committing things to paper, I decided to request to work from home the following week. When I was at Stonemore, it was way too easy to leave my desk and go out onto the estate. Whether I was weeding, planting, raking or coppicing, the more physical the job the better and the quieter my mind was. But now I had to focus; I needed to think about which partners we should approach, including charities and conservation experts; and there were some smaller projects at Stonemore that I hadn't nailed down yet. Callum cleared my working from home request, but later that day he came to find me.

I was working at Belheddonbrae, on my knees planting some newly arrived plug plants, when he appeared behind me and nearly made me jump out of my skin. 'Jeez Louise!' I cried, almost dropping the red campion plant I was holding.

'Sorry,' he said, smiling. 'You've got mud on your face.' He carefully brushed my cheek with his forefinger.

'What's up?' I said.

'Jamie just wanted to check you're okay,' he said, looking faintly awkward. 'I told him you're going to be working from home for a bit. There's not an issue, is there? Some other reason you want to be at home?'

'No, I'm fine,' I said, in a brittle, chipper tone, which he thankfully failed to catch on to.

'Great, I'll tell him that,' he said, assembling his vape.

'Pass me that trowel, would you?' I said.

He did and watched me fill the hole around the plug plant before I patted it into place with my hands, melding the plug with the damp, pre-watered soil. 'Also,' he said, with a gust of blueberry-scented vape fumes, 'Jamie said he wants a field of sunflowers.'

I glanced up at him, raising my eyebrows.

'His mother's favourite flower. Reminds him of his child-hood. At least an acre.'

I surprised myself by not even considering a yes. 'Nope.'

'Really?'

'Not part of the plan.' I started digging a hole for another plug in the finely turned soil.

'How can I persuade you? Can I make you a hot chocolate?'

I sniggered and rocked back on my heels to look at him. 'Tell him you've left it with me.'

Callum saluted. 'When you're back in the office let me know, and I really will make you a hot chocolate.'

He headed off and I carried on planting, listening to the birdsong and the murmur of the breeze through nearby shrubs. The conversation had turned a little cog in my brain. It was clear Jamie wasn't at peace with the idea of Belheddonbrae being a wildflower meadow, and the thought occurred to me that I could always make some reference to its past, even if it wasn't through a direct re-creation of the old garden.

Back in the office, and waiting for the hot chocolate from Callum, I composed a quick email to Emma, the archivist who worked in the house one day a week, in case she had any historical notes on Belheddonbrae's history.

As I clicked send, I heard a distant wailing noise, coming closer: a Tally distress call. She was making it as she descended through the house. She appeared, carrying Hugo clumsily in her arms.

'He's done a wee on the Boulle cabinet,' she shrieked, depositing him on the carpet where he gave her a dark look.

'He's normally so good though,' I said, stroking his ultra soft ears. 'Perhaps he needed to go out and they missed his signals.' Hugo looked dolefully at me and sniffed my garden-scented jeans. 'I'll take him out now.'

Tally stomped over to her desk. 'I'll have to get the conservator in *again*. It's the cabinet that was just cleaned! Lucinda is furious.'

'Hmm.' The idea of the perpetually sunny Lucinda being annoyed was suddenly, wickedly appealing to me. 'Good boy, Hugo,' I murmured to him, picking up his lead and delving in my drawer for some treats. 'Very good boy.'

Hugo looked up at me and licked his lips.

On my first day working from home I was bored by 3pm and was pushing womanfully on with the sustenance of a packet of chocolate digestives when I heard a car pull up. Racing to the window at a speed that would have put Hugo to shame, I saw Fi climbing out, carrying an enormous bunch of flowers in a gift bag.

'They're not from me!' she said as I opened the door.

'They were delivered to the office so I thought I'd bring them over.'

'Come on in, it's teatime,' I said, ushering her in. 'Luckily I haven't hoovered up all of the biscuits. You were just in time.'

She smiled and put her bag down on the sofa. As I clicked the kettle on, I turned and looked at her. There was something different about her face. A clearness in her eyes and skin; a vitality in her movements. Something clicked in my mind.

'Do you have news for me?' I said.

Her giggle was breathless, so uncharacteristic that I knew straight away. 'Are you a witch?' she said, unable to repress the smile spreading across her face. 'I might just be a tiny bit pregnant.'

The shriek that erupted from me was unexpected even to me, and Fi laughed as I jumped in the air and stretched out my arms. 'Oh my God! I can't even hug you, can I? You're too delicate. Don't pick anything up.'

'Of course you can hug me!'

'I promise not to squeeze too hard.' I embraced her and did an impromptu dance around the kitchen. 'Who else have you told?'

'No one. We want to keep it quiet until the twelve-week scan. It's just you and your witchy ways.' She grinned as I flung a handful of chocolate biscuits on a blue and white plate.

'I'm so happy for you,' I said, feeling the need to open

a bottle of champagne, then realising that was impossible because a) I didn't have any and b) Fi wouldn't drink any. 'Sit down, sit down.' I served her tea and biscuits then sat down opposite her, squeezing her hand.

'I don't want to talk about it too much, if that's okay,' she said. 'I don't want to count on it – so early.'

'Understood.' I raised my tea mug and we 'cheers'd' each other. 'I won't talk to you about it until you speak to me first. But I'm always here.'

'I know.' She touched my knee. 'Thank you. Now – er – I hate to be nosy, obviously – but who are the flowers from?'

The flowers. I'd completely forgotten about them, lolling in their gift bag on the kitchen counter in shades of cream and purple. I fished around in the bag and found the tiny envelope with the card, addressed to Ms Anna Whitlock. I tore it open and pulled out the card.

So you've blocked me. But I still miss you. Talk to me, Anna.
  Sean xx

'Anna?' Fi's voice broke into my thoughts. 'What's wrong, love? Your face is a picture.'

'I'm fine.' I pinned a smile to my face. 'They're from Sean. To be honest I wish he'd just do one. I'm impressed he remembered where I've moved to. Normally anything I told him was mysteriously wiped from his memory within thirty seconds.' I went back to the sofa and dipped a chocolate biscuit in my tea.

'They did the rounds before they got to the office,' said Fi. 'Apparently Lucinda thought Jamie had bought them for her so things got a bit complicated. I was glad to jump into the car and deliver them.'

I swallowed back questions about Jamie and Lucinda and moved the conversation on. We talked about books, TV and the glory of the warmer weather.

'I'd best leave you to your peace and quiet,' said Fi, after a while. 'Sorry to interrupt your blissful day working from home.'

'It was slightly too quiet actually,' I said. 'I almost missed Tally.'

'So you're finally feeling at home?' she said quietly.

'I wouldn't go that far.'

She grinned and we hugged and said goodbye. I faithfully promised to visit her and Richard for film night on Friday.

After she'd gone, I carefully clipped the leaves off my bouquet and emptied the sachet of plant food into a vase, mixed it with water, and slowly arranged the flowers. I even managed to impress myself with my own serenity. I finished the document I was working on, then noted the time and closed my computer down. It was just past five and a soft light was falling through the cottage window, lighting up the grey flagstones. Through an open casement I could hear the birds singing, nothing else.

As I chopped vegetables for dinner, I examined my feelings. Fi had brought big news to my little hideaway and I needed to check the chinks in my armour. But after a minute or two I realised I wasn't wearing any. There'd been no reason to defend myself, or to hide my feelings.

When Sean and I had been trying fruitlessly for a baby, and we'd started having medical investigations, every baby announcement had cut me. Whether it was a friend, colleague or acquaintance, it had always felt like a dagger to the heart. I knew the unworthiness of these feelings; the smallness that I had resented other people's babies because I couldn't have my own. But disliking myself for my feelings had made things even worse, and since I came to Stonemore I'd begun to accept that feelings were just that – neither good nor bad, just there. As long as I didn't actively do anything to distress anyone, as long as I didn't wish anyone ill, I could hold on to good Anna, true Anna, even if her inner voice was quiet and tinny like a turned-down radio.

In the past I'd got good at play-acting joy; congratulations were offered without hesitation, and even I knew the right expression to paint across my face. Sometimes acting – you might even call it lying – is the best and kindest thing to do, and I'd elevated it to a noble art.

As I cooked, I checked my feelings again. Once, twice, three times. And I found, astonishingly, nothing negative at all. When I'd danced for joy, it wasn't some pretence – an automatic performance to hide my pain. I'd been happy, really happy. The feeling was simple: a singing emptiness that left me feeling empty and full at the same time. No complex corners or shadows. No need to hide. My joy was as straightforward as my pain had once been.

Dinner was delicious. The landline phone rang twice that evening, but both times it was Sean, so I ignored it.

CHAPTER 15

It is a truth universally acknowledged that if a person has concentrated on taking home everything that might possibly be needed for working from home, a single vital thing will be left behind. For me it was the tiny memory stick I'd saved some plant lists on. I was planning to turn my attention to the parterre, with the idea of adding some herbs and flowers. My garden design instincts had been coming alive again; I'd been daydreaming about banks of English lavender, fragrant in the summer sunshine, and swathes of love-in-a-mist, with their spiky green foliage and soft blue petals.

Luckily I realised the memory stick was missing at the precise moment I opened my eyes on Wednesday morning, so once I'd showered and dressed, I decided to nip to the staff office before anyone else was around. Sure enough the office was empty, and I quickly found the stick, popping it into my purse and locking the desk drawer.

'A-ha! Trespasser!' I turned to see Lucinda standing there. I glanced at the clock – 8.10.

'Just came to pick something up,' I said, resisting the temptation to ask her why she was roaming around like she owned the place. 'See you later.'

'Anna . . .' There was a new note in her voice that made me turn towards her again. It was then I noticed what she was wearing, and it was decidedly non-Lucinda-like: a white outsized shirt over her jodhpurs. A man's shirt. Her hair loose, tousled – bed head. The conclusion flickered so quickly in my mind that I know I didn't keep the look of surprise off my face.

'Yes,' she said, biting her lip. 'I know you'll be pleased for us.' She gave a little giggle. 'Before long, I'll be here pretty much permanently.'

I was trying very hard to arrange my face into a cheerful expression and had the sense I was failing. 'Great news,' I said. 'But none of my business.' As her smile faded, I tried to recover it. 'I wish you and Jamie much joy,' I said, as though I was in a Jane Austen novel.

'I'm really interested in the work you're doing, just as I am in Tally's management of the art collection,' she said, a shade too brightly. 'So I'd love to get involved. In fact, any big decisions, I'd appreciate you discussing them with me as well as Jamie.'

'Right,' I said. 'Right.'

Her smile was acres wide now. Was it my imagination, or was she looking a bit shark-like?

'I can see I've blindsided you,' she piped. 'Is it a bit early for Miss Sleepyhead?'

I knew now that my expression was very much not positive and that I needed to get out of there. 'Totally. Much too early for me,' I said.

'Hello yooooou,' Lucinda cooed. Hugo had just trotted through the office door. He carefully avoided her outstretched hand and went into Callum's office.

'He likes me really,' said Lucinda.

'Of course he does,' I said.

I held my head high as I walked away from the house, resisting the temptation to break into a jog. Once I was through the deer park, I pulled out my mobile and messaged Fi. *Is Lucinda down to marry Jamie? She just implied she is very definitely the boss of me.*

I pressed send and slipped it back into my bag as it tried to find a signal. By the time I got into the cottage the landline was ringing.

'Anna, it's Fi.'

I told her what had happened.

'Crikey,' she said. 'I didn't realise things had gone that far. Jamie hasn't said a word.'

'I know we all knew they were seeing each other, but . . .' That far. I didn't think they'd gone that far. 'It's weirded me out, that's all. Sorry Fi. I'll see you later.'

I felt strange, and I didn't like it. Just for once, I didn't turn to the carbs to get me through my unsettled feelings.

I did twenty jumping jacks, brewed a pot of coffee, and settled at the kitchen table to focus on work. I ploughed through my emails with ruthless efficiency. Cal had forwarded an email from Jamie saying that he wanted us to put Stonemore forward for a new rewilding award sponsored by a well-known conservation charity. If we were shortlisted it would bring attention to the estate and garner positive publicity, plus possible sponsors for our projects. By half ten I'd absorbed the details of the award and was already drafting our submission.

When my phone chimed, my heart jumped. My startle reflex was getting too much.

> ROSE *I'm going to an art exhibition preview. There will be champagne. Should I go for 50s vintage look or 80s power broker, shoulder pads, etc.*

I smiled and typed a response.

> ANNA *Def 50s. Dior New Look, etc.*

> ROSE *Consider it done.*

> ANNA *Send pics. Love you.*

> ROSE *Ofc. Love you.*

When I put the mobile down, I felt restlessness move over me like an itch. Weirdly, I still didn't want to eat. Instead I changed into leggings and a t-shirt, laced up my trainers and went out for a quick run to the end of the lane and back. It was agony. When I got back inside, I leaned on the kitchen counter to catch my breath. But the fresh air and birdsong had helped.

I looked at my phone. Three missed calls from a number I hadn't seen for a while.

Jamie.

I sat down at the kitchen table, staring at the phone. Ignoring him completely wasn't an option. He was my boss, after all.

> *Hi,* I typed into my phone, *sorry I missed your call. Is there something up at the estate?*

I sat looking at it for a good three minutes, but no response came.

This was a good thing, I thought to myself. One of my self-help books had made a big deal out of 'sitting with difficult feelings', rather than trying to suppress them or (as in my case) eat my way out of them. It was a skill I'd been planning to master and it looked like I was going to get some advanced training in it. So I left the phone next to me and concentrated on writing the award submission, pushing away the difficult thoughts that crowded my head, including the idea of Lucinda and Jamie in bed together.

Two hours later I'd finished the first draft, without a meltdown or a single piece of toast in sight.

My dinner was cooking and I was so absorbed in the book I was reading that when the landline rang next to me, I snatched it up without thinking.

'Hi Anna.'

I froze at the sound of Jamie's voice.

'Anna?'

I cleared my throat. 'Oh, hi! Hi, sorry, wasn't expecting it to be you.'

'Sorry to call out of working hours. I did try calling earlier.'

'I saw. I've been writing the prize submission. I'll have something for you to see in the next day or so. Can I help you with anything? Nothing's gone wrong on the estate, has it?' I had clicked into smooth efficiency and helpfulness.

'It's not about Stonemore.' His voice was crisp. On edge. 'Lucinda said she saw you this morning.'

I paused. 'Yes?'

'I'm sorry if she upset you.'

I felt my stomach take a dive. 'It's really no business of mine who you're sleeping with,' I blurted out. I had meant the words to sound cheery, but somehow they hadn't come out like that.

He sighed. 'I'm not sleeping with her. We've had two dates. And she has no responsibility for the running of the estate, or the rewilding project.'

I frowned, thinking of Lucinda: her tousled hair, the white shirt falling off one of her shoulders, the sense of ownership she'd conveyed. And the word *permanent* had definitely been used at some point. 'But she's living at Stonemore now, right? I'm sorry, I'm just confused.'

His voice tightened. 'No. She came over last night and her car broke down. I'd drunk half a bottle of wine so couldn't drive her, and she couldn't raise anyone at the cab company.'

Oh right, I thought. *If ever there was a pretend phone call, that was it.*

'Anna?'

I blinked. 'Sorry, I must have got the wrong impression.'

We sat there in silence. For some reason I didn't want to hang up, and it seemed he didn't either.

'I saw the flowers. Very nice.' His voice was quiet, even.

I studied the grain on the pine kitchen table. 'Not really. They're from my ex. Trying to make amends.'

'Has it worked?'

'Nope.'

'Right.' He sounded hesitant. 'So that means we get to keep you a little longer?'

I couldn't help myself. 'If you play your cards right.'

I heard him laugh quietly. 'What do we need to do?'

'Oh, you know, the usual stuff. Regular picnic hampers from Fortnum and Mason's. A year's supply of coffee. Maybe a small sports car at Christmas.'

'I can offer you beagle service at your desk and access to a pony at all times.'

I laughed. 'Not sure I'll ever be getting on a horse again.'

'Not even if I ride with you and protect you from hedgerows?'

'I doubt you could guarantee my protection,' I said archly.

'I'd try my best.'

My breath hitched.

'Are you still there?'

'Yes,' I said. 'Still here.'

'I guess I should thank you,' he said, the amusement fading from his voice. 'It was what you said about background being so important that made me . . . take another look at what might happen with Lucinda. Romance is a busted flush. Look at my parents.'

'And to think you teased me about my family's age-old saying,' I said, in as bright a tone as I could muster.

'Ah yes, what was that crappy saying again?'

'You can't put a hot pan on a cold stove.'

'That's it.' He paused. 'No, it still doesn't make any sense.'

I bit back a laugh. 'Of course it does. You've just said it yourself. Certain types of people fit together.' I put on my poshest voice. 'It's all about the breeding.'

I heard him sigh. 'You're so chippy.'

'I'm amazed you even know the word.'

'Perhaps I know more than you think.' The slight roughness in his voice silenced me again. 'Is there a chance, Anna, that you might ever think of me as an actual human being?'

I swallowed hard.

'Anna?'

'I'm thinking.'

I heard the sound of his outbreath; I hoped it was a laugh.

'I've thought. Maybe. One day. If you try very hard.' It was meant to be a joke, but it sounded wrong.

'And you think *I'm* difficult.'

'I never said that.'

'You didn't have to.' Suddenly, I couldn't read his tone. His voice was soft, but we were in dangerous territory. I had the urge to keep him talking, to battle out the differences between us. At the same time there was a dull ache of awareness that this conversation was a dead end. One, he was my boss. Two, he belonged to Lucinda now – whatever he said, that had been made patently clear to me.

'I won't keep you,' I said. I could feel myself closing up, reverting to professional politeness. My telephone voice. 'Thanks for calling. I'll get the award submission to you tomorrow.'

The silence went on a beat too long. 'Thanks. I'll funnel any comments back through Callum.' He put the phone down without another word.

CHAPTER 16

'I know it's impossible,' the conservator said, 'but the beagle urine seems to have actually *helped* the piece a bit. It should still be cleaned, but strangely it seems to have improved it.'

'Goodness,' I said.

Somehow, despite everything, Tally had finally managed to arrange for the conservator to come when she was 'at the optician'. I messaged her. *Apparently Hugo has magic wee and has improved the cabinet.* She read it immediately, but didn't reply.

A message popped up from Fi. *All good!*

Her twelve-week scan. I sent three party popper emojis, a thumbs-up and a love emoticon, then turned back.

'Sorry about that. How long do you think it might take to clean it?'

As he ummed and aahed his way through his calculations, I opened a new email on my phone from Emma, the archivist. She'd attached a scan of an old planting plan for

Belheddonbrae, dated to before Jamie was born. One glance showed me it had the kind of detail I was looking for. I felt a thrill at the idea of tweaking the plan so that it was more meaningful for him.

The conservator and I had negotiated his hours on site, and I was making him a cup of tea with three sugars, when Fi danced in through the door.

I left the kettle and hugged her, then added a mug to the conservator's to make her one of the herbal teas she was insisting on having in place of her usual strong coffees.

'Thanks love,' she said. 'Although frankly I could do with some caffeine. I guess I won't though.'

'Ah, the parental burden of sacrifice,' I said, and she kissed me on the cheek. She looked dazzling: her hair and skin were transformed, and she was lit up with a bright, happy energy. There was no hint of morning sickness or tiredness.

'I don't mean to complain,' I said, as I tipped sugar into the conservator's tea, 'but we do seem to be doing most of Tally's work between us these days. She seems completely obsessed with working on recaptioning all of the paintings.'

'Yes,' Fi said. 'I think Lucinda's been on her back to do new things. I had to do the insurance check this month and take over the redesign of the guidebook.' She saw my widened eyes. 'I know, I know. I even took work home last week.'

'And I've been supervising conservators all over the place and raising purchase orders,' I said. 'I need to get back out on the estate before I lose my mind at Tally.'

My phone vibrated. It was Callum. *Suggest you come up to Claybeck asap.*

I was much better at driving off-road now, but that didn't stop me from grinding the gears as I took off from the gravelled area near the kitchen garden. Mica gave me a doubtful wave as I passed, and I managed to smile and wave back.

I began to enjoy the solitude as Stonemore retreated, and the track wound its way through the estate, edged by deep, lush grasses and bracken, the hills both brooding and vast but also vivid with summer colours: yellow and purple along with dark, dense greens and browns. I drove past a small area that had been replanted, glancing at the baby trees (okay, saplings, but I liked calling them that in my head).

It wasn't long before I saw Callum's Land Rover, parked at a short distance from the river. He got out and waved.

'Is everything okay?' I said.

'Yes, don't worry – just follow me,' he said. We climbed a rocky stepped path, then made our way quietly through the copse that led to the riverbank. Then he stopped and pointed.

I'd seen some of the dams the beavers had been building, but this was different. Situated in the midst of water stilled by their dam-building, was a dense mass of tangled branches, vegetation and mud. A smooth mound of, well, *mess* to the untrained eye – silhouetted against the cool, dancing light on the water.

I clutched his arm.

It was more than a beaver lodge. It was a beaver *palace*.

'Think they've settled in?' he said softly, and his face broke into the biggest smile imaginable.

My own smile answered his. I was so happy in that moment – every worry evaporated, pushed out by the sheer gloriousness of it. It was spine-tingling, and it was the kind of moment when, if we were going to do it, we should have wanted to kiss each other. Instead we just looked at each other, our faces bright with happiness, and absolutely no chemistry at all sparkling between us. And there was something about the look we exchanged that noted all of that, and declared that it was no problem at all.

'This is a good day,' I whispered, and as he nodded, I took my phone out and quietly took a picture of the lodge.

'I bet we get kits next year,' he murmured to me, and tears of happiness pricked behind my eyelids.

We left the pond and went back to our vehicles. Leaning against the bonnet of his Land Rover, both exhilarated, we took in the view: the hills and fields rolling away from us, divided into irregular shapes by walls and hedgerows; the perfect line of cloud at the horizon, and the intense brilliant blue of the sky. He nudged me. 'Are things alright between us?' he said. He kept his eyes on the horizon.

'They are,' I said. 'They absolutely are.'

'That's good,' he said. 'Because I think you might turn out to be one of the best friends I've ever had.'

'Oh, stop it!' I said, and gave him a shove as he laughed.

'If I message you the picture,' I said, 'will you show Jamie? I know he'd want to see this.'

He took out his vape. 'You send it to him, Anna.'

'No, it's fine, he wants everything channelled through you.'

I glanced at his face, returned to its normal serenity.

'You did this,' he said, and inhaled. 'He should see it from you.'

I went back to the office carrying my phone as though it held the co-ordinates for a treasure chest, or that week's lottery numbers. I kept opening the album and staring at that tangle of wood. I didn't know how I was going to share it with Jamie. For now, it was my secret.

'Tally!' As I entered the office, Fi's voice pierced the quiet with unusual impatience. 'What are you *doing*?'

'Just printing a sample of the MacRae Ancient tartan,' Tally replied, a slight whine in her voice. 'I'm on a mission for Lucinda, okay?' There was a desperate look on her face.

'You're using all the ink up! You do know that ink costs more than gold and saffron combined?' Fi stamped over and stared as dense squares of red checked with blue and green slowly edged their way out of the printer. 'What is it for, anyway?'

As I turned my computer on, I glanced up and saw that Tally was biting her lip. 'It's a secret,' she said eventually, looking as though she might burst.

'In that case, you'd better tell me right now,' said Fi, in a tone that brooked no argument. 'And it had better not be anything to do with a bloody reindeer.'

'What?' Tally said. 'No! We're going to have a ball.' She sounded huffy. 'That's *all*. Keep it to yourselves. Lucinda will kill me if she finds out I've told anyone before she's persuaded Jamie.'

'A ball?' Fi sounded decidedly irritated, probably envisaging the amount of organising she'd have to do and remembering the huge black hole in the diary the fete had been. 'I hope this doesn't mean you'll be working as Lucinda's unofficial event planner, Tally. I don't want to have to do your job as well as mine for the next three months. I do have a baby to grow, you know.'

'I don't know how I managed to get tangled up in all of this,' Tally said, fanning herself with a piece of paper. She looked at her phone. 'Oh, hang on,' she prodded at the screen laboriously. 'Lucinda says we're good to go, it's going ahead. So it's fine that you know, I suppose.' She looked as though she might faint with the stress of it.

'It doesn't mean we have to do all of the work,' I said, trying to be reassuring.

Tally sucked the air over her teeth in her usual precursor to a lecture. 'Anna, you need to understand. Lucinda is most likely going to be our new countess. I think we all need to do our bit to make sure she feels positively towards us, as her staff.' She closed her lips in a hard little line to indicate this feeling was non-negotiable. It was enough to make me want to headbutt the desk.

Fi picked up her phone and dialled an internal extension number, stabbing out the four digits. 'Can I come and speak with you?' she barked. Jamie must have replied in the affirmative, because within a minute or two she was gone.

Tally began to hum as she continued work on her mood board. I downloaded the image of the beaver lodge and set it as my screensaver. Then I attached it to an email.

Hi Jamie,

Congratulations on your new residents.

Best, Anna.

CHAPTER 17

The fact that a ball was following so hard on the heels of a fete was deeply exciting to Stonemore village. Despite Tally's attempt at discretion, by the time Fi had stamped upstairs to speak to Jamie, half the house knew. At the same time, Fi broke news of her pregnancy to Jamie so he decided to hire some extra admin support to ensure she wasn't run off her feet.

Slightly mollified, Fi returned to her desk and I watched as she demolished a handful of ginger biscuits.

'Honestly, she's a menace,' she said, looking darkly at Tally's empty desk (she'd gone to the haberdashery to get some swatches for bunting). 'Jamie knows we're meant to be saving money, not spending it. We need to put money aside to see to the drains next year. Never mind the roof.'

When I'd first come to Stonemore, I hadn't realised that managing the house was such a struggle. Apart from Jamie's flat, the upper rooms were dust-sheeted, with their radiators set to frost setting. Most houses of Stonemore's size would have had a housekeeper and an army of paid staff; instead the small staff did as much as we could, aided by the volunteers, and a contracted group of cleaners came in before opening hours. It wasn't uncommon to see Fi or Keith running with a bucket for a new leak when it was raining, or to see Jamie carefully cleaning a picture frame with a watercolour paintbrush, or inspecting brickwork on a ladder so tall it made me dizzy just looking at it. There was something about the quiet, uncomplaining way in which he did such work that had made me start to understand his role was a job as well as a privilege. I hadn't made a joke about poshness since our phone conversation.

Tally professed herself surprised when Jamie announced that he would be charging for entrance to the ball. Staff and volunteers could attend *gratis*, but he slapped a healthy price on tickets for other attendees.

'And he wants a *cold* buffet,' she moaned.

'It'll be fine,' I said. By this time, Fi had taken to completely ignoring her when she kicked off, on the grounds that getting stressed wouldn't be good for the little bun she had in the oven. 'People want cold food when it's a dance.'

'They should have the *option* though,' she wailed. 'Lucinda and I are as one on this.'

'I say this with a lot of love, Tally, but please shut *up*,' murmured Fi.

Tobias arrived at Stonemore just in time to save everyone's sanity. Fi put in a call to a temping agency and he turned up the next day, dressed sharply but coolly in trainers, jeans and jacket, and with a bespoke leather satchel that cost more than my entire wardrobe put together. On arrival at the tiny desk we'd squeezed in next to mine, he offered me a rhubarb and custard sweet, and I was sold.

Tobias was a recent graduate in Drama and Politics ('a classic combo,' he told me as we sucked our sweets), but he had the mind of a natural organiser and was completely unfazed by Tally, absorbing her monologues with a blank expression before bursting into a bright smile, and starting to make lists. He made tea, grasped our systems at the speed of light, and built strong relationships with our suppliers in what seemed like milliseconds. When the temp agency called to check his progress at the end of the second week, Fi blurted out 'you can never take him from us' in a voice so piercing we thought it was a matter of life and death.

When I told Tobias I'd expected him to be more dramatic, he rolled his eyes at me and said he planned to be a film director eventually, in which case he'd have to *manage* dramatic people rather than *be* one of them. 'And she's perfect practice,' he said, tipping his head in the direction of Tally's desk, which was piled high with swatches and magazines.

'What are you wearing to the ball, by the way?' Tobias said to us.

'Something glittery to drape over this.' Fi patted her baby bump – she was already showing.

'Glitter, excellent!' cried Tobias.

'And you?' I said.

He bit his lip. 'I might just have a second-hand Tom Ford suit in my wardrobe.'

'Oh my lord,' I said. 'You'll look fantastic.'

He held up a reproving finger. 'I'll have to countrify it. Maybe I'll fashion myself a pheasant-feather brooch.'

'Or you could just allow Hugo to cover you with a fine layer of beagle hair,' I said. Hugo was snoring on my lap – Jamie had had to go out for the morning.

'I'll consider it,' said Tobias. 'What about you, Anna?'

I sighed. Conversations like this were not my forte. 'Maybe I won't go.'

'Shut *up*!'

'Okay, okay. I've got a black dress I bought for work do's just before I left London,' I said. 'No, honestly. It's appropriate. A cocktail dress.' I caught his narrow-eyed glance. 'I'll pair it with killer heels and vampy red lipstick.' I'd sent this description to Rose by text, and she'd approved it.

'Mmm.' Tobias was not convinced. 'I'll bring you a brooch from my collection.' He was an avid collector of brooches from charity shops and flea markets. 'I will bring a red glass piece to match your lipstick.'

'Very kind.' Hugo shifted on my lap and I stroked his soft head.

'You do know,' Tobias leaned forwards, confidentially, 'that Lucinda is planning to recreate a dress from one of the portraits in the house? She's having someone in the village sew it. Tartan. Looks a bit biscuit-tin-like to me.'

'Really?' I glanced at Fi, who was rubbing her baby bump and looking very entertained.

'I know,' Tobias nodded. 'A real-life restaging of *Rebecca*. Although I checked and Jamie doesn't have a dead wife. It's his grandmother's portrait she's recreating. Which is less . . .' he paused to consider the right word, '. . . sexy. I said to Curtis,' (Curtis was his housemate, with whom he was secretly, or not so secretly, in love), 'if you wanted to make someone propose, would you dress up as their grandmother?'

I started laughing and quickly became hysterical. Even when Tobias, laughing himself, said, 'Hon, catch your breath, it wasn't *that* funny,' on I went, until Hugo sat up, glared at me, jumped down and ambled off to Callum's office.

'Oh dear,' I said, wiping tears of laughter from my face. 'I think I might need a change of scene.' I checked my face in my phone and saw there were rivulets of mascara on my cheeks. As I wiped them off, I didn't dare imagine the looks Tobias and Fi were exchanging.

I was still actively suppressing my laughter as I strode off to check on the conservator who was working on the Boulle cabinet. The thing was, I seemed to have shifted from finding everything terrible and tear-inducing, to wanting to laugh at everything.

I texted Fi as I walked, trying to shelter my phone from the seemingly never-ending summer rain.

ANNA *I keep laughing all the time. Is there a word for this?*

FIONA *Hysteria? Are you okay?*

It wasn't unpleasant, I just felt as though I was in delayed shock or something. There was also something very strange happening: I was starting to think well of Jamie. Even to quite *like* Jamie. Clearly Lucinda's obsession with marrying him had somehow tinkered with a primitive part of my brain. Also, we hadn't been alone in a room together for ages, and it was clear we got on best when we didn't actually speak to each other.

But I kept thinking about him watching the GPS when I got lost in the snow. And knocking the Jenga over to try to save me from embarrassment when I confessed to my childlessness. Not to mention him galloping to my rescue on a horse.

No-no-no, Anna, I said to myself as I stomped across Stonemore, *this is no time to be fostering ambiguous feelings towards a man you categorically loathed until about five minutes ago. Just deal with your issues, woman, and download a dating app.*

But that hadn't stopped me from studying the planting plan our archivist had provided for me, and incorporating some new elements to Belheddonbrae. Elements that I hoped would please him, because somebody had to cheer the grumpy bugger up. Make him crack out that sunshine-from-clouds smile.

I was making too much of this. It was a good thing that I didn't dislike him so much. We could develop a positive, friendly working relationship. At a distance.

The room the conservator was working in was roped off from the public, so I had to thread my way past several curious tourists before stepping over the rope barrier and going over to him. Yet again, the joy of leaping the rope, and striding across the room with an air of authority. I really had to master this tendency towards twattery.

'Alright, Anna?' Reg the conservator raised his magnifying headpiece. 'Sadly you appear to have forgotten my cup of tea.'

'Oh no! Sorry.' I wanted to tell him I'd been too busy daydreaming, but thought I'd probably hit my weirdness quota for the day. 'I'll go and make you one.'

'No, don't worry, I'm about to stop for lunch anyway. I should be finished today.'

'Great.' I noticed him glance over my shoulder and turned to look.

Jamie. As though my jumbled feelings had summoned him out of thin air.

I don't know how long we looked at each other, but when Reg cleared his throat I realised it must have been more than a few seconds. I got a hit of Jamie's musky aftershave. Had he always smelt that good?

Luckily, whilst I tried to gather my scattered thoughts, Jamie was introducing himself to Reg and chatting about the cabinet.

'So it's probably best not to let your dog pee on it in future,' Reg was finishing up. 'Even though it had an, er, positive effect this time.'

I decided to slip away and leave them to it. 'See you later . . .'

'No.' Jamie shot a look at me. 'I need a quick word. If you have a minute.'

I gulped audibly and nodded. Reg frowned questioningly at me. 'Laters,' I said.

'Er, okay,' he said.

I followed Jamie to the far side of the room. We were in the red salon, a drawing room decorated with red silk wallpaper and deep patterned carpets. Luckily it was the size of a tennis court, so we found a place discreetly distant from Reg and the tourists. He glanced back at them, caught my eye, and smiled. But I caught the sadness in his face and my sympathy for him blindsided me as much as his smile normally did.

'I thought you were in Newcastle,' I said, watching him as he looked out at the deer park, the light bright on his face. He looked every inch the earl in that moment: straight-backed, the aquiline lines of his face and mouth reminding me of every portrait in the place.

'I *was* in Newcastle,' he said. 'I'm thinking of thinning the art collection.'

'Really?' I was shocked. 'Tally hasn't mentioned anything.'

'She doesn't know.' He glanced at me, then back at the distant tourists, and I saw the flicker of worry there.

'Sorry, I didn't mean to tell you – or anyone. It's the bloody roof again. There's some urgent maintenance that needs doing and we don't have the money.'

'I'm so sorry,' I said.

'This makes a change,' he said, his mouth twitching into a slight smile. 'I thought you might have a reprimand for me.'

'Nope,' I said. 'No reprimand.' The air seemed to crackle between us. 'I mean,' I scrabbled for the right words, thinking of all the 'yes' moments I'd answered with 'no'. 'I know I'm quite negative sometimes, but I don't mean to be unsupportive.'

He was frowning. 'Are you joking?'

I blinked at him.

'Anna? You're one of the most can-do people I know. You're always thinking of others, helping other people.'

I stared at him, not knowing what to say.

'I wasn't saying you were unsupportive. Just that you occasionally – put me in my place.' His mouth twitched again, with something that might have been amusement.

I felt obscurely relieved, seeing his expression. I'd begun my 'No' journey thinking I wouldn't care about other people's opinions anymore, but it turned out I still did, even after months of mantras. 'And you don't mind?'

'To tell you the truth, I rather like it,' he said.

It was very hard to breathe all of a sudden. 'I'm sorry about the roof, anyway,' I gabbled.

'Forget I said anything about it. I didn't mean to foist my problems on you,' he said. 'Talking of problems, did I see you with a scythe the other day?'

'Yes!' I said. 'I love cutting back with a scythe.'

He shuddered. 'Do we even have insurance for that?'

I smiled. 'It's all in the technique. Don't worry, I won't lose an arm or anything.'

'You'd better not.' He looked away and gave himself a little shake. Then he glanced back and did a double-take. 'Why are you laughing?'

Yep, there I was, laughing again. 'Sorry. You just slightly reminded me of Hugo. You know, when he shakes himself.' I shook my own head. 'You know, his floppy ears.' I did my best impression of a beagle.

He frowned, and then out of nowhere, he cracked up. And my hysteria seemed to be catching because our joint laughter escalated until a volunteer steward popped his head around the corner and gave us a look of consternation. I covered my face with my hands and tried to gain some composure.

'Thanks for that,' Jamie said eventually, catching his breath. 'What was I even going to say to you?'

I wiped tears of laughter from my face. 'No idea.'

He leaned his forehead against the window. 'Oh, I know. I wanted to congratulate you. On the environmental submission for the rewilding prize. It's fantastic, Anna. And the beavers. The bloody beavers! It's an absolute wonder. Do you know the charity that arranged it emailed me? They said that it only went so smoothly because of all the work you put in – I'll forward it to you.'

I smiled. 'No problem. For a minute I thought you were going to make me redundant. Money saving and all that.'

'What? No. *No*, Anna.' He looked at me intensely.

'Stonemore will only survive by looking to the future. Don't go anywhere. Please.'

What could I say with that intense gaze pinning me to the spot? 'I'm not planning on going anywhere,' I said.

'Lucinda hasn't been interfering? Because if she has . . .'

'She hasn't said a word to me,' I said. 'She's mainly working with Tally at the moment.'

He caught my gaze with his; his eyes were blazing. 'The estate needs you.'

I took a breath. 'No one is irreplaceable.'

'I disagree. I realise sometimes we're at odds with each other. But you're brilliant at your job. The relationships you've built – we have people queuing up to work with us on our projects. You're *needed* here.'

The air seemed to thicken. Standing there, facing him, I felt my body tighten with tension. This situation was getting to me in a way I couldn't fathom.

'I have to go,' I said. And without waiting for a response, I turned and walked away.

As I stepped over the rope, a tourist tapped me on the arm, a young woman with a phone out, craning her head to look beyond me. 'Is that the earl?' she said.

I smiled. 'Yes.'

'Is he single?' Her eyes were wide with interest.

'No,' I said, thinking of Lucinda, and how right she would look in a portrait hung on one of these red silk walls. They would be what my mum used to call a handsome couple. 'I'm afraid he's not.'

CHAPTER 18

The rain didn't stop. It continued through the long August day, then hammered down during the night. I put extra blankets on my bed that evening; it was as though autumn had come early, and there was a sharpness to the air. The next morning I waded to work in wellington boots, in a gap between showers, the trees waving along my little lane as the wind got up.

All morning, yellow weather warnings for storms and triangular flood warnings flashed onto my laptop screen. I did what I always did in London: turned them off. But at half past three Callum appeared at my desk, kitted out for wet weather and a kit bag slung over his shoulder. 'The Madocs have phoned in. They need some help moving their animals and I'm heading off now. I'll have a walkie talkie with me.'

As he spoke there was a flash of lightning and an instantaneous crash of thunder.

'Do you want me to come with you?' I said, thinking *please say no*.

He grinned. 'Nah, I'll be fine. Log on to GPS if I'm not back in oh, six hours.'

I carried on working and we all tutted at each other about English summers, but there was something unnerving about the intensity of the wind and rain. At half four, Tally took a call from another tenant who said there was flooding. 'They said one of the fences has washed away along with a bank at Elder Edge. The Stonemore ponies might get out,' she said, a distinct note of panic in her voice. 'You need to do something, Anna.'

I sat very still, trying not to panic. The Stonemore ponies had been introduced to an area of the estate before I arrived: four Exmoors, with the right to roam over a specified area. But if they got out, and panicked in the storm, God knows where they would end up.

'I'm sure it will be fine,' said Fi, but there was a look of worry on her face and she picked up the phone and dialled Jamie.

He was down in five minutes, in full storm gear. I felt a little jump of tension at the sight of him, but he didn't look at me. 'Walkie talkie?' he said to me expressionlessly and I fetched him another handset and a set of keys for one of the Land Rovers.

'Surely Anna can do this?' Tally squawked. 'I mean, it's her job really. And you're hardly expendable, my lord, unlike her.'

'Er, thanks, Tally.' I said. 'What are you going to do, Jamie?'

'I'll work it out when I get there,' he said.

I took a breath. Time to put my big-girl pants on. 'I'll come with you,' I said. 'You might need help.'

'It's fine.'

'Tally says it's my job, so just let me come with you,' I said. 'Fi, can you keep an eye on Callum on GPS?'

'Of course.'

Jamie hadn't looked at me in the eye once since he'd walked in. Now he shrugged, and was gone before I'd even got my waxed jacket over my shoulders. 'I take it that's a yes,' I said to Fi, who was looking after him with dismay. I put my hand on her shoulder as I passed. 'Don't worry,' I said. 'Have one of those scones I made. The baby needs the extra calories. We'll be back before you know it.'

She squeezed my hand, smiling, but the worry hadn't faded from her eyes.

Jamie drove in silence at a speed which I didn't think was advisable, especially when we hit a bump and my head hit the roof. It was still pouring and the sky was the colour of dishwater; as I stared at it, a vein of lightning flashed across it accompanied by a crack of thunder so loud that I had to try very hard not to squeal.

'This weather is unbelievable,' I said.

'Just a bit of precipitation,' he said, eyes fixed on the track ahead.

Thanks to some fancy off-road driving, we got to the ponies quicker than I thought possible. But the report that had come in was not correct. There were some trees down but the boundary was still secure, and the sensible Exmoor ponies were all gathered in their shelter, munching hay, so they'd clearly recently been tended to. It took us 45 minutes to check the boundaries and shamble back to our Land Rover. Our journey back started a lot slower: the rain was flying sideways, the wind was blowing in huge gusts, and the windscreen wipers could hardly deal with the intensity of the rain.

'Is it my imagination, or is it getting worse?' I said, watching Jamie as he hunched forwards, peering through the water-lashed windscreen.

'Tiny bit,' he said, under his breath.

We'd gone barely 200 metres when at a turn in the track, and to the accompaniment of a rumble of thunder, we found a huge tree down in front of us. There was another flash of lightning and an immense crack of thunder that felt as though it was reverberating through my body. I swore under my breath.

I was just regaining my composure when I noticed that Jamie was hurriedly putting the Land Rover in reverse. I looked out of the nearside window and could see nothing but rain and the lowering clouds.

'I know another way back,' he said. We were weaving down the hillside on narrow tracks when he braked hard and we skidded to a halt. 'What the hell . . .'

'What's wrong?'

Finally, he actually looked at me. 'It doesn't normally look like this. I think there's been,' he cleared his throat, 'a landslide. Just a small one, obviously, but the track is . . .'

'Gone,' I finished his sentence for him.

I did the thing I always do in grave situations. It's annoying, but I can't help it. I started laughing. Then there was a crash of thunder and I stopped laughing.

'Are you alright?' he said. 'Anna, I think we're going to have to get out and take shelter. I don't know another way. My normal response would be to stay in the car but this weather . . .'

'It's fine.' I didn't want him to complete the sentence. I had a vivid vision of the Land Rover being taken out by a tree or a landslide and rolling down the vast hillside into oblivion. 'Woah . . .' My voice wobbled. I had opened my door. Two foot away was a sheer drop. 'Shit shit shit.'

'It's alright.' I felt his hand on my wrist, holding it. 'Climb out this way, if you're uncomfortable.'

I decided to throw dignity to the wind and scrambled over the seats and gear stick. He stood waiting for me. As I stood, dithering about jumping out, he put his hands to my waist and lifted me down so quickly and easily I didn't have time to think about it, other than how absurdly comforted I felt by his closeness. 'Okay?' he said, as I stood staring at him in the howling wind and rain.

'Fine,' I managed.

'Don't worry. There's a bothy a little way from here.'

'A bothy?' I echoed him stupidly.

He was opening the back of the Land Rover and pulling out its emergency kit bag. 'Here, you can carry the axe.'

'That sentence has never been said to me in my life,' I said, but received it and followed as he strode into the woods.

The forest didn't seem a great place to be in the middle of a storm so I hurried to keep up with him. The rain dashed into my face and branches swung violently. Everything felt muffled, and the air smelt clear and pure, but electric. Jamie loped ahead with his bloody tallness and long legs. I concentrated on not tripping over. Being clumsy whilst carrying an axe wasn't a great idea.

We emerged from the strip of woodland and came to a small patch of land surrounded by grey stone walls on three sides. The bothy was built of stone, and had a corrugated iron roof. Its green front door shone out, calling us in from the storm.

'Drovers would have stopped here way back when,' called Jamie to me. I followed him through the unlocked green door.

Never have I been more glad to be inside. As soon as he shut the door, I felt relief burst over me, and a telltale throb of a headache. The rain drummed madly on the tin roof. Jamie tried the walkie talkie but it released nothing but a burst of static.

'I thought it was meant to be long range,' I said. He shrugged and shook his head.

It was just one room: bare stone walls, the woodburner in

the fireplace on one side, a small stack of wood on the other. He was already on his knees, unpacking the kit bag. 'Anyone who stops here has to restock the wood before leaving,' he explained. 'I'm going to build a fire. We need to dry off.'

'Is there anything I can do?' I said.

'Check the bars on your phone near the window,' he said, taking his phone out and looking at it. 'Mine hasn't got any reception.'

I checked mine too – nothing.

'I'll send a text. Then if I do get any reception, it'll go,' I said.

He nodded, removing some chipped logs from the small store near the far window. 'Yes please. Send it to Callum and to Fi, tell them we had an issue and that we're at the Dalawick bothy. If conditions improve and it's still daylight, we'll hike down.'

Hike? I thought but didn't say. 'And what if they don't?' I asked.

He paused in the midst of fire preparation. 'If they don't, we'll stay the night.' He looked at me. 'And if you could take the look of horror off your face, that would be helpful.'

I opened my mouth to say it wasn't quite horror that I was feeling, then closed it again. In fact, I was horrified, but only because the idea of spending the whole night with Jamie, on my own, had unlocked a cacophony of feelings in me which I didn't want to look at too closely.

Jamie continued his prep. 'There's no sign of it stopping out there,' he said. 'I don't want to put us at risk – or anyone else, trying to get us. We'll be fine. You might remember, every kit has chocolate,' he waved a family-sized bar at me, 'and . . .' He went over to the far corner and wobbled a section of floorboard with his foot, before lifting it with his hands. It was a big bottle – he cradled it tenderly. 'We have whisky. Single malt. The Macallan. Good stuff.' He gave me the slightest of smiles, almost as though he was smiling against his will. 'Truce, Anna?' he said. 'I'll try not to get on your nerves this evening.'

'You don't get on my nerves,' I said, in a hollow voice. But he did. I was swiftly coming to the realisation that he got on every nerve, but not in the way he thought.

He returned to the fire box, lit a bit of paper with a match from a box in his bag, and the fire gradually began to take. Then he took out a fluffy tartan blanket. 'Take your wet gear off,' he said, then at the look on my face, 'your *outer* clothes. I'm assuming your coat protected you from the worst. Wrap up in this, get near the fire. I'm going to get some water from the brook.'

I did as I was told. As I sat watching the flames, I hugged myself and tried to still the thoughts that were racing across my mind.

I do not want him, I told myself. *I do not want Jamie*. The storm had shaken me up and I'd temporarily taken leave of my senses, that was all.

He came back with a jerry can of water. 'My grandfather used to bring me up here,' he said, offering me water with a dash of the whisky and a few squares of chocolate. 'He's the one who started the tradition of leaving a good whisky here. You never know, you might enjoy this – it's just like camping.'

'Nooo.' I was sucking the chocolate as unobtrusively as I could. 'I hate camping.'

He laughed and I blinked at the unexpectedness richness of the sound. 'I forgot, you're a city girl. Warmer?'

I nodded. I wished Hugo was here – he would have given us something to focus on. After five minutes of sitting watching the flames, I couldn't ignore something. 'Jamie,' I said. 'Is there a loo?'

'There's a shovel by the back door,' he said, without missing a beat. 'Don't go too near the brook. And be as quick as you can. I don't want to have to come looking for you.'

'Great,' I said. 'Don't have all the whisky. I'll want some when I get back.'

CHAPTER 19

At 9pm, when the light was gone, I sent another message saying we would meet Callum at the Upper Reaches at nine the following morning. By 10pm, the wind and rain had started to ease. We sat, cross-legged, watching the fire together, talking about whatever random rubbish I could come up with as I tried to keep our conversation light and impersonal. Against my will, I kept wanting to move closer to him to such an extent that I felt it was taking superhuman effort to stay in my place.

You are an insane woman, I told myself.

'You've been working here for a while now,' he said, startling me out of that particular reverie. 'Is there anything you want to know about the place? Or do you feel as though you know Stonemore back to front already?'

I thought for a minute. 'I do have a question for you, as it happens,' I said. 'Why do you have a pack of hounds?'

The smile was replaced with a frown. 'I'm sorry?'

'I mean, it's just a bit strange. With your green credentials and conservation plans, and *Hugo*. Does an old-fashioned pack of hounds really fit in with that?'

He narrowed his eyes. 'Hunting is a vital part of the local economy.'

'Riiight.' I narrowed my eyes in return and tipped my head sideways.

'Plus, I don't have my own pack of hounds.'

Eh? My eyes snapped back to his face. 'Yes, you do. I've seen them.'

'I think I would know if I had my own pack of hounds.'

I explained the location as best I could, to his impassive face. The high brick walls, the gambolling beagles.

'Did they look like finely honed athletes to you?' he said.

'I have no idea.' I'd waved at the people looking after the dogs if I saw them, but I'd purposely kept my distance from it all because it had made me uncomfortable.

'They're rejects, Anna. I thought you knew. We run a small sanctuary for the local area. We send some to a national charity when we get too many. Some people shoot their hounds when they get older or are injured.'

I stared at him. 'You mean you save beagles?'

'Not exclusively beagles. We had a wolfhound recently. Dropped off at the gate in a crate.'

I was dumbfounded. And it was clear he was not pleased. 'Now I've got a question for you.'

'Fire away,' I said.

'What on earth made you think that I was the kind of person who would own my own pack of beagles?' There was something in his face I'd never seen before. Could it be he was a tiny bit sensitive? Had I found the chink in his armour? Of course, it would be about dogs.

'I guess it's just the kind of thing the landed gentry does.' *Posh boy*, my eyes added.

'I see.'

'Sorry if I hurt your feelings.'

He snorted. 'You didn't. It's impossible for *you* to hurt my feelings.'

'Of course,' I said sharply.

We sat there in silence for what was probably a minute, but felt like two hours. I heard a sound of rustling, and a soft crack. His hand appeared in front of me, holding a single square of chocolate. I took it and put it in my mouth.

'Sozzo, as Tally would say,' he said softly. Hadn't I said that to him? On the night of the team-building evening? His memory was scarily accurate.

I narrowed my eyes comically at him. 'Another one,' I said.

'No.'

'Pleeeeease.' I hazarded a look at his stern face.

'You'll need some in the morning,' he said. 'Haven't you heard of delayed gratification?' and there was a slight glitter in his eyes. Dear Lord, I was *blushing*. I looked away.

'Sorry,' he said abruptly. 'I shouldn't flirt when you're stuck here alone with me.'

'Were you flirting? I didn't notice.'

It was his turn to blush. 'Thanks.'

I smiled, and nudged him in what I hoped was a blokey way. 'Sorry. And thank you. You seem really comfortable here.'

He nodded. 'I am. Like I said, I used to come here with my grandfather. And with friends from school and uni. I've got out of the habit of it recently. And my friends are all in London, making their way in the world.'

'Bankers?' I said, without thinking.

He raised an eyebrow. 'Some of them work in finance, yes. I envy them sometimes. No responsibilities, making their own money.'

I snorted. Perhaps the whisky was taking effect. 'It's over-rated. I'm sure they wouldn't mind having a ruined castle and a lovely manor house.'

He looked as though he wanted to say something, but didn't. Instead he nursed his cup of whisky and water.

'I'm sure it's not easy, having all of this to take care of,' I said half-heartedly.

'I wouldn't dare complain,' he said, and I saw a touch of bitterness in the line of his mouth. 'I know what people think. A lord in his manor house. Rich. No cares in the world. It's not worth mentioning the leaky roof, the thousands we need to make every week just to keep the lights on.'

'But you love it, right?' I said. 'It must be a labour of love.'

He thought about it; the slight frown on his face made my heart ache unexpectedly. 'I suppose so,' he said. 'That is, I've been raised to love it. But I also try not to become obsessed with it. My grandfather was obsessed – so was my father. It came first, above everything and everyone. I don't want to be like that.' I sensed a deep darkness in those eyes, which he was keeping fixed on the fire.

'It must be good to have those friends you talked about,' I said. 'They must understand.'

'Yes. From my schooldays. An experience like that tends to bond you with some people and divide you permanently from others. Although I wonder sometimes ...' His voice trailed off.

'What?'

'I think boarding school does something to you. Takes some vital, feeling part of you. Replaces it with coldness. When you're there, vulnerability equals death.'

'Yeah, so this chat is taking a dark turn,' I said. 'And you made me carry an axe here, for God's sake. Don't give me cause to regret it.'

His smile was back. 'You've mastered your own demise. Don't worry. I've just had too much whisky.'

'Me too! Perhaps some more chocolate?'

'No way.'

'Tyrant.'

'That's me.'

'Anyhoo,' I said breezily. 'You're one of the most eligible bachelors in England, aren't you? That's got to cheer you up.'

He gave me a chilly blast from those blue eyes. 'It wasn't exactly number one on my list of ambitions.'

'Oh for goodness' sake,' I snipped. 'Give me the chocolate.'

Sulkily, he broke a couple of squares off and handed them to me.

I devoured them like a wolverine. 'I saw those women queuing up at the fete just to have a minute with you. I realise it must be difficult to be so *wanted* and *desired*. Honestly, shall I get you a tiny violin? Some of us don't have potential partners cantering on our heels. And, by the way, don't worry, you're in no danger from me.' This was a blatant lie, but I said it as much for myself as for him.

He looked slightly interested by that. He poured a small measure of whisky into my cup. I tapped his. 'You too. You're not getting me drunk on my own, matey.' Although I had a slight feeling I might be drunk already.

'Well, as long as I'm not in any *danger*,' he murmured, helping himself to some more.

'It's perfectly possible for you to marry for love, like your brother has,' I said confidently.

'Glad that's all sorted then,' he muttered.

'George is your only sibling, right?' I knew I was being nosy but I couldn't help myself.

He nodded. 'I'm the heir, he's the spare. Dad was obsessed with Stonemore, and George and I were just the mechanisms by which he could ensure it survived and was passed on. Mother kept his attention for a while but then she got bored of him, and of this place, and took off to travel the world. Then she died.'

'I'm so sorry.' I fought the urge to comfort him in some way. Even touching his hand seemed impossible.

239

'There's no need.' He brushed it off. 'Also, I realise, it's not exactly normal to talk about it in such a blasé way.' To me he looked far from blasé, but I didn't want to contradict him. 'But neither of them really gave a damn about me or George. I lost count of the times we weren't collected from boarding school in the holidays. All packed up, sitting in the front hall with our trunks, just waiting.'

'How awful,' I said.

He bit his lip. 'It sounds like I'm trying to get sympathy.' He got up, collected more wood from the corner store. 'I'm not.'

'I didn't think you were.' Outside the windows, it was fully night now.

He put the wood down by the fire and sat down opposite me. 'All I'm trying to say is, I had to work very hard to dis-engage my emotions. To try and cut them off. I learned as a child that they were unhelpful things to have. I remember, arriving at boarding school, after my parents left, saying to myself, again and again, "I don't care, I don't love them." I'm not sure that's a healthy mantra for a seven year old to have.'

'Seven?' He must have heard the catch in my voice, and looked at me warningly: *no sympathy*. 'That's harsh,' I said. 'Sorry, Jamie, it is. For your parents to do that.'

He shrugged. 'I've been an adult for a long time now. I should have sorted my head out. Do you know – I'm not sure I want to tell you this, given how fucked up it is – but I can't even remember the last time I told someone – anyone – that I love them.'

240

My breath caught. I saw the look on his face – hesitant, ashamed.

'Not even Hugo?' I said, and smiled at the laugh it drew from him.

'Especially not him,' he said. 'He'd only take advantage.'

'I mean, I agree.'

'Sorry.' He smiled ruefully, adding the logs to the fire. 'You're not my therapist. I should definitely get a therapist, right? I haven't talked to anyone like this in years – if ever, frankly.' He paused. 'And now I'm sick of the sound of my own voice. Tell me about you. And if there's nothing dark, just make something up to make me feel better.'

I laughed, and gave him the edited highlights: Dad's departure, Mum's struggle to put food on the table, her insistence that Rose and I concentrate on our educations. He listened carefully, asking questions here and there, drawing more out of me.

'I was never bullied, not really,' I said. 'But when I started to get good results at school, one or two of the kids said things. About my background. The fact I didn't have a dad. It was quite a theme. I've always felt I have to prove myself, to somehow be . . .' I gave a hollow laugh. 'Unassailable. Perfect. Everything to everyone.'

He nodded. 'I understand.'

'For the record, I do actually think of you as a human being,' I said. 'Even though you're, you know, a lord.'

He smiled. 'Hallelujah.'

I steered the conversation back to work.

Sophie Loxton

'And you've concentrated on your career?' He was pulling a sleeping bag out of his kit bag, not looking at me. 'Because of . . .'

'My infertility?' I said, and saw his swift glance. 'It's okay, I don't cry every time someone mentions it. No, my discovery of that is a fairly recent thing. The man behind the flowers? We were supposed to get married. It didn't work out.'

'I know the feeling of things not working out.' He looked me in the eyes; there was a slight shyness in his normally unflinching gaze. 'Here.' He swung the sleeping bag towards me. 'Climb into this. We can't keep the fire going all night. Are you tired? You can go to sleep whenever you like.'

'A bit.' I checked my phone, then started to manoeuvre myself into the bag. Fi had replied to my first message, but I wasn't sure the second one had got through. 'Don't you have a sleeping bag?'

He grinned sheepishly. 'No. The emergency kit is packed for one. It's fine – you have it.'

I paused, midway through zipping it up. 'That's not fine! Let me give it to you.' I began unzipping.

'No, Anna. I mean it.'

His voice was so firm, I stopped in my tracks. 'I daren't disobey your Hugo voice,' I said.

He laughed.

'Shouldn't we . . .' I took a breath. 'Share it? If you get pneumonia and die, I'll never find my way out of here.'

He paused in the firelight. He looked unbelievably

242

handsome. We'd both drunk whisky. And now I was offering him my bed – or the nearest equivalent.

In my mind: sirens, red flags, red traffic lights. All totally ignorable.

'Best not,' he said, after a gap that was too long to be disregarded. 'But we can sit close together for a while, if you like.'

Awkward. I shuffled my bum along until I was sitting against his left side. Nothing elegant about it, and I almost shoved him as I landed next to him, but he seemed to find it amusing. 'Did you know,' he said, 'beagles lean against each other to show friendliness. To show you're part of the pack.'

'Really?' I fought the urge to huddle against him. 'I suppose Lucinda wouldn't like it if I said I'd been cuddling up to her boyfriend.'

'I'm not her boyfriend.' He looked down at me in a way that was meant to be imperious but looked straightforwardly comical. 'We're just – spending time together. Nothing serious.'

'Uh huh,' I said.

'We're not sleeping together,' he insisted, so strongly that I patted him on the arm in a motherly way.

'None of my beeswax, anyway,' I said.

'That whisky's gone to your head,' he muttered.

'Aye aye, captain,' I said sleepily.

I was more tired than I thought. Before long my eyes were closing of their own accord and my head was nodding forwards. Then I woke, out of a mini-sleep. 'Was my head on your shoulder?' I said, jerking up. I felt his hand briefly touch my head.

'Easy there. Kind of.'

Just as long as I wasn't sniffing him. Because he did smell delicious.

'Mmm.' I opened my eyes properly, sat up. 'Not sure if this is going to work. I'll end up drooling on you or something.'

'You can do whatever you like,' he said, and something about the quality of his voice made me look up, and into his eyes.

This wasn't a normal look. This was the look that I had been hoping to keep at bay all evening. That buzzing electricity that had crackled between us. I told myself to look away, but I couldn't. About a dozen red flags waved giddily in my brain. And all of my No's, my hold-backs, my just-be-an-ice-queens were fading out to the sound of pieces falling into place and cogs clicking into gear.

I wanted to kiss this man. I wanted, very much, to do more than kiss this man.

'Just out of interest,' he said carefully, finally dragging his eyes from me and looking at the dwindling fire. 'Why am I in no danger from you?'

I tried to steady my breathing, but there was no disguising the blush that was seeping its way into my face.

'About a thousand different reasons,' I said.

'Name them,' he said, and his voice caught on the words in a way that made me close my eyes and send up a little prayer to the gods of chastity.

'It's just, if we got together,' I scrambled, 'which we're obviously not going to do, it would be fine for a month or two,
but then we'd start to get irritated with each other. You'd
get annoyed I don't know the rules to polo or lacrosse.' He
was shaking his head. 'Or I'd curtsey wrong at an event and
all your mates would laugh at me. I call them mates, you
would refer to them as friends. A thousand things like that.'

'Not curtsey properly?' He was echoing what I'd said with
complete incomprehension. 'What the hell are you even
talking about?' I opened my mouth to speak and he put out
a hand. 'And if you even try and tell me that weird thing
about pans and stoves again, I'm going lose it.'

'Lose it?' I snarked, forgetting my resolution not to argue
with him. 'I can't imagine that.'

'Imagine it,' he said, and in one seamless movement he
pulled me towards him and kissed me.

It felt so natural. It was as though I had given in to a mag-
netism that I had been resisting all along. As my lips parted
beneath his, my whole body thrilled with a sense of anticipation, and I put my hand to his chest and pressed my body
against his. You know how I thought I wasn't up for lust
anymore? How Callum had proved to me that I'd stowed
that part of myself away, perhaps forever? I discovered in that
moment that I was 100 per cent up for it. That I wanted to
drown in it. That I was kissing Jamie – my boss, the grump-
iest man in Northumberland – so hungrily you would have
thought he'd been served to me on a dessert trolley. And
he was kissing me back with a passion to match my own.

When we moved apart, his blue eyes looked so dark in the firelight and there was a look of such hunger on his face that my breath caught and I pulled him to me again, just to taste his lips again, just to prolong this moment.

When we moved apart, he buried his face in my neck. 'Anna,' he said. 'You make me lose my mind.'

I ran my hands through his hair and I didn't even need to think about it; it wasn't a decision, it was just happening because it was meant to happen. There was no room for worry in my mind, no room for anxious analysis, only the space for the sensations: for the touch of his hands on my waist as he gently pulled me to him; the feel of his muscular back as my hands slipped under his shirt; and the taste of his mouth as his lips met mine again and again.

The rain drummed on the roof. When he said, 'Tell me to stop if you want me to stop,' and unbuttoned the first button of my blouse. I said 'Don't stop,' and I said it again about ten or fifteen times but who the hell cared because I wasn't counting.

His hands were slow, deliberate; he asked with each move of them as he undid my jeans, his thumbs skimming my hips, so that I made a sound that was barely audible but seemed to drive him on. After what felt like hours of aching caresses, I peaked so hard that it was ridiculous, because it felt as though my body had melted into liquid and nothing else, I said his name and tried to touch him and he said, 'Let's wait until there's a bed, Anna. I think we need a bed.' But his voice broke on the words. All we had was the folded blankets on the bothy floor. 'I want it to be better than this,' he said. 'A four-poster bed, at least.' He smiled at me and it was as though my heart – which I'd honestly thought was numb, if not dead – broke open.

I needed to hide what I was feeling from him. I had to hide what had just hit me like an avalanche. Trembling, and so feverish that I felt I would never be cool again, I curled into his embrace and said, 'What just happened?' My arms tight around his torso, I breathed in the scent of him. I hadn't realised how much I had wanted to do that until this moment. I was holding on so tight to him, and I didn't want to let him go. He buried one hand in my hair and stroked the length of me with the other.

'I've wanted to do that for a very long time,' he said, into my hair.

'In which case, we don't need a bed,' I said, determined to give him what he had given me, my hand moving over his rumpled clothes, down further, exploring, until his hardness was in my hand.

'Are you saying that you want me too?' he said, his breath hitching. Although considering what I was doing with my hands, I didn't know how he could doubt it.

'Yes,' I said. 'I want you.'

As he tilted his hips, and allowed me to continue, I saw the look on his face: a half smile, half shaking of the head, as though he could hardly believe what was happening. I watched him be caught in the tide of passion as my hand moved, gently then firmly, watching every expression pass across his face, responding to him, until he let go in a way I could never have dreamed, my name on his lips.

I woke with the light from the uncovered windows, to find Jamie lighting the fire again. I was cold and stiff and felt about a hundred years old, although he must have felt worse, as I'd largely been sleeping *on* him. As the memory of what had happened flooded into my head, it felt like a fever dream. His face, when he turned to me, was different: there was a softness to his expression as he leaned over to me that made my heart falter in my chest.

'Come on, old soldier,' he said, hauling me to my feet with an outstretched hand. When I landed against him – theatrically, I have to say, I'm only human – he took my face in his hands and kissed me, and I literally moaned because he had no right to kiss so well for someone I was definitely not meant to be with.

I was already rationalising things. We'd had a drink, right? We'd just been fooling around, right? Because what on earth was I doing, apart from destroying my career prospects and side-tracking a peer of the realm whose only purpose in life was to produce an heir and a spare? Also, he'd declared he was pretty much unable to have a functioning romantic re-lationship, so we could just press 'reset'. Couldn't we?

'I don't like the look on your face,' he said, looking alarmed.

'I mean, it's just my face,' I said.

'And it's a beautiful face, but you look – upset.'

'Not upset,' I said. 'A bit blindsided, but – Jamie, that was amazing.' I didn't have the guts to tell him that Sean had never brought me near to that level of abandon, so easily and in a way that I had completely lost control. This was no quick grope under the influence. There had been an edge and I had gone over it. The intensity of the night before hadn't been okay, or nice, or good enough. It had been back-arching, screaming-level pleasure. Like dying and being reborn all in one. And now I couldn't even look him in the eye. A grown woman, blushing.

We went out together to gather water. It had stopped raining at last. I looked at Jamie and saw, like me, he was glorying in the fresh air, bright-eyed and smiling, even with that hint of sadness in his eyes, which I had noticed yesterday and now couldn't unsee.

When I waved my phone in the air, a text plinked into my inbox. Callum. I imagined an inkling of concern, good wishes, etc, so when I saw his message I snorted with laughter.

'What does it say?' said Jamie.

'It just says "Okay",' I said, and began laughing hysterically. 'I mean, we've been missing for the night and he just says okay?'

'Did you sleep with him?' he said, and looked down when I glared at him. 'Sorry, I don't want to sound like a psycho, it's just – okay, I sound like a psycho.'

'No, I didn't sleep with him,' I said, and he let out a sharp exhale. 'Are you sleeping with Lucinda?' I countered. 'You were making such a song and dance about not doing it, I assumed you had.'

'I'm not a liar,' he said, and gave me a playful nudge. 'We were in a relationship a while ago. But we haven't been together in that way for a long time, and certainly not since I met you.'

'Then why are you dating her?' I literally wanted to kick myself for asking.

'Because it seemed logical,' he said. 'Sensible. I wanted you, and it was clear that you didn't want me, and it was driving me round the bend, so—'

'So you wanted to make me jealous?'

'I didn't think it was possible to make you jealous,' he said. His eyes were fixed on the floor. 'Look, can we get back to Stonemore? Can we get to a bed, Anna?' He looked at me with such intensity that I felt my stomach flip with desire. 'Then take it from there?'

Even taking a breath in was painful. 'I don't think it's going to be as straightforward as that,' I said.

We hiked down the hillside. Jamie had descended into silence, occasionally holding a hand out to me, but his gentleness felt like a stab in my heart. When I'd tried to explain to him that we should forget about what had happened between us, I'd made such a mess of it that he'd asked me to stop. 'We can speak later,' was the last full sentence he'd said to me before we reached the Upper Reaches. Callum was exactly where we'd asked him to be, and gave each of

us a cheerful pat on the back. We climbed into his Land
Rover and carefully negotiated the route back to Stonemore
very, very slowly as they discussed repairs and clear-up. As
we descended, my phone started chiming with morning
messages – Fi, Rose, my mum. I sent brief, cheery replies.

'I took the wee boy Hugo home,' said Callum to Jamie.
'He was not impressed by your absence.'

'Did he try and sleep in your bed?' said Jamie, then we
glanced at each other and both blushed. It was strange how I
was thinking of us as a 'we', as though invisible threads had
been spun between us. I had the feeling they'd been there
for a while. It was just that I was only seeing them now.

'Yes,' said Callum. 'But I chucked him out. No place for
a dog.'

'Er, quite right,' said Jamie, and for a moment I was filled
with the desperate need to laugh.

'You look deranged,' said Tobias, when I walked into the
office. 'I mean, like you had no sleep at all.'

'You try sleeping on the floor of a bothy,' I said grumpily,
hoping that he didn't notice my face turning seven shades
of crimson.

'No thanks,' he said, stapling a sheet of paper.

'Grab your stuff,' said Callum, breezing by. 'I'll drop you
home.'

'I'll see you later, Anna.' Jamie was walking past me,
not even a glance, just as though I was a stranger. But as he
passed me, he brushed the back of my hand with his fingers.

It took everything I had in me not to follow him. In a daze, I gathered my stuff together. I knew I'd upset him by suggesting our night together might be just that. I'd got into the habit of pushing people away, both to protect them and myself. He could understand that, surely? But deep down, I knew I was kidding myself. As I walked past Tally's desk to get my bag, I glanced at a framed image on the wall. I'd walked past it a hundred times. The family tree of the Mullhollands, stretching back four centuries – one unbroken line to the present. Dependent on one thing: children.

Suddenly, I found I was blinking back tears.

'Anna?' Tally was standing there, holding a mug of tea. She put it down.

'I'm fine.' I tried to steel myself. I wasn't in the mindset to endure one of her lectures. But she didn't lecture me. Instead she came to me and put her hands on my shoulders, in a stiff, but undeniably affectionate gesture.

'I'm so glad you're back,' she said.

And when she put her arms around me and gave me a squeeze, I found I was properly crying.

CHAPTER 20

I didn't sleep well. I kept waking up, and when I did, the memory of Jamie's touch made me cover my face with my hands. I lay in my bed in the cottage, listening to the sound of the trees rustling and the birds singing. I had been so uninhibited with him, had lost myself so much, and now I was blanking him, ignoring the three texts he'd sent me since we'd parted. What kind of slapper, my mother would have said, does that?

When he messaged me again, I messaged back. *Please come. Even if it's just for one night.*

It was exactly 8pm when he pulled up in the car, parking beneath a knot of nearby trees (this I was grateful for – I didn't particularly want my neighbours across the field spotting his car).

When I opened the door he was standing at the end of the garden path, looking around. The ox-eye daisies were blooming, and in the twilight they seemed to glow, pale circles of light.

'I don't remember it being this beautiful,' he said.

'I *might* have scattered some seed here,' I said. 'I told you wildflowers were beautiful. Country people call them moon daisies, because they shine at night.' But he was already striding towards me.

I only just got him in the door and closed it before he took me in his arms and kissed me. No whisky, this time, but it was just as dizzying, my skin tingling and my body melting even though I was tired and restless and completely sure that we were not meant to be together. Apparently there were parts of my anatomy that hadn't got the memo.

When we broke apart, he took my face in his hands and gave me a questioning look with eyes so bright it hurt to look at them. 'I'm trained,' he said, 'not to need anyone, or anything. Just to survive, lone wolf, all that crap. I can't tell you how many people I've successfully kept at a distance. So why do I need you?'

I shook my head. 'You don't. This is just a temporary feeling.'

'Anna, it's not.'

And then we didn't say any more.

At first, we took things quickly. There, on the sofa, tugging at each other's clothes, stealing kisses roughly as though we were playing at things. It was only when he grappled a condom from his wallet that I took a breath. 'I didn't think they sold those at Stonemore General Stores,' I said, as casually as I could.

'Under the counter. You have to say a password,' he said. I started laughing and could only stop myself by gently biting his shoulder. Which worked, because at that moment his hands found a certain place as expertly as if he had a map of me. I was half losing myself in the physical rightness of it and half wondering at how natural it felt – the way we anticipated what the other wanted. When – at last – he was inside me, it was as though my body released all its tension and melted into pure sensation, sending me into a whirling vortex of pleasure so intense I wasn't sure I could take it without passing out. Instead I dug my fingers into his back and made a noise I barely recognised.

'And I was worrying about me losing control too quickly,' he murmured, but I heard the roughness in his voice. We moved together, our hands entwined, first slowly and tenderly, then urgently, deeply. At the peak I was shaking so much he nestled his face against mine, tenderly. 'Are you okay?' he whispered, his breath catching on the words.

'I am,' I gasped, 'very slightly better than okay,' and when I heard him laugh grittily, I lost myself entirely, again, and so did he.

It was only afterwards that he lifted me and carried me upstairs to the bedroom, his mouth against my neck, my heart somewhere on the ceiling.

I'd felt pleasure before, of course, but that night with Jamie was at a different level. It was an unlocking of something far deeper. Once we reached the bedroom, our caresses were slow, deliberate and so exquisite they left my skin singing. I could think about nothing but us, in that room. The exquisite building and release, the slow juggernaut of anticipation, which left me gasping in its wake. And to see him losing control made my bliss even more intense. There was only this, now, more, again. With him deep inside me, our gazes locked together, there was no room for past pain or uncertainty. I felt uninhibited, comfortable and utterly wanted, and I did everything I could to make him feel the same. I fell asleep in his arms, pressed against his chest. This was what a fling was all about, wasn't it? This sense of desire coupled with belonging?

Wasn't it?

When I woke at 5.30am, I couldn't admit the night was over. Half asleep, I pulled him to me, telling him what I needed him to do, my voice describing every sensation and saying his name as I tumbled over the edge and he did too.

I opened my eyes and when I looked at him, he was smiling. He stroked my hair.

'I'm not sure how to recover from this,' I said, with a hollow laugh.

'You don't need to recover from it,' he said. 'This can be every day – well, maybe not every day. We might need to rest sometimes.'

I traced the strong curve of his arm with my fingers. 'I see your family tree every day when I go into the office,' I said. 'You know I'm not the person you're looking for.'

He stopped stroking my hair. 'Don't do this.'

'One of us has to be sensible,' I said, hardly knowing how I managed to say the words. 'One night is fine. More? It's going to be a heap of trouble in the long run.'

He disentangled himself from me and sat up, on the edge of the bed, his back to me. I put my hand out; touched his smooth, muscular back that I'd been clinging to only moments before. But he jumped to his feet, grabbed his clothes, and left the room. I heard him running down the stairs.

I followed him slowly, faffing around with my dressing gown and the flip-flops that doubled as my slippers. Crikey, I was weak at the knees after the night we'd had.

He was sitting on the sofa, buttoning up his shirt, his face like thunder.

'Hey,' I flip-flopped over to him. 'Don't go like this. I'll make some coffee.'

'This is so messed up, Anna.' He pulled on his shoes and started tying the laces. Mechanically, I got the cafetiere out and started spooning coffee into it, then put the kettle on. I was scrabbling for words. This night had been supposed to sort things out, make things simple, reset things.

'Come on,' I said. I went to him, put my hands on his shoulders from behind. He tensed, then touched my right hand with his own. 'Good,' I said. 'Just have some coffee, okay? Don't rush out of here. I want things to be alright between us.'

But as I poured the water and made the coffee, the reality of what I'd done started to hit me. We could have written off the night in the bothy as a fever dream, a mistake made under the influence. But I'd gone and invited him, my boss, to my house for a one-night stand. Great move. Then gone through with it, in the most ecstatic, chandelier-swinging way, before rejecting him in the middle of it. Excellent, excellent, couldn't have planned it better if I'd written it into a five-year plan. I blinked, looked at the kitchen in the cold morning light. It was as if I'd been drunk and this was the hangover.

'Here.' I took our mugs of coffee over and sat down next to him. 'It's almost six o'clock. I'm barely conscious.'

'You seemed pretty conscious five minutes ago,' he said. He was leaning forwards, his hands clasped together. I rubbed his back.

'I'm not sick,' he said irritably. 'I don't need your pity.'

'It's not pity.' I took a swig of coffee. It was too hot and burned my mouth.

'Let me get this straight.' He turned and looked at me. 'You enjoyed last night, didn't you?'

My mouth dropped open. 'Of course!' *Best sex of my life by a country mile*, I wanted to say, but I had enough metropolitan defensiveness left not to give him too much of a compliment. 'It was wonderful.'

'Thank you,' he muttered. 'So I wasn't dreaming then? It's not as if we just did it once, Anna.'

'I think we were into double figures,' I said. I'd been hoping to forge every detail of it into my mind so I could recall this perfect one night of passion when I was old and decrepit but I'd lost my mind and stopped counting.

'So my question is, why wouldn't you want more of that?'

Now it was my turn to stare into the depths of my coffee. The question hollowed me out. How to explain to him that I knew what would happen? How the children issue would corrode us, as time passed? That it was better to have one perfect night and remember us as that, rather than losing all hope and joy as the bitterness slowly crept in, like ivy growing over an unkept garden, choking all life out of it?

'Is it what I told you?' he said. 'In the bothy? Do you think I'm too fucked up?'

'No!' I put my coffee down. 'Jamie, no. This is nothing to do with that. It's nothing to do with you. This is all on me.'

'Right,' he said tightly, as though he didn't believe me.

'You have to trust me when I say that my fertility issues would change things,' I said carefully. 'Maybe not now, or even in a year's time. But eventually it would. And then you'd be left with nothing – no child, no happy memories, and even less time to begin again with someone else.'

'I don't believe that,' he said. 'Couldn't we at least try?'

'Let me ask you something,' I said.

He nodded.

'Have you always thought you'd have children?'

He swallowed. 'Yes.'

'And have you always liked the idea of having children?'

'Yes.'

'Exactly. This isn't about whether to plant dahlias in the garden, or paint the bathroom blue. This is fundamental. If you stayed with me, I'd take something away from you. And if we embarked on a relationship, and then you decided it wasn't working, you'd take something away from me. I've been there, Jamie. I can't go through it again.'

He looked at me properly then, deep into my eyes. Took my hand. 'Anna . . .'

I shook my head, my eyes prickling with tears. 'It's a no, Jamie. For both our sakes. You'll thank me in ten years' time.'

'No, I won't.' He picked up the mug and sipped from it. 'Let's just give it a chance. We can go as slow as you want.'

'I'm not having this conversation,' I burbled on, trying to maintain a superficially bright tone. 'It seems to me you have your countess right there.' I thought of Lucinda. Thought of how many times I'd subconsciously compared myself to her – tall, lithe, blonde, never a hair out of place. Whilst I crashed through life with my hair like a bird's nest, barely knowing my left from my right.

And there was her voice, of course. That perfect, cut-glass voice. The signifier of a class I would never feel at home in.

'What are you talking about?' Jamie looked bewildered.

'Lucinda, of course,' I said. 'I think she's perfect for you.' And I marvelled how sensible and in control I sounded.

'Let me get this right.' Jamie had put his coffee down, and he was staring at me with a granite-hard gaze. 'Yesterday, I told you things about my life that I've never told anyone. I did the one thing everyone's always telling me to do: let go. Let someone in. So I did. In every single way possible. And now you're suggesting I marry someone else?'

I sat very still and looked into the middle distance. The space between us seemed to stretch into miles. I could have reached out and touched him at that moment, but something kept me frozen to the spot.

'For God's sake, Anna . . .' He put his hand on my knee. 'Will you at least look at me?'

I wouldn't look at him. Instead, I groped for words that would put an end to all of the difficult feelings. I remembered a distant conversation with Rose, three cocktails into a long evening, when we'd concluded that my life should be about fun, about flings. About moving on. *It's just sex, Anna,* I remember her saying. *You need to chill out about it.*

I had to lie to him. It was for the best. It would save both of us more pain.

'I thought it was just about sex,' I murmured. I didn't look at him. I couldn't let him see the terror I felt at the truth. This had been so much more than that. Every touch had told a different story.

I cleared my throat and hammered it home. 'As far as I was concerned, this was a one-night stand.' The silence that followed my words seemed to have its own quality. I felt as though I'd dropped a heavy stone into a deep lake.

'Fuck this.' He got up from the table. I wanted to stop him but I couldn't move. Instead I watched him put his coat on, search for his car keys. Finally he found them and turned back towards me. His face was pale, his eyes blank. I wanted so badly to go to him, to put my arms around him. Instead I stayed there, arms folded over my chest.

'What a dreadful, horrible mistake this has been,' he said, staring at me as though I was a stranger. 'Let's just forget it, shall we?' He laughed bitterly. 'Everything through Callum, as before, eh?'

'I guess,' I muttered.

'Great,' he snapped. 'See you around.' But he didn't go. He stared at the door, and he hung his head. For a moment I thought he was crying. I sat forwards, trying to urge myself to go to him. Then he turned.

'You should know,' he said, and his anger seemed to have drained completely away. 'This was never just about the sex, Anna. I wanted this. I wanted *you*.' He yanked open the door and walked out.

I couldn't have spoken if I tried. Frozen, I barely registered the sound of the front door slamming behind him. I was still sitting there when the Land Rover started up and he drove away.

CHAPTER 21

I sat in my empty cottage. I sat in a daze for an hour after Jamie left, trying not to think about the previous night in all its gorgeous pleasure, or the morning with its sadness. And of course, in spite of my trying, I thought of nothing else, so when I accidentally chipped my mug as I put it down on the counter, I started crying.

I thought my crying days were over.

I didn't want to journal. I didn't want to speak to Fi or Rose. I wanted Jamie.

I had a shower and dressed, but there was no way I could muster the energy to put make-up on. And when Gerald the mouse flitted past, I couldn't even be bothered to throw a shoe at him.

In the end, I crumpled to the floor, and sat there, my back against the sofa. Willing myself to be strong, willing myself not to cry. I dragged my phone from the coffee table and dialled a number.

'Sorry to bother you, Fi,' I said, when she answered. 'Is there any way you can come over? I really need a chat. I'm Snookered.'

Twenty minutes later, she was there, arms wide open, ready to listen.

'I did think there might be chemistry between you,' she said quietly, when I'd confided in her. 'Do you really think there's no chance of things working out?' She sat beside me on the sofa, mugs of tea cooling on the coffee table nearby.

I shook my head miserably. 'No chance at all.'

She took my hand and squeezed it, nodding gently in acceptance of what I'd said. We sat there, in the silence. No need to speak, no need for me to justify anything.

There are moments when only a best friend will do.

Three weeks passed, and somehow I managed to avoid seeing Jamie. September came with all of the heat that summer had denied us. The Stonemore Ball was preceded by dry, bright days – days so bright, and so dry, that it seemed a precursor of a long spell of autumnal drought. Climate change was never far from my mind and I felt a faint dread as the days passed, a worry that all the work we'd put into the estate so far might easily be eroded by Mother Nature.

As the ball date neared, Tally was messaged by Lucinda at all times of the day and night. At any suggestion that Lucinda might appear, I would race to another corner of Stonemore and once, memorably, even hid inside a cupboard. In the final week we all directed decorators and caterers, briefed musicians and prepared attendance lists. It was like the fete all over again.

On the day of the ball, after we'd completed our final preparations, I went back to my desk to watch Forestcam and promptly fell asleep in my chair. I was woken up by Tobias an hour later, already in his Tom Ford suit, perfectly coiffured and smelling delicious. I trudged home rather more slowly than I should have done, and considered staying there – but I had to do this. I booked a taxi, then unzipped a clothes holder and dragged out a black cocktail dress that I'd bought not long before leaving London. After months in jeans, I was pleasantly surprised at how chic it looked: with a high halter neck that exposed my shoulders (I offered a quick thank you to the heavens for the manual work I'd been doing), the black chiffon skimmed my figure, ending in a subtle ruffle at midi length. I put on a pair of emerald-green high heels, which felt slightly like being on stilts after walking around in trainers and boots for so long. Then I made my way gingerly out of the front door to the taxi.

As I stepped into the portico of Stonemore, I could hear the noise of gathered guests and glasses clinking as I murmured my name to the lone security guard on the door, ignoring the buzz of the fourth *where the hell are you* text from Fi. Hopping up and down on a single leg on the doormat, I took off one of my high heels and emptied out a small collection of gravel that had found its way in as I clattered across the drive.

In the next room, a harp began to play, zooming up

and down the scales. Its trilling brilliance reminded me of fairytales, glass slippers, romance. All the things I had to wean myself off.

'There you are!' Fi appeared, draped in blue glittery fabric. 'Come *on*!' She squeezed my shoulder. 'Lucinda's about to make her entrance. And you look gorgeous, by the way.'

'You're a very kind best friend,' I said. We traipsed into the hall, and I grabbed a glass of champagne from a tray proffered by a waiter, keeping my head down. It was always a magnificent room but tonight its scale felt even more extraordinary; the lightwell flooded the stone and marble interior with soft evening light, and the polished wooden side tables were set with huge, flamboyant flower displays in blue and white vases, filling the room with scent.

The harpists, *plural*, were for Lucinda; they'd been one of her 'non-negotiables'. They were flying through some kind of dramatic classical piece. Still, people carried on talking. Then I heard an enormous *gong* from the far corner.

'It's Tobias,' Fi said under her breath. 'She made him hit the dinner gong. I haven't heard that in years.'

It was enough to still the crowd for a couple of seconds. And in that moment Lucinda swept into view on the top landing, between a set of pillars. At the side, I glimpsed Tally, who was desperately fiddling with the long train of the dress before diving out of sight. The gong sounded again, gathering the attention of anyone who hadn't heard the first one. Then I saw an annoyed-looking Tobias winding his way through the guests, landing between me and

Fi. '*Embarrassing*,' he hissed to us. 'I'm asking for a bonus for doing that.'

'Consider it done,' murmured Fi, sipping her elderflower cordial.

'Babe,' Tobias nudged me and whispered. 'What's this?' He made a twinkling gesture with his hands in my direction. 'You look as hot *as*.'

I was spared from attempting to accept the compliment when Lucinda paused on the top stair and tipped up her chin. Everyone looked up at her.

Her dress revealed her creamy shoulders, then was tightly bodiced before it fell away in a dramatic sweep to the floor and beyond. Yes, she had a train. Behind her, on the landing, was the portrait she had taken the idea from: Lady Georgina, a member of the MacRae clan, who had married into the family. Only the ancestor wore a black dress with a tartan sash, whereas Lucinda's dress was entirely tartan.

'Shortbread,' breathed Tobias.

He was right. She looked like a biscuit tin. A dazzlingly beautiful biscuit tin. She looked prettier than I'd ever seen her: her hair in glossy, loose curls that bounced as she moved, her face subtly made up and slightly flushed.

'I swear to God she was in hair and make-up for three hours,' said Tobias.

'And it was worth it,' I said. He caught my eye and nodded.

Lucinda had paused halfway down. She straightened her gown, and took a deep breath.

'Good evening, everyone,' she said. 'Please allow me to welcome you to the Stonemore Ball.'

Reflexively, I looked down at my feet. This was all too much. 'The earl and I,' she continued, and I felt Tobias nudge me in the ribs, 'are delighted to see all of you. I now call upon the earl to raise the toast.'

I heard people shifting behind me, and felt Jamie pass me. I got a brief hit of his aftershave and fought the urge to flinch with the pain I felt. I was aware of him climbing the stairs and taking his place alongside Lucinda. I couldn't look.

'Good evening,' said Jamie. I thought I heard the note of tension in his voice, but when I looked up he was smiling. My stomach fell two storeys. God, he looked amazing: dressed in black tie, white shirt pristine, tie as neat as if he'd measured it, the whole thing perfectly fitted to show the broadness of his shoulders, and the athleticism of the body I now knew all too well. I was so used to seeing him in work gear; this was a whole new dimension that would definitely be haunting my dreams. I looked back down at my drink and fought the desire to down it in one.

'As Lucinda said, we are grateful for your presence here this evening.' I felt Fi's hand on my back, a slight, familiar touch of comfort. She knew I would be finding this difficult.

'We'd like to open the ball with a country dance.' I didn't look up; I couldn't bear to think of him exchanging glances with Lucinda. 'Please do join us, it's easy enough to follow.'

I lasted one minute at the edge of the room. Long enough to see Fi and Richard take their places, laughing; long enough to wave at Keith and Mica as they made their way to the centre of the room; long enough to see Lucinda loop her train over her arm and settle into Jamie's arms. They began to dance together, both of them smiling, each step seamless. Jamie looked like an entirely different person to the tortured man who had stood in my cottage. It appeared that they had perfect chemistry. And I had brought them together. Yay me.

I looked around the room, full of smiling people dancing, drinking and having conversations. It was perfectly easy to slip away.

Outside, it was a cool but still evening, the sky darkening to a deep sapphire blue. Lines of cars were parked neatly on the grass beyond the carriage drive. I took some deep breaths, and tried to ground myself. I was alone. And it was fine, totally fine. I had no obligations to anyone; I also couldn't hurt or disappoint them. This is what I told myself as I stood there, drawing in deep breath after deep breath.

I don't know how long I stood there, breathing in the cool evening air. But it was crunching on the gravel that alerted me. I turned to see Jamie, with Hugo on a lead.

'I thought you were dancing,' I said.

'I was, but then I went up to see him. He gets stressed on his own. Did I tell you Lucinda tried to put a bow tie on him?' Hugo studiously followed a scent trail on the gravel.

I shook my head, unable to find words for once.

'Don't you want to dance?' he said.

I shook my head again. 'Don't really want to be here at all, to be honest.'

'In that case, couldn't you have turned up in a sack or something, rather than looking so fucking amazing?'

My eyes locked onto his. There was a hardness to his gaze that in the past I would have seen as coldness. But now I knew. He was struggling to hold his emotions in.

'I could say the same to you.' My hands had turned to fists and were gripping my dress, so intensely was I trying not to reach out and touch him. When I caught sight of his own hands, doing the same, my gaze met his with a force that should have been too much for two people to bear.

He swore under his breath. 'I need to tell you something.' He came a step closer. 'But, Anna,' the way his voice caught on my name almost undid me, 'just say one word, and—'

'Jamie!'

We both looked back. It was Lucinda, holding up her tartan gown in handfuls as she negotiated the gravel. 'They're playing a waltz – the one we practised. Come *on*!' There was a definite edge to her voice.

I heard a small sigh escape him.

'You'd better go,' I said. 'Do you want me to take him?'

He handed me the lead. 'I'll be five minutes.'

While Jamie and Lucinda waltzed away inside, Hugo and I wandered around the carriage drive, the distant music drifting out to us. The little hound seemed happy, his nose glued to the ground, his tail swaying.

When I heard footsteps on the gravel I was expecting Jamie, but turned to see Fi, a wrap around her shoulders. She smiled at me but I could see hesitation on her face.

'It's like Piccadilly Circus around here,' I said.

She looked around the empty drive. 'Er, right. You really have forgotten what London is like.'

'I'm a fully converted countrywoman,' I said. 'What's up?'

She folded her arms. 'I need to tell you something.'

'Jamie just said the same thing.'

'I guess he would.' She glanced over her shoulder. 'Look, they're announcing their engagement tonight.'

NO. There was a rushing in my ears. I dropped Hugo's lead, then quickly stooped to pick it up again before he cannoned off. 'How do you know?'

'Lucinda told Tally, and Tally told Tobias. He was sworn to secrecy but he's just had his fourth glass of champagne and would probably tell me his pin number if I asked.'

'Jamie asked her?'

She looked doubtful. 'Not exactly. Apparently they had a discussion yesterday, and came to a mutual decision.'

'How romantic,' I said tightly. I was glad I hadn't eaten anything because I definitely felt sick. And hot, like I was coming down with something. 'I have to go,' I said. 'Tell Jamie I had to take a phone call or something.' I pressed Hugo's lead into her hands.

'Anna?' She put her hand on my arm. 'I know it's quick. And to be honest, I don't think Jamie's making the best decisions at the moment. But you wanted him to be free, didn't you?' She saw the look on my face, and put an arm around my shoulders. 'Oh love. It's okay.'

I shook my head. 'No, it's not. But it will be. I just need some space. I'll see you tomorrow.'

I strode off across the carriage drive, headed down the quiet drive through the deer park. Put one wobbly foot in front of the other, again and again. I needed movement; I needed to shake off this feeling. Once out of sight, I took my high heels off and started running.

By the time I got home, my lungs felt scoured, as though I'd reached parts of them I hadn't exercised in years, and my feet were sore from the uneven, gravelly ground of the lane. Two words had pounded around my head as I ran. *My fault*. I had no right to get upset. I'd told him to marry her.

But he looked so unhappy.

And I felt so unhappy. And he was mine. He was bloody mine.

Just say one word, he'd said. Was he asking me to stop him?

I changed into tracksuit bottoms and a jumper, wiping the mascara trails from my face and ignoring the hon, where's you? texts from Tobias, who had, he informed me, moved onto the punch. I climbed into bed and burrowed into my fluffy white duvet, a steaming mug of tea on the bedside table beside me.

I wasn't sure I could bear to be around Lucinda if she was planning her wedding to Jamie. Although, maybe she'd be busy brushing up on her honorifics. Practising her signature.

Commissioning a sculpture of herself. I tried to laugh, but couldn't.

My phone buzzed. From Fi. *Announcement made, toast drunk.*

I sent her a face-covered emoji and took a sip of tea, all the time choking back tears. It was very simple. I needed to leave Stonemore. Not immediately. I'd wait and see if we were shortlisted for the award. Document the rewilding plan fully, ready for the next manager.

I opened the calendar on my phone and created an entry on today's date: 'T-14'.

Fourteen days to resignation.

CHAPTER 22

I came into the office the next morning to find Tally sitting at her desk, strangely quiet. I'd imagined she'd be cock-a-hoop that the ball she'd played such a central part in arranging had resulted in a dynastically significant engagement. But instead of establishing a new mood board for the wedding, or ordering commemorative mugs with Lucinda and Jamie's faces on them, she was softly tapping away on her keyboard with a pensive look on her face, pale and dressed down in jeans and a navy sweatshirt.

'Tobias's flatmate just called, he's going to be late,' she said, when Fi and I came into the office, having met by accident on the drive.

'I bet he is,' said Fi, switching her computer on and plumping up her chair cushion. 'When I drove him home, he said he was so drunk he couldn't see. I guess I'm on my own with the email enquiries this morning.' Fi received a wide range of enquiries, from lost property to whether the estate could be used for filming. 'Oooh good, there's only forty-three new messages this morning.'

We smiled at each other, but Tally didn't look up. Her glum silence infused the air.

'Are you alright, Tal?' I said, as Fi started typing. 'Lucinda must be thrilled. I hope she thanked you for all your hard work.'

Tally looked into her tea mug. 'No, she didn't,' she said quietly. 'She actually told me she didn't like the ring. I know I'm responsible for the art collection, including the jewellery, but I can hardly be faulted for that. Jamie asked for that ring. It was his aunt's. A square emerald, perfectly pretty. He didn't want to use his mother's, even though I had it polished and repaired.'

In my peripheral vision I saw Fi look up sharply from her computer screen.

'I'd assumed I would be helping to arrange the wedding,' Tally said. 'But she said she wanted a professional to do it.'

'Maybe she was a bit overwhelmed,' I said soothingly. 'Would you like another cup of tea?'

'Yes please.' She pushed her mug towards me. As she refocused on her computer screen, a sad frown settled on her brow.

She was out of the room when Fi returned from her morning meeting with Jamie. 'Something weird is going on,' she said. 'He's being so low key about it all. He didn't even want me to put an announcement in *The Times*.'

I choked on my coffee. 'Is that what posh people do?'

'Mm.' She sat down at her desk, looking worried. 'And the ring. I remember Roshni saying about it, ages ago. Jamie's mother had a diamond ring that was definitely going to be the engagement ring for whoever he marries. He's deeply attached to it. Why would he change his mind?'

'Maybe it's just as Tally said,' I muttered, highlighting a heading on my document and clicking bold. 'Either way, it's none of my business.' I saw her watching me as I carried on working, but I didn't care. I'd spent a sleepless night thinking about it. Trying not to remember him touching me. Trying to imagine a world in which he belonged to someone else. My jealousy was so piercing it was as though someone had rammed a stiletto into my heart. It was time for me to grow up, and whatever happened next, it was nothing to do with me.

We didn't have to worry about Tally's weirdness for long, because that afternoon, normal service was resumed, and she drifted through the office with a clipboard and earnest expression, saying she was going to supervise the movement of a painting.

'Could she *wear* more perfume?' groaned Tobias as he came in and put his satchel on his desk, moving very carefully. 'It's like she's in the room. And I'm dead.'

'That's a long hangover,' I said. 'What did you drink?'

'Everything,' he said. 'Last thing was a whisky mac. I think it was my fifteenth grown-up drink of the night.'

'Ah, to be young,' said Fi.

'And how are you feeling?' I said to her. 'Did bubba mind going to the party?'

'Not at all,' she said, grinning. 'I've never felt better in my life. Whatever the baby is doing to my hormones, I hope it continues.' She was looking ridiculously bouncy.

'Tobias.' It was Lucinda, and she was sweeping in as though she was still wearing a ballgown. There were no jodhpurs in sight. She was wearing a knee-length cotton tea dress and had her hair in a chignon. She still looked stunning but the whole get-up added approximately ten years to her age, partly because she'd also lost the sunny smile that had previously been a permanent fixture. 'I've been speaking to my mother.'

'Oh, Clarissa?' said Tobias, doing a full turn on his desk chair. 'We chatted at the party. She was marvellous.'

'Yes, well,' said Lucinda, looking distinctly peeved, 'she said you weren't acting entirely appropriately, I'm sorry to say. Please remember, when you're in public you are essentially an ambassador for the Stonemore Estate.'

Tobias seemed incapacitated. He put a new chewing gum in his mouth.

'Lucinda,' said Fi gently. 'I line-manage Tobias. Please do leave this with me. There isn't any need for you to be concerned with staffing matters.'

'Fiona, I intend to be fully involved,' said Lucinda. 'And please *do* deal with this. There will be other events in future, and I don't want to have to speak to Jamie about this.'

I saw uncertainty cross Fi's face and it flipped a switch in me.

'I think you *should* speak to him, Lucinda,' I said.

Lucinda switched her gaze to me. 'I beg your pardon?' she said.

'I think you should speak to him. The truth is, none of us work for you. We work for the Earl of Roxdale. That's what it says on my employment contract, which means anything we do is precisely nothing to do with you.'

'Anna, it's okay,' I heard Fi murmur, but there was no stopping me now.

'I suggest you go to Jamie right now and tell him about this conversation. Run it up the flagpole. See what he says. I think it might be quite illuminating for him to know how you've been bossing his staff around. Tally hasn't stopped running after you for the last three months, not that you've even bothered to thank her. She's here to look after the art, not you.'

She looked unimpressed. 'I think you'll find Jamie wouldn't be worried by me taking an interest in the way things are run.'

'And I think *you'll* find no one here is going to be bullied by you. Not Tally, not Tobias, not Fiona, and not me.'

Lucinda held my gaze for approximately three seconds then flounced out.

'That might be the best thing I've ever seen,' said Tobias.

I sat down, feeling suddenly drained. 'Well, I wouldn't try to emulate it. It's not the smartest move.'

Fi crossed the office and gave me a hug. 'I think you were very brave.'

Tobias carefully removed a croissant the size of his head from his satchel and bit into it. 'When the temping agency rang me and told me about this gig, I thought it would be dull, but I love it.'

'No need to mention the temping agency. I told you, you're staying here forever,' said Fi, stapling a handout together. 'Once you've finished that croissant, you're coming with me to do a volunteer briefing.'

'Will Beryl be there?' said Tobias. 'I really like Beryl. We danced at the ball.'

'Beryl is the local MP's wife, Tobias,' said Fi gently. 'Not one of our volunteers. So she won't be there.'

'Moving in exalted circles already, T,' I said, smiling at him. 'You little social climber. Maybe you've learned more from Lucinda than you have from us.'

I left the room as Tobias threw a pack of Post-it notes at my head.

I wasn't over my conversation with Lucinda. As I went into the cold bathroom, I gripped the sink and looked at my white knuckles. The annoyance was coursing through me and it wasn't dying down: a heart-scouring amalgam of sadness, jealousy and anger. There would be more days like these, I knew.

I thought of what it had taken to get me here; the change I had wanted to make in my life. I thought of the view from my kitchen window: the mist lying low on the ground, the sun low and bright, lighting up the windows of the cottage, the pinkish orange light picking out every detail of every tree and plant. I had come to Stonemore to find that serenity, that calmness. I thought of the photograph of me and Fi, as teenagers. I'd printed a copy and kept it inside the cover of my journal. I thought of our shining faces; the hope in my eyes.

I didn't want this level of anger and frustration. I was free in life, and wasn't life a game? I didn't have to stick if I wanted to twist.

I looked at myself in the mirror and wiped a stray spot of mascara from below my eye, doubled up the soft woollen scarf around my neck, and met my own gaze, standing tall.

It was time to twist.

I thought about messaging, making an appointment, but my blood was up. So I marched the now-familiar route up to Jamie's flat. As I passed through the back corridors, my fingers trailing along the walls with their peeling green paint, I heard the distant sound of Fi's voice as she addressed the volunteers.

The moment I rapped sharply on the door, I heard Hugo's volley of barks and I smiled, it was so bittersweet. It was his 'big dog' bark, incorporating a slight growl, just in case there was someone scary at the door.

Luckily I'd managed to put the smile away by the time the door opened. I saw the look of surprise on Jamie's face, but it lasted milliseconds before he read the expression on my face and steeled himself. That was fine – I could be steely too. In fact, I felt like pure steel at that moment.

'Can I speak to you?' I said. 'It won't take long. It's about work.'

'I didn't doubt it,' he said flatly. His hand on Hugo's collar, he opened the door wide and let me past.

In the morning light, the flat looked more dishevelled than I remembered. There were piles of books and papers on the dining table, a couple of wine glasses left unwashed from the night before, and Hugo set about shaking a piece of newspaper in his jaws. 'He's been in the recycling,' said Jamie.

That wasn't quite like the Hugo I knew. The faint scent of Lucinda's perfume hung in the stuffy air. I found myself tipping my head to try and see into the kitchen.

'My intended has gone to visit her mother,' said Jamie, a shade of sarcasm in his voice.

He gestured towards the dining table but I shook my head. 'This won't take long.'

'Okay,' he said. He folded his arms, and glanced out of the window at the first tranche of arriving visitors.

'I'm leaving,' I said.

His gaze snapped back to me. 'I'm sorry?'

I shrugged; there really wasn't much more to say. 'I'm giving my notice. Today.'

His lips had parted in shock. I made a mental note not to look at his lips and fixed my gaze two inches above his head instead.

'Where's your resignation letter?' he said.

'Oh.' I looked around as though it might appear magically from somewhere. 'I'll get it to you today.'

'So you didn't plan this? It's spur of the moment?' he said.

I frowned in irritation. 'No.'

'You're one of the most organised people I know,' he said. 'If you were serious about this you wouldn't have come without a nice, neat letter, perfectly phrased, naming your date of departure.'

I didn't quite like the way he was saying this – the note of bitterness in his voice. I tried to breathe steadily and to ignore the pounding of my heart.

'I'm perfectly serious,' I said, only the slightest tremor in my voice.

He was shaking his head. 'Why?'

I blinked at him. 'I've established things here. Time for a new challenge.'

He practically growled. 'Absolute rubbish. You've written a plan. You've been here – what? – nine months? And now you're going to leave us in the lurch. This will set the project back years.'

I managed a shrill laugh. 'Wow – emotional blackmail, that's great. I really should have stuck with the corporate world.'

I saw the brief twist in his expression. I'd hurt him. It was only there for a second though – the steel was back in a moment. 'You really should,' he said.

Ouch.

'I'll have the letter with you by the end of the day,' I snapped.

As I turned, something made me stop. A brief, high-pitched whine. It came again. It was Hugo. He was on the floor, under the coffee table. I'd never heard him make that noise before.

'God.' Jamie had his hands on his head. 'He can't stand shouting – or when people get . . .' he swallowed, 'aggressive. I'm not sure what he went through before he came here.'

The beagle made the noise again, a whine, a *please-no*, in dog language. Beneath the table, he was trembling.

'Oh, sweetheart.' I was on my knees before I had time to think about it. I reached under the table to stroke the small, soft spot behind his right ear. He ducked his head away. I felt the air shift, and Jamie was next to me, saying Hugo's name.

Hugo didn't respond. Instead he placed his head on his paws and gazed up plaintively at us.

Jamie rocked back on his heels. Our faces were inches from each other.

'Didn't I do what you wanted, Anna?' he said quietly. 'Isn't that enough to keep you here?'

When I looked up at him, his eyes were dark with sadness. I couldn't move; I could hardly breathe.

'I would have done anything,' he said.

'Please,' I said. 'Don't.'

The phone rang.

He closed his eyes and stood up, his face hardening.

'That'll be Roshni,' he said. 'She and George are checking in on me constantly. I have no idea why.'

'I'll go.' I stood ungracefully but quickly, glancing back at Hugo, who still had his head on his paws. I tried to ignore Jamie as he answered the phone, but before I got to the door, he waved his hand in my eyeline. 'She wants your number,' he said. 'She says she has a gardening question.'

'Fine,' I said flatly, with a shrug. Only then did I finally manage to get out of the door.

Luckily, I wasn't required to banter much that day. Tobias had decided to begin writing his 'Fiona manual' for covering her maternity leave, so was carefully taking notes and eating toast furiously. I kept to myself, and swiftly drafted a resignation letter which I emailed to Jamie, copying Callum in. Callum was absent for the day so I knew he'd only see it tomorrow. And I'd tell the others then, too. I couldn't face it now. Plus, I had three long months to serve as my notice period. I could argue I needed less, but I'd never reneged on a contract in my life, and the thought of telling Jamie I wanted to break the contract made my heart falter in my chest.

'What's up?' Fi was smiling at me. 'You look very pensive.'

'Sorry. Nothing,' I said, then looked down to see an unknown number ringing my mobile. I answered. 'Hello?'

'Anna? It's Roshni.'

I almost swore again. 'Hi there. How are you?'

'Fine thanks. What do you think about Cosmos?'

'Cosmos?'

'The flowers? My gardener is recommending them for our garden in London. Hundreds of them. In a shade called,' she paused, 'cupcake? Which doesn't sound very me.'

'They're beautiful flowers. Very elegant . . .' I was struggling. 'Romantic . . .'

'Excellent, I'll go with them then. On another note, why are you letting Jamie marry that gold-digger?'

With a single involuntary movement, I swiped my empty coffee mug onto its side and it rolled off the desk. Fi hurried to pick it up whilst Tobias took out one of his ear buds and frowned at me.

'Bear with me, I should take this outside,' I said, mouthing 'sorry' at Fi and clumsily crashing out of the office onto the front drive.

'I'm here.' I took a breath of fresh air.

'Great. And I'm waiting for your answer.' I heard a faint tapping and imagined her in her glass office in a City skyscraper, tapping a pen on the table.

'It's nothing to do with me.'

'*Au contraire*. He was wild about you, Anna. *Is* wild about you.'

I put my hand to my chest.

'Then, just as things look as though they're starting to fall into place, you slam the brakes on and he rebounds into the arms of his ex. And, let me tell you, George and I were very glad that she was his ex and we were hoping she stayed that way. But apparently you thought differently.'

I cleared my throat. 'Yes, I pointed him in her direction. But all that happened was he discovered she was right for him.'

'Come on, Anna. It's clear she just wants the house and the title. In fact, it's worse. Her *mother* wants her to have the house and the title. Ambition by proxy.' I heard the tap-tap-tap of her pen on the desk. 'The most tragic kind.'

I had no answer for that. Other than I hoped it wasn't true. The way Lucinda had looked at Jamie – that was real, wasn't it?

'The way she looks at him—'

'The way she looks at him is the way a dog looks at a bone. She wants it, she'll consume it, then she'll be off having affairs and doing God knows what. Do I really have to tell you this? Have you heard her mention anything about *him*? About who he is? Does she know what his favourite colour is? His favourite food?'

'Yellow, and arancini balls with extra spicy sauce,' I blurted out.

I heard Roshni sigh. 'Great, so *you* know. But does she?'

'I don't know.'

'Ask her. Ask her anything about him.'

I was silent.

'Look, Anna, it's okay if you don't want to be with him.'

'It wasn't that.'

The faint tapping stopped.

'I did want him – to be with him.'

She was silent.

'I couldn't ruin his life.' I picked at a stray thread on my jumper.

The tapping resumed. 'The children. I suppose I get it. What I don't get is encouraging him to rebound with Lucinda.'

'I wanted to help,' I said lamely. 'He's a sensible man.'

'Not at the moment. I'm going to do my best to slow this engagement down.'

'It's really none of my business. I'm leaving, anyway.'

She sighed again. 'He just told me. Just ask Lucinda what he likes. I have to go. Bye.' A soft click indicated her departure.

I could hear the beagles hallooing in their paddock as I trailed back to the office. I closed my eyes against the emotions that were battering me.

'You look sad,' said Tobias, as I sat down at my desk. 'Hon?'

'I'm leaving,' I said. There was no point in waiting – it was best everyone knew, asap. 'I have to serve three months' notice, so not yet.'

I avoided Fi's gaze, and batted away their questions. I could practically *feel* them swapping worried glances so I took a quick look at Forestcam then started working with an intensely focused efficiency that they didn't dare to interrupt. I was in the middle of a phone conversation with Keith about placing an order of bare root wild pear trees when a flash of movement outside the window caught my eye: Lucinda, leading one of her horses across the drive.

I was out of my chair in a second, feeling the eyes of my colleagues on my back, hurtling through the office door.

'Lucinda,' I said.

She turned and frowned. When I'd first known her, she'd done nothing but smile, but it seemed as though she was out of supply now.

'What's Jamie's favourite food?'

She looked up sharply, her eyes wide. 'What?'

I repeated the question.

'Why do you ask?'

'We were just talking about family members and their food fads. I'm just taking a quick straw poll. It's an event I'm thinking of running in the kitchen garden.' Wow, my lying skills were ramping up.

I saw her struggle with uncertainty. Then she gave a little sigh. 'Steak frites,' she said.

'Right,' I said. 'Thanks.'

I walked away from her, and away from the house. I needed to be outside. As I walked, I tried to put Roshni's words to the back of my mind. Surely Lucinda loved Jamie? How could she not? When I got to the Mulholland Oak, an ancient tree at the heart of the estate, I sat down beneath its branches, and stared out at the landscape I'd learned to love. With absolutely no idea what to do.

CHAPTER 23

The next month passed slowly as autumn settled over Stonemore. I talked myself into thinking Lucinda and Jamie's marriage was a good thing, and that Roshni had been mistaken. Meanwhile, the office had a muted atmosphere. Callum never reproved me for resigning, but the air of sadness he wore when he greeted me was reproach enough. Fi understood my reasons for going, but still asked me 'Are you sure?' every couple of days. In the evenings, I often took refuge in her and Richard's kitchen, like a clingy house guest who refuses to leave. I wanted to spend as much time with them as possible before I went. They had turned their spare room into a nursery, and I sat with Fi, browsing online for cots and musical mobiles, promising I would make regular 'auntie visits' once the baby had arrived.

After a Zoom interview with a conservation charity based in London – this time everyone turned their camera on, unlike the Stonemore one – I was offered a job. Rose offered to put me up until I could get established again, and I booked a storage unit for my stuff.

But somehow it still felt unreal, as though I was planning someone else's departure, someone else's life. When I asked Fi whether Jamie had started recruiting for my role, she just shook her head.

One thing Jamie had done was refuse Lucinda's request to hire an event planner for the wedding. Tally had commenced mood-boarding and thinking about menu choices, but I could tell her heart wasn't in it. Lucinda was planning a Christmas-themed wedding, to take place on the last day of December. When Tally started having a meltdown about colour schemes, I went out into the fresh air and worked on the estate.

I also unblocked Sean, and messages from him began to trickle through, often on Sunday evenings, when he'd always tended to feel a bit melancholy. I kept my responses friendly but distant, an approach I found remarkably easy to cultivate.

And I completely stopped journalling. Because even when I picked up my pen, I found there was nothing to write. All I felt was that old, familiar numbness.

'Congratulations.'

I looked up as the cream-coloured envelope landed on my desk in front of me.

It was Jamie. He was dressed for the outdoors, in a

check cotton shirt and indigo jeans speckled with mud, his hair uncharacteristically ruffled. He'd been spending a lot of time outside, either in the beagle enclosure or at Belheddonbrae. I was forever seeing him at a distance striding around the grounds. Whenever I saw him I ran away, even if I was mid-task and it meant startling whoever I was working with.

I took my headphones off and looked past his left shoulder. 'What's this?'

'We're shortlisted for the Acorn Prize. The awards ceremony is in London in six weeks.'

His expression was unreadable – he looked neither happy nor sad, and his blue eyes were blank and cool. I felt a brief shimmer of gladness at our success, satisfaction at a job well done. But it was immediately cancelled out by a wave of sadness.

'That's brilliant,' I said. 'Congratulations to you and Callum.'

'It's down to you,' he said. 'And whether we win or not, this will put Stonemore on the map as an estate serious about conservation. There'll be profiles in the press, and a big networking event the day before the ceremony.'

'And you and Callum will be brilliant,' I said, with my best magnanimous smile.

'Callum will be staying here.'

'No!' I said. I heard movement behind me and Callum appeared, nodding and vaping furiously.

'Can't stand the big smoke, Anna.'

'And you'll be within your notice period and can come.' Jamie's face was expressionless.

'I'm quite sure you don't need me,' I said, starting to type again. Anything other than looking at him.

'It's non-negotiable. I'm going to line up private meetings with some funders looking at investing in our project. Quite apart from the press we'll be doing, and the networking event. We'll need a full team.'

'But not Callum?' I raised an eyebrow.

'I like to play to my staff's strengths,' he said crisply. 'So it will be you, me and either Fiona or Tobias.' He glanced at Fi. 'Whichever you prefer. Roshni is going to arrange for us to have one of her company's corporate apartments for a reduced fee.'

'I'm coming with you!' cried Fi. I looked doubtfully at her baby bump, but there wasn't a flicker of doubt on her face. 'I've seen those apartments – they're lush. It can be my last big fling in the city and I can stock up on tiny shampoos in the luxury bathroom.'

'With my blessing, babe,' said Tobias. 'I can go to London any time.'

'That's settled then.' Jamie turned such a look on me that I glared back and was satisfied to see his jaw flex.

'By the way,' he said. 'I've noticed there are some changes to the planting scheme for Belheddonbrae. I saw the new plan in the potting shed – Mica showed me. These haven't been cleared with me, have they?'

'No.' I kept my eyes focused on my keyboard. 'I went to the archive. There was an old planting plan. From 1985.'

I glanced up and saw the date reverberate in his eyes. The year his parents had married.

'I can send it to you. I believe,' I kept my eyes from his face, 'your mother wanted to incorporate some of the flowers from her wedding bouquet into the planting plan. As a kind of reference to the wedding. I thought you might appreciate some of those being included. I apologise – I should have cleared it with you.'

When I looked up at him, he was staring at me. There was something about the way he was holding himself, the still aspect of his face, that made me realise he was struggling to hold his emotions in. That he couldn't speak.

'J!' Lucinda bounced in and placed a kiss on his cheek. 'Here you are! I have things to discuss with you.' She twined her arms around his torso and I felt every muscle in my body tense.

He nodded silently and went with her, Hugo weaving around his feet worriedly.

And now I was going to be sharing an apartment with him. This notice period just got better and better.

That night I had a glass of wine after dinner, and before I knew it, I was packing; if randomly throwing possessions into cardboard boxes can be called packing. My phone chimed regularly with excited messages from Fi.

> *We can relive our dancing days in London. Or,*
> *you can dance and I can watch with my feet up.*
> *Or, we can go for a bottomless afternoon tea.*

My responses mainly consisted of smiling emojis for a reason. Emojis worked where my words didn't. I'd been doing pretty well in my opinion, but when Lucinda shrieked with delight at something Jamie had said and wrapped herself around him like a car around a lamppost, I felt a stab of sexual jealousy so piercing that it had taken my breath away.

Even now, I couldn't get it out of my mind. The memory of us, our bodies locked together, hands clasped above my head as we moved in our own rhythm ... Therefore, the open bottle of wine.

My phone chimed again and I picked it up to see what Fi's next stage of excitement looked like.

> JAMIE *I meant it when I said congratulations.*
> *We owe our success to you. And I'm grateful*
> *for your kindness about Belheddonbrae. It*
> *means a lot.*

I stared at the words on my phone screen until the blue light hurt my eyes. It was a nice message, a kind message. So why did it hurt so much?

In the precise moment I clicked the screen off, the light flashed again.

> JAMIE *We need you in London, Anna. I don't*
> *think you understand how important you are to*
> *this project.*

I chucked the phone onto the coffee table and poured another glass of wine. When the phone started ringing, I felt proper fury. What did he want from me? Blood?

I snatched the phone up. Withheld.

'What *is it*?' I said.

'Anna?' said a male voice that definitely didn't belong to Jamie. 'It's me.'

I'd always liked Sean's soft voice. It was one of the reasons I'd fancied him. But it crossed my mind that he sounded slightly lacklustre. My tastes had clearly changed.

'Er, hi,' I said.

'Hi you.' Silence.

'What is it you wanted?'

'Have you been drinking?'

'One glass.' I looked at my second glass, half drunk, and wondered why he was calling me on a Tuesday rather than a Sunday. 'To what do I owe the pleasure?'

'I've just got home after a terrible date.'

I rolled my eyes as he told me about it. The gist seemed to be that he'd been running through the stock of available women in London, but there was no one like me, and that this was a deeply romantic compliment. I carried on sipping my wine and stifled a yawn. Then, when he'd finished, I let the silence sit between us.

'Have you,' he said eventually, sounding coy, 'seen anyone? Dated anyone – since we split up?'

'Yep,' I said.

'Oh.' He sounded crestfallen.

'Goodnight, Sean,' I said, and hung up before he could say anything else.

There was no chance of getting out of the trip to London. So I didn't protest – other than privately and repeatedly, to Fi and Rose – and six weeks later I found myself hurtling through the London suburbs, being driven by Jamie. Fi sat up front with him; I sat behind. I had bolted for the back seat in an attempt to keep my distance. We were studiously polite to each other.

We would have the evening to rest, then a packed itinerary: two full days of networking and press events before the ceremony, then plans to visit a couple of other conservation projects on the outskirts of London. As we drove, Fi was typing furiously on her phone in response to further requests for meetings.

The corporate apartment Roshni had arranged for us was in a smart Art Deco block on the north bank of the Thames. Jamie had been allocated a reserved space in the underground car park and when we walked into the reception, we were greeted by a bright-eyed woman in uniform who was so immaculately turned out I found myself fiddling with my hair. Ah yes, I thought, *London*. We all seemed to be feeling a bit shell-shocked. Jamie had handled the London traffic with aplomb but we'd already earned a tut from a commuter when we'd emerged onto the pavement as a group.

'I forgot everyone walks so *fast*,' said Fi, popping her

phone in her pocket as we attempted to keep up with the uniformed lady.

The apartment was extraordinary. It took up a floor of the building, was all cream and white, smelt of high-class incense, and was pristine. Every bedroom had an en suite stocked with bathrobes, toiletries and the fluffiest white towels I'd ever seen. When I noticed my bed had a TV screen built into the foot of the bed and a complimentary hamper of sweet treats, I almost cackled with delight.

'Oh my goodness.' Fi collapsed onto the sofa as I put a mini pack of cookies on the table. 'This is amazing! Can you massage my feet, Anna?'

'I told you not to wear new shoes,' I said.

She was already taking them off as she checked her phone and cackled. 'Poor Tobias, left alone with the inbox. He's had five events enquiries today alone.' She looked around the room. 'Just look at this place!'

'Roshni's really outdone herself,' said Jamie, taking out his phone and pressing a number. 'I'll call and thank her.' He drifted away and I heard him say, 'Thanks, sis,' when she picked the phone up.

'I know it sounds mean,' said Fi, once he was gone, 'but I'm glad Lucinda isn't here. Tobias has already messaged me three times to say what a nightmare she's being.'

'Why didn't she come?' I turned my hand over and inspected my nails. It pained me to ask, but I couldn't help myself.

Fi shrugged. 'When Jamie made it clear it would be all

business, she wasn't interested.' I looked up. She was gazing at me steadily. 'He really needs a – what's the word? – help-mate. Partner in crime. Whatever.' She sighed. 'It's not good. I'm worried for him.'

'It's really none of our—' I stopped as Jamie walked in. '—business.'

'All okay?' Jamie looked between us. He seemed weary.

'Perfect,' said Fi. 'Can we order pizzas in tonight?' She looked as though she was opening her eyes extra wide to try to stay awake.

'Of course,' Jamie and I said, in unison. We looked at each other.

'We must stop doing that,' he said stiffly.

I nodded, going to sit alongside Fi. 'How are you doing?'

Fi tilted her head onto my shoulder. 'Bit tired.'

'I was worried this might be too much for you,' Jamie frowned. 'Shall I call Richard? We can get you home, if you need to go.'

'I'm fine, stop fussing.' Fi smiled, but I saw the strain in her face. 'All I'll be doing is sending emails and making phone calls. It's you two that have to do all the hard work.'

'I'm lucky I've got the best team,' said Jamie. 'I couldn't have done any of this without you – both.'

I felt a stab of sadness so intense I couldn't speak. What was wrong with me? I looked down and gave myself a little shake. 'Who wants a cookie?'

'It's yours,' said Jamie. Then his phone started ringing.

He walked away to take it but I could hear it was Lucinda;

her voice was like a burst of static, cutting through the serenity of the room.

'Sorry? They said what to you?' I could hear the stress in his voice.

'She should be kinder to him,' I said, in a low voice.

But Fi was only interested in one thing: the last cookie. 'Sorry love,' she said. 'Bubba wants this one.'

I nodded. 'Fair enough.'

I've always been a fan of eating pizza on the sofa, so the evening should have been perfect. But Fi seemed exhausted and Jamie was stressed after his conversation with Lucinda, so we all ate and went to our rooms with less jollity than when we'd arrived.

Alone in my room, I lay on the king-size bed, sinking into the Egyptian cotton sheets and watching the news on the TV. Despite the luxurious surroundings, I was feeling listless. It was just after ten when my phone vibrated.

SEAN *Arrived?*

ANNA *Yes*

SEAN *Free tomorrow evening? I really want to see you.*

I thought of Jamie's face when he picked up the phone to Lucinda. I picked up the phone and typed.

Yes. 6.30 at Chandos?

It was a coffee bar we used to visit. I didn't need alcohol in the mix.

Perfect. Xx

I lay there, watching the usual scenes of doom and destruction on the news, glancing back at Sean's message. There was a time when the thought of seeing him would have pushed out every other thought, every other hope and expectation. It seemed ridiculous, a little sad, to me now, how much emphasis I had placed on our relationship. It had been the foundation of all my hopes. I think he sensed that, too. Which is why, when the news came that we would never have our own children, it had all been too much for him to bear.

Perfect, his message said. I turned off the news and stared at the ceiling. But was it, though? Was it, really? I closed my eyes against the word that appeared in my head.

No.

CHAPTER 24

I was up early, but Jamie was even earlier. I found him making tea in the kitchen, dressed in black jeans and his copper-coloured sweater. He waved his phone at me and I caught a glimpse of a disconsolate Hugo staring out.

'He ate one of my hiking boots,' he said. 'Or a bit of it, at least. Callum is taking him to the vet.'

'Oh, poor Hugo,' I said, taking the phone and staring at the large-eyed, *I'm sorry* look that was emanating from the screen. 'I hope he's alright.'

'Apparently he's wagging his tail and barking for his breakfast,' said Jamie. 'I'm told this picture captures his entire millisecond of remorse.'

'Love it,' I said.

'Ready for our meetings?'

I poured milk into my coffee. 'Born ready.'

'Roshni says only city wankers say things like that.'

I snorted into my mug as I headed back to my room. 'And she's absolutely right.'

My corporate persona clicked back into place as easily as it had left me. I took extra time over my hair and make-up (war paint was important), re-ironed my navy peplum dress, and painted my nails a classic taupe that indicated I meant business. I saw Jamie take a breath when I emerged from my room. 'I feel underdressed,' he said, but the content of his look made excitement bubble in my chest.

'You're an earl,' I said. 'As a rule, you don't need to dress up.'

'So you've learned posh people's rules now, have you?' he said.

'If you can't beat 'em, join 'em,' I said.

We stared at each other for a dangerously long minute. I wanted to kiss him so much I could hardly breathe. Luckily, this was the moment that Fi crashed out of her bedroom door.

'Sorry I'm late,' she said brightly. 'I was just chatting to Richard. He said he might pop down this evening.'

'Pop down?' I said. 'It's a seven-hour drive.'

'Mm,' she said. 'Any coffee in that pot?'

'My friend Mike says beavers are destructive,' said the man who had looked me up and down when he walked into the room and was still periodically glancing in the direction of my breasts. 'What next, wolves? Lions?'

'I'd be on board with wolves,' I said, raising an eyebrow. 'But to address your first point – or should I say, *Mike's* point – beavers are a keystone species in our isles. They engineer their surroundings, certainly, but only in positive ways. Their dams increase wildlife diversity, improve the water, and act to prevent flooding.'

He curled his lip and folded his arms across his chest. I offered to show him the film of our beavers taken by the local wildlife trust, but he cut me off.

Jamie sat forward and fixed him with his coldest gaze. 'It's clear you're not listening to my colleague,' he said, in a rough voice. 'Perhaps you'd clear the slot for someone who's serious about conservation.'

The man scrambled to his feet and exited so quickly, I thought he was going to trip over his feet.

Meanwhile, I fought the urge to fan myself.

'Well, he was a waste of time,' said Jamie.

'We never had a chance,' I said. 'His board has told him to come and meet us because they're upping their green credentials, but he's a dinosaur. He'll just go back and say we're certified tree huggers, or something similar.'

Luckily, the next three meetings went well, and one possible sponsor lit up when Jamie incidentally mentioned the beagle sanctuary. 'My son loves Snoopy,' she said. 'He's into retro cartoons.'

'If he loves Snoopy, he'll really love Hugo,' said Jamie. 'I can offer a complimentary visit to the beagle sanctuary for sponsors who commit for eighteen months.'

'She actually wrote that down,' I said to him after she'd gone.

'You do beavers, I'll do beagles,' he said, and we grinned at each other.

'Am I imagining this,' he said, 'or are these meetings going really well?'

'They are,' I said. 'I certainly think we've got a chance to get some sponsorship for our pine marten project, or some of the smaller regeneration plans. In the end you can never tell until they sign on the dotted line, but it feels positive.'

He was nodding, his gaze catching mine.

'I like this,' he said quietly, then closed his eyes with a little shake of his head, which was the cue for me to stare at the table and slightly move my chair away.

'Who's next?' I said brightly.

He consulted the list. 'A seedbomb provider.'

I relaxed. 'Brilliant. At least they'll be on our side.'

'Am I doing enough?' he said.

'I'd be disappointed if you were chatty,' I said. 'There's nothing quite like a strong, silent earl glowering in the corner of the room to put pompous corporate guys off their stride. That "my friend Mike" guy would have mentioned wolves in the first sentence if you hadn't been here.'

I saw a glint in his eye but luckily, before he had the chance to reply, the door opened and admitted representatives of the biggest seedbomb company in the United Kingdom.

We arrived back at the apartment to the smell of burning toast. Richard was making Fi her favourite comfort food:

cindery toast with butter and jam. 'She's lying down,' he said. 'Don't worry, she's fine. I guess she wasn't prepared to feel rough two months out, after having such an easy ride for the last seven. I'll stay the night, if that's okay?'

'Of course,' said Jamie. 'And she's been a star. She hasn't stopped sending me emails all day.'

Richard grinned. 'I think she's most annoyed that she won't get to go dancing with Anna.' He disappeared off into Fi's room bearing his toasty treasure.

Jamie's phone chimed and he looked at it. 'Hugo's fine, it seems,' he said. 'Apparently his beagle digestion has coped with the boot. We could open the champagne?'

We stood and looked at each other. 'Although that's probably not a good idea,' he said. Neither of us looked away.

There was a knock at the door. Irritation flickered over Jamie's face, then he looked at his watch and swore under his breath. 'I forgot. Press.'

'Bloody hell.' I levered my feet back into my high heels as he went to the door.

The journalist was a petite, classically styled redhead with highly labelled jewellery, clothes and handbag that she wore with slightly dishevelled carelessness. She was authentically Sloaney and introduced herself perkily as 'Juliet, from *Country House* magazine.' She was accompanied by Jack, a faintly scruffy photographer who looked as though he'd rather be anywhere else than here. They seemed a tight enough pair though, with relaxed, sibling-like body language, and they brought a faint miasma of cigarette smoke with them.

'Anna,' I said, shaking their hands. 'I was just about to put the kettle on. What would you like?'

'Coffee please,' said Juliet. 'Mine's black. Jack likes milk and two sugars.'

The photographer grinned. 'Any posh biscuits?'

Juliet elbowed him in the ribs.

'We're all out, I'm afraid,' I said. It was true; Fi had been going through them like a forest fire through dry tinder. 'I'll be back with the drinks in a minute.'

Jamie gave me a grateful look as I passed him. As I put the kettle on, I could hear Juliet chatting to him. Jamie was bringing up the rewilding plan, talking about the beavers, the work we were doing to diversify the woodland, and the plans he had for young people from disadvantaged backgrounds to get work experience in land management. We had talked about this plan a lot in the last day; I heard the pride in his voice as he described it, without a hint of uncertainty or trademark grumpiness. He sounded . . . hopeful.

'Wonderful, wonderful,' Juliet was saying. 'But also, I wanted to do a kind of *personal* viewpoint, too. What does Stonemore *mean* to you – how do you *feel* about it?'

Silence fell. I left the kettle boiling and stepped into the living room. I could see Jamie's face. He was temporarily frozen, lost for words. His smile had faded to nothing. I remembered his words about boarding school: he'd been trained not to express his feelings, not to show them. *Vulnerability equalled death.*

'I think the rewilding is wonderful,' he said, catching on

the word she'd been using. 'I think it can only be a good thing.'

Juliet tilted her head and frowned. 'Um, well, yes ...' she said.

I couldn't bear the look on Jamie's face. Like a schoolboy called out by a teacher; as though he knew things were going wrong, but he didn't know how to fix it.

'The earl thinks of his ancestors every day,' I said, loudly enough to make everyone turn. Satisfied I'd got Juliet's attention, I continued. 'He knows he's the custodian of something far greater than him. Stonemore is a jewel in the crown of Northumberland. It's been a fortress, then a family home, for centuries. But now, Jamie's in a position to ensure it's much more than that. It can give back to the land and the people who have nourished it. What we're doing is new, but if the first earl woke up and walked out into Stonemore's acres, he would still recognise it. We're taking care of the present for the sake of the future, but also to honour the past.'

Juliet had directed her mobile's microphone towards me and was scribbling notes, smiling. After a minute we all looked at each other.

'Yeah, what she said,' said Jamie, and we all laughed.

'Teamwork,' said Juliet, making another note. 'And I understand congratulations are in order.' She looked up and smiled. 'When's the wedding?'

'Oh.' It was my turn to freeze; the shock of it gut-punched me. I looked at Jamie for help.

'This isn't . . .' He paused. 'This isn't my fiancée.'

Jack looked up from adjusting his camera, a slow smile dawning on his face as he looked at Juliet's stricken expression.

'Oh . . .' Juliet looked backwards and forwards between us. 'I'm *so* sorry. I just assumed—'

'My fault entirely,' said Jamie. 'I didn't introduce you properly. Anna is our rewilding manager at Stonemore.'

'Pleased to meet you again,' Juliet said with a smile. 'But – is your fiancée here at all, Lord Roxdale? We'd love to get a picture of the two of you. Our readers would love the romantic angle.'

'No, she's not,' said Jamie. And, as if to fill the resulting silence, 'She's not really a city person.'

'I'd best be getting ready for this evening,' I said, and left them to it.

As I freshened my make-up and got changed into jeans and a cotton Oxford shirt, I heard the soft click click of the camera and the perky voice of Juliet as she directed Jack. Then the door slammed as they left.

I sat on the edge of the bed. The day had taken it out of me. Being with Jamie all day had been harder than I'd imagined. Every so often, the atmosphere had crackled between us like the air before a storm, and my desire for him – a desire so strong it felt like a physical force – had come in waves. I'd had to *adult* very hard to resist doing something unwise; I knew the slightest thing might trip that hair trigger. I'd had the sense that even if I'd just brushed his hand with my own, it would have been game over for both of us. I sensed it in him too: a certain rigidity to the way he held himself, the way compliments had slipped from him as though he hardly intended to say them. The steely, just-breakable toughness of his blue eyes.

I closed my eyes against the thoughts in my head, stood up, and sprayed on some perfume.

I came out to find Jamie inspecting a slice of cold pizza he'd just extracted from the fridge. 'This looks less than appetising. Shall we go out for dinner?'

God, that sounded good. Dinner with Jamie as opposed to coffee with Sean. I realised I'd been dreading it. 'Sorry, I'm meeting someone.'

'Oh, right.' He put the pizza back and looked at his feet, seemingly to avoid my gaze. 'I forgot, London is your natural territory, isn't it?'

I shrugged. 'A bit. Have a good evening.'

'You too. Take care out there.'

I smiled. 'There aren't any wolves.'

'If you aren't back by midnight, I'll come looking for you.'

'Thanks, Dad.'

He smiled, but when I got to the door I turned and looked back at him. He was turned away from me, fists clenched, staring at the floor.

In the lift I checked my phone again.

TOBIAS *Lucinda is driving me mad. MAD!
She's in here every five minutes. She actually
made Tally cry.*

ANNA *What?!*

TOBIAS *Yep. Tally's gone home. I doubt she'll
be in tomorrow.*

ANNA *Cripes. Well done for hanging on in
there. You haven't used our code word so I
assume you're not at your limit.*

We'd decided on the codeword 'banana' to signal if things were getting out of hand and Fi or me had to get involved.

TOBIAS *Believe me, I'm almost there. BTW
that Darren bloke's been in to look at one of the
pictures. He tried to flirt with Tally and Lucinda
at the same time. He's unexpectedly creepy.*

I sent a nauseous emoji as the lift doors opened. He sent me a 100 per cent emoji.

Chandos was a coffee bar on a small street near Pimlico, halfway between Sean's workplace and where I used to work. As I neared it, the familiarity of the streets worked its way into me and I felt a veil of sadness-tinged nostalgia fall over everything. There was the tapas bar we'd gone to on our second date, and there was the near derelict house we used to wonder about – OMG, there was the tabby cat we nicknamed Arthur!

I stood to look at the cat. He was lying on the wall in a patch of fading sunlight. He looked at me with a distinct air of disdain.

'I see you've found Arthur.'

I turned. Sean. It was surreal to see him in real life, so close. Over the past few months he'd morphed into a voice on a phone, a series of text messages. In my mind he'd grown smaller, like a picture on a TV screen, thanks to all my meditation exercises. But now he was beside me, and the overwhelming feeling was one of familiarity. I knew that look on his face – that mixture of gladness and uncertainty. I knew the type of pomade on his hair. Why he'd chosen that tie to go with that suit.

'Hello, you,' he said.

We embraced lightly, like friends. There was the scent of him. The number of times in the days after our break-up when I'd pressed my face into a sweatshirt of his, to get a hint of that familiar smell. But now I felt – nothing. Was this shock? Was this the numbness of those terrible months after the break-up, reasserting itself, warning me to protect myself?

As we walked into the coffee bar, he was talking, talking. Somehow his voice kept fading out as I focused on putting one foot in front of the other. But it was fine, because he didn't seem to need my input.

' . . . so I said to Kelly, there's no way I'm working on that project . . .'

' . . . to that restaurant, but it was an awful evening, not like when we were there . . .'

Had he always been like this? I thought, sipping the strong black coffee I ordered. Had he always used me as a sounding board, not caring whether I replied or not?

'Anna?'

I focused on his face.

'It's so good to see you again. I've missed you so much.'

I smiled weakly. He waited, his eyes questioning.

'I've missed you too,' I said. It seemed simpler just to say it. And it was partly true. I'd missed him a lot – so much – at the beginning. I'd obsessively thought over our relationship, my brain bathed in a cocktail of sorrow and anger. But, gradually, that had lessened. With every plant I'd put in the ground, every joke of Tobias's I'd laughed at, every time I'd been booped by Hugo, that cocktail had lessened in strength. And there was Jamie.

Jamie had been something entirely new. Grumpy, maddening, hilarious, and so utterly gorgeous just the thought of him tumbled me into delirium. Yes, I'd rejected him – for his own sake. But in this moment, I was homesick for him.

I looked down to see Sean tracing the outline of my fingers on the table.

'How's things with you?' he said.

Finally, a question about me! I thought, and realised I would have said that out loud to Jamie with a fair dose of sarcasm. But not to Sean. I edited myself with Sean. I always had.

'Fine,' I said, and took another sip of my coffee.

He nodded, as though I'd said something profound. I could tell he was holding something back; he was excited about something. Weirdly, this made me even calmer.

'Hasn't changed much in here, has it?' I said, looking around at the retro banquettes, all red leather, chrome and Formica.

I needed a therapist. This man, this love of my life, was positively boring me, and was making me boring too. I was boring myself.

'Anna,' he said, in his gentlest voice. 'I'm ready.'

And with that, he took a small box from his jacket pocket and put it on the table.

I swallowed hard. 'What's that?' I said.

The thing is, I knew what it was. I knew it because I recognised the box: blue leather, gold tooling, and with a small chunk knocked out of the leather where I'd thrown it across the room.

The box contained my engagement ring. *Our* engagement ring.

He was smiling; I was sinking. Couldn't he see it on my face? How could he misread this situation so completely?

'I'm ready for us to move on,' he said, putting his hand over mine. 'Together.'

I cleared my throat. 'Can I have some water please?' I called to the nearby waiter. He nodded and went off to the kitchen.

I started coughing. It was as though my throat had closed up. Sean rubbed my back and I stifled the urge to elbow him in the face.

Why so angry, Anna?

This would need next-level journalling when I got home. It would need craft supplies: glitter, watercolours, possibly even papier mâché.

The water came, I drank and descended into silence.

'What d'you say?' he said, as though we were joking around. He opened the box, and at the sight of the familiar diamond cluster I felt sick to my stomach. I slammed the box shut.

'Hey . . .' He looked wounded.

'Explain,' I croaked, and had to take another sip of water. 'Explain what you mean by move on.'

'Oh.' He hadn't prepared for this. Lord, he really had me down as a pushover. But then he had known yes-girl-Anna, three-bags-full-Anna, embrace-the-power-of-yes-Anna.

'It's been difficult,' he said. 'For both of us. I know. Processing what happened. The fact is, I thought I could move on, but I can't. I'm in love with you, Anna. I'm ready to accept you – as you are. I can live without kids. As long as I've got you.'

I swallowed hard. 'So,' I said, 'let me get this right. You've road-tested a hundred other women but they're just not quite right. So you've decided to forgive me for something that was never my fault in the first place.'

I could see him processing the words, and it was taking

a long time. He was a smart guy, but something wasn't computing.

'I never said forgive,' he said. 'That's not what I meant. And I thought this was what you wanted? You wanted us to stay together.'

I realised I was tapping my foot. I was sitting on a bubbling cauldron of emotion that was threatening to erupt at any moment.

'It was,' I said. 'But I'm not so sure now. You're fine with it now, in this precise moment, but what about in five years? Ten? Every Christmas, when the TV is showing ads with little kids and perfect families? I reckon you'll milk it for everything it's worth.' I adopted a whiny, high-pitched voice that I didn't recognise. 'Ooh, Anna, I'm so sad about not having babies, you'd better buy me a Porsche to make me feel better!'

He flinched. 'Why are you being so horrible?'

'Maybe I *am* horrible, Sean. Or maybe honesty hurts sometimes. Anyway, this is me, the real Anna, nice to meet you. You were pretty horrible back in the day too. Turns out humans often are. You say you're ready to accept me, like some consolation prize. I tell you what, why don't you pop yourself back on Tinder and try out some more *laydeez*, give yourself a real run at finding happiness?'

'This isn't you. You're hurt, I get it. I've been hurting too. But we can get over this.'

'Okay.' I took a breath. 'You say you want me as I am. What is that, exactly?'

'What do you mean?'

'What do you love about me?'

'Um . . .' He sat and thought for so long I thought I was going to have to order another coffee.

'Your eyes,' he said. 'I love how they shine when you're happy.'

'And?'

'You're a great hostess. You have lovely skin. You like cooking. You're clever. You're kind.' There were actual tears in his eyes. 'You always pick me up when I fall.' He nodded. 'Metaphorically speaking.'

I nodded back. 'That's nice. It's not quite right, though. You missed a few key qualities out. I'm sarcastic, Sean, really sarcastic.'

He frowned. 'No, you're not.'

'Trust me, I am. I'm a narky cow. I don't like cooking nearly as much as you think I do. I don't naturally have clear skin, I just wear make-up. I swear a *lot* even if it's only in my head. Some days, I don't shower. I prefer dogs to people.' I looked at him, whirled my hand. 'The list goes on, and on. All the things you don't know about me. And that's not all your fault. It's partly mine. When we were together, I lost myself. No, I gave myself up – hands in the air.'

'I never—'

'I know you never asked me to. I just – did it. From day one. Saw what you wanted, and gave it to you. First date: Mexican food. I don't really like Mexican food, but I wanted to please you so much I convinced myself I liked it.' I handed him a napkin. His eyes were getting moist. He'd need to blow his nose in thirty seconds.

'You got one thing right though,' I said. 'I did pick you up when you fell. But what happened when I fell?'

He blew his nose.

'And it was my first fall, Sean. When we found out I couldn't have children. I'd worked so hard to keep things the way you liked them. Always to be strong, happy Anna – great at work, fun to be with, effortlessly efficient. Then I fell. It was a big fall, I get that. Huge. But you let go of me, the minute it happened.' I had to pause, take a breath. 'You let me fall into the gutter.'

'It was hard for me too,' he said.

That was the line I'd always played in my head – poor lad, imagine. But now something in me had hardened.

'Not as hard as it was for me,' I said, drinking the rest of my water. 'You had options. One hundred of them, as it turned out. I didn't.'

'So you're saying there's no way back for us?' His tears had dried. A tiny voice in the back of my brain noted how quickly his tears had dried. I could have wept for England when we split. I looked at him, taking in every detail of his face. He looked so – ordinary.

'That's the thing,' I said. 'I don't think there is a way back.'

'I see,' he said flatly.

I stood up as he put the ring box in his pocket. I kissed him on the forehead as though he was a child – our child.

Who would that child have been? I thought. Then I blinked away the tears that sprung into my eyes. And I left the Chandos coffee bar, and the life we had built together, him sitting there, looking at his empty cup. Until that moment, our life had still been waiting for us, an empty but furnished apartment, lights on, waiting for us to walk back in the door. But now, I turned the lights off, and the vans were coming, to empty it.

CHAPTER 25

As I walked into the tube station, I could feel my phone vibrating in my pocket, and I ignored it. I sat down in the hairdryer-like heat of the underground carriage and tried to calm myself. I was trembling. I'd been relatively calm when I was talking to Sean but now the numbness had worn off. I'd messaged Rose on the way to the tube and she'd insisted on meeting for an emergency debrief, but I didn't want to dissolve into a jelly the moment I saw her.

My phone had hooked onto the underground's wifi and I could feel it blowing up. What on earth? Sean wouldn't be this persistent. Were seedbomb manufacturers really sending me excited emails at half seven in the evening?

> TOBIAS *Fi's turned off her phone and I need to tell you guys something or I'm going to burst. It's not life-threatening but it's* 😬.

Anna hon pls call.

Anna please.

Banana.

BANANA BANANA BANANA

The moment I was outside of the underground station, I called Tobias. He answered in two rings. '*Thank you!* I was about to combust.'

'What's wrong? Has something happened?'

'*Er, yes.*' I heard the crunch of gravel; he must be outside Stonemore. He lowered his voice to a whisper. 'I'm working late,' he said. 'I wanted to get the rotas done for the next three months to surprise Fi.'

'You sound like a spy,' I said. 'Do you have to whisper?'

'Yes, I do!' he hissed. 'She could be anywhere!'

'Do you mean Lucinda?'

'Yes!'

He continued: he'd been working late, Tally had been absent most of the afternoon after her run-in with Lucinda, etc, 'that creep' Darren had been working on one of the minor paintings.

'They didn't know I was there,' he said. 'I went up to check that the gift shop was locked, and there they were, in the grand salon.'

'Who?'

'Lucinda and the creep. By the Caravaggio. Kissing.'

I almost dropped my phone. 'What the fuck?'

'You see,' said Tobias triumphantly. 'You're whispering now!'

I was walking down one side of a Georgian square. I spotted a bench on the other side of the railings and went to sit down, swearing under my breath.

'So what do we do?' said Tobias.

'I don't know,' I said.

'Ask Fi. She'll know.'

'No.' I instinctively wanted to protect Fi. 'It's too much. She's tired and stressed.'

'We have to tell someone, and whoever that someone is they have to tell Jamie.'

I looked at a pair of urban seagulls fighting over a half-eaten sandwich. London was so picturesque these days. 'Do we?' I said.

'Anna, *that woman* has just ordered an eight-foot wedding cake. What a bitch! Cheating on him and bankrupting Stonemore at the same time. Are we going to let her get away with that?'

'It's none of our business,' I said lamely.

'*Really?!*' Tobias was definitely not whispering now.

'Tobias,' I said. 'Go home, have some dinner, relax. You've told me. I'm going to think about what to do.'

'Hmm,' he said. 'It's true, I haven't eaten. I'm feeling extra hangry.'

'So trust me,' I said.

''kay.'

'Speak tomorrow. Night night.'

'Humph. Night.'

My mind was whirling as I put the phone away and headed for the pub I'd agreed to meet Rose at. I saw her from a distance, looking impossibly stylish, with her camel-coloured raincoat tied at the waist and the most glorious bag I'd ever seen tucked under her arm. My heart swelled at the sight of her; my sister was what I missed most about London. I crossed the road and trotted straight into her arms.

She squeezed me then searched my face with her eyes. 'How was it?' she said.

I gazed back at her and shook my head. 'I don't know where to start.'

I tried to come into the apartment as quietly as I could, but I had the feeling my entry was about as subtle as breaking a window. The Art Deco front door needed a full-strength shove to close it.

Seeing Rose had helped, but afterwards I hadn't felt ready to go back to the apartment. Instead I'd found a bench by the river for half an hour. Long enough to feel a bit weird and vulnerable, sitting alone in a city.

I wondered now if it would disturb everyone if I made a cup of tea. Sod it. I needed one.

'Hey Cinderella.' It was Jamie.

I swore and put my hand to my chest. 'Couldn't you have made a noise or something, rather than creeping up on me?'

'There are four of us staying here,' he said. 'It wasn't likely to be empty.'

I filled the kettle and turned it on. 'Sorry. I'm a bit jumpy.'

'Good evening?'

I looked at him. There was a half-smile on his face, but his eyes were blazing with a strange warmth. *Jealousy*. My mind told me it, even as I tried to logically deny it ('He's not jealous. Why would he be? Don't be ridiculous, Anna'). But he was. And there was a part of me that was thrilled about it. Ridiculously thrilled.

I looked into his eyes. I hadn't allowed myself a look like that for a while, but I drank him in with my eyes. Screw it, if Lucinda was going to cheat on him, I was allowed to look at him. As I looked, I remembered the way he had touched me; I remembered how lost we had been in each other, the way he had said my name in a voice rough with desire. He stared at me; I saw in that look exactly what he wanted to do. He took a step back and I saw him catch his breath.

'It wasn't a great night,' I said, thinking of Sean. 'But it was necessary. Some ends to tie up.'

He nodded, looking at the floor. 'I hope you're okay,' he said softly.

'I am. Tea?'

'Best not. Much as I'd like to sit up and chat.' He turned away.

'Jamie.'

He turned back. Tobias's words were echoing around my head. Why on earth would Lucinda cheat, when she had this man? But perhaps she didn't have him, not really. It would be so easy to tell him – just to say the words. But how much would I be telling him for my own sake? It would be easy to fall into his arms, into his bed, right now. But telling him would be like flicking a domino over in rows of dominoes, and send circumstances spiralling off in all directions. It wasn't the time or the place.

'What's wrong?' he said.

'Sorry,' I said. 'It's nothing that can't wait. Just a work thing.'

'Right.' His expression faded to blankness. 'Goodnight.'

I heard him go to his room, closing the door softly behind him. I checked the kitchen for comfort food, but it seemed it had all been hoovered up by Fi, Richard and Jamie. The only thing left was the bottle of champagne sitting forlornly in the fridge, waiting for something to celebrate.

CHAPTER 26

Richard left to return to Stonemore at 7am; the only sign of him going was the epic slam, which was obligatory when exiting the glam apartment's front door. 'He's got an important meeting tomorrow,' said Fi, foggy-eyed with sleep, as I made her a tea an hour later. 'And once we've got the prize ceremony out of the way, you've just got to visit that project, haven't you? I can stay in the car.'

This wasn't like Fi. Every time we asked her, she said she was fine, but all of her bounciness had departed. I thought about telling her what Tobias had said, but dismissed the thought in under a minute and gazed at my phone gloomily.

TOBIAS *Anna! Help me. What do I do? The creep is back.*

ANNA *Sit tight. I'll sort it.*

I thought it through. The ceremony was at lunchtime, thank goodness, and then we'd be on the road to visit the project outside London. Jamie suggested we drive through the night to get home, rather than staying another night in London as originally planned. 'I think Fi needs to get home,' he said, and I agreed.

'Got your outfit planned?' I said to her now.

She nodded and smiled. 'Might need ironing though.'

'I can do that.'

I watched her face brighten as Jamie entered with croissants.

We needed to get home. We could sort everything out once we got home.

Home. Stonemore. That's how I'd thought of it, automatically. I should have felt more at home here in London – galvanised by the city, alive to its excitement and opportunity. As I'd sat by the glittering river the night before, I'd just wanted to get back to Stonemore. I wanted, not the freedom of London, but to be hemmed in by the stone walls of my cottage. Wearing jeans and a jumper dusted with beagle hair rather than designer clothes and shoes that made me sashay as I walked. I wanted to breathe the clean air, check the meadow, complain about the weather.

TOBIAS *A nice lady called Roshni called.*

ANNA *You didn't tell her, did you?*

TOBIAS *Ofc not! What do you think I am?*

ANNA *We're coming back tonight. We can sort everything when we're back.*

We readied ourselves for the awards ceremony with trepidation. Fi decided against the glitter and went for a deep blue structured dress that looked high fashion rather than a tent, paired with flat shoes. I'd gone for a deep, rewilding appropriate green, fitted to the waist then flowing out in an A-line shape, with vertiginous heels. And Jamie was in a perfectly tailored blue suit, looking hotter than any man had the right to look. Shoes polished, crisp white shirt, and artfully stubbled. 'I don't want to look like a Hooray Henry,' he explained, when I teased him about the shadow on his face. Tactfully, I didn't tell him that my stomach had flipped with desire at the sight of him.

His phone had fallen silent. Apart from the obligatory morning photograph of Hugo, sent by Callum, there were no frenzied updates from Lucinda, no 100-decibel phone conversations where she complained about altercations with the florist. She was clearly occupied with Dirty Darren. Did the woman have no taste?

The ceremony was in an uber-trendy eco-hotel in Knightsbridge. Inside, everything was white, and there was a lot of smoked glass. It was also aggressively perfumed. Fi put her head on my shoulder as Jamie signed us in.

It began with an hour-long drinks reception. Fi did a

lot of smiling and nodding from a chair whilst Jamie and I progressed around the room, making small talk and handing out business cards. I'd always hated networking on my own account, but acting on behalf of Stonemore, I was as efficient as a military-trained operative. 'God, you're good at this,' Jamie murmured to me at one point.

'Don't praise me, I'm in so much pain from these shoes I might start crying,' I whispered.

He choked into his drink.

Luckily the hour sped past and we were shown into the ballroom where a three-course lunch was set. The room was decorated with wildflower arrangements and vast amounts of foliage. 'Is that an actual *tree*?' murmured Fi, clutching me on one side and Jamie on the other. 'How much money do these people have?'

'As long as they're on the side of the angels,' I said, and allowed a passing waiter to refill my glass. I was sticking to elderflower cordial, partly out of solidarity with Fi, partly because I was worried about getting tipsy and hurling myself at Jamie with warnings about Lucinda.

Lunch flew, and then the ceremony began properly. We watched carefully as a lifetime achievement award was given to a tree expert who had contributed to the understanding of root systems. Then we were on to the agricultural section.

'When are we up?' said Fi.

'It won't be for a few minutes,' I said. 'They've got the whole of agricultural, then it's heritage, which includes us.' She gave me a thumbs-up and nipped off to the loo.

The projects were truly inspiring – from the independent cheesemakers to an initiative that was recycling vegetable matter for fuel. It wasn't like a TV awards ceremony where people thanked everyone from their agent to the person who took them to school when they were five; here people were sometimes brusque to the point of incomprehension, but everyone looked really pleased. It was heartwarming to watch. One farmer couldn't speak, receiving his award whilst blinking back tears.

'Highly unusual,' I whispered to Jamie. 'I've learned that true country folk are usually as tough as winter ground.'

'What, like me?' he said, with a rueful grin that pierced my heart.

The agricultural section finished and they began to play a succession of snapshots of the heritage projects, including one featuring a drone shot of Stonemore executed by George.

'It looks fab,' I said to Jamie.

'Do not tell him that,' he whispered.

Fi arrived back at the table just as they were reading out the nominations for our award. 'Just in time,' I said to her, with a smile. She tried to smile back, but I could see immediately that something was wrong. Jamie had turned away, watching the stage.

'What's up?' I whispered.

She looked at me, her eyes shining with tears. 'I'm bleeding,' she whispered.

'And the winner is, the Stonemore Estate First Steps Rewilding Project!'

Applause rang in my ears. Jamie turned to look at me, smiling as he rose to his feet. Then he saw my face, and Fi's, and the smile faded to a frown.

'You go,' I mouthed to him. With a curt nod, he turned and weaved his way through the other tables to get the award. My neighbour nudged me and congratulated me. I stretched my mouth into a smile – somehow, without any thought, I found myself thanking him. On the other side, I clutched Fi's hand, clammy and trembling, in my own.

Jamie's speech may not have been the shortest on record, but it was a close thing. I didn't catch a single one of the handful of words he said. Then he bounded back down through the applauding guests.

'What's happening?' he said.

I explained as quickly as possible. 'We have to get her to hospital – now.'

I held Fi tight in the back seat as we sped through the London streets, Jamie driving with a set jaw. She wept against my shoulder and I couldn't bear to feel how much she trembled in my arms.

'It's going to be okay,' I said, again and again, absorbing her shivering as Jamie dialled Richard on the hands-free.

'Hi?' Richard's voice in the car, innocent and curious, sent Fi into a volley of sobs. 'Hush, hush, hush,' I said to her, as though she was a child.

'Richard, it's Jamie. You'd better get back here. I'm driving Fi to hospital. She's bleeding.' Jamie spoke crisply, definitely. When a cab pulled out in front of him, he put his hand on the horn.

'Oh my God. Can I speak to her?'

Fi opened her mouth to speak, but nothing coherent came out.

'Fi? *Fi?*' Richard's voice was frantic.

'Richard. Richard!' Jamie's voice: relentless, firm, calm. 'Just get in the car if you're not in it already, and drive back. Don't take any risks, eyes on the road. We're taking good care of her. Do you understand?'

I heard him swallow. 'Yes.'

'That's good. We'll see you soon.'

'I'm hours away.'

'We'll see you soon, Richard. Remember what I said.' He named the hospital and gave him the co-ordinates. 'Drive safe.'

'Okay.' Richard's shell-shocked voice brought fresh tears to my eyes.

Jamie raised hell at the hospital. I'd never seen people move so fast; they were out in a minute with a wheelchair. I ran alongside Fi down the white corridors, then stood at the edge of the room as the medics did their thing. Fi had stopped crying. Deadly calm, I could see hope and despair fighting in her eyes. When a doctor started to speak, in a slow, measured voice, I came forwards, seeking to understand him when she might not.

Baby is in distress.

Emergency caesarean.

Baby small, but viable.

Would she give consent?

'Her husband's hours away,' I said, my mouth dry.

'Just do it,' said Fi. 'Save him.'

Him. I choked back a sob. Her and Richard's secret: they were expecting a little boy.

'Can my friend come in with me?' said Fi. Her temporary calmness was dissolving; I could hear the tremor in her voice.

'Of course,' he glanced at me. 'You'll have to get gowned up.'

I stepped out of the room for a moment. The corridor was busy, the hospital full of the ceaseless activity of human life. When Jamie took me gently by the shoulders, I started and stared up at him.

I repeated what the doctor had said. 'The baby's small but viable.'

'Viable? Jesus Christ.' He let me go and turned away, then back. 'Are you alright?'

'Yes, I think so.'

He enfolded me in his arms. Just for a moment, I breathed in his warmth, the scent of him. It felt as though we were clinging to each other, holding onto each other's strength.

'Anna?' A nurse had appeared. 'Follow me to gown up.'

Jamie released me, and we stared at each other. We nodded at each other, then I went.

*

It was the longest minute in the world. It felt like the longest silence, even amidst the frantic activity of the medical staff. I leaned over Fi's head, stroking her hair, as her son was taken out of her and carried over to a trolley.

Waiting, waiting, holding my breath, Fi trembling. The silence, the terrible silence.

Then, a wail.

I heard Fi gasp, saw her frantic terror alchemise into joy.

'Show baby to Mum,' I heard someone say.

And there he was. Red-raw, enraged, bellowing into the air, and utterly perfect. Placed on Fi's chest for a moment, he quietened. I looked at his eyes, the bright blue of a summer sky, looking out at the world. Here he was. Life could begin again. But it would be utterly changed.

They rushed him away to an incubator.

'He just needs a little bit of oxygen,' said the doctor as they began to stitch up Fi. 'He's in good hands.'

I wanted to grab hold of him and say: *Promise me everything will be okay. Promise me.* Instead, I stroked Fi's hair as they sewed her up.

Outside the theatre, stripped of my gown, I sat down on a plastic orange chair. I was still wearing the clothes from the ceremony, and the high heels. It was as though I was suddenly conscious again, and back in my body. My feet were killing me and my shoulders were in knots. Jamie appeared, carrying a paper cup. 'They said you were out. Drink this. I asked for extra sugar.'

I took a sip. Hot chocolate. 'Thanks,' I said. 'Although obviously it's not a patch on Cal's.' The joke was a poor one, but he smiled weakly. 'He can make you a special one when we get home,' he said. 'How is everything? Fi?'

'She's fine,' I said. 'And he's fine.' I leaned against him. I didn't care about being subtle.

He nodded. 'I saw them bring him past. He was yelling pretty hard.' He put his arm around me.

'He'll see the saplings become adult trees,' I said. 'If he grows up at Stonemore.'

Jamie stroked my hair. 'And I bet he'll like the sunflowers.'

I laughed croakily. 'Sunflowers won't like the acidic soil at Stonemore, or our high winds,' I chided him. 'But there's going to be a whole field sown with meadow buttercups. I know you wanted a blaze of yellow.'

I saw his face twist with emotion. He held me tight to him. Then it was natural to drop a kiss on my head, my forehead, then my lips. And I kissed him back. It was the tenderest, sweetest kiss. After a moment we parted and I nestled into the crook of his neck, defenceless against the tide of emotion that was suddenly threatening to overwhelm me.

'I'm sorry,' he said. 'I shouldn't have kissed you.'

'Don't worry,' I said. 'What happens in maternity stays in maternity.'

By the time Richard arrived, Fi had slept for two hours and was so outwardly calm and happy she claimed to be 'embarrassed' she had been so stressed. The baby was to be called Ross, 'and I know he will be alright,' she said, almost defiantly. Richard was less certain; I could see the worry on his face, and as they took their place beside the incubator, I could see he was shaking.

The medics were cautious but said the signs were good. Weighing in at a mighty four and a half pounds, Ross was big for a preemie and all the signs were positive that his early entry into the world wouldn't affect his long-term health. They were just giving him a 'little bit of help'.

'It's strange,' I said, as Jamie drove me back to the apartment so we could pack up our things and get Fi's stuff. 'I just loved him – little Ross. The moment I saw him. Not like Fi and Richard do, of course. But the urge to protect him was so great.'

'Yes,' said Jamie quietly. 'I felt the same about my nephews.'

I watched his face as he drove. I could see he was carefully building up his defences again. Watching his quiet resolve as he navigated the London streets, I realised that I loved him. I loved this man. Posh boy. Beagle boy. Earl. Whatever. He was just Jamie to me, and I loved him so much I thought my heart might break again. When I started crying, unable to contain it anymore, he put one hand towards me and clasped mine for a moment. 'Ross and Fi will be okay,' he said. 'I know it.'

I nodded, tears streaming down my face. I wanted to tell him everything. How I'd shied away from being near babies. The baby showers I couldn't attend, or the ones I did, only to end up sitting numb on the tube home afterwards, winded by the pain. I wanted to tell him Stonemore had started to heal me. That I'd found new things to love. That a meadow full of wildflowers told me that my life wasn't worthless, and I wouldn't be traceless.

That seeing Ross born had made my heart swell so much it hurt, but that the pain was a kind of beautiful pain. A way in to being that baby's aunt, an elder of some kind.

I wanted to tell him that I loved him, just so he knew. That I wanted him in every single way it was possible to want a person. That the connection I'd felt with him hadn't gone away, as much as I'd tried to break the threads binding us. That I hadn't used him, shaken him off, moved on. What had happened between us would always be there, a tiny shard lodged in my heart. It hurt now, but one day, like the children I'd never had, that shard would shine as bright as a gemstone.

But telling him that would just be for my own sake, wouldn't it? It would be a selfish thing to do.

So instead, I blew my nose, wiped my eyes, and pulled out the glass vase Jamie had stowed in the glove box, etched with the prize name. 'Where will you put it?' I said.

'On one of the twenty-five mantelpieces at Stonemore,' he said.

'As long as I can dust it.'

'That's the thing though,' he said, indicating right and waiting for another car to pass. 'You won't be there, will you?'

*

It was an overnight drive back to Stonemore after we'd dropped Fi's stuff off at the hospital. Richard was being provided with a bed by a local charity who kept facilities for parents, and wouldn't accept Jamie's offer of extending the apartment booking. 'I'm closer to them here,' he said. I let myself have an hour with them, holding Fi's hand and cooing over Ross, but they needed time together as a family. I could always practise being 'weird obsessive auntie' once Ross was home. We left them with hugs, kisses and the contents of the hospital gift shop. This included an enormous teddy intended to stand guard over Ross's incubator, which had to be moved within five minutes due to health and safety concerns.

I convinced Jamie to alter his insurance so we could take it in turns to drive. 'If you do the whole thing, you'll end up falling asleep and we'll plough into the central reservation at 4am.'

'Thanks for your faith in me,' he said dryly.

'You're only human, I'm told,' I said.

So we drove and slept, drove and slept. After a few hours we agreed we needed to stretch our legs, so shared a sleepy coffee break in the neon bright café of a service station at midnight. We were quiet. Companionable, but quiet. I could sense the unsaid words building up between us. And there was a feeling growing in my chest. Heavy weather. An urgency.

Tobias's Lucinda complaints had stopped once I'd told him about Fi. I gave him regular updates about her condition, and received sober 'Thank you x' texts in response. I knew he didn't want to burden me but I also itched to ask what the situation was.

And I knew, at any moment, I could tell Jamie his fiancée had betrayed him.

'Is Lucinda expecting you?' I said, sipping from my paper cup of coffee, which was so weak it looked as though the water had just been shown the coffee granules before they'd mutually agreed to part.

He blinked, as though the question surprised him. 'I think so. I called and she wasn't there, so I left a message with Tally to tell her I'd be back and for her not to wait up but go home. I just want to get back and go to bed.'

I nodded. A cleaner pushed a mop around the beige tiled floor, bobbing his head to the music coming from his head-phones. I felt as though I would burst. This went beyond Lucinda; beyond Sean.

'I want to stay,' I blurted out. Jamie's eyes darted to my face, but in an instant he looked away again.

'You're just tired,' he said. 'It's been an emotional day.'

'Don't you want me to stay?'

His eyes kindled and fixed on my face. *There you are,* I thought.

'You know the answer to that question,' he said grittily.

'So why the reticence? Am I to understand you won't let me withdraw my resignation?' *God, I was being bold. Did this coffee have Cognac in it?*

'I don't know.' He put the lid back on his cup.

I drew in a juddering breath. Saw Stonemore being erased from my life. My raw, middle-of-the-night feelings threatened to tip me into another crying fit.

'Fair enough,' I said, looking down. 'I can still visit, I guess. Excuse me. I just need to pop to the loo.'

In the deserted bathroom I locked myself in a cubicle and allowed myself a brief sob. Crying at midnight in a service station loo. Wasn't there a country music song with that title?

I came out of the cubicle, ran cold water and washed away what was left of my make-up. The water made my eyes marginally less puffy. I put some lip balm on, sprayed some perfume from a tiny vial I found in my bag. Not bad. I mean, I looked as though I'd been on an all-night bender, but I was making an effort.

Jamie was waiting outside the toilets, sadly inspecting a coin-operated ride-on train for children as though he was considering having a go.

'I'm fine,' I said to him. 'Consider that conversation not had.'

He passed a hand over his eyes. 'There's a lot I could say,' he said. 'But it wouldn't be fair on anyone.'

I nodded, and waved my hand as though to indicate *blah blah blah*. 'Let's hit the road.'

CHAPTER 27

I knew I was home when I heard Jamie saying my name. I woke, bleary-eyed, in the back seat of the car, my neck cricked, my lap covered with a grey fleece blanket.

'I thought I was supposed to drive the home stretch,' I said, rubbing my eyes.

'You were fast asleep. I didn't want to wake you,' he said.

We were parked up outside my cottage. I opened the car door as Jamie got out and started unloading my case. The sky was a dense blue–black, the stars bright and clear. The trees were still and the Gothic details of the cottage were bathed in pale moonlight.

I landed on my feet with a squelch. *Still muddy, then.* I clomped up the pathway and unlocked the door, Jamie following quietly behind. He put my case down on the hearth carpet, looked around as I turned the lights on.

We stared at each other.

'Thanks,' I said. It felt like an ending. I wondered if we would ever be alone again. Here, like this. And there was only one thing I wanted to do. I walked quickly across the room, wrapped my arms around him, and buried my face in his chest. Just to feel him, just to smell him.

He froze for a minute, then his arms closed around me. I felt his breath in my hair.

'How long before you go?' he said, his voice rough.

'Ten days.' My voice was muffled against his shoulder.

'Anna.' His fingers were running through my hair. 'You've got no idea how much I want you to stay. How much I . . .' He buried his face in my hair and swore under his breath. 'This is wrong. I'm not being – honourable.'

The moment snapped. The atmosphere changed. We'd passed some kind of midnight – our carriage had turned into a pumpkin. We couldn't stand here for ever; and there were too many obstacles for us to go forwards.

'I have to go,' he said, gently disentangling himself from me.

'She doesn't love you,' I said. I was tired and sad and I couldn't hide it any more. But the words felt wrong as they left my mouth. It wasn't my place to tell him this.

His gaze had flicked back to my face. I suppose he saw the guilt there, the hesitation.

'She doesn't need to,' he said. 'Wasn't it you who said to me us aristocrats aren't like other people? And with my ice-cold heart, I'm lucky I've found someone to put up with me.'

My heart twisted. 'You deserve more than that,' I said, and caught the barely perceptible shake of his head.

'Goodnight, Anna,' he said.

Sleep should have been impossible, but I slept like the dead. When I woke up, the morning was in full swing and I realised I'd forgotten to set my alarm, reaching over and turning the clock towards me.

9.45.

I swore under my breath, swung out of bed and padded across the boards to find my phone. The room looked as though I'd got undressed whilst drunk – clothes everywhere and my phone on the dressing table, where I never normally left it.

Six missed calls from Tobias.

Three messages from Tobias.

> TOBIAS *Where are you? Major drama here:*
> *BANANA*
>
> *What point is there in having a code word if you*
> *don't reply?*

As I stared blankly at the screen, a new message popped up. It was from Roshni.

> ROSHNI *Did you know?*

I hit Tobias's number. He answered in three rings, his voice crackling as my wifi sluggishly connected us.

'Hi stranger,' I heard Tobias say breathlessly. 'You will not believe this.'

'Edited highlights please. I can get details later. Everyone's alive, aren't they?'

'Just about. But Lucinda's got *burned*.'

I sat down on the bed. 'What happened?'

'From what I can gather, when Jamie got back to the house last night, Lucinda was in the flat.'

I frowned. 'And?'

'And she wasn't alone.'

My sleepy mind ground its gears. I put my hand to my chest. 'Shit. Not?'

'Darren.'

I put my hand to my mouth. I wanted to weep at the sheer monumentality of it. Jamie, arriving home, exhausted and run through the emotional mill, to find—

'They weren't . . . ?'

'I'm not sure, but it must have been bad – the engagement's off.'

A kind of squawk escaped me.

'Anna! Are you alright? You sound like you're having a coronary.'

'I'm fine, I'm fine. How's Jamie?'

'I don't know. Haven't seen him. I got half the story from Callum and the rest from Tally.'

I suddenly remembered the message Jamie had left with Tally. 'Was Tally there yesterday?'

'What? Oh, yeah. But she was avoiding Lucinda like the plague. I think she suspected what was happening.'

I sat very still. Good old Tally. She hadn't given Lucinda the message that Jamie was coming home. It was against her code not to do something Jamie had asked her to do; it must have been hard for her.

'And where's Darren the Dreadful?'

'Who knows? He's had the good sense to feck off somewhere.'

'God almighty.' I could feel the beginnings of a headache. I told Tobias I would be there in 45 minutes. As I rifled through my wardrobe looking for something to wear, I messaged Roshni.

ANNA *I didn't know the half of it.*

ROSHNI *We're on our way.*

The estate office was quieter than I thought it would be. Tobias was the only one there, drumming away at his keyboard with an intense look on his face as though he was programming code for MI5.

'Emails,' he said. 'I'm cancelling some of the wedding stuff. The amount of crap she ordered, it'll take a week at least. Tally's gone home with a migraine.' Beside him was Tally's thick ring binder entitled WEDDING – EARL. At the sight of it, my stomach lurched.

'Where is Lucinda?'

'Gone home. She came to groom her horses earlier and Pat threw an egg sandwich at her. She was on her lunch break and said it was the only thing she had to hand.'

'Bloody hell. Bit extreme. So word's got around then?'

'I might have been responsible for that. I set up a WhatsApp group with the staff and volunteers whilst you and Fi were away.'

'For gossiping purposes?' I raised my eyebrows.

'No! But they needed to know. Look, I didn't share any details.' He waved his phone at me. I took it and looked at the message he'd sent.

> *FYI Lucinda has betrayed the earl and will no longer be lady of the manor. Please feel free to punish her as you see fit.*

I gave it back to him. 'Don't demonise her, Tobias.'

'She demonised herself!'

'True, but she's going to be devastated.'

'She's not. That's the weird thing. She didn't even really seem that bothered.'

I goggled at him. Not bothered? At losing Jamie? I'd been crawling around on my knees for the last few weeks unable to function, and she was waltzing off without a care in the world.

'This is almost enough to make me start smoking again,' said Roshni, wrapping her fleece-lined coat tight around her as we sat on the antique bench in Belheddonbrae, cradling cups of tea that Mica had brought out to us. Roshni and George had arrived at half three, without the children this time.

'Chocolate is my vice,' I said. 'Luckily, Tobias cleared out the staff biscuit stash in my absence, otherwise I wouldn't be able to speak to you because my mouth would be full.'

She grinned but the smile faded quickly. 'What a mess.'

'Yep.' I glanced at her. 'Is that one of those designer dry robes? What the hell? Not a drop of water for three miles.'

She looked sheepish. 'I just grabbed the first thing on the way out of the door.'

'Bloody Londoners.'

'Humph.' She snuggled further into it.

'How is he?' I said. I'd been thinking constantly about whether to text Jamie. But why would he need a text from me? It would be like rubbing salt into a wound.

'I mean, fine, kind of,' said Roshni, her eyes fixed on the landscape. 'But it's like he's completely withdrawn. He was already going that way, even when they were engaged, but now it's complete. Like he doesn't feel anything. And that worries me. The boarding school training, kicking in. Good old Hugo, though. Every time Jamie sits down, he leaps into his lap and gazes adoringly at him. It brings him back into the world again.'

'We don't deserve dogs,' I said. 'Plus, Hugo never liked Lucinda.'

'Exactly!' said Roshni. 'Even the dog knew she was bullshitting. Honestly, my brother-in-law has spent his whole life being treated like a trophy to be won rather than an actual person. It's exhausting watching so many women throw themselves at him like lemmings over a cliff.'

'For the record, I think she did have feelings for him,' I said.

'Are you insane?' Roshni widened her eyes at me. 'The moment she got with him, she stopped paying her stable bills and started harping on about Mummy and Daddy not having enough money to do up the rectory. Don't tell me to be soft on a gold-digger.'

'Fair enough. But her life is here. She stables her horses here.'

'I know. She's messaged Jamie. He says he's fine about it. Couldn't care less.'

I caught her eye and she fiddled with her sleeve. 'Exactly. Weird, no? So help me, gilts and bonds and City boys are about a hundred times easier to deal with than all these *feelings*.' She held an imaginary cigarette in her elegant, tapering fingers.

'I'm sure Jamie's glad you and George are here.'

'I think so. I don't know. George is going to get in touch with some of their mutual friends, arrange some visits. Jamie needs company that isn't just beagle-shaped. I've told him if he doesn't agree, I'll pay someone to kidnap him and deliver him to our house where he can babysit Kes and Jake.' She sighed.

'I told him I wanted to stay here,' I said. 'On the way back from London. He said it wasn't a good idea.'

Roshni smacked her own forehead with a flat palm. 'What is wrong with you two? I could knock your heads together. And why couldn't you just be together, in the first place?'

'I swore, when I came here, I'd learn to say no to things,' I said quietly. 'I was always such a "yes woman". Saying no to the relationship with Jamie was part of getting over that.'

She narrowed her eyes. 'So you're a recovering people-pleaser?' she said.

'Something like that.'

'Only, you wanted to be with him, didn't you?' Her eyes searched my face, her gaze clear and analytical. 'That's the impression you gave me.'

'Yes,' I said quietly. 'I did. But—'

'But nothing. Why didn't you just put your own happiness first?'

The question floored me. I found myself counting my breaths again. 'I was scared,' I said. 'And I wanted to protect him. Stonemore means so much to him.'

'He can protect *himself*,' she said. 'And he can protect Stonemore. But he can't make himself happy.'

She leaned against me, and nudged me. I glanced at the questioning look on her face.

'We're not going to get together,' I mumbled.

'Whatever,' she said, tipping the remainder of her tea onto the ground. 'I've got to get back.' She got up from the bench and headed off in the direction of the house.

'Nice dry robe,' I called after her.

She gave me a cheerful two-fingered salute. 'Just think about what I said, Anna,' she called. 'I mean it.'

The wedding was harder to cancel than you might think, and emails weren't enough. Phone calls and difficult conversations were required. The following day Tobias got fed up of taking the flak from suppliers so handed the ring binder back to Tally, whereupon she burst into tears. Her bossiness had dissolved so completely I ended up sitting outside on a bench with her, my arm around her as she sobbed onto my shoulder. She seemed more devastated about what had happened than either the bride or the groom. So of course, I offered to take over cancelling things.

'Sucker,' mouthed Tobias at me, before launching into a version of 'If I Only Had A Heart' from *The Wizard of Oz*.

It was so strange, deconstructing Lucinda and Jamie's wedding, gaining glimpses of what it would have been – tartans, roses, evergreens, many many candles (so many, it would definitely have constituted a fire risk – Tally really was the worst collections manager in the world). I could picture it all so clearly, and at the same time it seemed impossible that it had existed at all, even if only in Lucinda's imagination.

It was, I was told, too late to take back the deposit for the cake, as the fruitcake layers had already been baked and were 'resting' and being 'fed' daily with syringes of single malt whisky. 'Single malt,' I muttered to myself, and saw Tobias shake his head. I arranged for the tiers to be delivered once done – the thought of it perhaps being a massive christening cake for Ross crossed my mind.

The news of the broken engagement had finally reached Fi, and she had called me for a technicolour conversation in which she called Lucinda every name under the sun. Then Ross started crying and she had to go. 'We should be home next week. Give Jamie my love,' she said.

Give Jamie my love. The truth was I had no idea what to say to him, but I knew my silence would start to look like coldness. After I'd hung up on the final cancellation call I was prepared to make – to the people who were making handmade favours out of timber cut at Stonemore ('It was a fallen tree, Jamie insisted we didn't cut any down, don't you get on your high horse,' Tally had bleated), I sat to compose a message to Jamie. One of Callum's hot chocolates had found its way onto my desk.

'Have you seen him today?' I said to Cal, going into his office and shutting the door behind me.

'Yes.'

'How's he doing?'

Callum looked pained, as though he wasn't equipped to examine the intricacies of the human heart. 'Alright,' he said.

I sipped the hot chocolate and licked cream off my upper lip. 'Anything else to add?'

'Not really,' he said, looking uncomfortable. 'I'm not good at this stuff. He seems fine. Roshni and George are there.'

'Righty ho.'

'Oh, and the Tamworths are arriving next week.'

I turned back. We'd been discussing introducing some Tamworth pigs to a small area of the estate. 'Really?' I heard the eagerness in my voice.

'Will you be here?' He was looking at his computer screen, avoiding my gaze. I knew that move – I'd done it enough myself.

I felt empty. My last day was due to be next Friday. So I would see the Tamworths released and then have to leave them. 'I hope to be,' I said.

He nodded. 'Well, enjoy that hot chocolate. You've earned it. Single malt in an effing wedding cake.' He widened his eyes at me, and started assembling his vape. 'There's a reason I intend never to get married.'

The thought of Jamie's sadness stayed with me all day. I tried to focus on other things, and met with Keith and Mica to discuss how the volunteers were getting on with the parterre maintenance. But that evening, after avoiding my feelings all day, I took a sip of wine, and pressed send on a message to him.

> *I'm so sorry about what has happened. If there's anything I can do, please let me know. Ross is doing well and Fi sends best love.*

I looked around the room, at the boxes of my possessions. The log burner was built to a blaze and I was wrapped up on the sofa. I couldn't bring myself to carry on packing. I wanted to dig my heels in like Hugo did when he decided he wasn't going anywhere without a treat.

I looked back at the phone. Jamie had read the message, but there was no indication that he was online or typing. I put the television on. There was a moody drama about a murder on, but I couldn't concentrate. When my phone plinked, I snatched it up. Tobias had been busy – it was from Roshni.

> *Single malt in a wedding cake? Don't let me near that woman or I'll murder her.*

I rubbed my forehead and put it back down. I couldn't sit here, waiting. I needed to do something.

I left my fireside behind, put my heavy coat on, and went out into the cold winter night. I took a torch to navigate the muddy, hollowed lane, all the time telling myself I was being stupid, even as I crossed the deer park and the manor house came into view. I wasn't sure what I was doing, or why.

I came to a halt in the carriage drive of Stonemore, the proud, Neo-Classical house in darkness apart from the lit windows of the flat. I stood there, looking up.

I needed to see him, that was all. No, not *needed*, I could survive without him – I *wanted* to see him. I wanted to make sure he was okay.

It was freezing. I stamped my feet on the ground and huddled into my coat.

And then, there he was. Standing at the window. Dressed in black rollneck sweater and jeans. He was looking back at somebody – Roshni or George, I guessed – and speaking. There wasn't a trace of a smile on his face. He looked so sad. Then he turned and looked out into the night, in my direction.

I was standing in darkness, in a dark coat. Could he even see me? I raised my hand, held it there for a moment.

He frowned for a second. Looked intently. Put the hand that wasn't holding a mug to the window for a brief moment, in an echo of my gesture.

Then something changed in his face. He put his hand down, turned, and walked away.

Fool that I was, I waited for a few minutes to see if he was going to come down. But there was also a part of me – the truth-telling part – that had turned as cold as the night air. There had been something in the way he had turned away that reminded me of what Roshni had said. Completely withdrawn. Frozen.

I took myself back to the cottage, and put a few more possessions in my boxes.

CHAPTER 28

The office had always been a cheery place on Fridays, but even Tobias was looking muted the following day, and Tally phoned in sick. Even the weather felt low; by midday the sky was darkening and it felt several degrees colder. I was just telling Tobias he could take the afternoon off when something caught my eye – a flash of white and tan at the window.

I got up from my seat and went to look out at the gravelled carriage drive. It was Hugo. No collar, no lead. He was standing on the drive, scenting the air.

'What the hell,' I murmured, opening the door as softly as I could. I had no treats at my disposal – getting him to come to me would have to rely on affection alone.

'Hu-go,' I called, in my softest, sweetest voice. He turned and looked at me, his tail flickering into life. 'Good boy!' I said. 'Such a good boy. Hugo, come!' He raised a paw to take a step forwards.

The child came out of nowhere – a demob happy toddler, just released from her parents' car after a long journey day-tripping to Stonemore.

'Goggy!' she shrieked at the sight of the beagle, charging towards him, little arms outstretched.

Hugo looked at her with his bright, seal-pup eyes, and assessed the situation.

I called his name again, but his eyes didn't move from the child.

He tipped his head.

Then he turned.

And he ran.

Boy, that dog could run. He ran with an ecstatic, joyous energy, galloping out into the acres of Stonemore. There was no way I could keep up with him, but I tried anyway – pounding across the drive to the first gate. By the time I reached it, he was long gone. 'Shit,' I said. '*Shit!*'

I got back to the office to find Tobias already tapping a message into the house group chat for everyone to look out for Hugo. Almost at the same moment, Roshni came running into the office. She was dressed in colourful workout gear and was holding a phone. 'Have you seen Hugo? George opened the door for a split second and he was gone. I think he was trying to find Jamie – he's gone for a run.'

I explained what had happened. 'Fuck,' she said. 'On top of everything. He doesn't have a tracker on, does he?'

I shook my head, dialling Callum. Tobias had sent out

his SOS but all the responses coming in were negative. No one had seen Hugo.

We went out in different directions, clutching phones and estate walkie talkies. I walked along the verge of the road that ran around the perimeter of the estate. I could feel the panic rising in me as I scoured every hedgerow and stone wall for a sign of him, calling his name. The cars that drove past seemed to be going much too fast. The thought of him being knocked down made me feel sick and shaky. At one point I caught a glimpse of figures on a far hillside, looking, heard the faintest suggestion of their shouts. I was sure one of the figures was Jamie.

We all searched for hours. But there was no sign of Hugo.

'He'll come back when he gets hungry,' I said, when we all gathered in the staff office at four, but I could hear the uncertainty in my own voice. The light was already fading and Hugo's dinnertime was 4.15. By this time he'd normally be sitting by his bowl, waiting for his food.

Everyone had worked hard. We were cold and tired. I half expected Jamie to appear, to thank everyone. Instead, George stood on a chair and gave a little speech, whilst Roshni and Tobias handed out cups of tea.

'Where's Jamie?' I said to Roshni.

She gave a little shake of her head. 'Still looking.'

As the volunteers drifted away and Tobias said good-night, Callum and I carried on working at our desks, as though by mutual agreement. Every so often, I glanced out into the darkness, as though that flash might pass by the window again. At 8pm, Cal came in.

'It's time to go home,' he said. 'Sitting here won't bring him back. I know that dog and he's a canny one. He'll probably have made eyes at a stranger and is snoozing by someone's fire as we speak. He'll be back tomorrow.'

I nodded, suddenly unable to speak. Cal watched as I shut down my computer.

Back at the cottage, I checked the garden for the little beagle, even though he'd never visited me. Then I fell asleep on the sofa. I stayed there all night. At 8am I was woken by a text from Roshni.

> *Is he with you?*

I blinked sleep from my eyes.

> *Hugo? No.*

> *Not Hugo. Jamie.*

I sat up. *No?*

'I even checked with she-who-must-not-be-asked,' said Roshni, when I got to the flat. 'He messaged George at 11pm yesterday, said he would be back soon. But if he did come back, he went again. His bed hasn't been slept in.'

'We were fast asleep after the day looking for Hugo,' said

George. He ran a hand through his thick hair and it struck me how much like Jamie he looked in that moment. 'What if he's lost? What if he's fallen? The weather forecast says it might snow.'

'He knows the estate like the back of his hand,' said Roshni. 'You've said it a thousand times. He's fit, strong and sensible.'

'Accidents happen though, don't they?' said George tightly.

I looked at them both. 'Have you messaged him this morning?'

'Of course. It didn't arrive,' George said miserably.

It was then we heard the noise: the hallooing, a cheering. We ran to the window.

Callum stood on the forecourt, a bundle in his arms.

'I've got him!' he shouted, when George levered open the window. 'I've got the little bugger. He's fine!'

The bundle was Hugo. And he was very muddy indeed.

We all took off down the stairs at the sight of him.

'I found him in the roots of the Mulholland Oak,' said Cal, when we reached him. 'I was driving around at first light.'

I snapped Hugo's collar around his neck and clipped on his lead, before Cal put him down on the floor. Hugo looked up at us all, and wagged his tail.

'Is it me, or does he look extremely pleased with himself?' said Roshni.

'Aye, he does.' Cal looked down sternly at him. 'I'll give

him breakfast and a bath, then we'll get him checked out at the vet.'

'You're a *massive nuisance*,' said Roshni to Hugo. He looked into the middle distance as though she hadn't said a thing.

'Now all we've got to do is find my brother,' said George. 'At what point can you notify the police of a missing person?'

I closed my eyes against the tension in the air. Jamie. Missing.

'I'll google it,' said Roshni. 'And let's convene a search party. Think about the routes he might have taken.'

'None of the Land Rovers are out,' said Cal. 'Wherever he's gone, he's walked. I'll go and get an estate map so we can make plans.'

'Excellent. Thank you.' Roshni put an arm around George and he rested his head on her shoulder. 'Any ideas about where he might go, my love?'

'Not really. He could cover quite a distance. He took one of the old kit bags, and the bottle of the Macallan from the living room,' George said.

The Macallan, I thought. *That whisky has a lot to answer for. Surely not . . .*

'I have an idea where he might be,' I said.

They turned and looked at me.

Half an hour later, Callum, Hugo and I were rattling our way up the hillside in Cal's ancient Land Rover. Hugo was freshly bathed and I held him in my lap, although occasionally he would launch himself onto his back legs and gaze out of the window at the hills and streams, as though he longed to be exploring them. Back at the house, Roshni and George were briefing the search party, just in case I was wrong.

The promised snow hadn't materialised but the sky was lead grey and menacing. When we got to our destination, I kept a strong hold on Hugo's lead as he jumped down beside me, and I hoisted a kit bag on my back despite Callum's offer to take it. We set off along the muddy track, our faces brightened by the cold.

At a clearing in the woods, we saw it: the little bothy where Jamie and I had spent the night, smoke rising from its chimney.

Callum caught my eye. 'Let's see,' he said.

Hugo and I went first. I knocked on the green door and turned the handle. At the same moment as I opened the door, Jamie appeared in front of me, surprised and glum-looking; Hugo went mad with joy, barking and bouncing on his back legs. Jamie's face creased with joy. 'Ingrate,' he said, crouching and inhaling the smell of Hugo's scruff as the beagle booped at him with his nose. 'Where the hell have you been, little hound?'

'On adventures,' I said, trying desperately to stop myself from keeling over with relief. I leaned back out the door and gave a thumbs-up to Callum. He nodded, and a smile broke across his face. 'One hour,' he said, and headed off back through the woods.

I closed the door and turned to look at Jamie, suddenly feeling shy. He had scooped Hugo into his arms, and was rubbing the little dog's chest. Then he gently put him down. 'Was it you who guessed where I was?' he said.

I leaned back against the door. 'Yes. George said you'd taken the Macallan. That was the clincher.'

He nodded and smiled, still not meeting my eye.

'I've got treats,' I said. 'Plus my own supply of chocolate, so you can't ration me this time.' I pulled out some folded blankets from the kit bag and put them on the floor. Hugo immediately claimed the pile and lay down on them. I laughed.

When I stopped laughing, I looked up; Jamie's eyes were bright and fixed on my face. His beautiful, electric blue eyes, so much like the sky over Stonemore, but filled with a feeling that flipped my heart.

'I thought I'd lost him,' he said.

'Nothing's lost that can't be found,' I said.

'Is that one of your mum's weird sayings?' he said, and as we started laughing, he pulled me to him. 'Can I kiss you?' he said. 'Even if it's for the last time?'

I answered by kissing him first.

It was just like the first time we'd kissed; like lighting a touchpaper. And we didn't stop, couldn't stop. He lifted me up into his arms and I wrapped my legs around his waist, until Hugo started barking and we broke away from each other, breathless and laughing.

'It was never just about sex,' I blurted out, and saw the

361

astonishment on his face. 'I love you. I know it's inconvenient, but I love you.'

'I love you too.' He said it without hesitation. Then he pulled me to him again and kissed me passionately. 'I've wanted to kiss you again, for so long,' Jamie said. 'You drive me insane. I can't tell you, Anna.' He pressed his face into my neck whilst I played my fingers over his neck, his hair.

'I need to sit down before I fall down,' I said. I was trembling with adrenaline, with relief, with absolute desire. We sat down on the folded blankets and Hugo squirmed beside us, burying his nose in the side of Jamie's thigh. 'Tell me it's not the last time,' Jamie said.

'You're not getting rid of me that easily,' I said. 'By the way, do you realise you just told me that you loved me? I mean, after all that fuss. See how easy it was?'

'Ridiculously easy,' he said softly. 'Thanks for the therapy. You can go now.'

I shoved him and he pulled me to him. 'I can't believe you're here.' He planted another kiss on my lips. He handed me his tin mug and I took a sip of whisky; warm, fiery and soothing. 'Luckily I'd only just poured my first.'

'It was an emergency,' I said. 'George thought you were lying at the bottom of a sheer drop.'

'What? Really?' He shook his head. 'Oh no, poor George. I didn't think.'

'I'm sure he'll forgive you.' I allowed myself to stroke the side of his neck with my thumb. It was as though I had to ration these moments – too much joy would kill me.

His eyes flickered back to my face. 'I've made such a mess of things. When I got back, and I saw Lucinda with that man – it was like I woke up from a dream. What was I thinking? Me and Lucinda? Poor woman. I failed her on every count. I couldn't even bring myself to go to bed with her.'

I choked on my second sip of whisky. 'What?'

He shook his head. 'Said I wanted to wait, it was romantic, etc. But the truth was, I couldn't touch her. Not when we were fresh in my mind. I tried very hard to get over you.'

I handed him the mug back and he took his own sip. 'But I wasn't over you. And when we were in London, I realised I really wasn't. It hit me like a sledgehammer. When you went out – to see your ex, I presumed – I was so jealous, I didn't know what to do with myself. And being in that apartment, so close to you. The number of times I almost reached out and pulled you into my arms. When I saw you outside Stonemore the other night, I couldn't bear it. I couldn't bear to think of what I'd lost. I didn't need your pity.'

He put the mug down, took my hand, turned it over and kissed it. 'Can we just, please, be together.' Then his expression changed. 'This isn't pity? You're not just here to get me off the hill and back to Stonemore?'

'Don't be ridiculous.' I took his face, stared into his eyes. 'I'm in love with you, Jamie Mulholland. I've tried not to be, but I've failed. And yes, we can be together. Because ...' I paused, and saw him tilt his head at me, watching me. I remembered Roshni's words, and the way they had cut through everything with their truthfulness. I'd been so proud of all my '*no's*'. But in the end, I'd been saying no to happiness – mine and his.

'Because?' he said.

I stared at him. 'Because I want you for myself,' I said. 'I want to be happy. And I think that might make you happy, too.'

I saw the smile dawn in his eyes as I said it, even though the words sounded strange to me.

'Then it seems we don't have a problem,' he said. He tipped my chin up where I'd looked away. 'I tried to follow your instructions,' he said. 'I tried so hard not to love you. But I can't do all this – I can't be here at Stonemore, I can't be myself – without you. You think I haven't considered the children thing, but I have. I've thought about nothing else since the moment you told everyone. And I've made my peace with it. I'd rather have you – there's not a shred of doubt in my mind. Anna, promise me you won't go.' It cost him to say it, I could see that – to drop that high, cold guard.

'I promise.' I curled up against him. Felt his arms tight around me. Did I really dare to do this? Did I dare to be happy, really happy?

It was too late. I already was.

The fire was ablaze as it had been on that evening we'd been stranded. 'They say there's going to be snow,' I said, staring into the flames.

'I'm not scared of the snow if you aren't.'

'I'm scared of the shovel, and of your strict chocolate rationing,' I said. 'Callum's coming back to get us in,' I checked my watch, 'forty-five minutes.'

'Maybe we should make good use of the time.' He nuzzled my neck, and I could feel goosebumps running over my body.

'Not in front of Hugo,' I said. The beagle's eyes were balefully half open, as if he couldn't bear to take his eyes off his newly found master.

'Awkward,' said Jamie. 'He's supposed to be my wing man.'

'Oh, he is. Look how he brought us together.'

'Anna?' Jamie handed me the mug again. 'You're going to need another sip.'

I sipped dutifully.

'I know this might seem sudden, but I've never been surer of anything in my life. Will you marry me?'

'Marry you?' I said faintly.

Jamie held my gaze. 'Yes,' he said. 'I'm not scared if you're not.'

'Marry you?' I said. 'And Stonemore with its leaky roof? And Tally with her endless lecturing on etiquette? And this smelly beagle?'

He held my gaze, and I could see he didn't know whether to smile or frown at me.

And I thought of my cottage, my self-help books, my journal and its No, inked in bright colours again and again and sprinkled with glitter. And I looked into the eyes of this astonishing man, and thought how strange it was that even when you wanted nothing to do with it, life had a way of seeking you out.

'Yes,' I said.

EPILOGUE

We were married at Stonemore on the coldest Valentine's Day you can imagine, with snow a metre deep outside. The celebrant had started their journey early that morning, and came the last part on foot, trudging up the long drive of Stonemore with a bright and determined expression ('as long as I'm away by twelve, I can get to the next one'). In the grand entrance hall, Jamie took my hand and promised to love me always, and I to love him. We were surrounded by the people we loved the best: Fi, Richard and Ross; Rose, my mum and stepdad; Roshni, George, Kes and Jake; a handful of close friends including Callum, Tobias and Tally (who had to be forcibly stopped from trying to plan a much bigger wedding). And Hugo, who danced around us and almost tripped both of us up several times during the ceremony. He looked perfectly nice without a bow tie, obviously.

We didn't buy anything expensive for that wedding,

other than the rings: no tartans, no evergreens, no scores of candles. And I couldn't have been happier. Jamie lit a silver candelabra on the hall table and as the snow flurried outside, we made our vows in the quiet hall, in air that seemed filled with warmth and happiness despite the cold weather. Afterwards, we ate sausage and mash in the flat, with Hugo cadging chunks of sausage from pretty much every guest. For afters, we'd planned to hoover up a chunk of 'Lucinda's bloody wedding cake', as the gargantuan construction had come to be known; tiers of it had served as everything from Ross's christening cake to the staff Christmas party cake, and it still wasn't gone. But when I came to dish it out, I found that Jamie had bought a different cake instead: a light sponge, frosted with fondant icing and decorated with hearts. 'Something new,' he said to me, with a smile (I'd borrowed my shoes, and worn a blue brooch, for luck).

If anything has surprised me, it's how easy marriage has been. How straightforward it is to wake up every day and love Jamie, and find that he loves me. It's true we've had to extend the flat slightly, and get some proper storage (I can only have my shoes eaten by Hugo so many times), but I've had no problem being that strange thing I thought I'd never be – a wife. And I'm an excellent dog mum, even if I do say so myself.

And Lucinda? She married Darren in the wedding dress she intended to become a countess in. Of course she did! Sometimes she even appears in our lives – in emails asking to rent a paddock for the summer. I hope she's happy. We all deserve our chance at happiness.

Despite my fears, it turns out Stonemore doesn't feel empty or like a house without a family. If there isn't Ross rampaging about it (he particularly loves crawling under the visitor ropes in the red salon), on any given weekend you'll find Kes and Jake following their Uncle Jamie like shadows, learning about the estate that they will one day inherit, chasing beagles in the enclosure, or greeting house visitors. On every weekday, there is the family we've chosen for our-selves: our friends, the volunteers who care for Stonemore, the staff (and animals) who make it our home. And there is, of course, the land. I love all of it: every bramble yielding its berries for our blackberrying trips (leaving a share for the birds, of course); every dog rose with its pale pink flowers; every precious oak – from the ancient Mulholland Oak that stands tall and proud in the heart of the estate to the hand-ful of modern saplings. The wildflower meadow flourishes at Belheddonbrae, and in summer delighted visitors walk their way through the mowed paths amidst a blaze of white, yellow and purple flowers. When I give tours, I point out the vividness of the purple melancholy thistles, and ask them to listen for the ticking of the yellow rattle which tells me summer is ending and it's time to wield the scythe again for the hay cut.

I should add that the roof still leaks. 'Can you imagine doing this for the rest of your life?' Jamie said to me one day, a grim expression on his face as I handed him another bucket for a brand-new leak in the roof. I put the mop over my shoulder and walked on with him, my hand on his back as we traversed the back corridor with its green peeling paint and slightly musty smell, leaning into him as he hooked his arm around my waist and pulled me close.

'Don't take too long to answer,' he murmured into my hair. 'I'll be thinking you're having second thoughts, Lady Roxdale.'

I kissed his cheek lightly, glorying in his scent, his closeness. 'No second thoughts at all, my lord,' I said.

'Sure?' He put the bucket down with a clatter as we reached the place.

'I'm sure,' I said, smiling up at him. 'I've always been wild about you.'

ACKNOWLEDGEMENTS

Huge thanks to my editor Clare Hey for her enthusiasm and skill, and the team at Simon & Schuster UK who have worked so hard on this book: Aneesha Angris, Sara-Jade Virtue, Laurie McShea, Sarah Jeffcoate, Pip Watkins, Olivia Allen, Maddie Allan, Robyn Ware, Katie Sormaz, Rachel Bazan, Karin Seifried and Gail Hallett. Thank you also to Clare Wallis for copyediting and Celia Killen for proofreading.

Gratitude and adoration to my agents Jane Finigan and Daisy Parente at Lutyens & Rubinstein. Without your support, and, let's face it, straight talking and skill, *Wild About You* would have remained my secret. I am also grateful to Sarah Lutyens, Lily Evans, Anna Boyce, Prema Raj, and Tara Spinks at L&R.

This book is dedicated to Emily Kidson and Siân Robinson, who read it as a favour when it was barely even a first draft. I'm so grateful to you both for your encouragement, as I am to Deborah Roberts Schultz who heard me murmur coyly about it for many months without telling me to be quiet.

Huge thanks to the friends who have cheered me on even when I wouldn't share my pen name. You're smart people, so you've probably guessed it by now. Amanda, Lucy, Ruth, Natalie, Sophie L., Sophie C., the Leopards, Goldsmiths' friends and the always amazing Bookworms – please know how grateful I am. Ditto, Barry and Fiona. Sorry Fiona, I nicked your first name entirely by accident.

Big love to the writing friends who have supported me: Melanie Backe Hansen, Sophie Hardach, Jason Hewitt, Kate Mayfield – thank you for the brilliance. Antonia Hodgson, I am so grateful to you for our writing days, and for letting me make bad coffee in your kitchen.

This book was begun in the reign of Bertie, a beagle cross whose name is written on my heart; and completed in the reign of Badger, a joyous furball. I am grateful to the charities that made these additions to our family possible – Battersea Dogs and Cats Home and TAG Pet Rescue.

To my family, as always, love and thanks: Mum and Dad; Lisa, Samuel and Harrison; Angela and family. And, as always, huge thanks to my husband Aelred, for his love and support, which makes everything possible.